EDGE *of* EXPOSURE

An Entanglements Novel

BOOK 5

Gina Marie Martini

PAGE PUBLISHING
Conneaut Lake, PA

First originally published by Page Publishing 2023

ISBN 979-8-88960-462-4 (pbk)
ISBN 979-8-88960-472-3 (digital)

Printed in the United States of America

The Entanglements Novels by Gina Marie Martini

Edge of Exposure
Lethal Revelations
Love Affair: Tommy's Memoirs
Moonlight Confessions
The Mistress Chronicles

In loving memory of Edward J. Martini, whose radiant smile and warm personality would light up any room he entered, momentously touching the lives and hearts of others.

ACKNOWLEDGMENTS

I am blessed to have friends who took the time to read my story in advance and offer feedback, an essential part of the process. Many thanks to Darlene Ashford, Donna Barent, Joanne Colavolpe, and Sally Diglio for your attention and kind words of encouragement.

I would like to thank my friend, Michele Wasef, RN, for assisting me with some clinical details that enhanced the authenticity of the storyline.

CHAPTER 1

The spotlight, once an enchanted friend, flickered brightly with a blaring heat that enveloped and guided me to fame and fortune. Darkness, the enemy of anyone in show business or politics, cast shadows of fear, doubt, and the excruciating death of one's career. My world revolved around both the Hollywood and political scenes, like the Earth orbiting the sun.

The shimmer of light that surrounded me had burned at maximum intensity. An eclipse couldn't evade the blinding flashes of cameras, the humming of microphones, and scathing tabloid scandals.

Drained and exhausted, I escaped from living in a fishbowl, starting over with a new identity and life, existing on my terms.

Dwelling in darkness became a welcome change of pace.

*****

Paris in November! Tourism slowed this time of year, allowing the locals to admire the beautiful, thriving city without an onslaught of visitors. Traffic was still horrendous as I waited patiently in my silver Peugeot hatchback for the neon green Renault Clio in front of me to wake up and drive through the green light. I slammed on my horn, disrupting Elvis's "Heartbreak Hotel," encouraging the Clio to move at a steady pace along the bank of the Seine. I bee-bopped along to my idol's soulful melody on my way to work.

The Musée d'Orsay, one of the most popular museums in Paris, displays artwork and sculptures dating between the mid-nineteenth and early twentieth centuries. Originally, this structure was used as a train station before transforming into the extraordinary museum it became famous for today, welcoming millions of tourists annually.

I parked my car and shuffled to the employee entrance in the back. Even in the cool month of November, a line of tourists waited outside the main entryway in formation maintained by belt dividers near the statues of an elephant, horse, and rhino.

The old railway station vibe existed like you were floating through a long, illuminated tunnel to catch your train, passing by magnificent sculptures and rooms containing masterpieces of pure beauty. The massively high ceilings carried voices, and the prancing of feet echoed as folks meandered through the vast area, halting between exhibits.

As a tour guide, I created a unique itinerary packed with a wealth of knowledge for my guests to absorb, enhancing their experience of each exquisite piece.

"Good morning, Charisse," my friend and coworker, Juliet, said as she skated past me.

"How about lunch?" I suggested.

"Oui! One o'clock at our usual spot?"

I nodded. My typical lunch with Juliet consisted of a quick snack from the museum's café and sitting outside on the steps that led to the Seine. We admired views across the waterway like the Louvre, and, of course, the grand Eiffel Tower could be spotted from anywhere in the city.

I rode the escalator up to the fifth floor. Each day before my first tour began, I liked to spend a few quiet moments in my favorite part of the museum—the impressionist section. This area displayed the works of geniuses such as Claude Monet, Auguste Renoir, and Edgar Degas. But there was one piece I cherished most, a piece that once belonged to my family, *the Boulevard Montmartre at Twilight, 1897,* by Camille Pissarro.

My coworkers might have noticed my attraction to this painting since I visited it daily. I'd never share its mysterious connection with my grandfather, Sergio Ursini. This piece by Pissarro was stolen during the Second World War. My grandfather acquired it in the early 1940s. Grandpa's knowledge of art and love for this painting rubbed off on me. My desire to become immersed in the intricate details of masterpieces and the artists who created them motivated me to attain a college degree in art history.

Unfortunately, someone ripped the Pissarro painting off my grandfather's wall. For several years of my adult life, my purpose progressed to a search and rescue mission. I proved successful in retrieving the art, eventually returning it to Grandpa. That was until my situation went sideways. Someone I trusted had double-crossed me. My options were to selfishly hide the painting or give it up, hoping to prevent criminal charges or a massive scandal that might have sent me to jail. The methods I used to procure it wouldn't have been construed as legal.

Years later, my past crept up to bite me. I had no choice but to anonymously ship the painting to this museum in Paris, far from my adversary's reach. It belonged here on the fifth floor with other work by Pissarro and his impressionist peers rather than stored away in hiding for no one to appreciate its beauty.

Seeing this painting daily triggered bubbles of excitement. I felt my grandfather's spirit beside me whenever I stood in this spot. I glanced at my watch and quietly uttered, "Shoot!" Time to start my day.

Momentarily, I stopped for a peek through the grand clock window to watch a few people race along the busy street below, snapping photos of the prominent building I had the pleasure of working at a few days a week. Although I didn't consider this job I adored as *work*.

My love of art flourished into passion, becoming an essential part of my childhood in Las Vegas, Nevada. The circumstances that brought me to Paris in 2010 were devised of love and survival.

CHAPTER 2

At the end of my workday, I found my way home to 27–29 Rue de la Roquette. A twenty-minute drive could double in time during the prime tourist season from May to September. In the off-season months like today, it might take a mere fifteen minutes unless road construction or an accident interfered. Luckily, I arrived home promptly this Saturday, November 17, 2018.

Using the rearview mirror, I touched up my mocha-shaded lipstick and tossed a brush through my light-brown hair, a new color I thought I'd try, although I missed the natural ebony shade I wore when living in the US.

My move to Paris not only meant changing my appearance, but I also had to change my name. Thus, Charisse Yvette LaSalle became my identity in France with citizenship and a background in art history. My birth name, however, was Victoria Grace Ursini. Sylvia Ursini, my mother, adored celebrities and the glamorous lives led by her idols. Her life revolved around the opportunity to become famous and make a name for herself in the shimmering spotlight.

She named me Victoria after a soap opera character from *The Secret Storm* in the 1950s and Grace after the beautiful Grace Kelly, following her successful movies like *Rear Window* and *To Catch a Thief*.

My husband's Peugeot sat in the space next to mine in the parking garage. He beat me home for a change. In public, I referred to him as "Tim," "honey," or "babe." Tim McGee was the name he used when we relocated to Paris, abruptly parting from our home and families in Las Vegas.

Tim established himself as an English-speaking tour guide. He purchased a moderately sized catamaran to cruise visitors along the Seine, showing off the many beautiful sights the antiquated city offered. My husband had a vivacious personality, entertaining his guests with funny stories and details about the renowned attractions, but he didn't speak French very well. He could get by with basic words and attempt to strike up a conversation with the locals. Often, he'd receive strange glares as if he insulted someone with a slip of the tongue. Many people spoke English here, and the need for English-speaking workers in the tourism industry proved vital.

Tim had been visiting France regularly since the 1970s, so he picked up a lot of knowledge about the culture and the residents. He taught me how to blend in following our dramatic move from the US.

Riding the elevator up to our apartment, I reflected upon the surprises my honey always had up his sleeve, especially on a day like today—my birthday. It was difficult to come to terms with hitting my sixties, well over the hump of middle age. My forties and fifties didn't bother me. Sixty-something just sounded *old*.

Back in the US, I had established myself as an actress, Sylvia's dream career. I mainly featured in science-fiction films, starring in seven movies. They weren't major motion pictures, but my dream had been fulfilled. A sci-fi TV series I starred in, *Rising 51*, filmed in Las Vegas, was how I met the love of my life in 2005.

At that time, Tim was known as Tommy Cavallo, the owner of the Montgomery Hotel and Casino in the heart of Vegas along the exhilarating Strip. Our worlds collided when we met, but I happened to be married to someone else. A lonely woman in a tainted marriage fell in love with an extraordinary man. But my marital ties strangled me in ways I couldn't divulge, hindering a relationship from blossoming with Tommy.

Back then, the spotlight kept me warm and toasty, but its rays of duplicity often shined through, especially with a possessive husband who adored the luminous glow of that light.

Husband number one, Jeffrey Atkins, debuted as the mayor of Fernley after we married in the '90s. He climbed his way up in the political ranks to become the governor of Nevada. Divorcing Jeffrey took time, money, and multiple risks. We lived beneath the microscope of his political campaign. The chilling part was that Jeffrey knew my secret about the Pissarro painting I had swiped off the wall from the home of a dangerous drug dealer, Trey Winters. Jeffrey collected evidence of my crime, blackmailing me into staying bound to him legally. As a result, our marriage had transformed into a raging sham—a turbulent rapport based on disgust, anger, and extortion.

Tommy helped me escape my marriage and potential larceny charges associated with the regrettable situation I had launched with Pissarro's eminent painting. My divorce drew negative attention throughout the state. Tommy had his own problems in Vegas too—trepidations that endangered his life.

Shortly after my affair with Tommy had been exposed, death threats were received, and a car bomb demolished Tommy's sports car. We weren't certain if Jeffrey had been behind the threats Tommy received, but he was a likely suspect. With help from trusted allies, we changed our identities and moved to Paris for a chance at a happy, quiet life together in 2010.

Despite the happiness we established, we missed our friends and family. Tommy's family was advised of his "death." A man as popular as Tommy Cavallo in Las Vegas couldn't walk away free if he maintained ties to his prior life with many formidable enemies: nemeses with the means, motive, and strong desire to slice his throat.

Sylvia and my brothers, Kirk and Tony, knew I had left the country to start a fresh life away from my vindictive ex-husband. I didn't want Jeffrey to find me or threaten me with a jail sentence about the theft of the Pissarro painting, even if its current home was on floor five at the Musée d'Orsay. My family knew of the alias I used and my location, but they had no idea that Tommy was very much alive and living with me. I trusted my relatives, but because the people closest to Tommy believed he had died, my family had been recited the same tragic piece of fiction.

I stepped off the elevator and approached the door to apartment 1150. We felt safe and secure using our Tim and Charisse covers in Paris for the last eight years. Still, Tommy always locked up our home tightly.

Thanksgiving decorations garnished the interior door with a lovely orange and gold wreath and plastic pumpkins. Tommy and I typically adorned our home with the flavors of each American holiday. I expected him to approach me with a delicious meal he prepared or announce reservations at Maison Marcil, a new bistro that opened on the city's west end, especially since I had tossed a few hints about the five-star reviews it had earned. I grew antsy, wondering what he planned for my birthday tonight.

"Babe? You home?" I spoke a bit loudly. Tommy wouldn't admit to it, but his hearing had faded over time. I found myself repeating words. Some of the challenges of aging were dealing with aches, vision impairments, memory lapses, and hearing difficulties. Tommy had several years on me, so he had a head start in dealing with the dysfunctions of aging. His job and a younger lady in his life helped him to feel more youthful than the number of years he'd lived. Tommy matured gracefully, with dark strands that peppered his gray hair and his muscular build softening just a bit, still being able to drive me wild.

In strolled my love to greet me at the door with a peck on the cheek, wearing jeans and a casual pine-green T-shirt. "Hi, honey. What's for dinner?" he asked.

My eyes bulged. Was he experiencing a senior moment, forgetting my birthday? Previous birthday blitzes he arranged brought me to some lovely areas in France, like Monet's gorgeous home in Giverny; medieval Rouen; the spectacular Palace of Versailles; charming, artsy Montmartre; and the mighty Mont St. Michel. Initially, we chose not to travel outside France while adapting to a new lifestyle, separated from our loved ones.

After seeing many remarkable spots in this country, Tommy coordinated a trip to Berlin to learn more about World War II. Parts of the Berlin Wall remained standing, haunted by past sins and fractured by freedom. Checkpoint Charlie, the Holocaust Memorial, and Bebelplatz, the underground book-burning memorial, served as reminders of the catastrophic events that led to the staggering death of millions.

Last year, we visited Russia, seeing Giulio Romano's original *Love Scene* masterpiece hanging at the Hermitage Museum. Tommy had recreated that piece for me in a smaller size that hung on our bedroom wall. St. Petersburg was a lovely city with numerous attractions to enjoy, like Catherine's Palace, Peterhof Palace, and the Church of Our Savior on Spilled Blood.

This year, though, he asked me what was for dinner.

"What's wrong?"

I shrugged and said, "Uh, I thought we'd go out tonight."

"I'm beat. I had an incident on the boat today. Some lowlife was picking pockets. It wasn't a local gypsy. He was a guy from Baltimore."

"Did he get arrested?"

"Yeah, I let the police handle it. Called it in on the radio before I docked. Two cops escorted him off. I had to hang around to give them a statement. Hauled in some nice tips, though," he uttered with pride.

I merely nodded to appease him.

"Sorry, I didn't make dinner, babe. I guess I fell asleep after an exciting day."

My mouth opened to express my anger, but Tommy instantly took hold of my hand and chuckled, interrupting the start of an argument. He draped his arms around my waist and pulled me in for a sweet kiss. "Happy birthday, sweetheart."

I released a breath, feeling somewhat relieved he didn't forget. "You remembered?"

"Have I ever forgotten? You're in for something special."

"Really?"

"Reservations have been set for weeks at that new restaurant you've been hinting about." He smirked.

I giggled. "I guess I wasn't very subtle."

"We've been together long enough for me to pick up on your cues. That pickpocket incident threw me off track. Working with the cops and giving a statement prevented me from getting home early enough to shower and change. How about we take this opportunity to save time and shower together?"

I wrapped my arms around his neck and leaned in for a kiss. "Not sure we'll actually save time showering together."

*****

Still reeling from the smoldering shower encounter, I slipped into my royal blue dress. My legs wobbled as I stepped into my Christian Louboutin rhinestone pumps.

Tommy smoothed out his silver tie against his favorite black suit, a look that harmonized with his hair.

We arrived at Maison Marcil a few minutes before eight. Glistening chandeliers sparkled over our heads as we strolled by a roaring fireplace set in the back that released a blaze of heat. A piano player tickled the ivories to a smooth-sounding French song. We strode past a gorgeous bar with colorful bottles lined in a pleasing, 3D triangular format as the host pulled a chair out for me to sit beside a window with an incredible view of Montmartre's Sacré-Coeur Basilica lit up in the distance.

The sound of my cell vibrating grabbed my attention. Email messages from my best friends, Bridget and Claudia, chimed in, wishing me a happy birthday. Kirk and Tony also sent me birthday text greetings. They were nine hours behind Paris time. I had plenty of time to respond.

I ordered seafood crepes with a fresh side of vegetables and salad. I chose to live a beef-free lifestyle since I first modeled for a clothing designer back in college. The only meat I consumed was fish. Tommy selected the traditional confit de canard—roasted duck with au gratin potatoes. The warm, crisp baguettes tasted heavenly, and our meal proved savory and delicious. He always ensured his food excluded any type of wine or alcohol; the French loved to drench cuisine in liquor, and Tommy stopped drinking long before we met. He continued to manage his sobriety; however, it never bothered him if I ordered a glass of white wine. I rarely drank alcohol, but since it was my birthday and I wasn't driving, I treated myself.

Despite feeling delightfully stuffed and buzzed, Tommy had arranged for a cherry layer cake set within a dark-chocolate shell to be brought to the table by waitstaff performing "Joyeux Anniversaire," the French's version of "Happy Birthday." I thought I'd splurge, indulging in a delectable taste of sugar. My modeling days were long over. No one monitored the numbers on the scale anymore—except me. This magnificent cake, topped with twinkling candles and sprinkles, stated *Joyeux Anniversaire, Charisse.* The moist confection tasted as rich and delicious as it looked. I might have eaten more than just one bite.

Tommy smirked this delightful grin he always wore when he was up to something. He raised his glass of ginger ale, prompting me to lift my glass of Chardonnay. "Happy birthday, baby. I love you."

"Aww, I love you too. Thank you for bringing me here! This place is fabulous!"

"We're not through celebrating. You haven't opened your gift yet."

His secrecy forced a big smile from me. "Hmm, you mean I'm getting something else besides what you gave me in the shower?"

"Oh, the shower was good for me too. But I'm talking about your birthday present. Let's get out of here."

*****

We arrived home at ten thirty. I whipped off my glittery pumps the moment I entered our apartment. We recently changed the color of the walls to a soothing shade of sage green. I still admired the fresh coat as I gazed around this little nest we called home. The cream curtains hanging above the sliding glass door of our balcony were open, displaying a mesmerizing view of the shimmering Eiffel Tower with the dark evening sky as a backdrop.

Before meeting Tommy, I had never experienced the splendor of Europe. France was the perfect placc for me to live and work as an art history buff. I'd love to explore Italy, but Tommy had roots there. His life had been threatened. Any place we traveled needed to be in a region where he didn't have a hotel or acquaintances. We might have altered our appearances and changed our names, but we could be recognized if we visited familiar settings. I wouldn't put his life in jeopardy by taking foolish risks.

"Get comfortable, birthday girl!"

I stood before the balcony, watching thousands of lights gleam around the Eiffel. This glorious vision never got old.

Tommy returned and handed me a deep, square box, gift wrapped in various shades of purple with a spiral bow dangling green, purple, and yellow ribbons.

"Wow! Should I guess what's inside?" I asked as I took a seat on the leather sofa beside him and shook the box to gauge what the package might contain.

"You can try, but I won't tell you. You might as well open it."

Acting like a five-year-old, I tore through the paper and flung the remnants playfully around the living room, making him chuckle. I lifted the top of the box to find another wrapped gift box inside. "Is this like those Russian wooden dolls where I keep finding more packages within a package?"

He smiled but offered no hints.

"I love this!" I shouted, tearing into another box. Inside were papers and a booklet. "What's this?"

"I'm not saying a word."

"A travel catalog?" I guessed, flipping through the pages to see that the travel company specialized in tours of China. "Oh my god! China?" I screamed, then jumped off the sofa, dashing into his arms, and positioned my frame atop his lap. "Babe, this is amazing! Did you book a trip?"

"Well, don't get too excited. I haven't booked anything yet. Between our work schedules, we have to figure out a good date. China is not a spur-of-the-moment getaway like other vacations we've taken. I know you've always wanted to see the Great Wall."

"Yes, plus Beijing, Shanghai, and Hong Kong. Oh, there's so much to consider."

"That's why I didn't want to plan this without your input. So I'm promising you a trip to China in 2019, and you can plan the entire itinerary. I'll have someone cover my tours when we're away."

"Well, Remi has been a big help to you. I know you have no desire to re—"

"Don't say it! Don't say the R-word. I wouldn't know what to do with myself if I retired."

"You said the dreaded R-word." I laughed.

He brought me in for a snuggle and kissed me as passionately as the first time our lips met in 2005.

The travel brochures called me. I grew eager to impulsively pick something tonight when my cell rang, displaying Sylvia's number across the screen. I raised my pointer finger to Tommy. He knew he needed to remain quiet when I answered, "Hi, Mom!"

"Happy birthday, Victoria! Aunt Lucy is here with me."

"Happy birthday, princess!" My sweet aunt's voice resonated in the background. Aunt Lucy always referred to me as "princess" since I was a child.

"Thank you, ladies!"

"Are you doing anything fun to celebrate your birthday?" Sylvia asked.

"Well, I had dinner with a *friend.*"

"That sounds nice. Where did you go?"

"A new, swanky restaurant. The food was delicious! I treated myself to a slice of cake."

"Good for you!" Aunt Lucy said with a giggle.

"What are you two girls up to today in Vegas? Anything special?" I questioned.

"I'm dragging your aunt out of this apartment for some fresh air. Maybe we'll go trolling for men." A hearty laugh gushed from Sylvia's lips.

I couldn't help but chuckle, watching Tommy cover his mouth to hold back his laughter. "The men in town better watch out for you two temptresses!"

"Your mother wants to drag me to the Flamingo later. Honestly, you were just there last night, Syl."

"Lu, you gotta get out more. Live a little."

Sylvia and Lucy were inseparable sisters who looked alike, but their personalities drastically differed.

My eyes glanced at the China travel guide, instantly distracted. "Mom, Aunt Lucy, thanks for calling. I'm still celebrating my birthday with a friend right now. I'll call you tomorrow, Mom."

"Love you, Victoria."

"I love you too."

"Your mom and aunt always make me laugh. I wish I could meet them in person instead of eavesdropping on your conversations with them."

"So do I." I sighed for a moment but picked up the China brochure, energized to scan through the multitude of options.

"There's another present in that box, ya know."

"Another gift? What?" I put the travel book down and glanced within the large box. Beneath the crunch of multicolored polka-dot tissue lay a gift box wrapped in patterned red paper with white rosebuds. I tore at the pretty paper to find a flat white package with colorful circular images across the bottom. It read, "Explore Your Roots."

"A DNA test?"

Tommy nodded. "This one has great reviews. It'll tell you your health risks as well as where your roots are from."

He meant well with this gift, but my stomach danced a salsa just thinking about it.

"Honey? You've mentioned doing one of these tests, yet you never bought one. All you have to do is spit in a tube and mail it to a lab. Who knows what you might learn?"

I smiled. "Thank you, honey—for this and the vacation."

"You're upset. I'm sorry." His eyes drooped in time with a frown.

"No, this was so thoughtful. I've lived my whole life without knowing about my full genetic makeup. What if this leads to disappointment?"

"What if it doesn't?"

CHAPTER 3

I had stuffed the DNA kit inside a dresser drawer. Whenever I came across it in search of a blouse, I'd stare at the small white box with colorful images painted across the package. *Explore Your Roots.* I knew who I was, despite my questionable paternity.

I grew up in an environment where truth could be construed as fantasy fiction. Sylvia Ursini flaunted an expansive imagination, barring no limits. At seventeen, she graduated from Las Vegas High School. She fell back on her childhood tap dancing and jazz background to establish herself as a showgirl at the Flamingo on the Strip—the hotel Bugsy Siegel founded in 1946. Sylvia spoke as if she had met and befriended Bugsy, saying things like, "Oh, yeah, Bugsy was a great guy and so good-looking!"

I didn't realize the depths of Sylvia's embellishments until I became old enough to establish a historical time frame. Bugsy Siegel had been viciously murdered in 1947. Shot to death in the home of his lover, Virginia Hill. Sylvia would've been at the tender age of fourteen. She couldn't have known the man.

According to Sylvia, she lied about her age to dance at the Flamingo as a teenager. If she didn't have pictures of her performing in her fanciful costumes, wearing stunning headdresses with hundreds of feathers and sparkly jewels, I wouldn't have believed her.

She was a gorgeous woman with an hourglass shape, possessing an exotic Italian look like her parents: long, black hair with bouncy waves, hypnotic chocolate eyes, and full red lips that practically glimmered when she smiled. It was her exuberant personality that added to her sex appeal. Unfortunately, she never had a long-term relationship or a husband.

Sylvia talked about meeting many notable people at the Flamingo. In the early '50s, Dean Martin and Jerry Lewis were comedic geniuses. She provided tremendous details about them and her alleged affair with Dean Martin before my birth. Dean already had two marriages and a slew of children by the time I was born. Sylvia kept a framed black-and-white photo of her with Dean on the vanity table. She had at least met the legendary singer and actor. Whether or not they were actually involved was another puzzle I'd never solve.

One evening at the curious age of seven, she was brushing my long layers at the vanity table. I reached for that picture of Dean with his arms intimately wrapped around her waist and asked if he was my dad.

From the reflection in the mirror, I watched her cheeks turn pink. Her red-painted lips curved into a mischievous smile. She didn't answer my direct question, but she never said I was wrong, either. I thought that wicked smile she wore said it all. I'd stare at his photo in search of a resemblance. One snafu in my theory—Dean Martin didn't have dimples like me. None of the Ursinis had similar, deep-set dimples.

As a child, Sylvia's stories fascinated me. She was quite a storyteller with a captivated audience—me, a naive little girl who thought the world of her glamorous mother. I adored her up until about age twelve. As I grew up, I grew wise to her inflated versions of truth and watched her flirt relentlessly with men. Something about her sultry eye glances, flashy long lashes, and the way she shook her beautiful figure everywhere we went easily triggered attention. Many chased her around, but none of her relationships lasted more than a few months.

In spite of her lust for a man's touch, she also became involved with the church. She'd dress me up in lovely outfits and shiny shoes. On holidays, we wore fanciful gloves and hats.

When I turned thirteen, my birthday present was the announcement of her pregnancy. My brother, Kirk, was born on May 7, 1968. Kirk Douglas shined on the big screen in *Champion* and *Town Without Pity*. He had been Sylvia's favorite actor at that time, so she named my brother after the talented, handsome man—Kirk Douglas Ursini. Whoever Kirk's father was, he never kept in touch with him or Sylvia.

Seventeen months after Kirk's birth, my brother, Tony, entered the world on October 12, 1969. Tony was named after the popular actor Tony Curtis, remembered for his starring roles in *Some Like It Hot* and *Spartacus* alongside Kirk Douglas. Tony's father, Burt Ianni, was a Vegas local. I knew Burt tried to make the relationship work, but Sylvia could be difficult. Even though she always wanted or needed a man in her life, Burt and Sylvia didn't make an ideal love connection. Tony was the only one of the three of us who knew his father and maintained a relationship with him, using his last name.

Three children born from the seeds of three different fathers was scandalous for that period.

Sylvia loved dancing on the stage, charming the men in the audience, and hearing the energetic whistles and cheers, but eventually, she surpassed the maximum age of a showgirl. Vegas entertainment preferred women under thirty in the spotlight. At some point, she switched to a hostess position at one of the Flamingo's restaurants.

My relationship with my grandparents became vital. My grandmother always had an ailment stemming from her struggle with mental illness. Grandpa, though, was strong and healthy. He'd take me to museums or have my brothers and me help out at the market he owned in Whitney. That market gave him a break as a caregiver to Grandma. Grandpa fit comfortably in the role of the family fixer.

Sylvia managed to keep our family home intact with enough clothes to wear and food on the table. We didn't have much money, but we never felt poor. She was also big on education. She didn't go to college, but she insisted I attend. My brothers didn't have much interest in education past high school, but Sylvia strongly encouraged them to be educated.

Kirk chose plumbing as his career trade. He married too young at the age of twenty to a wild child named Lacy, then divorced her before his twenty-third birthday. He had several relationships through the years, but nothing long-term. Kirk stood about six feet, two inches, strikingly handsome with a rugged, athletic build that women loved. He was always in jeans and fitted shirts that highlighted his structured physique. He had dark sable hair, rich brown eyes, and an olive complexion, inheriting the romantic Ursini Italian look. He had a soft spot where Sylvia was concerned and took after her with remarkable fairytale-telling ability.

Tony joined the Marines as soon as he turned eighteen, like his father. My youngest brother had black hair and eyes that gleamed crystal blue like Burt's. He was much shorter and stockier than Kirk, standing about five feet, eight inches. Tony was loving and protective toward his family, but he wasn't trusting in nature. And he would've wanted to save me from the abominable marriage to Jeffrey I had erroneously entered. To avoid a bitter dispute, I never divulged my marital problems to Tony until after I left Jeffrey.

Today, Tony lived with Leann, his long-time girlfriend. They hadn't married, and it didn't seem like they cared about the legalities of a legal union. Perhaps growing up with a wacky, single mother and a father who never married deterred his interest in marriage and children. Tony worked as a casino dealer at Mandalay Bay, and Leann was an executive assistant to one of the vice presidents at the same casino.

During my younger years, I had engaged in several short-term relationships with bittersweet endings before meeting Jeffrey Atkins. I thought that man would be the answer to all my problems. Boy, was I wrong.

Eight Months Later—July 2019

Families are like branches on a tree.
We grow in different directions, yet our roots remain as one.

—Suzy Kaseem

CHAPTER 4

Our trip to China quickly developed. I wasted no time coordinating the agenda. I couldn't wait to see the Great Wall, visit museums, and shop along Nanjing Road and Chenghuangmiao bazaar in Shanghai, see the Terracotta Army, the Bell Tower, and Drum Tower Square in Xi'an, and witness Hong Kong's spectacular Victoria Peak and Stanley Market.

Usually, when Tommy and I visited foreign countries, he preferred to rent a car and explore the magnificent sites on our own. China, however, would be a unique experience. He never allowed his mature age to dictate the activities we wanted to do, but the Chinese culture was unchartered territory for him. Tommy had no clue how to navigate the waters, which was the reason he selected a prominent tour company to escort us on this fantastic journey.

As the days drew near, I found myself breathless when speaking to friends and coworkers at the museum, like a burst of caffeine shooting through my veins, describing our upcoming adventure.

I barely slept a wink last night, restless about the appallingly long flight to the Asian continent. At 6:00 a.m., I rolled over to wake my lover with a sensual kiss against his neck and earlobe, stirring a fire within us. A delicious, early morning romp was a splendid way to start the day.

With two hours to go before heading to the airport, Tommy cleaned out the refrigerator and prepared to make one last dumpster run before leaving our home for two weeks. I checked my suitcase, ensuring we had sufficient supplies and our medication. My belly rumbled with restless nerves.

My cell rang at seven. Even telemarketers didn't make calls this early. My brother Kirk's name flashed across the screen of my iPhone. "Kirk, hey," I answered pleasantly.

He sounded out of breath as he spoke. "Vic, I know it's early, but—"

"Early? I'm up, getting ready for my trip."

"Trip? Oh, were you leaving *today*?" His rapid speech and labored breaths sounded like he had just run a marathon.

"What's wrong?"

"I'm at the hospital. It's Mom." Kirk elaborated; the fast tempo of his tone sounded sincerely stressed.

"Kirk, take a breath and tell me what happened."

Tommy quietly approached, so I placed Kirk on speaker.

"Mom was in a car accident. It's bad, Vic. Really bad. She's in surgery right now to stop the internal bleeding. She might not make it!"

"What?" The thought of Sylvia's death seemed unreal. A vibrant, mature lady in good health should live years longer.

Tommy placed his arm around me and kissed my forehead.

"What have the doctors told you? Where's Tony?" I asked. I'd feel better speaking to someone who didn't stretch the truth like a bungee cord.

"Tony's on his way to the hospital. I got a call from an officer at the accident scene. When I arrived at the hospital, they told me she was unconscious and banged up badly when brought in." His typical burly voice turned to whimpers when he continued. "If they can't stop the bleeding, w-w-we could…lose her."

Although I held some animosity toward her because my paternity had been an unsolved mystery my entire life, I never imagined losing her. Sylvia was too strong a woman to let a car crash end her life at eighty-six. My brown eyes set on Tommy's gray ones, unsure what to do or say.

He read my thoughts and clicked the mute button so Kirk wouldn't hear his voice. "I'll call the tour company to postpone our trip. We can reschedule China. You have to get to Vegas and be with your family. They need you."

Still in shock, I felt like crying, but the tears didn't flow. I texted Tony to fill me in when he arrived at the hospital. Tony understood why I contacted him after speaking with Kirk. We both saw the pattern of similarities between Kirk and Sylvia's quirky exaggerations. When Tony contacted me, he confirmed the dire situation. Her delicate life was in jeopardy.

What if I didn't make it to Vegas in time? Time to say goodbye.

*****

I sat unusually silent on the drive to Charles-de-Gaulle airport. The suitcase I had packed for China was tossed in the back seat to take on this impromptu Vegas trip.

"Honey, are you gonna be okay on this flight alone? I wish I could go with you, but—"

"You can't be seen in Vegas, honey. You're supposed to be *dead*. I'll feel better once I see Sylvia for myself."

"I called Danny. He'll meet you at the airport. If you or your family needs anything, my son will help."

Tommy already stated this twice before we left the apartment, probably feeling as jittery as me. "I know, babe. Please don't worry."

"Don't worry? If the press finds out you're in town, they might hound you for a statement. And your ex—" Tommy's teeth clenched at the thought of Jeffrey pestering me. "Once Atkins knows you're in town…well, I don't trust him."

"Jeffrey won't come after me, especially if the media is present. He already made himself look like the pompous ass that he is. He wasn't reelected as governor. He has no power or leverage over me anymore."

"If I have to fly down there to keep him away from you, I will."

"Absolutely not! No matter what happens, you cannot show your face in Vegas. And please don't argue with me before I hop on that plane. I can't deal with all of this if I thought you were angry with me."

He parked the Peugeot, grabbed my luggage, and walked me inside the airport near the check-in at American Airlines amid the hustle and bustle of travelers.

After my luggage had been checked and my boarding pass was in hand, I inched toward Tommy's sad expression and slipped my diamond ring and wedding band off my finger. "You'll need to hold onto my rings."

Tommy stared at the sparkling diamonds in his palm, smirked, and nodded. "Yeah, no one back home knows you got hitched again." His head lowered. "I'm gonna miss the hell outa ya."

"We'll FaceTime every day. It'll be like we're together."

"I'll know the difference when you're not snoring beside me," he teased.

"You'll miss my snoring as much as I'll miss your icy toes brushing up against me."

He chuckled and drew my body close to him for a sultry kiss and lengthy hug. As our foreheads touched, he said, "I hope your mother is okay. Call me as soon as you land. Love you."

"Love you more."

CHAPTER 5

The first flight was long and uncomfortable. Booking a last-minute flight meant I sat between two strangers in coach with a wailing baby behind me. My thoughts drifted to Sylvia. Was she still in surgery? With a two-hour layover at JFK in New York, I dialed Kirk's number, but he didn't answer. Tony's cell went straight to voice mail. I left them messages and hoped to hear some news before my flight headed to McCarran International Airport.

In the ladies' room, I glanced in the mirror at my chocolate hair color with red tones. I changed my hair color multiple times since I left my life as Victoria Ursini behind. The bleached look didn't go over well with Tommy, reminding him of his ex-wife, Sadie—a lovely blonde. Their rocky marriage ended in disaster in the '80s. When I switched up my appearance to this rich auburn shade, Tommy's gray eyes perked up. He'd never come out and say he hated that light-gold shade on me, but I could sense his dislike.

I picked up an egg and cheese sandwich at a deli counter to control the belly rumbles, then attempted to contact my brothers again. Kirk and Tony still weren't answering their phones as I sat nervously at gate thirty-two. I left another message and sent a text that I'd be on another plane soon, desperate for an update. Perhaps no news meant good news. I called Tommy through FaceTime while impatiently praying for an optimistic status on Sylvia.

"Hi, honey. Are you in New York?"

"Yeah, the waiting is killing me! I can't believe my brothers haven't responded to my messages."

"Maybe they don't have an update yet. Your emotions are running high right now. Stay calm. You've got another long flight. Maybe you should take one of your sleeping pills," he suggested.

"Uh, my sleeping aids. Damn, I think I left them on the kitchen counter." I glanced at my watch, wondering if I had time to run into a store to pick up a bottle of melatonin. But an announcement for boarding to Las Vegas billowed through the vast space of adjacent gates. So I said farewell to my love, blowing him a kiss, when a text from Kirk rang in.

"Mom survived the surgery, but she has a long road ahead of her. Her life is on the line. Your presence will help."

Tony texted a more mellow message, saying, "Mom's okay. We're waiting for her to wake up. We have to keep our cells off in the ICU."

My fingers tapped across the keypad of my cell, replying, "Thank god. I'll meet you at the hospital after my plane lands."

I released a breath of relief, grateful she survived the surgery.

*****

After the plane landed at McCarran, Tommy's son, Danny, texted that he was waiting in the cell phone lot and that he'd meet me at the passenger pick-up area in his white Lincoln Navigator.

When I retrieved my luggage, I texted back, teasingly saying to look for an old lady with dark-reddish hair, a cream-colored blouse, and black paisley pants, carrying a burgundy suitcase.

I spotted the enormous SUV approaching and sent a wave, hoping I had the right vehicle since the windows were tinted. Danny jumped from the car to greet me with a warm hug. "I'm sorry to hear about your mom, but it's good to see you." He took a step back and fiddled with his blue tie.

"It's nice to see you too. Thank you for picking me up." He looked as handsome as his father, remarkably similar in size and shape but with more youthful features.

"It's no trouble, Vicki. I have flexibility as one of the owners of the Montgomery. It doesn't feel the same without Pop running the place anymore, though."

"Tommy is so proud of all you've accomplished, managing the legalities of the family business. Does your family know about—"

"About you coming to Vegas? Not yet. You were highlighted in Pop's autobiography as his love interest before his *death*." He used air quotes to highlight the word death. "My wife has been curious about you since she read Pop's memoirs." He grabbed my suitcase and tossed it in the back of his large vehicle. "Hop in, and I'll get you to the hospital."

I ruminated on past events as Danny drove through familiar, hectic streets. Tommy had written his memoirs, which were published with the hope of identifying the man responsible for the death threats against him. We prayed the culprit would be exposed and put behind bars. Maybe we wouldn't need to live on a different continent, far from our families, if the threat could be neutralized.

Danny read Tommy's memoirs when the book was first released in January 2011. He believed someone murdered Tommy, and he put himself in grave danger, determined to bring a killer to justice, angering ruthless gangsters and other criminals. In 2013, after a couple of brushes with death, Tommy couldn't allow his son to think he was deceased any longer. He brought Danny into our secret world as Tim McGee and Charisse LaSalle-McGee. However, Danny's mother, wife, and four children had been kept in the dark about Tommy being alive, like my family and the Vegas community.

"How's your mother doing? Pop told me she was in a car accident," Danny acknowledged, disrupting my thoughts.

"I spoke with my brothers while I waited for my luggage in baggage claim. She's still unconscious, but fortunately, she survived emergency surgery."

"That's good! How was my pop when you left? I mean, it's been the two of you living in Paris together for several years."

"Your pop will be fine without me for a short time. Once my mother is back on her feet, I'll head home. We can test that cliché about absence making the heart grow fonder."

Danny laughed.

When we arrived at Sunrise Hospital, he pulled up to the main entrance.

"Do you need anything from your suitcase, Vicki?"

I held up my large, black Michael Kors tote. "I've got every-thing I need for now in here."

"I'll drop your luggage off to you later so you don't have to lug it around the hospital." He studied my face as if I had a piece of spinach crammed in my teeth. "Something's off with your look. Oh, it's your beauty mark."

I quickly flipped down the visor and gazed at my reflection in the small mirror. I had covered the beauty mark nested within my dimple to the right of my lips—another disguise for my Charisse identity. I used a wipe from my tote to remove the caked-on makeup I had grown accustomed to using daily. I turned to Danny. "Is that better?"

"Yes, now you look like the Victoria Ursini I've seen on televi-sion, except for the reddish hair." He chuckled. "Text me the address where I should bring your suitcase later. You can use one of my cars while you're in town."

"That would be wonderful, Danny."

"I'll say a prayer for your mom."

I kissed his cheek. "Thank you, Danny, for everything. I'll be in touch when I can."

CHAPTER 6

My pulse quickened in time with a vexing flutter in my stomach as I entered through the automatic hospital doors that swung open at my presence. A photo was taken of me for the visitor badge I clipped to my blouse. The woman at the information desk provided me with directions to the elevators that led to the ICU.

"ICU room 5," I muttered as I gingerly stepped off the elevator and walked dimly down a hallway past rooms with patients hacking, moaning, or complaining. Some slept peacefully. The brazen smell of disinfectant suddenly overwhelmed my nostrils. The sound of machine bleeps echoed from all directions.

A few paces ahead, I noticed my youngest brother, Tony, stretching his legs in the hall.

"Vicki!" he shouted when spotting me. His blue eyes softened in time with a gentle smile as he approached. Outside of using FaceTime, we hadn't been on the same continent since I left the States in 2010.

We embraced, squeezing each other tightly. The warmth of his arms felt so welcoming. I didn't realize how much I missed seeing my family in person. "Oh, Tony. You look great!" Except for some puffiness beneath his eyes from staying up all night, he looked handsome. His biceps felt larger, as did his midsection.

"Thanks, sis." He took a step back to take a better look at me. "You always look beautiful. I like the red hair. It's different."

I nodded as my smile faded. "How's Mom? Where's Kirk?"

Tony pointed inside the room where the image of Kirk holding Sylvia's hand didn't distract me from witnessing her bruised body, lying as still as a corpse. I had to catch my breath before advancing toward Kirk and placing an endearing hand on his shoulder.

He stood to hug me. His muscular arms squeezed around my petite frame. "It's good you're here, Vic."

Slowly, I inched nearer to Sylvia, peacefully sleeping in the bed. A tube with oxygen flowing plugged her nose, helping her to breathe steadily. A mountain of regret swept through me, thinking I should have found a way to come home sooner. I never thought the invincible Sylvia Ursini would let a car accident bring her down. "Hi, Mom. I'm here." I clutched her hand, but she didn't flinch from her immobile position.

Her russet-shaded hair looked recently colored. She always maintained routine hair appointments, manicures, pedicures, and facials. Sylvia kept up with the latest fashion trends. She refused to wear matronly clothes, adding more years to her appearance. She looked outrageous in skinny, ripped jeans and lattice-sleeved tops, but maintaining her sexy showgirl image was essential to her. No one would have guessed her to be in her eighties. A few nips here and a couple of tucks there, and she looked like the younger woman who lived within her aging physique.

Tony leaned against the doorframe. "You must be exhausted after your long flight."

I was ridiculously overtired, though I sat on a plane for fourteen hours. My stiff limbs required movement.

"Where are you staying?" Kirk asked.

"I thought I'd stay at Mom's house. I still have a key. Hey, why don't you guys go home? Get some rest. Shower. I'm here now, so I'll stay with her. You've been here all night."

"No, I'm staying," Kirk insisted.

"Kirk, you'll be no good to Mom if you're exhausted," Tony said.

Kirk shook his head. "You can go if you want, but I want to stay longer."

"The nurse told us only one visitor at a time. Vicki's here, so give her some time alone with her, Kirk."

Emotions charged my brother, Kirk, whereas logic ruled Tony's actions. Tony managed to convince Kirk to take a break. They kissed Sylvia's pale cheek before driving home to refresh and recharge.

Feeling unbearably exhausted, I stood beside Sylvia and brushed my fingers against her forehead. I thought some light music would liven the mood in this ominous room. I clicked on the Dean Martin playlist on my iPhone, starting with "Ain't That a Kick in the Head," followed by "Mambo Italiano," before a pretty, fair-haired nurse entered.

She whispered, "Hello. You must be Ms. Ursini's daughter. Your brothers said you'd be coming."

"Yes, I'm her daughter, Vicki. Do you have an update on her condition, nurse—?"

"Tara." She pointed to her name tag. "I need to do a quick check now, if you don't mind giving me a moment, please."

"Of course. Is it okay if I keep the music on?"

"Anything to encourage her to wake up."

"You think she can hear the music and my voice?"

"It's very possible. As long as the music doesn't disrupt anyone, feel free to play it. And by all means, talk to her. Let her know you're with her." She sent me a lovely smile.

I moved out of the way for Tara to check Sylvia's pulse and review the numbers flashing across the screen of the machine affixed with wires to Sylvia's arm and chest. The nurse jotted some notes in the chart she carried while speaking, "All set for now. According to the nurse-on-a-stick, her numbers are encouraging."

"Why hasn't she woken up?"

"It's normal for her to be unconscious post-surgery and with a head injury. All we can do is wait. It could be a minute, an hour, or another day until she wakes."

"Thank you for the update, Tara," I said before she bounced back to the nurse's station.

"Well, it's just you, me, and this *nurse-on-a-stick*, Mom." I chuckled at that name, staring up at the machine that captured her vitals. "Nurse Tara thinks you might hear our voices." I interrupted Dean's version of "King of the Road" and pushed the chair closer to the side of the bed, where she lay still and quiet. "Seeing that you're a captive audience right now, I wanted to tell you…I'm sorry. Yes, you heard that right. I'm sorry I haven't visited you in person for so many years. Phone calls and sending you money to help pay your bills shouldn't have compensated for my absence."

The beeps made by the nurse-on-a-stick steadied, distracting my one-sided conversation. I grasped her hand and whispered, "I know you didn't understand why I've been so secretive about my life. I led you to believe I avoided the media and Jeffrey. There's so much more to it, but I'm happier than I've ever been. I finally know what love is. You used to warn me about love. You'd say, 'Love could be wonderful, but it requires two-way communication, honesty, and a ton of patience.' I wish you experienced having someone to count on and plan a future with. Someone to be by your side through thick and thin like I found."

A light swish from Sylvia's finger was felt. My eyes were fixated on the hand I held. "Mom? Can you hear me? It's Victoria."

Perhaps that flicker was wishful thinking.

"Oh, Mom, I'd love for you to wake up and tell me that amazing story when you were Gregory Peck's good luck charm at the roulette pit. Or oh, oh, oh, when Ava Gardner got jealous because Sinatra hugged you and called you *sweetheart*. That's a fantastic story!"

Her fingers came to life, gently gripping my hand. This time, I was sure that I didn't imagine it. "You *can* hear me."

I sprang from the bed, raced to the door, and shouted, "Nurse, I think she's waking up!" I moved closer to Sylvia and clasped her hand again. "It's time to wake up, Mom. Tell me about the time when Milton Berle called you on stage to participate in his comedy act."

Nurse Tara rushed in, with another nurse lagging behind.

I inched back so they could examine her while I eagerly explained, "Her fingers moved, and she squeezed my hand!"

Tara held Mom's wrist, feeling her pulse. "Ms. Ursini, can you hear me? Can you open your eyes?"

"Mom, these ladies would love to hear about your years as a famous showgirl."

"Wow, you were a showgirl?" Tara asked, presuming Sylvia understood her words.

"A *famous* showgirl. Performed in hundreds of numbers. Met numerous celebrities. She could sing, dance, and act. She was a brilliant performer!"

Sylvia's lids began to twitch. Spreading flattery like butter on warm bread encouraged her to wake.

"Oh, here she comes." Tara turned to her clinical partner and muttered, "Page Dr. Sherwood."

Within seconds, the nurse raced from the room, and I heard the announcement for Dr. Sherwood to go to ICU room 5.

"Tara, wait until you hear my mother's stories about Dean Martin and Jerry Lewis."

"Really? Oh, I can't wait, Ms. Ursini. You actually knew those stars? Wow!"

Sylvia's eyes blinked a bit until she stared straight ahead with those pretty brown eyes, focusing on the sterile room, the hovering nurse, and me.

I smiled and tried to stand closer, yet out of Tara's way. "Mom, I'm here. It's me, Victoria."

Sylvia blinked hard before her eyes swerved to Tara, rechecking her pulse.

"Welcome back, Ms. Ursini."

"Mom, you're at the hospital. You were in an accident, but you're okay."

A look of confusion washed across Sylvia's face.

A man wearing dark-blue scrubs and a white lab coat feverishly entered the room. He gave me a serious nod before looking into the open eyes of his patient.

As they examined Sylvia, speaking in clinical riddles, I stepped behind them to text Kirk and Tony the good news. Then I texted Tommy.

After what felt like a prolonged examination, Dr. Sherwood introduced himself, verified I was immediate family, and said, "She has a lot of healing to do, and I have tests to order to confirm there's no further internal bleeding, but it is encouraging that she's awake. I'll check in on her shortly and before the next round of tests."

"Thank you, Doctor."

Once the doctor and Tara exited the room to move on to see other patients, I plastered a full smile on my face and sat beside a silent Sylvia. Her eyes eerily followed my every move.

"Mom, do you need anything? Can you speak?"

She merely blinked.

I took hold of her hand and kissed her knuckles. "Squeeze my hand if you can understand me."

She managed a docile clasp.

"You were in a car accident. Do you remember? Squeeze once for yes, twice for no."

Sylvia's eyes closed for several seconds, then pressed my fingers together once feebly.

"Good, you remember."

She pulled her hand from mine and used her fingers to remove the plastic cylinder from her nose.

"No, Mom. Keep that on. It'll help you breathe."

"Victoria," she said in a raspy, muddied tone, filled with exhaustion. She cleared her throat. "S-s-stop fussin' s-s-so much. W-w-why are you h-h-here?"

I was thrilled she started to act like her tough, ornery self. Although she didn't sound happy to see me.

"I flew home to make sure you were okay after the accident. Can I do something to make you more comfortable?"

"Damn t-t-truck came out of nowhere. H-h-hit me on the side." She grabbed her midsection, releasing a heartbreaking moan. Tears welled up in her eyes.

"Try not to move, Mom. Between your injuries and surgery, you're bound to feel achy for a while. Kirk and Tony were here all night. They're on their way back to see you."

"You shouldn't h-h-have come b-b-back," she stuttered. "That ex-h-h-husband of yours. Con-d-d-des-s-scending p-p-prick."

I knew Sylvia didn't care for Jeffrey after what he had put me through. Initially, she loved that I married a wealthy politician; anything that shined a spotlight on her and her family made Sylvia happy. Learning Jeffrey had blackmailed me to stay married to him instantly altered her initial perception of him.

She added in a weak tone, "He c-c-calls me—angry. Wants to know w-w-where you are. Stay away f-f-from him."

"Don't worry about Jeffrey, Mom. I'll make sure he doesn't harass you anymore." Her statement completely shocked me. She never told me Jeffrey had been bothering her.

"Go back…h-h-home. Don't look back." She grabbed her stomach, groaning in agony.

"I'm not leaving until I know you're okay."

Sylvia stirred in the bed, trying to sit up. She slumped back into her pillow when she realized she hadn't the power to switch positions. "Listen…to…m-m-me." Her voice sounded frail as she gasped between slurred words.

"Mom, let's get you some oxygen." I attempted to place the tube inside her nose, but she fiercely brushed my hand away, proving her strength was returning.

"Do *not* s-s-sell my h-h-house. You m-m-must k-k-keep the house," she blurted breathlessly.

"The house? I wouldn't sell your home."

Sylvia shook her head back and forth in frustration. "Promise me y-y-you won't sell m-m-my house!" She reached for my hand and clenched it with surprising firmness.

"Okay, don't worry. No one's selling your home. Please put the oxygen tube back in and rest," I insisted while gently securing it in place.

This time, she didn't fight me. She closed her eyes and drifted off.

I sat back in the chair and blew out a heavy breath, reassured she woke with a mild spurt of energy. A quirky sensation passed through my heart, but I felt grateful she would recover.

CHAPTER 7

Kirk and Tony barreled inside the hospital room.

"Mom!" Kirk shouted, racing to her side.

I stepped aside so he and Tony could each have time to speak with her. "It hurts her to talk. I asked the nurse to up her pain meds."

Nurse Tara had already informed me that a steady dose of morphine flew through one of the tubes attached to Sylvia. The wary look in Tara's eyes discouraged me when I explained the pain Sylvia expressed when trying to hold a conversation. She sought the doctor's approval to adjust her medication.

After several minutes of visiting with Kirk and Tony, the cocktail of pain meds eventually knocked her into dreamland. Tara expected Sylvia to sleep for hours, and they needed to run further tests. She insisted we go home to rest ourselves.

Tony offered to drive me to our childhood home.

I encouraged Kirk to come to Sylvia's house with us. It would be like old times, reminiscing on fun childhood memories about growing up, Ursini style, and running through the aisles at Grandpa's market, startling his customers.

Still, Kirk declined, clearly exhausted from the traumatic day.

*****

Spending time alone with Tony allowed me to catch up on his life with Leann, working at Mandalay Bay, and his golf game. Leann and I never really hit it off as friends, but Tony loved her. Although they were never married, Leann was considered family.

"So who's the mystery man?" Tony asked with a crooked grin.

It pained me that I couldn't share elaborate details about my marriage to Tommy. I couldn't say anything to my family or friends about my personal life. I feared I'd slip and mention the name of my supposed deceased lover. "Mystery man?"

"Aside from Mom's injuries and the excruciatingly long flight you endured, you're glowing, Vicki. I have to wonder if you're no longer just hiding out from the media and Jeffrey in Paris. Maybe some Parisian gent is responsible for that happy glimmer you're radiating."

I couldn't help but smile without confirming his suspicion aloud.

"After all this time, you could come home, ya know. Something or someone is keeping you in France. My money is on a guy."

"I love my life in Paris, Tony. I've adjusted and made friends."

"You don't have to justify yourself to me. Eventually, you have to come out of hiding. It's been years since your divorce. The media keeps busy with politics, for the most part, these days. They may not pay any attention to your affair with that hotel tycoon slash author or Grandpa's painting you miraculously retrieved before he died."

"I know you read Tommy's memoirs."

"He really loved you. It's a shame he died so suddenly. Look, if you did meet someone else in Paris, I'm sure Tommy would be happy you moved on. You only live once, Vicki. Happiness looks good on you." He smiled large enough to make his blue eyes sparkle.

As we pulled around the corner of Orchard Lane, our childhood home came into view—a cute blue ranch nestled on a quarter acre of land. An enormous cedar tree took up the majority of the front yard, with its oversized roots emerging through the green grass.

"Whose car is in the driveway?" Tony questioned.

"A friend of mine dropped it off for me to use while I'm in town."

"That's a *Mercedes*. Nice friend."

"It's Tommy's son, Danny. He texted me, saying he left it here for me to use. My luggage is in the trunk. Danny was kind enough to pick me up at the airport earlier."

Tony slammed on the brakes when he parked. "Really? I'm surprised you've stayed in contact with the Cavallo family."

"Several years ago, he was determined to speak with me to learn about his father's death. How could I deny his request? Danny is a good man with a lovely family. I let him know I was coming to town, and he offered to help."

Tony's brows raised. "Will you be okay here…alone?"

"This is our home, blooming with memories. I always feel safe here." I drank in the warm air as I gauged the front yard beneath the massive cedar tree. The wicked heat turned the grass to straw, so I made a mental note to search for the sprinkler in the shed tomorrow.

"Where'd he leave the car key? I'll help you with your luggage."

Danny's text explained he placed the key in an envelope and slipped it inside the storm door.

Tony practically drooled when checking out the luxurious red Mercedes before popping the trunk to collect my luggage while I opened the door to enter my safe haven.

Tony plopped the bags in the living room and looked around the quiet space. "Feels cold in here, like the AC is set to 50 degrees," he said, forcing a shiver to rush up my spine.

"I'll adjust the thermostat. Thanks for the ride. Want some coffee or tea?" I asked as I approached the central air device to raise the temperature.

He shook his head. "Think I'll go home and try to sleep."

I nodded, understanding. "I'll meet you at the hospital in the morning."

Tony turned to leave but stopped suddenly. "I'm really glad you're home, Vicki."

"Me too."

After the door shut behind him, I glanced around the room. Sylvia bought a new living room set, and the walls were painted in earth tones, a different look from what I remembered. Maybe she used the money I sent her every month to refurbish the place. I had the means to help her live comfortably throughout her retirement, but the checks I sent didn't compensate for my absence.

Her vintage white china dinnerware with dainty mauve flowers and gold trim hugging the edges was still displayed in the antiquated cherry hutch in the dining room. The fragile pieces could stand a thorough cleaning by hand.

The floors needed vacuuming, and the tables required polishing. A mountain of laundry overfilled a basket in her bedroom. Dishes were piled in the kitchen sink, waiting to be washed.

I tossed some clothes in the washing machine first and raised my sleeves to rinse the dishes before filling the dishwasher. I swept the white tile floor, then decided to make a cup of hot tea when my cell buzzed. Tommy called by video.

"Hey, honey." It was so nice to see his face on the small screen. "It's a bit early in Paris."

"I told you I can't sleep well without you. I wasn't sure if I'd catch you alone after a long day of traveling and spending time at the hospital. I saw your text about Sylvia waking up. You must be relieved."

"Very! The nurse basically kicked us out so she could get the rest her body needs to heal. Is it possible to feel exhausted yet wired at the same time?"

"After what you've been through—yes. Did you take your meds today?"

"Uh, with the time change, I forgot." I reached for my purse and pulled out the prescription bottle to take my daily dosage.

"Where are you now?"

I lifted my cell and introduced him to the home where I grew up at 67 Orchard Lane. "Oh, let me show you the lanai and the backyard. Sylvia maintained this gorgeous peony bush." I stepped into the lanai, scurrying around a white wicker seat with an aquamarine cushion to reach the porch swing, large enough for two, adorned with tan and bright blue pillows. "She loves to sit out here on this swing and stare into the yard at the beautiful white peonies she tends to. There was always something dramatically peaceful about her flowers." The rest of the yard could turn to hay, but she tended to these peonies like they were her children.

I flipped on the light switch to cast a shimmer across the backyard before stepping near the small, treasured garden. "Look at how perfectly lovely these peonies are." I held the delicate, creamy white petals with a touch of pink in my hand and breathed in the sweet fragrance. Her voice echoed through my head—a flash of a memory of Sylvia pruning this bush and telling me, "Happiness blossoms from within. Tend to your garden and pluck the weeds." A reminder that I was responsible for my own joy. Always take care of myself and remove the negativity in my life, including people with pessimistic energy.

Tommy's voice snapped me back. "Pretty flowers, babe. Why'd she plant the bush in that spot away from the house and off to the side? It looks out of place there."

"Hmm, I never thought about it. Perhaps she wanted to enhance the garden but didn't get around to it, or she lost interest. I told you, honey, Sylvia had a unique way of thinking. She might have ADHD. I'm not sure I'll ever understand how her mind operates."

Tommy and I reconnected while I sat on the swing, sipping my tea, recovering from stress, jet lag, and the nine-hour time difference from France until I decided to go to bed.

CHAPTER 8

Lurking

A white Ford Focus sat at the end of a long driveway obstructed by a row of pine trees. The 2012 model was the only decent car he could afford. The man needed a reliable vehicle, and this Ford had a mere 30,000 miles on it. The air conditioning unit emitted a burning scent, but the heat of July in Nevada could melt his flesh without it. Sweat glistened beneath his Los Angeles Clippers cap from squally nerves, not the hundred-degree temperature.

The monstrous estate always took his breath away. He'd never been inside, but he drove by the place numerous times throughout his life, thinking about the residents within. Why did they own such an impressive mansion with vast acreage while he lived in a one-bedroom apartment, sharing space with ants and cockroaches skulking in the walls?

Through binoculars, he watched the homeowners beneath the well-lit entrance. A woman with salt-and-pepper hair and her husband, a blowhard in a Brioni suit, sauntered out the front door.

The well-dressed man snapped his fingers at one of the servants, who instantly produced his briefcase. A black Audi sedan with tinted windows pulled up to the couple. The driver stepped out and opened the back door for his passengers to enter. They seemed to be in a hurry as the driver jogged around to the front of the car, slipped into the lavish front seat, and sped off.

Before the main gate at the bottom of the drive opened for the couple's exit, the man lowered his Clippers cap and drove several paces behind the luxury vehicle to track how they'd spend their evening.

CHAPTER 9

With nerves as squishy as Jell-O and my body still adjusting to Nevada time, I managed only a few hours of sleep. At six, I dashed out of bed, made a cup of English breakfast tea, and finished Sylvia's laundry. I had plenty of time before visiting hours began to boil an egg and toast an English muffin from the freezer. I looked and felt like a new woman after a hot shower.

I drove Danny's Mercedes to the corner pharmacy for a few items, including an over-the-counter bottle of melatonin gummies, to ensure I rested this evening. I couldn't take regular sleeping pills, fearing an adverse reaction to my daily medication.

At 9:00 a.m., I arrived at the hospital carrying a small bouquet of lovely white peonies I picked from the yard, meant to cheer up Sylvia and brighten her room. Perhaps she'd be awake, keeping the nurses in stitches with her phenomenal stories from her showgirl years.

That strong disinfectant aroma drifted through the ICU as I strode down the corridor. Men and women in scrubs scrambled from the nurses' station positioned in the center of the area. Breakfast trays were being collected from rooms.

I smiled at Nurse Tara, who sent me a friendly wave in return.

"We need help! Hurry!" A familiar, frantic voice was heard shouting, sounding like my brother, Tony.

I picked up my stride to room 5, only to witness a swarm of clinicians racing inside. A loud, menacing sound buzzed.

Tony dashed in and stood behind Kirk when a firm, deep voice announced, "Code blue!"

I spun around Tony's frame to witness a nurse nudge Kirk's arm, shouting at us to step outside. Another nurse attempted CPR, her hands pressing rhythmically atop Sylvia's chest, chanting, "One, two, three—"

I tugged at my brother's shoulder. "Kirk, let them do their job. We can't be in their way."

Kirk punched low at the air with his fist and staggered out of the room.

Tony faced me and said, "Mom was awake and talking a little. The doctors planned to run more tests, but she gasped for air, and that damn machine beeped steadily. Jesus, what if Mom doesn't survive?"

"How can you be so negative, Tony?" Kirk grumbled as he paced in a half-circle.

"Kirk, we have to be prepared for the worst. I don't want our mother to die, but that car crash was severe. She's in the ICU, not a recovery room after one of her *cosmetic* surgeries."

"Stop!" I snapped.

"I'm sorry. I don't mean to sound harsh. I can't believe this is happening." Tony positioned himself against the window frame outside our mother's room, observing the health professionals through the open blinds do their job. Dr. Sherwood darted in, calmly and politely requesting stats from the nurses.

Kirk and I made our way beside Tony. The three of us, side by side, watched the horror show play out before our eyes until the faint, lengthy beep of that nurse-on-a-stick penetrated the air around us.

The doctor mumbled, "Time of death: 9:19 a.m."

The peony bouquet escaped from my grasp and dropped to the floor. "No!" I shouted, glancing at my Apple watch. Nineteen minutes after nine—the time of her...*death*.

Kirk barged into the room with Tony and me on his heels.

"I'm terribly sorry, Mr. Ursini. We've done all we could." He recited composed, practiced words regurgitated countless times to other families.

"What caused her death? She woke up yesterday. You said her vitals were encouraging. Keep doing CPR or whatever you have to do!" Kirk insisted.

"I'm sorry, Mr. Ursini. Your mother is *gone.*"

"She can't be—" I muttered between the fingers covering my lips, ill-prepared to accept her death.

A serene sound of silence exhumed.

Tony skated past the clinical team to sit beside her body.

Kirk's surprised expression froze in place, in denial of her dreadful fate.

Nurse Tara entered the room and approached Kirk. Her lengthy lashes blinked slowly. "I'm so sorry for your loss." She glanced at Tony and me. "If there's anything you need."

"Thank you, Tara," Kirk replied, barely making eye contact before he rushed to Sylvia's bedside.

This wavering feeling danced through my stomach and around my racing heart. I exhaled resignedly, inching my way nearer to her. Slowly, I sank beside her on the bed and gripped her left hand. A hard lump burned in my throat when I uttered, "Mom, you lived an exuberant life. Now you can sleep with the angels."

I couldn't believe that one coherent moment with Sylvia yesterday would be my final conversation with her. After wrapping my head around this tragic news, I needed a moment to process the unthinkable. I needed Tommy. "Excuse me," I mumbled to my brothers. "I need some air."

Somehow, I found my way to the elevators that led to the main lobby and exit. My fingers trembled as I tapped my cell in search of Tommy's number. It took a moment for my brain to translate the time difference. I sat upon an unoccupied bench and sighed before pressing his number, anxious to hear his voice.

"Hey, babe. How are you? I didn't want to call because—"

"She didn't make it," I spat out, interrupting his sentence.

"Oh, no! I'm so sorry. What happened?"

"I suppose her injuries werc far more critical than anyone realized, thanks to that car accident. Luckily, I got to speak with her yesterday, not realizing what little time she had left. She rambled on about Jeffrey and some silly nonsense with the house."

"You know, there's a reason for that time you spent with her, even if she wasn't quite coherent. You needed to see her. I'm sure she was happy to see you too, baby. What can I do? I wish I could come there and—"

"I know that's not possible. I need to wrap my head around her death. Oh, she was always a bit *reckless,* but that added to her charm. She wasn't like the other moms when I was growing up. I feel guilty, harboring a fair amount of bitterness toward her for keeping my paternity a mystery. Did I tell you she started teaching me about healthy skin care when I was ten? 'Take care of your skin when you're young, Victoria. You'll thank me when you're old and gray someday. But not *really* gray because you'll dye your hair, of course.'" I smiled, reminiscing about our blasé discussions regarding beauty secrets and fashion trends.

"Between Sylvia's good looks, genetics, and the skin care advice she gave you, you don't look your age at all, honey, or maybe I just think you're beautiful no matter what."

Tommy always knew how to elevate my mood, especially during such a strenuous time, facing a great loss and mounds of guilt. Guilt for not visiting her sooner when I had the chance to make peace with her. Sure, I called her every week and sent money to allow her some financial freedom during her retirement years, but it didn't make up for the time apart.

My throat felt scorched, and my head throbbed an angry beat when Kirk, Tony, and I said our final goodbyes to Sylvia privately before stepping away from her lifeless body. This seemed like a dream that I struggled to wake from.

Pulling Kirk from her bedside was challenging, but Nurse Tara assured Kirk that she'd take care of Sylvia personally. Tara had a soothing way about her that reassured my somber brother. As Sylvia's health advocate, Kirk had the accountability of signing some papers. Tony stepped out of the room while I watched Kirk mindlessly scribble his initials and signature across some pages, still and insufferably quiet.

Tony returned, explaining, "I called Aunt Lucy to tell her the news."

"How'd she take it?"

"Horribly. She planned to visit Mom today. I offered to pick her up later this morning. You know, she's been sleeping a lot. I'm not sure whether it's from age or one of her many health conditions."

"Maybe we should check in on her," I suggested. "I was looking forward to seeing her in person, but not under these circumstances."

"She's eager to see you too. She sounded so upbeat when she heard you were flying in."

"Perhaps we should stop by Aunt Lucy's apartment."

"You two go. I'll meet you there after I wrap up here," Kirk affirmed.

I tapped Kirk's shoulder and nodded, understanding his need for solitude. "We'll see you there." I cocked my head to the side, encouraging Tony to follow me to our cars for the drive to our aunt's home.

*****

Aunt Lucy's apartment dwelled a few miles from Sylvia's house. He led the way in his truck while I followed him in the Mercedes.

Multiple sclerosis, one of Aunt Lucy's ailments, a debilitating condition that hit her hard with her first severe episode in her early fifties. MS affects the central nervous system, preventing the brain from communicating with the rest of the body and causing numbness, weakness, and tremors. Some people endured vision problems and the inability to walk. My aunt struggled until she had access to a new injectable drug shortly after her diagnosis, delaying the further progression of the disease. Her body had already gone through the agony of an outbreak with uncontrolled movement in her fingers, feet, and legs. The treatment allowed her to get some functionality back. These days, though, she required the use of a sturdy walker.

Sylvia helped her sister with physical tasks around her home that Lucy couldn't manage without difficulty. The last time I spoke with Sylvia, she feared Lucy might need to move in with her or go to a nursing home. Only time would tell how much longer she could live in her apartment alone.

Lucy was the younger sister, sharing the same features as Sylvia. They could pass as twins up until Lucy's diagnosis. Lucy was strong-willed like my mother but less rambunctious. She loved telling stories about how she'd have to reel Sylvia in when she was either angry or acted on impulse—typically related to men.

We dialed her apartment number to be buzzed in. Red, white, and blue decorations in honor of the Fourth of July holiday were scattered across the lobby walls as we inched our way through the hallway.

We knocked upon Aunt Lucy's door, where a floral decoration with bright-colored tulips and buzzing, pollinating bees hung. The wheels of her walker dragging across the carpet on the opposite side of the door were heard. When the door finally opened, Aunt Lucy's brown eyes were moist and swollen from shedding tears. Her puffy silver hair had been pulled back with a large clip. She wore tan slacks and an oversized lavender blouse. The smell of coffee filled the room as we entered and took turns hugging our sweet aunt.

"Oh, it's so wonderful to see you, princess."

"I wish it were under better circumstances, Aunt Lucy. You look wonderful."

"Oh, you're just being polite! I can't stop crying. What little sensation I have in my face feels heavy and bloated."

I shook my head and wrapped my arms around her petite frame snugly. "You're beautiful." She was as lovely as Sylvia, without the face-lift, manicure, and hair color. If she didn't have difficulty walking, you'd never know she fought an autoimmune disease or battled a mental illness like her mother, horrible conditions that ran in my family.

"The coffee is ready. I'm boiling water for tea, Victoria. There are some Lipton tea bags in the cupboard." She pointed to the exact place where I'd find the tea.

"Sit down, Aunt Lucy. I'll get the milk," Tony said after filling a mug with coffee.

"I can't believe my sister is *gone*!" She wept through each word. "Tell me about this accident she had, and what happened in that hospital?"

A moment of deep contemplation overpowered me. "You know, Mom mentioned a truck coming out of nowhere and hitting her."

Tony drizzled milk into his mug and added, "Before you arrived, Vicki, a couple of Metro officers came by the hospital to check on her. They said they'd stop back to speak to her today if she was able to give a statement. An ambulance rushed Mom to the hospital from the scene. She was unconscious, so no one heard her side of the story. Vic, she told you about it?"

"Only that a truck came out of nowhere. She remembered the accident but was in pain and couldn't speak without discomfort. I wonder how the other driver is and whose fault it was."

Aunt Lucy stood, though I wasn't certain why. I had just poured boiling water into our mugs and slipped in the tea bags.

"Do you need something?" I asked her.

"I just can't sit still, I guess. Oh, there are some Italian cookies in the jar. You know I love my sweets."

"I'll get them," Tony said. He grabbed a plate from the cupboard and spread a few pignolias, shortbread cookies dipped in ganache, and Italian rainbow cookies to fill the dish.

Aunt Lucy took an excruciatingly long time to sit and get comfortable before she snatched a pignolia cookie and dipped it in her tea. "Where's Kirk?"

"He'll be along soon. He stayed behind at the hospital to sign some papers. Maybe he needed to see Mom again," I explained, feeling worried about Kirk. He was the closest to Sylvia. Since depressive disorders ran in our family, I worried Kirk's grief might trigger a flurry of emotions and extreme sadness.

I learned to manage my moods with a prescribed daily dose of lithium. Taking this drug meant I needed to limit alcohol consumption and drink plenty of water. Years ago, I discovered the hard way that medication compliance was vital to my health.

My aunt became my savior, picking up on the subtle symptoms I exhibited because she battled bipolar disorder too. Manic depression was the common term when she was diagnosed. Severe shifts in moods left her feeling worthless, holding back tears one moment, then suddenly racing to an overly energized invincibility, demonstrating irrational actions.

I ought to know.

An orange cat jumped up on the table, startling me. "Oh, hi there, pretty kitty."

"Ginger, get down! You know you don't belong up here." Aunt Lucy scolded her cat.

"Hey, Ginger." I reached out for her to sniff my hand, and she brushed her thick orange coat against my arm in response, begging me to pet her.

"Ginger is very friendly. Giselle is hiding somewhere. You might see a flash of black-and-white dash by. She's a skittish tuxedo cat but very nosy. She loved when your mother came over." Aunt Lucy wept.

Tony tapped her hand in sympathy while Ginger purred in complete bliss for the attention I gave her.

Aunt Lucy dried her eyes and blew her nose, using a tissue she had tucked inside her pants pocket. "Did I ever tell you about the time when I first brought your Uncle Gary home to meet your grandparents and your mother?"

We'd heard this story a hundred times before, but we encouraged her to tell it. As she retold the tale with impeccable detail, I thought my aunt had an unhealthy obsession with her ex-husband. At some point, Uncle Gary vanished from our lives. I remembered him clearly. Gary Connors was a handsome construction worker with a muscular physique, jet-black hair, turquoise eyes, and chiseled features. He'd pinch my cheeks when I was little. I couldn't recall the last time I saw him. I was in college at the time. Sylvia told me not to ask questions because it would upset Aunt Lucy. Kirk and Tony were very young. If it weren't for Aunt Lucy's endless stories, they wouldn't remember Uncle Gary at all.

Aunt Lucy had had a bit of a mental breakdown after Gary left her. She couldn't care for her house by herself, compelling her to move in with Grandma and Grandpa at some point after her husband's disappearing act. She never remarried. It was obvious she never got Uncle Gary out of her heart.

Tony and I chuckled at the end of Aunt Lucy's meticulous version of Gary's introduction to the Ursini clan. She might suffer from the pain of MS and a behavioral health condition, but her mind still seemed sharp.

A loud buzz echoed through the house, causing me to jump, comparing that ominous sound to the nurse-on-a-stick that specified Sylvia's time of death.

"That must be Kirk in the lobby," Tony said. He buzzed him in and stood near the doorway until Kirk walked in, met our aunt with solemn eyes, and gave her a loving squeeze and kiss on the cheek.

"My sister was so fortunate to have three generous, loving children to help her."

I felt remorseful, hearing those words leave my aunt's lips. Sending Sylvia a monthly check helped her with financial security, although I didn't feel present in her life. But I could be here for her now. "I know Mom had a will. Does anyone know where it is or what her wishes were?"

"I know where she kept important papers in the house," Kirk replied. "I'm sure we'll find her will when we go there later."

"She told me she added your name to the house and her bank account a few years back, Kirk. Because of her age, she thought it would be wise, and I agreed. If anything happened to her, one of us could access her assets. What about her funeral? Did she want to be buried or cremated? We can organize a nice service at the church." Suddenly, I thought about everything that needed to be arranged. Flowers, music, the burial, and writing an obituary. Pressure in my mind and pain in my heart mounted. My head might explode.

"The Pine Rock Cemetery for Christians near the First Congregational Church is where she'd want to be buried," Aunt Lucy said matter-of-factly.

"That makes sense. She always attended Sunday worship," Tony added.

"Is Reverend Gordon still the pastor? Oh, wait. Is he still alive?" I asked. Pastor Gordon Steele had run the church since I was a kid, but he'd be up in his late eighties or possibly ninety by now.

"He's alive, but he retired several years ago. His son now runs the parish," Kirk answered.

"Josh or Drew?" I questioned, surprised by the notion.

"Pastor Joshua Steele," Kirk replied. "He's a little more open to modernization than his father was."

"Josh and I went to school together." My mind drifted, thinking about the fifth grade and my crush on Josh then. After I finished college and moved out of Sylvia's house permanently, I didn't attend church any longer. I lost touch with the Steele family unless Sylvia brought them up in conversation.

Tony reached for a pignolia, saying, "I'll notify the church today. Maybe they'll see us tomorrow to help plan the necessary arrangements."

"While I was at the hospital signing paperwork, I considered the Riverside Funeral Home for the service and burial. I know the funeral director. He's hired me for some plumbing jobs and referred me to his friends and clients. I'd like to give back."

Thankfully, we had ideas and a reasonable starting point.

CHAPTER 10

A cloud of emptiness and remorse loomed through our childhood home when we entered, knowing Sylvia would never return to her sanctuary filled with an abundance of memories. Shades of guilt and sadness toyed with my mind as tears drizzled from penitent eyes. The notion of no longer seeing her charming smile and vivacious energy when telling a great story from her past suddenly hit me. She drove me crazy, always exaggerating details, but her tales kept people in stitches.

Kirk headed toward her bedroom with Tony a few paces behind. Without much thought, I moved to her favorite spot on the lanai and soaked in the lovely view of her peonies. The day was balmy, with a bright sun shining over those dainty petals. I envisioned Sylvia in her large sun hat, gingerly pruning the peony bush.

When my brothers stepped into my peripheral view, Tony asked if I still liked mushrooms and olives on pizza. Kirk looked preoccupied, perusing a folder stuffed with documents he had gathered.

"I just need a moment." I shut my eyes again, drinking in visions of Sylvia. She had shown me the proper way to apply mascara when I was sixteen. She always gave good beauty advice. Sylvia exercised before it was cool or proper for a woman to visit a gym. Her hourglass shape and youthful appearance were important for her to maintain. Her voice sounded gentle and kind the first time my heart was shattered over a boy. I visualized her sitting beside me, saying, "He wasn't the one, Victoria, so don't waste your time sulking. Love is out there for you. I promise! When you find it, you'll know it, and it will be everlasting!" She emoted those words with such faith and enthusiasm for a woman who never maintained a long-term relationship.

"Vic, you okay?" Kirk asked.

My eyes opened, and I spotted him sitting across from me at the white patio table, settling into the plush aquamarine cushions. I nodded. "You found her will?"

Kirk held up the paperwork. "Yes. I knew the combination to the safe in her bedroom."

I glanced at Tony. "I'm suddenly feeling a little hungry. Mushroom and olive pizza sounds great."

Tony smiled, confirmed Kirk's choice of sausage and pepper toppings, and placed the order.

"Mom named Vicki as the executor," Kirk said, surprising me.

Kirk did a lot for Sylvia, but perhaps because I was the oldest, she elected me with the honor. "Go ahead, Kirk. You read it."

Kirk rambled through the legal jargon, skipping some irrelevant language, then got down to the basic verbiage we all understood. "She lists her main assets, which are the house, its contents, her bank accounts, and her Chevy, to be split equally between the three of us."

Divvying up everything she owned evenly came as no surprise.

"The car's destroyed, but we can submit an insurance claim," Tony added.

Kirk quietly weeded through more legal talk. "Okay, she named a few possessions she specifically picked out for us to have. Anything else we wanted to keep, we can pick and choose, I suppose. The first item listed is the antique hutch and the china dinnerware. Mom wants Aunt Lucy to have that because that piece originally belonged to their grandmother."

"Oh, yeah. I recall Mom talking about them squabbling a little over Nana's hutch. I guess that piece should be kept in the family."

"Vic, she wants you to have her gold locket that has a picture of you and Mom together in it."

I clasped my chest and felt my eyes fill up. "I love that piece."

"Mom also wants you to take the Monet replica you gave her for her birthday a few years ago."

I nodded. "She knew I loved art. It's the piece hanging over her bed."

"Hmm, this is interesting. She wants *me* to have her diamond ring with the gold filigree." Kirk's lips curved in sync with his rising brows.

"She wore that ring all the time," I stated.

"It's probably a sign from her, encouraging me to settle down." Kirk laughed. "I highly doubt it would go with my plumber attire."

"For Tony." Kirk paused and chuckled. "He always made the best damn martinis. He admired my Waterford crystal martini glasses and decanter set. Anytime he makes one of his special cocktails, I hope he thinks of me."

"Mom loved a good martini. So does Aunt Lucy. How about I break out that set now and shake us up dirty martinis? Aunt Lucy used to say, 'The dirtier, the better!'"

Kirk and I laughed in stereo.

"Wait, there's more." Kirk continued, "To my dear friend, Beverly Perrin, who *surely* passed before me. But *if* she's still alive and raising hell, she should do it in style. I want Bev to have my tiara with the rhinestones and crystals given to me by Desi Arnaz when I won the Vegas showgirl pageant back in 1960. Desi emceed the event. He was such a flirt!"

We burst out in laughter.

"Hmm. There's a separate piece of paper with a note that she attached with a paperclip. She dated this note just a few days ago. It says, 'To my beloved children: I wasn't the kind of mother who baked cakes from scratch, sang the ABC song, or hovered over you like those typical, dull mothers. My moral compass might have taken me down some rocky paths, but in spite of my spirited ways, I loved you all very much. I've written each of you a personal letter from my heart. Because you are all unique, so are my words to you.'"

Kirk fumbled through the large manila envelope. "I don't see any letters."

Tony and I followed Kirk to the bedroom to check the safe. She had legal documents like her social security card, passport, and birth certificate, but no personal letters.

"You'd think she would have kept them with her will," Tony stated definitively.

I shrugged. "I'm sure when we clean out this place and figure out what we're going to do with it, we'll find the letters she mentioned."

The pizza arrived as Tony created his special martini recipe. I filled my crystal glass with iced tea instead of the potent concoction Tony whipped up.

"Let's raise these lovely martini glasses to Sylvia Ann Ursini, a nontraditional mother and a hell of a woman. May she liven up heaven with her fantastic showgirl dance moves and wild stories! Salute!"

Our glasses clanked together in amity.

CHAPTER 11

Instead of celebrating with fireworks and a picnic on July 4, my family and I discussed the autopsy results, which explained Sylvia died from a hemorrhagic shock caused by the injuries she sustained in the accident. Despite emergency surgery, her body continued to bleed from within.

What happened to Sylvia on her last night, freely driving her Chevy Impala through the desert where she lived her entire life? She was a youthful eighty-six-year-old who should have had a few more years ahead of her.

Tony said he drove with her a few times to assess her driving skills and ensure her reflexes remained solid. She had no idea he was testing her. We avoided having that problematic conversation someday, taking away her car. Sylvia assured me she only drove to the grocery store, Aunt Lucy's apartment, the Flamingo casino with Beverly on Fridays, and church. The church was the farthest distance from her home, but she knew the route well. The street where her car was found would not have been on the way to any place she frequented.

Kirk spoke with Detective Boyle of the Las Vegas Metropolitan Police Department, questioning who drove the truck that ultimately took Sylvia's life—the truck she swore came out of nowhere and crashed into her side.

Boyle advised it had been a hit-and-run accident. No other vehicles were at the scene. The road she traveled on had few lampposts to light her way along the dark, desolate stretch. The cops found no witnesses, but evidence showed dark-blue paint from another vehicle within the dents it made in her car. The driver of the dark-blue vehicle would face charges, possibly vehicular homicide. The angle from which her car had been hit was suspected to be a taller vehicle like a truck or SUV. At least now they knew it was a truck, which could narrow their search, thanks to Sylvia's statement to me. She experienced too much pain after surgery to offer any additional details.

At the time of Sylvia's awakening, I didn't know someone had fled the accident scene or that we would be looking for the person who caused her death. Given her age, I falsely assumed that she bore responsibility for the accident.

I didn't pack funeral attire, so I brought Aunt Lucy to Nordstrom's the afternoon before the funeral to shop for appropriate outfits. I selected a black-fitted dress with ruffled sleeves and a scoop neck to highlight the gold locket Sylvia left me. I noticed my aunt staring at the price tags before she considered trying something on. I insisted her dress would be my treat and to stop looking at the tags. She chose the first dark-gray dress she tried on.

My aunt took gradual strides with her walker, taking a break after every tenth step. She let out a huff, exhausted from the lengthy time it took for her to change. It pained me to watch her frail figure struggle.

*****

Visitors were welcome to arrive at the Riverside Funeral Home on the morning of Monday, July 8, to pay their respects.

A limousine was hired to drive Aunt Lucy, my brothers, and me to the funeral home, church, cemetery, and lastly, to Ricciardi's Ristorante for lunch. Anyone attending the services would be welcome to join us afterward for a hearty Italian meal.

The quiet drive to Riverside felt maddening. None of us knew what to say along the way. Tony repeatedly mentioned how badly Leann felt for not coming around while we planned the services.

My last conversation with Leann was years ago and had become so heated, I thought she'd slap me. Surprisingly, Leann agreed to drive her vehicle to the services, so she could take us all home when this abysmal day concluded.

When we arrived at the funeral home, an ache filled my stomach, throbbing against my insides from my bowels to my throat as we exited the air-conditioned limo into the excruciating summer heat. Clouds spread across the vast sky, preventing the sun from peering through, yet the dry July air felt insufferable. Kirk and Tony assisted Aunt Lucy in departing the vehicle while I unfolded her walker and secured it for her to grasp.

Approaching from a black Hyundai Accent was Burt Iannl, Tony's father. He looked really good for a man in his mid-eighties. He dressed in a light-gray suit with a blue bowtie, spouting class. I noticed he walked with a slight limp. He shrugged, saying, "I don't know what to say, kids. I'm sorry this happened to your mom."

Tony leaned in and hugged his father. Kirk warmly shook his hand, then embraced him. Burt became a surrogate father to Kirk, being a mere seventeen months older than Tony. Often when Burt picked up Tony for overnight visits, Kirk excitedly tagged along.

"Victoria, you look gorgeous," Burt said as he wrapped his arms around my waist.

"It's good to see you again, Burt. You're looking pretty gorgeous yourself! Are you working out?" Physically, he appeared healthy and robust.

"I take Dad to the gym with me twice a week. He *tries* to keep up with me," Tony teased. It always felt good to hear one of us refer to a man as "dad."

Leann parked her white Honda CRV in the lot and tentatively drew near. She said hello to Kirk and Aunt Lucy, intentionally kissing their cheeks and draping her toned arms around them, offering condolences. Her blue eyes blinked in my direction. She bobbed a head full of platinum blond waves before giving Burt and Tony her attention. Her boobs had grown another cup size since I last saw her, I noticed.

"Hello, Leann. I'm glad you could make it." I smiled, tabling my animosity.

"I'm family, Vicki. Of course, I'd be here for Tony," she retorted, then she clasped Tony's hand tightly and nudged him away from me.

I sucked in a deep breath to calm my nerves. Between the impending view of Sylvia's body and the passive-aggressive greeting from Leann, I silently prayed for solace and patience.

Light classical music sounded through the speakers as we entered the building. Men in dark suits welcomed us in whispered, sincere tones. Kirk's connection, Mr. Ramirez, showed us to the room. A guest book sat beside a short stack of prayer cards on a podium for people to sign in.

My heart raged like a desert storm, and my head suddenly felt heavy and dizzy when I witnessed the cherry casket we had selected to lay Sylvia's remains. Her vibrant spirit no longer resided within the flesh laid out before us. Aunt Lucy and I had picked out a deep purple dress that looked stunning against her olive complexion and russet-colored hair. The makeup artist made her look beautiful, adding subtle tones to the layer of foundation cemented to her face that was heavily bruised from the crash. Sylvia would be pleased with the results.

We all stood around the casket, releasing tears and saying prayers to ourselves, wishing our mother to rest in peace. I stepped away to observe the setup of the room, with about twenty empty chairs waiting for friends to occupy. Several flower arrangements were situated on either side of the casket and along the mantle. I couldn't help but read the cards to see who had sent the lovely sprays. We added a statement in the obituary that in lieu of flowers to please donate to the soup kitchen the First Congregational Church supported, a cause close to her heart. She often volunteered her time there. Still, some friends sent flowers.

My brothers and I compiled a wide array of photographs Sylvia kept in albums. We selected numerous family pictures that held cherished memories. Some favorites included photos of her childhood with our grandparents, her days dancing at the Flamingo, and snap-shots with her celebrity acquaintances. Tony and Leann assembled these memories into a large-framed collage that captured the essence of her life.

In strolled a couple, possibly mid-sixties. It took a moment for me to realize the man's attire and somewhat recognizable facial features—Pastor Joshua Steele and, presumably, his wife. Josh first approached my brothers and my aunt. He stopped momentarily when his hazel eyes met mine.

"Victoria!" he uttered with exuberance. "It's been a long time, hasn't it?"

"Too long, Josh. It's nice to see you."

"I wish it were under happier circumstances. Your mother was so proud of you and all you've accomplished. If it weren't for you, some children wouldn't have art or music programs from your time as our state's first lady. Oh, perhaps that's not a good subject to bring up." He made an awkward expression, lifting his lids and stretching his lower lip.

"I take great pride in my achievements when I was married to Jeffrey. Thank you for acknowledging my efforts."

His wife cleared her throat and tugged at his arm.

"Oh, forgive me. Surely, you remember Debbie, my wife."

It took a moment to make the connection. "Deborah Paquet… from high school?"

"It's me, Vicki. I'm Debbie Steele now. It's lovely to see you after…well…not *too* many years." She cackled.

Debbie Paquet was rather quiet and shy in school. Her clothing always looked like it had been purchased at a local thrift shop or donated. We weren't close, but we traveled in different circles. Josh was part of my clique. I felt a tad curious as to how they got together and married.

I lost touch with many school friends, mostly because I dealt with the hopeless feelings triggered by bipolar disorder. Eventually, I learned how to properly control my moods through medication compliance, but it took years to succumb to treatment.

"We were at a retreat with about twenty-five parishioners up in Hawthorne. I expected your mother, but she didn't show. I assumed she wasn't feeling well. I had no idea about her accident until we returned from our getaway. Debbie and I didn't hear the news because this retreat was technology-free. You know, I would've gone to the hospital or at least met with you when you scheduled today's service."

"Oh, we understand, Josh. Your assistant was quite helpful in organizing the details. You said my mother planned to go to this retreat?" I had to ask since we wondered where Sylvia had been driving on the night of her accident.

"We left after Sunday service concluded. Sylvia didn't attend worship that day, but we waited for her in the church parking lot. Eventually, we called her when she didn't show up on time without calling."

Debbie chimed in, "I left a message and never heard back from her. We figured she wasn't up for the trip."

"Hmm," I murmured, curious why she suddenly changed her plans.

"If there's anything you or your family needs, you know you can come to me, to us." Josh looked lovingly at his wife. "Your mother was a special woman. She'll be missed. I'll pay her an honorable tribute at the service later."

"Thank you, Josh. Reverend. Pastor?" I chuckled, unsure what to call him.

"Dearest Victoria, we go back a long way. You can call me Josh."

Many people drifted in and out to pay their respects. Most knew Sylvia through the First Congregational Church. I felt a little out of touch with the people in her life today, but it also felt good to meet so many who adored her. Her induction with this church in the '60s turned out to be a blessing. She still possessed erratic and impetuous traits.

A woman I recognized strode into the room as if floating on air, dabbing a tissue beneath puffy eyes. "Aunt Bev's here," I whispered to Aunt Lucy, who huffed and rolled her dark-brown eyes. Technically, Beverly Perrin wasn't my aunt. She was Sylvia's best friend who also danced at the Flamingo. The pair had been inseparable since the first grade.

Beverly secreted a sassy spirit, pretty and petite, with a different look than Sylvia. She still bleached her short waves platinum blond. Her straight posture and grace exhibited confidence. Aunt Bev's strong demeanor melted when she saw Sylvia's body up close, resting in the casket. She kissed her forehead and wept.

Kirk gingerly stepped near her and opened his arms, allowing Bev to fall into his firm grasp. Tony and I made our way over to welcome her.

Aunt Bev hugged and kissed us all with mounds of sympathy oozing from her soul. "I can't believe she's gone. And from a car accident, no less. Tell me, what did she hit, or did she fall asleep at the wheel again?"

"Fall asleep? Aunt Bev, did our mother fall asleep when driving?" I tried to keep my voice down to prevent others from eavesdropping. I glanced at my brothers, whose eyes bulged as wide as mine. Sylvia didn't reveal an incident like that to any of us, but apparently, she had confided in her best friend.

"Mom always kept it together. She was sharp and alert," Kirk insisted, always in defense mode when it came to Sylvia.

"It only happened once…that I know of. She blamed some medication that made her drowsy. She lost her bearings for a moment. No one got hurt. That night, I think she had been driving home from one of those spaghetti dinners the church organized."

"This is the first time we're hearing this," Tony said.

"Syl would've been embarrassed to tell you. You know, I was just with her the Friday before it happened—we played Bingo after a meal at the Flamingo," she said in rhyme. Her eyes swerved to Aunt Lucy. "Hi, Lu!" she shouted with exuberance.

Aunt Lucy waved with two fingers—no hint of a smile showed. I had never noticed such friction between them before, but they weren't usually in the same room together. The tension grew thick enough to sink my teeth into.

Kirk found a seat for Aunt Bev to sit comfortably.

Unlike Aunt Lucy, Beverly seemed healthy and strong, walking without the use of a cane or walker. I suspected she had a face-lift, like Sylvia, because she had no severe wrinkles for a woman in her mid-eighties. Even if she followed the same healthy skin regimen Sylvia taught me, she'd have more evidence of life shown on her face and neck unless cosmetic surgery erased the years.

"Hi, Vicki!"

I turned my figure in the direction of a familiar voice and noticed my two best friends from college, Bridget Hanson and Claudia Chavez.

"Oh! You came!" I shrieked and embraced them. Inside, a happy dance erupted.

Claudia and I were roommates in college, and Bridget lived in our dorm; we became as close as the three musketeers. Bridget hailed from Henderson, a more upscale community. Claudia originated from Arizona. They both regenerated their lives in California post-college. Bridget, a self-proclaimed, renowned artist, followed her husband's career and family to Sacramento. Claudia secured a teaching job in Walnut Creek.

Although we parted ways geographically, we stayed in touch. We saw each other a few times a year before my relocation to Paris. Afterward, I needed to limit my conversations with them to emails and texts. They understood I carefully avoided the media after my affair with Tommy had been exposed, and my very public divorce from Jeffrey captivated headlines. As my best friends, they sympathized with my need to avoid the spotlight and vowed to protect my privacy, believing I lived in Montana, a rumor I started when I changed my identity.

Tommy encouraged me to fly to California and meet up with them. He didn't expect me to leave my whole world behind when I chose to create a new identity in France. However, I felt safer staying by his side.

Bridget placed an arm around my shoulder. "I'm so sorry about your mother's passing, Vicki. Wow, the memories I have whenever we'd meet up at your house. She was so much fun!"

"And cool! She gave the best advice about boys." Claudia laughed.

My friends spoke about their love lives with Sylvia more often than I did.

Claudia's eyes lit up beneath wisps of light-brown curls. "We really need some girl time to catch up."

"We'll be at the Venetian for a few more days," Bridget added.

"Well, then we need to meet for lunch on the Strip before you head home. I've got to stay in town until my mother's estate is settled."

"Perfect." Bridget glanced behind her and noticed several people waiting their turn to pay their respects. "We'll be in touch, Vicki. Again, I'm so sorry about your mom."

"Yeah, sweetie. I can't wait for us to reconnect this week." Claudia draped her arms around me.

It was a pleasant surprise to spot Tommy's son, Danny, enter and stop at Sylvia's casket for a quick prayer. He fiddled with his navy and gray striped tie when he shuffled in my direction. "I'm sorry about your mother, Vicki." Danny turned toward the lovely redhead standing by his side in gray slacks and a black silk blouse. "This is my wife, Bianca."

"It's nice to meet you. I'm so sorry for your loss," Bianca repeated the same benevolent words I'd listened to for the last hour.

I smiled. "Thank you both for coming. Bianca, it's a pleasure to meet you despite the circumstances."

"We would love to have you over for dinner. I mean, if you're in town a little longer and would like to meet our family."

"That's a lovely offer. I'd like to meet your children and get to know you and Danny better. Thank you."

My mind wandered, hoping I wouldn't slip about my life with Tommy in Paris over shrimp cocktail. Tommy might feel a little jealous that I could spend time with the family he adored and missed. God, I missed him! If only he could be here in person, standing by my side the way Leann glued herself to Tony's hip. Daily video time with Tommy became vital to my sanity throughout this gruesome week.

I introduced Danny and Bianca to my family a moment before I noticed Jeffrey's obtrusive presence. My ex-husband had a fetish for red ties. He loved power. Wearing red boosted his typically elevated confidence. He had aged with a multitude of white strands blended with his natural brunet color, still flaunting an arrogant, calculating look. I turned my head to avoid eye contact.

Sylvia told me before she passed that Jeffrey kept in touch with her, angry he couldn't find me. He harassed her, hoping she'd tell him my location. Fortunately, she protected my secret hideaway in Paris.

Danny must have witnessed the brief direction of my serious gaze. His head swerved the same course. He mumbled, "What's he doing here?"

I smiled half-heartedly and whispered, "I won't make a scene at my mother's funeral." I tried to get Kirk and Tony's attention with a slight wave of my hand.

Too late.

They spotted Jeffrey as he neared the casket. He made the sign of the cross and genuflected like the Catholics. Simulating remorse, he closed his eyes momentarily to pray, though I doubted his prayers were for Sylvia's spirit. Jeffrey's wish would be to rattle me. He feigned a sorrowful look as if being filmed for the evening news.

Jeffrey strode toward Kirk and extended his hand in sympathy.

Kirk said nothing, ignored his hand, and turned his chin.

Jeffrey's arrogance pushed him to move to Tony, who I suspected wanted to slug him. Instead, Tony followed Kirk's lead and calmly rejected his hand. He projected a seething glare from his blue eyes. Tony's lack of height didn't mar his confidence to tackle Jeffrey if necessary.

Tony's threatening expression didn't dissuade Jeffrey from greeting our aunt. "Aunt Lucy, you look marvelous!" Jeffrey bent to her level, seated in a comfortable chair, and tapped his cheek to hers, making a loud, smacking kiss sound, though his lips never touched her flesh.

My aunt squirmed in her seat but politely thanked him for coming.

"I'm terribly sorry for your loss. I know how close you and Sylvia were," he said.

If my dear aunt had the strength and agility to run from Jeffrey, she would have.

When Jeffrey stood, he positioned his stance directly in front of me, meeting my bitter emotions through a phony joyful guise. "Victoria. It's been a long time." He grinned that political, shady smile I learned to detect. "Sylvia was quite a woman and my mother-in-law for many years. I just had to make an appearance today."

"And you have." I expected my blatant reaction to his presence to be obvious, despite displaying my dimples.

"I kept in touch with Sylvia. You know, assuring she had everything she needed."

"Hmm, I heard you mostly inquired about *me*." I took a step away and spread my hands apart widely. "Here I am, Jeffrey. What do you want from me?"

The painted smile he wore grew from ear to ear. He moved close enough to kiss my lips but turned his chin to the side of my face. His lips gently brushed against my cheek. His warm breath heated my face, combatting the icy chill flowing up my spine. Then he whispered ever so softly, "I'm gonna bury you deeper than the six-foot hole awaiting your mother's body."

Tony and Kirk moved closer, building a wall of protection, standing on either side of me. If they had heard what Jeffrey whispered, they'd pummel him to the ground and start a brawl. Jeffrey loved playing the victim, but I wouldn't give him the satisfaction.

"Well, I look forward to the challenge. Thank you for coming." I revealed a devilish grin, not to attract any further attention to the distressing moment.

The few guests in the room knew I cheated on Jeffrey with Tommy, thanks to the media stoning during an election year when Jeffrey lost his position of power, painstakingly stepping down as governor after a mere one term. There was nothing gracious about his loss. People who read Tommy's memoirs would have learned about Jeffrey's manipulations to keep me tied to him. Some believed

Tommy's version, but Jeffrey secured a wide array of supporters who referred to the allegations as *unfounded*.

I refused to show fear of his irrational threat. He had been run out of the governor's mansion, and he lost me. Jeffrey was a sore loser.

More guests entered the line of friends and acquaintances, but my brothers stayed close to me with Jeffrey nearby, ignoring the spectators who waited in wonder if an argument might brew.

Sylvia loved drama. She might have appreciated this touch of theatrics at her funeral.

Danny stepped in to alleviate the situation. "Mr. Atkins. It's *interesting* to see you again after all these years." He placed a firm arm around Jeffrey's shoulder. "I insist you let me escort you out."

Jeffrey didn't fight Danny's polite request.

CHAPTER 12

The First Congregational Church dwelled on Willow Street in North Las Vegas. On this cloudy day, the black stone exterior of the church appeared more intense with a haunted facade. A gray steeple, tall and dramatic, extended to a point with an old, ornate cross perched at its top—just as I remembered it.

As we staggered inside, the sparkling lights illuminated the space enough to consider wearing sunglasses. The walls were bright white with gold trim enlivening the dark wooden pews.

A spiral staircase polished to perfection led to the organ and choir loft high above us, proudly situated with a view of the parishioners and the lovely white marble altar. The tinkling of the organ keys echoed a chilling yet beautiful hymn with a familiar rhythm from my childhood. Kirk selected the music, knowing Sylvia's preferences.

As we trailed along the center aisle to take our seats in the first pew, I took note of the floral arrangements with white Asiatic lilies and creamy roses accented with white and pink peonies and greens that adorned the altar.

My stomach continued to rumble as Pastor Josh stepped to the podium and welcomed everyone, declaring the service a celebration of the life and times of the incomparable Sylvia Ann Ursini, friend to all attending. He spoke about her time spent cooking and cleaning in the soup kitchen. She used to help the Sunday schoolteachers keep the children engaged in religious discussions. I felt more surprised hearing that she participated in Bible study. The church's activities became an integral part of her life—more than I realized.

After she retired from her hostess position at the Flamingo, Sylvia kept busy by helping with meaningful community events sponsored by the church. I felt a strong sense of pride, listening to Josh praise her devotion to worthy causes.

Josh offered the crowd the opportunity to speak about Sylvia in remembrance. Kirk worried he'd become too emotional, and Tony didn't feel comfortable speaking before the crowd. Since I had grown accustomed to giving speeches, I advised Josh I'd be the final speaker on behalf of the Ursini family to say a few words, reflecting on her life.

A few churchgoers described their encounters with Sylvia, commending her efforts to help others, while some expressed their fondness of her stories about the celebs she had brushed elbows with in her youth.

Aunt Bev talked about their long-term friendship, keeping their times at the Flamingo at a PG rating. She fussed with the tiara Sylvia bequeathed to her upon her puffy platinum blond hair and laughed, saying, "You had to rub it in, Syl, didn't ya? She won this gorgeous first-place tiara, while I got a lousy fourth-place ribbon. I couldn't believe it when her son, Kirk, brought me her cherished prize. She wore this sparkly crown at the Flamingo every night! She wore it to the market and probably slept with the damn thing. Oh, excuse me, *darn* thing." The crowd chuckled as Bev stared up to the heavens, regretting the use of a curse word in church.

When Beverly's speech ended, and no one else stood to speak, I woozily strode from the pew to stand in the center aisle, where Josh met me and slipped the microphone into my palm.

I cleared my throat as I sought the words I rehearsed, but then a memory chimed through, and I chose an impromptu modification. I gazed into the crowd of unrecognizable faces. "My brothers, Kirk and Tony, our Aunt Lucy, and I thank you all for coming. Today, we celebrate an extraordinary woman who raised three children as a single mother. She didn't have a husband, but she had the Ursinis, who *always* stood by each other. People used to look down on her because she had children without wearing a gold wedding band. I think she should have been honored for her bravery in pushing back on societal norms.

"It warmed my heart, listening to the stories some of you shared about our mom. Knowing she shined such a joyous light on others is simply remarkable. Thank you for sharing those precious memories with us.

"Our mother wasn't like other moms. She could cook, but she wasn't an extravagant chef. One day, she baked cupcakes for my second-grade class in honor of my birthday. They looked perfect! I mean, *really* perfect, flawlessly decorated with rosebuds and sprinkles. The kids at school said, 'Wow, your mom bakes the best cupcakes ever!' I felt so proud. Later in life, I learned that the birthday cupcakes she actually made sank in the center and looked more like pancakes."

The crowd chortled.

"To make her daughter happy, she ordered three dozen cupcakes at the bakery, threw out the boxes they came in, and placed the gorgeously decorated cupcakes on her best serving tray." I paused to giggle. "Ya know, I'm still proud. She knew her faults and limits, but she didn't let her imperfections hold her back. She turned that deficiency into a positive result and a joyous memory for me. We can learn something from that. No one is perfect, but we all bring something special to the lives of others.

"My mother went out of her way to make her children and others happy because of her genuine heart and love for her family. She considered all of you family too. I speak on behalf of the Ursinis when I say that our hearts are saddened by this loss, but we are committed to keeping her memory alive with stories like the ones you've heard today."

Mindlessly, I walked to Josh to hand him the microphone. My legs felt a bit numb when I stepped back to the bench with my family, who smiled with praise for the loving message I conveyed to Sylvia's community, taming the bits of resentment I still carried.

Before worship concluded, Josh's hazel eyes beamed as he floated toward us. "I can feel Sylvia's presence here with her adoring children, her sister, and all her friends. Can you envision her smile? Hear her infectious laugh? I can. She's in a place now where she'll always be by your side Kirk, Tony, Victoria, and Lucy. I arranged to end today's service differently than usual. Allow me to introduce our dedicated organist and minister of music, Mr. Terrance Fontaine." Josh pointed up to the choir loft.

The reverberation of parishioners' bodies turning rang loudly as their heads looked up toward the back of the church to the loft in unison. A man with golden hair sat at the organ high above us. I couldn't see his face, but his fingers pecked at the keys to a song everyone knew, "Stand by Me," by Ben E. King. Terrance sang beautifully with the choir behind him in their red and white cloaks, backing up his vocals. Soon the crowd chimed in, singing the melodious tune. The cadence of a hundred voices echoed around us.

A tear was shed from my eye in time with my racing pulse. I took hold of Aunt Lucy's hand, and we both began to sing the soulful lyrics. Kirk and Tony joined in as well, Kirk maintaining a beautiful tenor voice. Sylvia encouraged Kirk to join the church choir when he was a child. The imagery of Kirk as a little boy, singing in that loft with Pastor Gordon, Josh's father, praising Kirk's talent sprang to mind. Tony and I weren't as talented in the singing department. Tony was more athletic, and acting was my calling.

CHAPTER 13

The time had come to bury Sylvia's body in the shiny cherry casket—her final resting place. The Pine Rock Cemetery service ticked by more quickly than I imagined. Josh said a few words, followed by a prayer. Specks of sunlight peeped through the gloomy sky. I lifted my chin to witness a widening gap through the gray atmosphere. The clouds suddenly parted for the sun to magically slice its way through, casting beams of orange and yellow as if heaven chose to open its gates for Sylvia during Josh's divine words.

We had arranged for white roses to be handed out for guests to place atop the casket before the service concluded.

"The Ursini family invites you to join them for lunch at Ricciardi's. You may place a rose down with Sylvia before you leave." Josh gently patted the top of the casket and stepped backward.

As people inched near the casket, spreading the flowers across the top, I realized this would be my final goodbye—like the last momentary conversation I had with Sylvia at her bedside. So much was left unsaid. Did I tell her I loved her? I couldn't recall. What little Sylvia had left to say to me, she said it—wanting me to be safe from Jeffrey; telling me about the truck that hit her, causing her untimely death; and not selling her house. Did she worry we would stick her in a nursing home, presuming she'd survive that horrible crash?

Aunt Lucy appeared tired from standing but refused to use her wheelchair today. She kept one in storage in case she needed it. At some point, the MS might not give her a choice. I assured my aunt sat on the small seat attached to her walker while friends plopped their rosebuds atop Sylvia's final resting place.

Once the crowd faded, Tony assisted Aunt Lucy, who took small, cautious steps forward. Tony closed his eyes, saying a silent farewell.

Aunt Lucy kissed the tips of her fingers, then placed them delicately on the casket before tears flew from her eyes. "You were something else, sister. My trusted friend and confidant. I don't know what I'll do without you, but *the bond of sisters lasts forever*," she emphasized. "We'll always be connected." Aunt Lucy glanced at me before her eyes veered to Kirk and Tony. "Did you know your mother checked in on me every day?"

We all knew Sylvia had evident concerns about her sister's ability to manage independently. When I spoke with her by phone, she'd tell me about her visits with Aunt Lucy, taking out her trash, changing the cat litter, and helping with other chores. I'd look into hiring a cleaning service to assist my aunt until the time came when she couldn't live alone. Aunt Lucy had no children to help her make decisions. She would need us. When I returned to Paris, I couldn't be here for her like her sister had been. Kirk and Tony would check in on her, but probably not daily.

Tony helped our aunt to the limo while I crept to Sylvia's remains. I delicately placed a white rose on top of the others. My fingers trailed along the smooth surface of the casket. I found a way to whisper with a hard knot in my throat. "I'm sorry I wasn't around more, but it's obvious how many people appreciated and adored you. I hope you know that in spite of my *issues*, I love you, Mom."

Kirk's hand brushed against my shoulder while a stream of tears rushed from my eyes. "I can't say *goodbye*. How about, see ya later?" I reached inside my purse in search of a fresh tissue to wipe the tears from my face and blow my nose. I stepped aside from the coffin beneath a lovely acacia tree with yellow blossoms to allow Kirk a moment alone with her.

*****

We arrived at Ricciardi's, a popular Italian restaurant that served a variety of traditional delicacies like burrata cheese, fried squash flowers, scungilli salad, and osso buco. Coming from an Italian heritage, Sylvia would love that we chose this restaurant with such a succulent menu. Aunt Lucy recommended an assorted Italian cookie tray with angel wings for dessert.

People took their seats, ordered drinks, and spoke in quiet, somber tones, pending the buffet-style entrées to be served.

I grew tired of keeping a smile intact as if tattooed on my face. Always appearing happy became challenging for me, especially when secretly managing bipolar disorder in the spotlight. I stepped toward the medley of photos that Tony positioned against an open wall atop an empty table. I couldn't help but stare at the photo of Sylvia and Dean Martin, still wondering if I shared any of his features besides my natural shade of raven hair and dark-brown eyes. Maybe I still felt angry that she wasn't honest with me about my father. My anger had suppressed through the years. I developed a good life. What difference would a father have made? A gaping hole in my existence became filled with an energizing acting career, the warm, dazzling attention I once loved, and now Tommy and his devotion to me. It was time to drop the resentment and hostility. Emotions that strangled my heart prevented me from appreciating the life Sylvia gave me, bearing all responsibilities of three children.

Loving recollections sprang to mind to the point where I momentarily forgot where I stood until Aunt Bev gained everyone's attention with the clinking of a knife against her water glass. With a boisterous voice, she shouted, "I realize this is a funeral. We all loved my friend, Syl. She always enjoyed a good soiree! Don't you think she'd want this to be more of a lively party instead of this depressing, teary-eyed gathering? Pastor Josh, in church, you said we were celebrating Sylvia Ursini's life!"

Josh smiled and nodded.

"We need some music, and I came prepared." Beverly took out her cell phone and placed blue-rimmed reading glasses over her eyes. "The last time I saw Syl, she hummed along to this old Elvis song. She loved Elvis! Victoria, your mother and I introduced you to the king when you were a baby. We taught you how to jitterbug!" Aunt Bev whisked her spry body to perform some jitterbug steps. She showed off some pretty good moves at her age. "Remember how you danced around, holding that hairbrush, singing at the top of your lungs?" She clicked her iPhone to play Elvis's "Hard Headed Woman."

Aunt Bev pushed two chairs together, grabbed my hand, and led me to stand on top of one of the chairs. Even at her age, she managed to pull herself atop the other chair. The two of us belted out the fast-paced tune. Aunt Bev knew how to liven up a grim day. She was right. Sylvia would want us to have a great time in her honor. She reminded me that Sylvia's love for Elvis Presley's music rubbed off on me. I held quite an assortment of Elvis souvenirs collected throughout my life.

Tony grabbed Leann and danced along to the music with her, triggering others to use the open space between tables as a dance floor.

Kirk grabbed Aunt Bev's hand to help her down from the chair, then he proceeded to attempt some quick-paced dance moves. He didn't hold a candle to Beverly's agile movements, but he managed to keep up with her.

When the song ended, Aunt Bev laughed then shouted at Kirk in between deep breaths, "Kid, you're gonna...be coming...to *my* funeral next...if I dance like that again."

Aunt Bev and Sylvia were best friends for a reason. Suddenly, I felt Sylvia's presence with us as if she laid a hand against my shoulder, whispering an Elvis Presley quote, "Live each day as if it were your last. It's written in the stars; your destiny is cast."

When the food was served, the waitstaff wore broad smiles, giggling about the entertainment we provided them. Beverly kept Elvis's greatest hits playing throughout dinner at a soft volume.

I noticed Aunt Lucy sitting quietly in the back corner of the room. I wandered in her direction and filled the empty seat beside her. "You okay?"

She showed a slight grin.

"You don't care for Beverly, do you?"

"Hmph! Is it that obvious?"

"A little."

She whispered, "That woman always made trouble for your mother since they were in school. If Sylvia got caught smoking in the girl's bathroom, Beverly was with her. Sylvia got caught shoplifting knickknacks from the drug store once. Beverly put her up to it. Skipping school, drinking under the bleachers—Bev was the instigator. She got your mother to dance at the Flamingo all those years ago."

"Well, Mom loved that time of her life. Besides, I'm sure you have some wild, teen angst stories like that too, Aunt Lucy."

She chuckled and shrugged. "I guess it doesn't matter anymore, now does it?"

"Sounds like you've got some outrageous tales. Wanna share?" I raised my brows.

"Some things should be taken to the grave, Victoria. My sister should rest in peace."

"I hope whatever you're keeping quiet about isn't something like…who my father is."

A look of surprise smothered my aunt's face. "Oh, Victoria. That's not what I meant." She sighed. "Your mother dated a lot of men in those days."

It seemed strange to me that my aunt claimed to have no knowledge about my biological father. I glanced at Aunt Bev, laughing with Tony's father, Burt. Now that my mother was gone, perhaps Beverly would open up. My mother must have confided in one of them about my biological father. Sylvia was gone. If Aunt Lucy and Beverly died, no one would be left to fill in the blanks in my life. Today wasn't the time for arduous queries, but soon and before I returned to Paris.

I paid the bill after our guests offered their last sympathetic respects before leaving.

Burt offered to drive Aunt Lucy home, who looked incredibly drained after such a long, emotional day. There was no need for her to sit around and wait for the other guests to depart while my credit card was processed.

Suddenly, Burt flew back inside. "Tony! Victoria! Cameras and reporters are assembling outside."

"Reporters?" Kirk stormed to the door to peek outside.

"And Vicki's ex-husband is on camera now, firing them up, whining about being treated *less than cordially* for making an appearance at his mother-in-law's funeral."

Leave it to Jeffrey to pour whiskey on fuel. At least he waited until after Sylvia was buried before he incited a media frenzy. I hadn't been seen on camera since Tommy's presumed death and my divorce in 2010. I had no use for such exposure or to explain why I had an affair, leaving the distinguished governor's mansion for a Vegas business tycoon whose "death" made national headlines. Since I returned to town, being spotted because of Sylvia's death was inevitable.

Tommy was concerned about this all along. I hid from reporters for years, allegedly in Montana. I couldn't have the press or outsiders learn about my life in Paris. Tommy would be found alive and accessible for his enemies to take a shot at him. I tried desperately to stay under the radar to ensure Tommy's safety. Traveling home was a risk I needed to take for Sylvia.

I collected my credit card from the waiter and said, "They won't leave me alone as long as I'm in town, and they'll follow me everywhere I go now. I've got to deal with this. Maybe they'll get off my back or show some sympathy today of all days."

"What will you say?"

"I guess it depends on what questions they ask. My marriage to Jeffrey ended years ago. I'm no longer acting. If they want to rip me a new one because I cheated on my pompous ass for a husband years ago, let them."

A million thoughts raced through my mind as I inched my way to exit Ricciardi's. The clock on the wall displayed three thirty-five, which meant I could be on the six o'clock news.

I'd been trained to handle reporters with negative perspectives, although I'd been out of the spotlight for years, out of practice for an impromptu inquisition. I opened the door and held my head high, but I wasn't alone, walking down the lengthy cement steps to the halfway point. Kirk stood to my left. Tony was on my right.

I noticed Leann and Burt helping Aunt Lucy take cautious steps with her walker along the wooden ramp to Burt's car, but their eyes were fixated on me.

Reporters simultaneously shouted, "Victoria!"

"Ms. Ursini, a statement, please!"

One journalist inserted a sympathy note, saying, "I'm sorry to hear about your mother's passing. Please give me a moment!"

My eyes spotted Jeffrey in the crowd, wearing that heinous politician's grin that made him look like a snob. His constituents believed he acted with confidence, fighting for the community. The fact was, Jeffrey loved power, money, and the intense drama tendered by the limelight more than people.

As I stood on the steps, my eyes scanned the crowd below me. I wasn't merely facing reporters. Many people were scattered through-out the parking lot, holding signs of my photo with a giant red X slashed through my face. Another picture of me from one of my movies with my mouth opened wide enough to see my tonsils, mid-scream, displayed a witch hat drawn atop my head with my face smudged with green paint and a bubble pointed at my lips as if I were saying, *I'll get you, Governor, and your little dog too*. They were haters and supporters of Jeffrey, either personally or politically.

The mob swelled around my body, holding microphones on long poles to reach me. Cameras snapped, and blaring red dots of video equipment shined into my eyes.

I stood silently at first, attempting to calm the jitters bouncing around in my stomach. I recalled a statement Sylvia once told me shortly after earning my first role in a film; I was about to promote my work as a new actress on the *Arsenio Hall Show*. To subdue my nerves, she said, "Victoria, you're in control. You're in charge. Never let them see you sweat."

I pointed to the News 5 reporter because she showed remorse for Sylvia's passing.

"Cassie Rayburn from News 5. Thank you, Ms. Ursini. Again, so sorry to hear about your mother. How's your family holding up?"

"We're doing our best to get through this very difficult, emotional time. Thank you for asking."

"You've been out of touch for quite some time. Can you shed light on where you've been and what you've been doing since you left Las Vegas?"

"I choose to live a quiet existence these days. I retired from acting."

"Did you retire because of your affair with Tommy Cavallo before his death?"

"Well…uh." My brain froze, incapable of thinking of a snappy reply. "I simply needed a break." I pointed to a stocky man with a crisp, golden beard to deviate from the affair question.

"Ms. Ursini, Damon Kappas from Channel 3. Governor Atkins said he had been shut out of your mother's funeral today. He made a kind gesture to pay his respects, and you denied him the opportunity." His statement sounded more like a harsh criticism than a question.

"I can assure you that the *former* governor had sufficient time to pray for my mother's spirit and offer his condolences to my family and me."

"So there are no hard feelings between the two of you anymore after you divorced him because of your affair with Tommy Cavallo? And what about the Pissarro painting you stole from a man named Trey Winters? Any comment about your involvement in that crime? A crime you got away with."

I could feel the dampness from the sweltering fire that filled my insides. *Never let them see you sweat.* Sylvia's voice ripped through my head as if standing beside me, speaking directly into my ear, and I forgot his acrimonious questions. I pointed to another gentleman, praying I wouldn't hyperventilate as my heartbeat sped, thumping loud enough to disrupt my thoughts.

"That valuable painting by Camille Pissarro was astonishingly sent to a museum in Paris. It's quite a coincidence that you fell off the face of the earth at the same time it landed in France. Experts acknowledged it had been shipped from Nevada."

I attempted to relax my arms in a comfortable position. But I didn't feel comfortable. "I'm afraid I'm unable to answer questions about the Pissarro painting. Look, this has been quite a difficult day for me, and—"

"What about your relationship with Tommy Cavallo? His book references a steamy tryst and a deep hatred for your ex-husband. Mr. Cavallo implied that the two of you concocted a scheme to damage Governor Atkins's reputation. Did you and Mr. Cavallo conspire to ruin his chances for reelection? An election that was *stolen* from him."

"That's absurd!"

"Not as absurd as this interview," someone muttered on camera for all to hear.

My heart pounded with wicked intensity. I'd been ambushed, unprepared to properly articulate responses. Their questions were bitterly biased but not necessarily unfair, considering the damage I instigated in my past.

Another journalist shouted, "You've developed a reputation for being a thief and a liar. What do you have to say about that?"

I had had enough. A bout of rage possessed me. "A thief and a liar? How dare you show up and attack me like this after I just buried my mother!" Venom darted between adverse words. "You should all be ashamed!"

Kirk and Tony each took an arm and quickly escorted me to Leann's vehicle while Jeffrey's supporters chanted hateful quotes like, "You're a has-been!" "Go back to Montana!" "Slut!"

I couldn't believe I had lost control. I let them see me sweat. The comedic look on Jeffrey's face, gloating about my humiliation, was now drilled into my memory. He secured and controlled this riot. He coordinated media inclined to despise me, and his supporters carried a grudge about the election he lost years ago. Jeffrey fantasized about the power the White House offered, and they all blamed me for damaging his reputation, preventing his longtime dream from coming to fruition.

CHAPTER 14

After this emotionally charged day, I washed away my anger and resentment about the stunt Jeffrey pulled by soaking in a long, hot bath. It was past 2:00 a.m. in Paris when I texted Tommy. He probably slept peacefully in our charming apartment. But on the off chance that he saw my message, he'd call me back.

I slipped into Sylvia's warm, cream-colored, fluffy bathrobe, fixed myself a cup of tea, and sat on the porch swing on the lanai, gently swaying. The lovely peonies caught my eyes—a tranquil view to calm my frazzled nerves. Though I felt much more serene, I couldn't help but allow my mind to deviate to the beginning of my relationship with Jeffrey, romanticizing his behavior pattern to fulfill my desire for love, saying "I do," and imagining a happy ending.

In the '80s, I picked up several professional modeling gigs. Jeffrey and I were introduced by my agent at the time. He wasn't my type; pretentiousness and arrogance weren't flattering characteristics, in my opinion. He tried too hard to impress me with his career aspirations, but his charisma and eloquence earned a friendship that grew in time. Jeffrey loved art and visiting museums, a common bond that connected us. He helped me get a few commercials for popular products like Tide and Pantene shampoo. That famous Pantene line, "Don't hate me because I'm beautiful," boosted my career. After that successful commercial, Jeffrey allied me with a new agent, Natalia Espinosa.

Natalia offered me a remarkable opportunity. Science fiction wasn't my first choice, but I nudged my foot in the door in a supporting role on a series made for television titled *Nick of Time*. The show featured the main character, Nick, an inventor of many disastrous ventures. The time machine he built, however, actually worked… to some degree. There were many issues with that machine, as he learned throughout the three seasons of the show's longevity. I played the part of a love interest from the 18th century. Would Nick choose to live in the reality of 1990, or would he elect his love for my character from 1783? We'll never know because the series ended with a cliffhanger just before Nick made such a complex choice.

Jeffrey and I had grown closer by then. He fired up the charm and stood by my side, supporting my career. The man knew what he wanted—me in his life and in his bed.

In my late thirties, none of my relationships before Jeffrey lasted. My friends were married with children, and I became concerned I'd grow old and without a partner like Sylvia, hoping for love to bloom as pretty as her peonies. I wasn't managing my mental health properly, either. I went off my medication several times throughout my life, convincing myself I didn't need it anymore once my moods were in check and I felt better, but I wasn't better. There was no cure to heal those funky cells in my brain, thanks to inheriting my grandmother's defective genes. Bipolar disorder was a cruel fate to accept, unable to defeat it or disclose it publicly. No reputable producer would hire an actress with such a disturbing label.

Jeffrey pledged his love and commitment with an enormous diamond in 1993. My manic moods were in overdrive. I made a lot of bad decisions when off my medication; one of them was accepting Jeffrey's proposal. The idea of marrying the prospective mayor of Fernley seemed enticing while my acting career heated with additional film credits with top billing.

The sun began to set when my cell buzzed, turning off the recollections of a dismal time in my past. Seeing Tommy's face on my phone eased my troubled mind and severe tension.

"Hey, honey. I just woke up and saw your text. How was the funeral? Are you okay?"

"I've got a lot to fill you in on."

CHAPTER 15

When the sun exposed its rays over an enchanting Nevada morning sky, my body ached upon waking from the constant twisting and turning battle through the night.

Tommy's blood boiled, hearing that Jeffrey not only attended Sylvia's funeral, but he had also made a mockery of it, persuading the media to unexpectedly hound me with questions. Jeffrey considered I'd be off my game. Unfortunately, I proved him right. I thought I could handle a spontaneous interview. Instead, my amateurish responses to the harsh critics made me look like a fool on the evening news.

Tony volunteered to help Aunt Lucy with some chores this morning, then he'd pick up lunch and assist with the cleanup effort before he returned to work later this week. Kirk offered to help me clean out every room of Sylvia's house, starting promptly at eight this morning. We had tough, poignant decisions to make. What would we keep, discard, or give to charity?

By the time nine forty-five rolled around and Kirk hadn't shown up, I called his cell and texted him, with no response. I worried about his state of mind. He got through the funeral okay yesterday, but a new day without Sylvia around could trigger bleak sensations. I continued my daily meds to prevent an emotional breakdown, but what did Kirk have to stabilize his moods?

I peered through the blinds and released a breath of relief. No trace of Jeffrey's fans holding vicious signs or the paparazzi streaming live videos. So I hopped in the red Mercedes and drove to Kirk's apartment a few miles away.

*****

A young woman in a blue business suit breezed out the main entrance but held the door open for me to access without buzzing Kirk's apartment for permission.

The elevator took me to floor four rather slowly. Kirk's apartment dwelled at the end of a long hallway. The rose-toned walls brightened up the place. It looked rather feminine, with pretty floral paintings positioned between each apartment entrance. Number 444, Kirk's *lucky* apartment. He hypothesized the consecutive fours were a sign of luck from the universe, which made me smile as I knocked hard upon the steel door. The sound of footsteps resonated after I banged harder, intent to uncover what delayed my brother this morning.

He opened the door, winded and barefoot, wearing comfy lounge pants and no shirt.

I moved past him to enter. The place looked tidier than usual. Kirk wasn't a neat freak, but he wasn't a slob, either. I recalled his place always looking cluttered with laundry, and I habitually tripped over his size fourteen work boots. "I was worried, Kirk. You said you'd be at Mom's house at eight. It's nearly ten. You didn't answer my messages."

"Oh, shit. Sorry, I got delayed. Let me grab a shower, and I'll meet you there." He raced to the door and opened it, eager for my exit.

I squinted and asked, "What's up with you this morning?"

"Kirk! You coming back to bed?" a sensual-sounding voice called from his bedroom.

"Ahh," I whispered.

He smirked.

"Okay. I'll get out of your hair."

"Hey, where did you run off to?" The woman's voice grew louder when she stepped into the living room. Her familiar face looked startled when she saw me. Her body appeared different, wearing nothing except Kirk's unbuttoned dress shirt from yesterday's funeral, barely covering her flesh. I had only witnessed Nurse Tara Marsh in scrubs—a less seductive look than the lovely woman standing before me, blushing and clutching Kirk's shirt to conceal her bare breasts. "Oh! I didn't realize—"

"It's okay, Tara. I was just on my way out." I couldn't prevent my smile from widening.

"Well, actually, I should get going anyway," Tara muttered between her fingers pressed against her lips.

"Don't leave on my account."

"My shift starts soon." Her face shimmered like a Red Delicious apple when she turned and tottered back to the bedroom, tugging the ends of Kirk's shirt.

I mouthed the words, "I'm sorry," to my flustered brother and let myself out.

*****

An hour later, Kirk's truck pulled into the driveway. I had finished emptying the hall closet and the bathroom vanity, mostly discarding toiletries. Sylvia's bedroom was next on my list when Kirk stormed in. "Really, Vic. You just show up unannounced?"

"I'm sorry. I had no clue you and the pretty hospital nurse got *close*. I like her."

He shrugged and shook his head.

"You don't care if I like her?"

"It was just one night. I couldn't sleep after the funeral, so I went to Duffy's pub, and she was there."

"She seems like a nice lady. Just go easy on her."

His brows narrowed when he faced me. "What does that mean?"

"You don't give women a chance. Look at you; you're gorgeous and in shape. Women must throw themselves at you, but you've never given anyone much of a chance after you divorced Lacy like a hundred years ago."

"Don't go there."

"It's just an observation. I like Tara. Maybe you should try dating and see where it goes. Don't keep playing the love 'em and leave 'em game."

"Where's Tony with lunch?" He clumsily changed the subject.

"It's only eleven, but I'll get off your back. I'm ready to start going through Mom's room. Do you want to tackle the garage? There's a lot of old junk and tools in there. Maybe you or Tony can use some of that stuff."

"I'll wait for Tony to help in the garage. I'll start in Tony's old bedroom. She used that room for storing things she didn't need often. I suppose she couldn't part with all the junk she accumulated through the years. What are we gonna do with this place? I mean, we grew up here. This is home. Even without Mom, it still feels like *home* to me."

My shoulders drooped as a thought lingered. "You know, you live in that small apartment. Tony and Leann have a house. I'm going back to Paris. If you have an interest in this place, maybe we don't have to sell it."

Instantly, Sylvia's voice echoed in my mind, saying, "Promise me you won't sell my house."

"Think about it," I encouraged.

And I could tell he was, watching his dark eyes peruse the room.

I felt like I was invading Sylvia's personal space, rummaging through her dresser drawers, discarding her undergarments, and determining what clothing might be worthy of donations versus a dumpster. This wasn't a job to give my brothers. She had several shirts with tags on them, a new package of socks, and a leopard-print pajama set folded with pins keeping it in place that could be given to charity. Since Sylvia and Aunt Lucy wore the same size, I put aside a gently used sweater and a few blouses she might like. A pair of Nike women's sneakers looked hardly worn, but Sylvia wore a size six. One difference between the Ursini sisters was their shoe size. Aunt Lucy had large feet, wearing a size nine like me.

The bottom left dresser drawer contained a couple of men's faded dress shirts, socks, and boxers. I put the items in the garbage bag to evade the imagery of Sylvia entertaining a man in her life. No men in her age group attended her service except for Tony's father, Burt. Nah. That relationship ended decades ago.

An hour of cleaning passed when I heard the front door open, and the aroma of something greasy filled the air. "I'm here!" Tony called out.

My stomach rumbled, happy that food had arrived. I raced to the kitchen to see Tony with containers from one of my favorite childhood hangouts. "Yes! You went to Zeke's Char Pit!"

"You're looking kinda thin, sis. Figured you could go for the deep-fried shrimp and cheese fries."

"My skin may hate you later, but I love you right now." I grabbed three plates as he set the bags down.

Kirk entered the kitchen. His face was as pale as a ghost.

"Bro, I brought us ribs and chili-cheese fries."

"You gotta see this!" Kirk shouted enthusiastically.

I grabbed a piece of crispy fried shrimp from the container and stuffed it inside my mouth, enjoying the crispy texture and mouthwatering seasonings as Tony and I followed Kirk to the spare bedroom he had been cleaning. I hadn't eaten a thing all day, and I couldn't wait to taste those disgustingly greasy yet delicious cheese fries.

"Look at this!"

"A laundry bag?" Tony scoffed.

"An old laundry bag from decades ago. How long ago did they stop making laundry deliveries?"

"I recognize the name, Mae's Whites. Yeah, there were radio ads back in my day that had a catchy jingle for Mae's." I started to hum a few bars when Kirk disrupted me.

"Forget the laundry bag. Check this out." Kirk removed a manila envelope from the old white bag. He lifted many large bills from it, then moved to the twin bed with the periwinkle blue spread and dumped the rest of the contents out. The clicking sound of coins blanketed a small portion of the bed.

I pushed my way in between my brothers. "Wow, that's a lot of cash and casino chips!"

Tony started juggling a few black chips labeled $100. "Woo-hoo!" When he took a closer look at the chips he held, his happy glow vanished. "Jesus, these are from the Thunderbird. What the hell is Mom doing with chips from a casino that no longer exists? And why didn't she cash them in years ago? They must be worthless now, but they look cool."

Kirk waved a few bills around. "Look, *old* money from before the government changed the style of the president's faces in the '90s."

"Maybe this is what she meant in the hospital," I whispered my personal thought aloud.

"What do you mean?" Kirk asked.

"When Mom first woke up after you left the hospital, she said something that struck me as odd. She was adamant that we not sell her house. It doesn't explain why this money isn't in the bank or her safe."

"I found it in the crawl space inside the closet, hidden behind a large box."

"Oh, yeah, I used to hide my *Playboy* mags in there." Tony laughed.

"Did she ever discuss money with you?" I asked.

"Not with me. Vic, we know you helped her financially because you had the means. Kirk and I helped her with chores around the house so she wouldn't have to hire people. We all pitched in to take care of her in our own way. What's the deal with this money?" Tony voiced the rhetorical question we all wondered.

"We should take it to the bank," Kirk suggested.

"Yeah, then we split it. First, let's see how much is here. There's a mix of bills. Could be thousands!" Tony declared, rubbing his palms together.

"She has bank accounts. Why'd she hide this money in the crawl space? Something's off," I said, divulging my concern.

Tony continued to play with the casino chips. "And these chips—the Thunderbird closed in the '70s, I think."

"Perhaps as we clean up the place, we'll find something to shed light on this small fortune." I hoped.

"Yeah, maybe there's more lying around. Let's count it!" Kirk merrily shouted.

My stomach howled. "I think I'll enjoy my shrimp and cheese fries first." I texted Tommy as I left the room, enlightening him of the secret stash we found hidden in an old laundry bag. He responded with several question marks. For the first time in his life, my husband was speechless.

CHAPTER 16

Stalking

The Ford Focus parked a row away from a silver Infiniti SUV off Freeway 15. The driver's fingers pressed the tip of his Clippers cap and lowered it to conceal his eyes. He watched the family's movements from a short distance. The man with thick hair the color of butter, the father, looked strong and virile. His wife, equally tall but slender with an athletic physique, could play in the WNBA if she wasn't weak and submissive, bossed around by her husband.

She'd be no problem, he thought. Her husband, however, was a different story. Powerful and wealthy with connections. This rich family wouldn't see it coming.

He'd been watching them interact at home and in public, absorbing their routine every day and evening. They had five children ranging in age from one to sixteen. He had been learning their schedules and habits.

Did hubby realize his wife was screwing her yoga instructor? Did wifey know that her husband brought their sixteen-year-old son to a brothel in Pahrump?

He still had much to gain before he put his plan in motion. His eyes watched the family stroll into Giovanni's Bistro. A nice family dinner out at an expensive restaurant. They'd enjoy a good meal tonight while he fine-tuned his plan.

CHAPTER 17

Danny offered to assist me with the probate court process and the legalities of managing Sylvia's estate, validating her will, and the disbursement of her possessions.

I needed to escape the madness of Sylvia's home. I spent the day stuffing trash bags and stacking boxes labeled "garbage" or "donation." Kirk and Tony had to get back to work and their lives. Once Sylvia's estate was settled and my family was okay, I could hop on a plane and return to Paris with Tommy.

Sylvia's house appeared smaller, with everything she owned stacked in piles. It felt claustrophobic. This place became too cluttered to have Danny meet me here. I also didn't want to run into the media or people from Jeffrey's orbit in public, like at the Montgomery, where Danny spent his days. He not only owned shares of the hotel and casino business his father perfected, but his additional function was VP and general counsel for the hotel. Danny had a great deal of experience reading wills and handling probate court, which certainly came in handy for me now.

Danny invited me to his home for dinner and to meet his children. Tommy felt ecstatic, though mildly envious, that I got the chance to spend time with his grandchildren, who believed he was deceased.

I left early for the drive to Summerlin, given the anticipated freeway traffic. I decided to make an extra stop at Callie's Sugar Factory, a bakery that made a variety of deliciously flavored cupcakes daily, like peanut butter explosion, cookies and cream, and chocolate bonanza. Tommy told me how much his grandchildren loved cupcakes from that particular patisserie. Even with the additional stop, I breezed through the gated entrance of Danny's property a solid twenty minutes before seven.

Several cars were parked out front of the massive mansion where Danny's family lived. The smell of a freshly mowed lawn tickled my nostrils as I stepped along the colorful cobblestone pathway. A vivid garden, rich with pink hibiscus, red azaleas, orange begonias, and white gardenias, forced me to stop in my tracks and enjoy the beautiful imagery that trailed aside the elongated front porch, enclosed by a gray cement wall. Butterflies fluttered their magical wings while bees buzzed in pollination heaven with the hot sun still shining in the early evening hours. My smile grew wide. Danny's home oozed with warm, positive energy. If I could, I would sit on his porch and watch the beauty of nature all day. I found gardening to be one of the most relaxing, creative exercises—an activity I missed, living in a Paris apartment.

The front door opened before I reached the porch steps. A couple of women were on their way out, and the sound of several voices could be detected from indoors. I smiled and casually said hello to the ladies exiting. They reciprocated with a friendly nod and smile. I must be earlier than I thought if Bianca had guests.

The pretty lady with strawberry blond strands noticed me standing on the opposite side of the screen door and signaled me to enter with a wave of a hand. "Vicki! Welcome," Bianca said as she approached and gave me a gentle hug to prevent my dropping the box of cupcakes. "Oh, the kids will love that you brought dessert from Callie's!" Her enthusiasm to see me and the cupcakes induced a chuckle.

"I thought they'd enjoy a sweet treat. I'm sorry, I'm early. I didn't know you had other guests."

"Let me introduce you to Danny's family, the Meades, on his mother's side. They've been trying to leave for the last thirty minutes. I had a little get-together this afternoon, and we ran late." She took the box from my hand. "Aunt Lisa, this is Vicki Ursini."

It took me a moment to make the connection. Lisa was Danny's aunt, his mother's sister. We shook hands upon introduction.

"How about I take those yummy-looking cupcakes to the kitchen for you," Lisa said before glancing at her wristwatch. "Then I have to get going. It was a pleasure to meet you, Vicki."

"Same here, Lisa."

She introduced me to Danny's cousin Abby, a thirty-something-year-old, who resembled Lisa, her mother. She seemed in a hurry, tap-dancing around my body to leave, apologizing for rushing out because she had to pick up her son from soccer practice.

A few yards from me stood Sadie, my husband's ex-wife, speaking privately to another woman. Tommy's disdain for Sadie eased as he aged, but he hadn't seen her to trigger the remnants of anger he once carried. Meeting Danny's mother came as a complete surprise. A throbbing sensation jolted against my temples when we made eye contact. She was a lovely woman who didn't look to be in her early seventies, with short blond hair mixed with white subtleties. Mild wrinkles surrounded her eyes and lips. Rather petite, but her potent expression pierced through when she stepped toward me. Her deep blue eyes scrolled up and down my body before her brash grin transitioned to a smile. "You must be Vicki. I recognize you from TV. Hank, my partner, and I enjoyed *Rising 51*."

"Thank you. It's nice to meet you, Sadie. I guess I arrived early. I didn't mean to intrude on your party."

"Nonsense!" Bianca said. "In fact, let me introduce you to Eve." Bianca signaled the attention of a heavyset woman in her mid-forties, with brown curls and light touches of bright pink hues blended in her locks.

"This was such a wonderful experience," Sadie said as Eve inched closer for an introduction to me.

Eve's lips rubbed together while her shadowy eyes squinted, focusing on my face as if deep in thought.

At that moment, Danny raced in with four children barreling past him, running in several directions upon entry. They seemed accustomed to the pandemonium, ignoring the disorder. Danny made his way around, greeting family members until he spotted me. "Hi, welcome to my life!" He looked at Bianca. "Didn't you say your party was ending at six?" He gave his beautiful wife a kiss. He left a peck on his mother's cheek, then opened his arms and hugged me, whispering, "Sorry."

"Don't be. I just met your mother and was about to meet Eve."

Eve eerily continued to stare without saying a word.

"Eve is doing her *thing*," Sadie added, tapping my arm with her elbow.

"Her thing?" I asked, wondering what her *thing* was.

Danny rolled his eyes. "Mom, Bianca, how about we start—" He twisted his arm and hand in a circular motion, signaling them to wrap things up.

"Shh! A woman's voice is speaking," Eve bellowed, causing the background conversations to immediately cease. The air flooded with a chilling silence.

In my confused state, I feared moving as all eyes fell upon Eve.

Bianca whispered to Danny loud enough for me to hear, "We tried to reach Pop, but he didn't come through again. Maybe with you here—"

"Babe, please," Danny responded impatiently as his eyes reached mine.

"Oh, she's a *medium*." I verified with surprise before someone shushed me.

Bianca silently spoke in my ear, "She's incredible, really. Danny isn't a believer. I hoped that by having her here in our home, maybe Tommy would come through."

If Tommy came through, Eve's credibility would be rubbish, at least to Danny and me.

Eve announced, "Oh, she's a spirited woman for sure. Everyone else singing through my thoughts got shoved aside for this spunky lady. She's got an amazing laugh and strong personality."

"Is it my mother again, Eve?" Sadie asked. "Danny, it was amazing! Grandma spoke to Aunt Lisa and me. She reunited with Grandpa in heaven. Grandpa said that Grandma met him when he passed two years ago and introduced him to the glorious kingdom of heaven. Eve made his transformation sound so peaceful."

"Uh-huh." Danny rolled his gray eyes in my direction.

"It's a different woman—a motherly figure—connected to *her*." Eve's finger stiffly pointed at my chest. Her eyes widened. "Did you lose your mother recently?"

I hesitated to reply. I mean, my mother's funeral made the news, thanks to Jeffrey's media attack. I merely nodded and attempted to smile, though I might have failed.

"She's a hot ticket. Feisty!" Eve laughed. "She loved to perform on stage and tell an enthralling story."

More information that anyone could learn. Although it wasn't like Eve expected me today and prepared to learn about my personal life.

"I see pink and gold colors. Wait! She mentions a treasure. She says, '*Think, Victoria, about my treasures.*'"

If Sylvia really was speaking to me through Eve, she must mean the bag of old bills and casino chips we found. I didn't understand the pink and gold colors. The chips were black and worth a hundred dollars each, but they certainly could be classified as a treasure. I wouldn't divulge my suspicions to the people in the room, so I absently bobbed my head at Eve. "I think I understand." The tension in my neck grew. I turned my back on Eve, hoping to break this unsettling spell. I had been in show business for a long time, like my mother. I smelled a charlatan, but I couldn't explain how Eve knew confidential information. Bianca hadn't given Eve my name, yet she said *Victoria* during this spontaneous reading.

"Your mother says don't sell the house. You promised."

My head instantaneously snapped back. How could she have known about Sylvia's dying wish for me to keep the house? Did Eve genuinely have the ability to communicate with the dead?

"Cardinals appear when angels are near. Cardinals appear when angels are near." Eve sang the phrase like a melody from a dark musical. "She's gone now, Victoria, but she's always with you. Seeing a cardinal will be a clue that her spirit is near."

"A bird?"

"Her words, not mine. Cardinals are a sign from the other side that your angels are with you."

The air grew cold and silent when Bianca's voice disrupted the mystical moment, "Can you check on Tommy Cavallo again? I mean, with both Vicki and Danny here—"

"Bianca, stop. Please," Danny begged, but Bianca waved her hand, discounting his plea.

Eve sluggishly lowered her head, looking as though she had fallen asleep in an awkward position. When her head darted up in a spine-chilling way, her eyes drifted to Sadie. "Your mother returned, my dear." Eve paused while the dead chanted sentiments through her head. She spoke to Sadie as if she was the only person in the room. "Your mother tells me Tommy isn't there."

Danny's gray eyes instinctively met mine. Eve proved to be rather inconceivable with the few details she revealed. But if this woman told the entire room that Tommy was still alive, the ripple effect would be disastrous.

"Okay, Eve. Thank you. My wife and I made plans this evening. Tell my grandma Meade I love her, and thank her for stopping by," he said in jest, then glared at his mother. "Mom—"

"I get it. Let me say goodbye to my grandchildren, wherever they ran off to, and I'll be out of your hair." Sadie turned to face me. "It was nice meeting you, Vicki."

"Yes, a pleasure, Sadie." I shook her hand, undecided if *pleasure* was the best word to describe our introduction.

Sadie snuck up close and whispered in my ear after Danny nudged Bianca into the kitchen. "Eve is pure magic! I could tell by the look on your face that she struck a nerve about your mother. I'm not sure what she meant about Tommy. Well, it's not like he was close to my family. Maybe their *wings* haven't crossed in heaven yet. I'm sorry for *your* loss. Your mother's death, of course, but also Tommy's." Her words sounded genuinely sincere.

She called out to her grandchildren for hugs goodbye before she left.

The aroma of tomato sauce and eggplant filled the air. Bianca created a rigatoni casserole, eggplant stuffed bread, and a garden salad for dinner, knowing I didn't eat meat. She prepared the meatless meal prior to Eve's entertaining performance. Bianca released a hearty laugh, saying, "When the Meades get together, it's difficult to part ways. I expected them to leave long before you arrived, Vicki."

"I was happy to meet the entire family." I bit into the warm, soft bread with thin slices of eggplant and mozzarella. My taste buds danced with each delightful nibble.

Meeting Tommy's grandchildren was a wonderful encounter. I met Emma and Kristina when they were babies. Tommy used to invite me over when he babysat the girls. They were too young to speak or remember my presence at that time.

Emma now teetered on the edge of thirteen, the spitting image of her mom with strawberry blond hair, porcelain skin, and a toned, athletic build. Kristina favored Danny's looks with chestnut hair and gray eyes. At ten and a half, she bossed around her siblings, ordering them to pick up their toys and dictating which TV show they'd watch later. The twin's looks always stumped me in the photographs Tommy would share. TJ and Tyler were eight and a half and quite a mix of their ancestral background. Blond hair and the oval shape of their faces resembled Sadie. They had the same gray eyes as Tommy and Danny, but their small nose and high cheekbones favored Bianca.

Danny encouraged the kids to take pictures with me, reminding them of the cool sci-fi movies I starred in. TJ and Tyler loved my film, *Robots from Space*. They were old enough for Danny to explain that I had been their poppy's girlfriend before he died, so I was *family*.

"I really miss Poppy." Emma blinked hard to control the tears filling her eyes. Her obvious pain tore at my heart. She and Kristina talked about their memories of swimming in his pool and playing with a variety of Barbies and board games he had bought them.

Tommy never met the twins in person, who argued over who should take a bath first tonight.

Bianca placed the box of Callie's cupcakes on the dining room table. The unique sugar combinations triggered the four kids to bounce to the table to choose their favorites.

"I want cookies and cream!" Kristina shouted with insistence and grabbed the cupcake from the tray.

"Me too!" The disappointment on TJ's face shimmered when he spotted Kristina take the cupcake he wanted.

"I bought two of each flavor," I announced, approaching the table to calm the impending argument. Tommy recommended I order two of each to avoid fighting. Although he watched them grow from a distance, he remained in tune with all aspects of their lives through Danny.

Emma politely allowed Tyler to pick his favorite plain vanilla cupcake before choosing vanilla with strawberry frosting for herself.

Over coffee and tea, Danny told some delightful tales about growing up as Tommy Cavallo's son, and I laughed at each story he shared. Bianca finished Danny's sentences in a way that seemed he expected her to chime in and contribute.

"I know of some children in need of baths!" Bianca shouted in a loud, teasing manner.

"No! Not yet, Mommy!"

"I'm coming upstairs to get you ready." Bianca threw a wink at me.

"Go ahead, Bianca. Danny and I need to discuss my mother's will, anyway."

We relaxed comfortably on the brown leather sofa. Danny spread some papers about the coffee table and explained the tedious probate process to me in layman's terms. He believed he could get through probate quickly enough so we could finalize Sylvia's estate.

A fruity, clean scent followed TJ and Tyler down the stairwell after their baths to give their father a hug and kiss goodnight.

"How about you two say goodnight to Vicki?"

"Goodnight, Vicki," the boys said in stereo and blessed me with a brief hug before they dashed upstairs in their red and blue super-hero jammies.

"You have an amazing family, Danny."

"I'm very lucky, and I won't take them for granted." He twisted his head to look upstairs, ensuring his family wasn't in hearing range.

"You don't have to say it. I know. They sure do miss Tommy."

*****

After expressing my thanks to Bianca and receiving a generous hug from Emma and Kristina, I hopped into the car and anxiously dialed Tommy at 7:00 a.m. Paris time. He loved hearing about my evening with his family. Danny already sent him the pictures he took.

"There's one with you, Danny, and the kids together that I'm going to frame. I love it!"

"Boy, does Emma miss you. Her weepy grin and wobbly chin nearly made me cry. They all miss you, but Emma really feels the loss."

"Uh, it tears me up inside, but it is what it is."

"I know. It was so hard not to talk about you in front of them. I don't know how Danny does it. Oh, Bianca is into psychics."

Tommy snickered. "Is she?"

"She had a medium over, hoping to talk to *you* from the other side."

He released a surge of laughter. "Yeah, what did *I* say?"

"Actually, I waited for this woman to make up some nonsense, but she claimed to speak to Sadie's mother, who said you weren't there."

"Really? Huh. Suzanne Meade was as sweet as apple pie. I always liked her. You know, I never said this out loud, but I think my pop had a crush on Suzanne." He laughed.

"A crush? What makes you say that?"

"I noticed the way he looked at her. But she was married to Sadie's father, Fred, his Army pal. Anyway, was my ex there?"

"Sadie acted quite welcoming as we spoke. Bianca's psychic party ended when I arrived, so she was on her way out."

"Hmpf."

"I understand your distrust and animosity. You were in an unhappy marriage, but you have to let that resentment go. You won't see her again."

"I'd rather talk about when you're coming home."

A sigh flew from my lips. "Danny's helping me settle the estate through probate court. Sylvia's house is almost all packed up now."

"Can't your brothers manage the rest?"

"There are a few final things I need to handle, like ensuring my aunt is taken care of. I'll talk to her about arranging for one of those companion-type services. You know, the people who come to your home, keep you company, and ensure you have a hot meal and a clean home."

"Okay, I get it. I just miss you like crazy."

"I miss you too, babe. I hope to be on a flight to Paris in a week or so. Can you handle being away from me another week?"

Reluctantly, he replied, "I'll manage."

"And if that Miranda Hurley from apartment 1018 flirts with you—"

"There's no one else for me, sweetheart, not even that spicy Miranda Hurley."

"Oh, so she's *spicy*?" I pulled the car into the driveway as Tommy laughed. "I'm home now, and you've got to get ready for your day on the river Seine. Love you!"

"Love you more."

As I neared the door, jiggling my key, a sharp spark of light whipped through the picture window in the living room—from inside the house.

My head snapped toward the driveway and street. No vehicles were parked except for the red Mercedes I drove. Was I seeing things? I inserted my key in the lock and slowly turned the knob to enter. No sooner did I flip the switch when I witnessed the figure of a person holding a flashlight dash from the living room to the kitchen.

"Hey! Who are you?" I shouted such a stupid question as if this hooded burglar would tell me. A loud crash sent shivers up my spine. Do I follow this person, dial 911, or run in the opposite direction to avoid a potential attack? In a split second, I decided not to run away.

I obviously scared the thief, who tripped over some boxes in the dark and darted out the kitchen door.

Cautiously, I inched near the open door to shut it, and reached for the lock, but the chain and doorknob were busted—the thief's entry point. I flicked on the outside light from the lanai and spotted the shape of that man staggering through the backyard with a lopsided sprint, like he had injured himself. The loud crash I heard must have been the falling of the once neatly stacked boxes scattered across the kitchen tile haphazardly.

Kirk and Tony arrived minutes after the police. I sat in the middle of the brightly lit living room, constantly peering over my shoulder. The crook left empty-handed unless he crammed something into his pockets I couldn't see. He wore a plain, dark, long-sleeved shirt and black pants. A black ski mask hid his features that would offer clues regarding his age, race, and hair color. His body was definitely masculine. Maybe he weighed 190, with an estimated height of five-eleven. The image left in my mind was that of approximately seven seconds and before my instinctive fears materialized.

I gave an officer my statement. They searched the place to confirm if the burglar had an accomplice. No one was hiding in a closet, under a bed, or in the basement.

"You can't stay here, Vicki. I'll replace the broken lock, but we don't know what that thief wanted," Tony worriedly stated.

"Are you sure about that?" I whispered so the officer standing ten feet from us couldn't hear. "This might have something to do with that *laundry bag* we found."

Kirk called the officer over. I thought he'd tell the cop about the money and old casino chips we found yesterday. Instead, he asked if he could look around and see if anything of value had been stolen.

I assessed the boxes spread across the floor. The pile hadn't shrunk. Although a few boxes showed torn newspaper pulled out and old clothing hanging from the top as if they had been combed through. Sylvia's valuables had been bequeathed and out of the house except for some furniture, the Monet painting still hanging on the wall, the locket she left me dangling from my neck, and the laundry bag with money and chips.

Kirk returned from Tony's former bedroom and nodded with wide, optimistic eyes, his way of telling us that the money and chips remained in the hidden crawl space.

I waved my hand to the burly officer with a crew cut and serious expression. "Officer, my mother kept a large sum of cash in the house and some old collectible casino chips with an unknown value. It's possible the thief was after the cash. Maybe I interrupted him before he found it."

"How much cash?" he asked with raised brows.

"A fair amount. We stumbled upon the money while cleaning out the place after she died." I intentionally neglected to divulge the sum totaled ten thousand dollars and a few thousand in chips.

"Yeah, some older folks don't like banks for some reason. I'll check to see if she ever reported a break-in before."

The officers left after securing the back door to prevent another burglary until Tony replaced the lock.

A throbbing ache beat against my temples. Stressed over disrupting a thief, settling our mother's estate, and the continued anguish about my crappy interview thanks to my ex-husband, which hit the news, making me the joke of late night comedic talk show hosts. "Kirk, take the laundry bag and deposit the cash when you can. Your name is on Mom's bank account."

He nodded hazily in agreement. "You know, I was giving what you suggested some serious thought, Vicki. I haven't been able to focus on much else. I think I am interested in buying you guys out of Mom's house and living here. There's a part of me that doesn't want to sell it. It still feels like home."

"That sounds like a great plan, Kirk." Tony's words offered encouragement.

"There's one thing I have to do if I move in here."

"What's that," Tony asked.

"Mom never put in a pool. When we were kids, we begged for one."

"I know. I never learned how to swim. The blistering summer months were insufferable unless we went to Grandpa's house to use his pool," I added.

"Burt had a nice pool. He'd take me with Tony often, especially during the summer." Kirk reflected and paused, thinking about happy childhood memories. "A friend of mine started a pool business. He's been in the industry for years but recently branched out independently. He can use new customers, and I bet he'll get the job done quickly."

"Mom added your name to the deed, Kirk. Technically, the house is yours, no matter how long the probate court takes. If you want the house and a pool, go for it," I said exuberantly.

Kirk's face beamed, wearing a broad smile.

An agonizing throb attacked my temples. "My head is pounding. I need to lie down."

"Vicki, stay with Leann and me tonight. At least until the lock is replaced."

He was right. Leann and I would have to tolerate each other for one night.

I texted Danny, asking if I could get a room at the Montgomery under an assumed identity on their most secure floor, starting tomorrow night.

Naturally, he was curious as to why I suddenly needed a hotel room, but he confirmed it wouldn't be a problem.

CHAPTER 18

I woke up early to the scurrying of feet in the hallway outside the guest bedroom. Tony and Leann attempted to keep their voices at a low tone while my lids lifted at the sound of whispers through the thin walls. My sleeping pattern had been off, given the stress in my life and the severe time change. Last night, though, I slept somewhat peacefully thanks to the melatonin. My mind immediately shifted to the reason for sleeping in Tony's guestroom; the image of that masked man roaming freely in Sylvia's house stirred my anxiety. Without that sleeping aid, I would have tossed and turned all night.

The clock radio told me it was 6:05 a.m. I dreaded returning to Sylvia's to finish cleaning, storing, and discarding. Since Kirk decided to move in, he might be apt to keep some of the furniture.

I made lunch plans with Bridget and Claudia today on their last day in town before flying back to California. I looked forward to seeing them, despite feeling violated after the break-in.

The smell of burnt toast and coffee brewing awakened my senses. A cup of hot tea would soothe my worries for a few moments. I tossed on my robe and headed to the kitchen.

Leann appeared too busy fiddling with Tony's cell to notice me standing behind her.

"Good morning." I intentionally spoke loudly, causing her to jump.

"Oh! Morning, Vicki." Tony's phone juggled between her fingers before dropping on the kitchen table.

"Whatcha doing?" I asked, hoping to hide my suspicious nature.

"Tony got a text from work, so I was—"

"Planning on telling him he received a text?" I wanted to ask why she was snooping at his messages, but as a guest in her home, I bit my tongue.

Her fair skin turned a mild shade of pink. "He's taking so long in the shower. Maybe he'd hurry up if he knew someone had contacted him. It sucks to have only one bathroom. This place is too small." She found a way to change the subject while subtly complaining that my brother couldn't afford a larger home, or perhaps she wanted to blatantly hint that my presence crowded her.

Tony raced from the bathroom, dressed in his black and gold casino attire, looking handsome. "Morning," he said as he picked up his phone.

"You got a text," Leann advised before biting into an overdone piece of wheat toast.

He looked at his cell as confusion washed over his face. "I don't see a new text. Maybe it was an email." Tony glanced at his watch. "Gotta run. Vicki, are you sure you want to go to a hotel? You can stay as long as you'd like."

Leann gasped, then urgently charged to the bathroom.

"I appreciate your offer, Tony, but I'll be fine at the Montgomery. Danny will ensure I have security."

"Don't worry about Leann. She's really fine with you staying here," he mumbled.

"Hmm, nice try, but it's best I go to the Montgomery until I feel safe staying at Mom's house again. Well, now it'll be *Kirk's* house. Go to work, so you're not late. Once I have my tea and a shower, I'll be out of Leann's way."

CHAPTER 19

Driving up the Strip brought back a host of fond memories: the grandiose hotels, popular celebrity-owned restaurants, crowded streets, and people in dazzling costumes trying to make a few bucks. Locals typically avoided the Strip because of the brutal traffic with brazen taxi and Uber drivers. I flew down a side street to arrive at Tommy's former hotel, the Montgomery, which was divided into three main wings, representing the countries of England, Ireland, and Scotland.

Tommy's pop, Rocky Cavallo, envisioned a luxurious resort back in the '60s while adding sculptures, murals, and elegant decor that highlighted the magical experiences of each great land. People came in from off the street to view a towering Big Ben, kiss the Blarney stone replica, take a boat ride in the man-made lake they referred to as Loch Ness, and meet Nessie herself, a massive, animated statue of a long-necked, dinosaur-like creature.

Tommy carried an abundance of pride in his hotels. Although he enjoyed his current career as a Paris tour guide, I wondered if he missed the excitement and creativity of owning the Montgomery.

I ran a few minutes late, but I texted Danny that I had just parked in the back lot where some employees had entered. Danny thought it would be in my best interest to maintain discretion. After my humiliating debacle with the press, I abhorred the spotlight. I wanted to wrap up Sylvia's affairs and return to my quiet life in Paris with Tommy.

Danny stood outside with Phyllis Santore, Tommy's former assistant and my biggest fan. She looked adorable in a two-toned black and forest green suit. Her brown eyes glittered with happiness as I approached her.

"Phyllis! I'm delighted to see you." We exchanged a warm hug.

"Oh, Vicki, it's great to see you again. I'm terribly sorry about your mother." She brushed her white bangs and repositioned her red-rimmed glasses after releasing me from her vigorous embrace.

"Thank you, Phyllis. How are things at the Montgomery?" My eyes wavered back and forth between Danny and Phyllis.

They responded in stereo, "Busy!" Then they chuckled simultaneously.

Another man, stocky in frame, wearing a gray-striped suit, stepped out and nodded at me. He faced Danny with friendly brown eyes and said, "All clear."

"Vicki, this is Bobby Lubitski, Rob's son. Do you remember Rob?"

"Of course. Nice to meet you, Bobby."

Danny added, "Rob and Jack retired, leaving their children in charge now."

"The Montgomery is truly a family business," Bobby said. "I'm happy to help you out while you're in town, Ms. Ursini."

"Call me Vicki, please. I'll be here for a few nights, maybe longer."

"Did something happen at your mother's place?" Danny asked in front of Phyllis and Bobby as they nudged me along through the back entrance to the service elevator. I recalled using this same path many times when Tommy and I met in seclusion, an attempt to keep our clandestine affair contained years ago. It worked for a while until Jeffrey discovered my betrayal, falling in love with another man.

If I startled Danny with the truth about why I suddenly chose to stay at the Montgomery, he might inform Tommy about the break-in at Sylvia's house. I couldn't worry Tommy, especially since he was too far away to help. "I'm feeling a little claustrophobic with the mountain of boxes to be discarded. My brother, Kirk, decided to keep the house and move in."

"I see." Danny's smirk told me that he surmised suspicion.

"Maybe once we clear out the place in a few days, I'll check out."

"Stay as long as you'd like," Phyllis kindly stated as she fiddled with her glasses.

The top floor of the Montgomery had numerous suites and top-notch security clearance. Only those with celebrity status held the proper key card to access the area. Additionally, a private casino with gaming tables and slots was open if we had the itch to gamble. A strong aroma of coffee and pastries came from the social room as we glided past it.

The England wing had the best view of the lively Vegas Strip, especially at night when the buildings gleamed with flashing lights and the streets crammed with thousands of tourists and entertainers.

Suite 1800 was a beautiful room with shades of lavender wallpaper offset by royal purple bedding. A small kitchen area with a sink, mini-fridge, microwave, and coffeemaker, complete with beige granite countertops, gave a homey vibe. A living room with a tan sofa, matching loveseat, large-screen TV, coffee table, and a desk covered the essential aspects of a relaxing home away from home. Atop the coffee table sat a small fruit basket with two apples, two oranges, two bananas, and a branch of red grapes.

"This is a fantastic room. I don't need all this space or special treatment outside of security."

"We're delighted you like it. Phyllis and I have to get to a meeting in the Scotland wing." Bobby glanced at his watch. "In ten minutes. It's been a pleasure, Vicki."

"Thanks, Bobby." I shook his hand and gave Phyllis a friendly hug.

I moved to the balcony to view the busy street below. I could feel Danny's eyes upon me, though my back faced him. "I'll be sure your pop knows that the change in leadership didn't take away from the quality and dazzling perks the Montgomery offered when he was in charge."

"Wanna tell me why you're keeping this from Pop?"

"I don't want to put you in the position to lie for me. I'll probably only be here a few days, but I'm not certain. There's no need to make a special phone call to discuss this with him. Although, when we FaceTime later, he'll figure out I'm not at my mother's house." I sighed, realizing I wouldn't be able to keep this from Tommy after all.

"My father has a sixth sense. It's none of my business, and I won't outright tell him, but if he asks me, Vicki, I won't lie."

"I'd never ask you to lie. I don't want him to end up flying out here."

"Is it that bad? Bad enough for him to risk his life, showing his face in Vegas?"

I shook my head. "I don't know yet. But you know how protective he is."

"And I'm equally protective of my family, which includes you."

"Someone broke into my mother's house. We don't know what they wanted. We think the burglar left empty-handed. It startled me, that's all. Metro thinks the thief might have targeted the house, knowing my mother died without realizing I was staying there."

"Okay, I get it. A random burglary sucks, but my pop would understand that. I can't see him losing his mind about a break-in."

"I don't trust Jeffrey. Neither does Tommy."

"You think Atkins had something to do with it?"

"I have no proof—only trivial theories. One thing my mother complained about before she died was that Jeffrey called her frequently, wanting to find me. The thief wasn't Jeffrey, but he could have hired someone. Do you see how paranoid I've become? I can't blame every negative moment in my life on Jeffrey."

"I'm glad you contacted me. You can stay here for as long as you need."

CHAPTER 20

Claudia and Bridget's flights were scheduled to depart before five. I planned to meet them for lunch at a French bistro in the mall attached to the Venetian, the beautiful Italian-themed hotel, beyond the entrance for gondola rides.

We laughed over tasty crab puffs drenched in a creamy white sauce about our college days and a few daring escapades.

Bridget exposed lovely diamond drop earrings as she tucked her natural silver hair behind her ears. She described her thirty-seven-year marriage to Derek and the numerous times she considered bailing on him due to his overindulgence with alcohol, though the term *alcoholic* never left her lips. Her fingers played with the diamond tennis bracelet suspending from her wrist while describing an upcoming African safari trip. She and Derek lived in a cozy Colonial and enjoyed regular visits from their two children and three grandchildren. She shared several family photos on her cell, eagerly showing off the branches of her family tree. In her spare time, she continued to create lovely paintings for the pure pleasure of it.

Claudia had two sons from different marriages. Her oldest had a daughter that Claudia helped raise. Her granddaughter lived with her, though she hadn't revealed why her son couldn't raise his daughter as a single dad. I had heard he got sucked into drugs, another statistic of the opioid crisis. Her younger son recently married a woman whom Claudia spoke fondly of. They had been trying to conceive. Claudia rambled, elated to have another grandchild in the near future.

Since she retired from her teaching career, she and her husband, Alex, found hobbies they enjoyed together. She said it really strengthened their marriage when they chose to play golf and dabble in photography. They started taking nature hikes and snapping pictures of butterflies, wildlife, flowers, and waterfalls.

Suddenly, I felt their eyes fixating on me, waiting for an update on *my* life. I couldn't tell them I lived in Paris, mention my marriage to Tommy, or discuss working at the Musée d'Orsay. If only I could share the photos of Tommy and me atop the Eiffel Tower or standing before the Mona Lisa. Instead, I fibbed about the big, gorgeous Montana sky, breathing in the freshest air that rivaled no other place I had lived before. I chuckled about flirting with cowboys and taking horseback riding lessons. I tried not to sigh through such expressive, dishonest words. Arbitrary deceit via email and text messages had become second nature, though still challenging. But lying to their faces seemed more uncomfortable than I imagined.

"Reading your emails gave us some relief that you were doing okay, hiding from the political blowout and media circus after you left Jeffrey. The world had heard about your love for Tommy. We understood your secrecy then. Seeing you in person after all these years is just wonderful!" Claudia shed a tear as she spoke. "Vicki, we are your very best friends. You can open up to us."

"You know, we read Tommy's book. You always seemed to avoid our questions by email. Were the details true? Come on, spill," Bridget playfully insisted before sipping from her glass of Cabernet.

I smiled at their lighthearted need for drama. The past, as told by Tommy, with the hope of discovering who wanted him dead, was public knowledge. I couldn't discuss my present, but the past was fair game. "Tommy had this unmatched, entertaining quality. Our love was powerful and passionate. If he lived today, I'm sure we'd still be together. He loved to tell a story, and he had quite a doozy to share with the world—even the complicated parts that included me.

I miss him a lot." I paused to blink away a tear. Perhaps I acquired Sylvia's talent for exaggeration. "By the time Tommy's book had been released, I *finally* left Jeffrey, and, as you know, I needed to evade the public, the press, and specifically *Jeffrey*."

Bridget's facial expression softened as she clutched my hand and sighed. "What was that ambush after your mom's funeral? How could he do that to you?"

"Jeffrey loves theatrics and mayhem, especially if it hurts me in some way."

Claudia raised her glass to sip the sweet Moscato and said, "You handled yourself just fine under the circumstances."

"You're being far too kind. It was horrible! I was unprepared for haters on the day I buried my mother. Jeffrey always loved to surprise me," I grumbled with whirling sarcasm.

"We felt awful when we learned about your love for Tommy, knowing he died. But it sure sounded more like someone wanted him dead. I mean, the media exploded with possibilities based on Tommy's memoirs. What do you think happened? You must have a theory." Bridget twisted her gray strands, waiting for my answer.

I paused before speaking. "I really can't say. My attorney advised it's in my best interest not to talk about such notions or entertain the media with whimsical concepts. Please don't take my silence personally, I trust you both, but I really loved Tommy. I have to honor my love for him and abide by my lawyer's recommendations."

They nodded, although Bridget's brows raised, seemingly put off that I wouldn't share secrets with my best friends like I used to.

"Your aunt Lucy looked terrible, struggling to get around. She's nothing like Sylvia. Your mother was a spitfire, Vicki!"

"Aunt Lucy copes with her conditions. I'm sure she's feeling lonely, missing her older sister. They were so close."

Claudia nudged Bridget's arm. "Remember that summer day after classes ended when we went to see Vicki at her mom's house? You weren't home, Vicki. They had a nasty fight!"

Bridget's fingers brushed against her chin, thinking. "Geesh, Claudia, are you talking about back in the '70s? You've got the memory of an elephant."

Claudia continued, "We knocked on the door. They must not have heard us over their own shouting."

"Oh, now I remember!" Bridget swiftly turned her body toward me with impending excitement. "Your mom and aunt were *screaming* at each other."

"Well, uh, sisters have arguments. I know of a few battles they had over the years, usually about me. My aunt always came to my defense if I argued with my mother." I giggled.

"No, this was *vicious*, Vicki." Claudia's light-brown waves whipped to her right at Bridget. "I guess we never told her."

"It sounded way too crazy and personal, and we didn't want to cause trouble," Bridget stated. "But now, so many years later, it doesn't matter. Your aunt accused your mom of sleeping with her husband. She acted wild, angry, throwing a large pot at your mother!"

My cheeks suddenly flushed, like a hot flash creeping up on me. "Aunt Lucy actually threw a *pot* at her?"

Sylvia always acted on impulse. Uncle Gary was a good-looking man, but would she have had an affair with her sister's husband? I didn't want to believe that. "I think I'd remember an argument of that nature." Shock must have shown across my face.

"You weren't there, Vicki, and we didn't interrupt them. We decided to leave and meet up with you afterward, probably at one of our prime spots."

"Oh, that Irish pub we liked…O'Reilly's Bar and Grill." Claudia proved to have a fantastic memory. "We didn't want to upset you, but that was a lifetime ago. Sounds like they got over it if they remained close."

"I'm sure they did," I mumbled, unexpectedly worried about Sylvia's relationship with her sister's husband.

From the moment I said goodbye to Bridget and Claudia at the restaurant, I wondered if they were wrong or if vital details escaped their memories. Did Sylvia sleep with her sister's husband? Was that the reason Uncle Gary made a hasty exit from our lives? Honestly, I couldn't recall the last time I saw him, but it would have been sometime during my college years—mid-seventies.

CHAPTER 21

A sick feeling in my gut grew with intensity when I turned down Orchard Lane. Visions of the burglar hobbling off into the dark night produced a lump in my throat as I parked in the driveway. Rather than allowing fear to control me, I focused on washing the dinnerware from the hutch and boxing it up before Kirk and Tony transferred the piece to Aunt Lucy's apartment. There was still some additional packing to do while my brothers worked their day jobs.

I had been in Vegas for two weeks, the time meant for my China vacation. I had also requested an extended family leave of absence from the Musée d'Orsay, explaining Sylvia's accident and my need to take care of her while she recovered. I didn't believe she'd actually *die*.

When filming *Rising 51*, I learned several karate moves when battling the actors playing the villainous characters. But those combat scenes were choreographed by a black belt in karate who consulted the actors and stunt doubles on fight scenes. I closed my eyes, hoping to channel my character, the tough CIA agent Lexi Thorpe, and use those moves to protect myself.

As I stepped along the concrete walkway, a feather descended. A rustling sound compelled me to look up and observe a bright red cardinal fussing on a branch of the great cedar in the front yard. *Cardinals appear when angels are near*, the verse Eve had recited several times. "Hi, Mom," I playfully mumbled. I shrugged, carefully slipped my key into the lock, and slowly turned the knob.

My head snuck inside the crack of the door, observing mountains of boxes and dead silence. Although sunlight filled the room through the large picture window, I instinctively flipped on the light switch and inched my way through every room—except the basement. I stood near the basement door and pressed my fingers on the knob, but the heebie-jeebies stopped me from entering the dim, unfinished space. I shook my head back and forth, thinking how silly to feel afraid in the house I grew up in.

An alarming buzz rang—my cell. I jumped a mile as goose bumps mystically sprang up my arms. Kirk's name and number displayed. "H-h-hey," I stuttered.

"Hi. I wanted you to know that my buddy, Cam, might stop by to measure the yard for the pool. He thinks he can gather a crew to start digging soon. He gave me quite a deal!"

"Wow, that's great!"

"Cam's looking forward to the work and some referrals. I didn't want you to freak out if you were at Mom's house and saw a car pull up or a strange guy in the yard."

"Yeah, that might have startled me. Hey, where exactly is he digging? He won't wreck the peonies, will he?"

"Er, about that. That plant is in an awkward spot and would be too close to the pool."

"Hold on. Can we salvage it? Maybe someone can uproot it carefully and replant it in another spot in the yard. It's thriving and so lovely."

"Okay. Okay. I gotta get back to work. I'll ask him if he has resources who can relocate that shrub. I'm sure he's had customers with similar requests."

"Listen, I'll pay to save Mom's peonies." Kirk started to say something, but I cut him off. "Don't argue about it. It's my request, so I'll pay for it."

He grumbled, "Okay. Thank you."

"Ya know, now that you're moving in here, I can get going. I mean, the house is nearly all packed up. We can wrap things up this weekend."

"I'm sure you want to get back to your life. Not that I won't miss you."

"I'll miss you and Tony too, but I need to get home. I'm still working, you know." I omitted the real reason for returning home— Tommy. "I'll make the arrangements to fly home Monday or Tuesday. That way, we'll have one more weekend together with Aunt Lucy. We need to discuss making plans to help her. If Mom took care of her, Aunt Lucy would need someone to fill that void."

"Yup. Gotta run, Vic. I'm being paged. Talk later." The call dropped.

A creaky sound caused me to jump out of my skin. I stood from the kitchen, peering down the hall. My eyes focused on that basement door. Then a rattling noise in the wall belted sharp and loud. Probably the usual plumbing noises my brain normally ignored. Somehow staying at Sylvia's house alone wasn't enticing. The hutch could wait another day. I swiftly grabbed my pocketbook and dashed out the door.

CHAPTER 22

Tommy and I spent a good chunk of Friday morning catching up. Eager to feel the comfort of his arms around me, I booked an Air France flight for this coming Monday evening, which made my husband very happy.

I had been researching various services for the elderly in preparation for an arduous in-person discussion with my aunt to gauge her reaction to receiving assistance. One option was to leave her apartment. Summer Wind, an upscale assisted living facility named after the Sinatra megahit, yielded great reviews. Aunt Lucy couldn't afford the place, but I could help her. I had her name added to the waiting list, which wasn't terribly long, probably because of the high cost. The amenities, service, and cleanliness added value. Ginger and Giselle would be welcome because small pets and service animals were allowed.

My afternoon plan consisted of tackling Sylvia's china set. I refused to let a few sporadic noises deter me from completing the task of washing every plate, cup, bowl, and platter, then polishing the lovely hutch to restore its beauty until the chime of my cell disrupted this hefty chore. "Hi, Tony."

"Well, you won't believe this, but what are the chances your lawyer friend, Danny Cavallo, could help us out of a jam?"

"Jam?" I groaned.

"Our brother got himself arrested."

"What? Why?" I couldn't articulate a clear sentence, but Tony understood my shock.

"You know that laundry bag of money we found? Kirk didn't deposit it. He, apparently, used some of the cash, and, well, are you sitting down?"

"Just tell me what happened."

"The money is counterfeit."

"Counterfeit? How could that be?" I shouted in utter shock.

"It explains why Mom didn't put it in the bank."

"Doesn't tell us why she had it or where it came from."

"He needs us to bail him out, Vic. I don't have the funds."

"I'll take care of it. Where is he?"

*****

I drove to the Metro station on Martin Luther King Boulevard, where Kirk awaited a bail hearing. Danny explained my options regarding bail and agreed to meet me at the station.

Kirk's face shimmered red and glossy when I stepped into the police box with Danny trailing behind me.

"Why did Tony call you?" he asked with irritation, sounding defeated.

"Because I have the funds to bail you out of here and get you proper representation."

"How are you doing, Kirk?" Empathy streamed through Danny's words.

"I'll be fine once you get me the hell out of here." Kirk's gray suit looked wrinkled. His striped, blue tie dangled crooked around his neck. Wearing a suit was an uncommon look for my blue-collar brother. His disgusted tone was another unusual characteristic, but given the circumstances, I couldn't blame him.

"For the record, Kirk, criminal law isn't necessarily my specialty, but I'll help to the best of my ability, even if it means giving you a recommendation for another attorney. How about you give me the gist of what happened?" Danny glanced at me in a questionable manner.

"Oh, well, can I stay?" My eyes drifted to my brother. "Kirk?"

Kirk released an awkward-sounding breath, "Yeah, you can stay, so I only have to tell this bullshit story once."

I pulled out a metal chair and sat beside Danny, across from Kirk.

Kirk snickered, still peeved that he sat in lockup all night. "I had a date last night."

"Oh, with Nurse Tara?" I asked, intrigued. That explained why he wore a sharp-looking suit.

Kirk made a sour expression because I interrupted the very beginning of his tale. "Yes, Vicki, with Tara." He rolled his eyes. "I wanted to take her someplace nice. I should have used my credit card to pay for the meal, but there was all that cash we found at Mom's house, so I stuffed a couple hundred in my wallet. When I paid the check, Tara and I were so wrapped up in our conversation that time just ticked by. All of a sudden, a police officer arrived at our table and placed me under arrest for trying to pay the bill with counterfeit money." His fingers stroked through his thick, sable hair.

"Oh, no, Kirk," I said with a sigh, realizing this demeaning incident happened in front of Tara.

"It was humiliating. They handcuffed her, but I insisted this was all on me. They took her information because she *associated with a potential felon* and eventually let her go. I tried to explain where I got the money, but they wouldn't listen."

"Vicki explained how you found the money, cleaning out your mother's house, Kirk. Where's the rest of it?" Danny questioned.

"At my apartment. I know I should've brought it to the bank like we discussed, Vic. With my work schedule, I never got there. A bank teller probably would've suspected it was fake. It sure would've saved me from spending the night in a fuckin' jail cell." Kirk pounded his fist against the table.

"Do you have a criminal record, Kirk? Anything at all?" Danny asked, expressionless.

"Me? No."

"That's a plus. You have proof of your mother's untimely death. You were with your siblings in the house when the money was found. None of you knew it existed. Why would you have thought your elderly mother would have had counterfeit money lying around her home? If you were a counterfeiter, why wouldn't you have made more modern-looking bills? It was old money, which was probably why the restaurant manager had to check it thoroughly. It was an innocent mistake on your part. I can make sure your restaurant bill gets paid so the restaurant will drop any charges they may have filed. Did you use that money to pay for anything else?"

Kirk shook his head. "No."

"You know, when that burglar broke into the house, we assumed he might have learned of our mother's death and broke in, not realizing I was staying there. I told the officer that night that we found a large amount of cash. He even joked about how some older folks didn't like banks." I began ransacking my pocketbook and pulled out his card. "Officer Scott Kane. I'll write down the case number for you. There were also some old casino chips from the Thunderbird that closed decades ago. We figured they weren't worth anything."

"This gives me a strategy," Danny explained directly to Kirk. "Hang tight through the hearing. Vicki will post your bail, but rest assured, I really believe I can get these charges dropped."

"Thank you, Danny." A slight glimmer of hope shined across Kirk's face.

Within an hour, Kirk was released on bond with the expectation that we'd return with the remaining counterfeit money and chips for the police to hold onto while they continued their investigation.

The evening news at six flashed Kirk's mug shot across the screen, citing, "The brother of former Governor Atkins's wife, actress Victoria Ursini, arrested for a counterfeit scam."

Scam, really? The media preyed on the weaknesses of people in the spotlight, starting with family members. Kirk was humiliated further on television because of his relation to me.

The strength of a family, like the strength of an army, lies in its loyalty to each other.

—Mario Puzo

CHAPTER 23

I arrived at Sylvia's home around nine Saturday morning, feeling tired regardless of the melatonin gummy I took to knock me out last night. My body continued to beg for rest. This abominable sleeping pattern I dealt with often left me cranky, despite the lithium pulsating through my system. My daily dose performed some kind of magic trick, controlling this anxious flow of energy and reducing fear and paranoia brought on by bipolar disorder.

A truck with a tree relocation logo sat in the driveway. Before construction began for the pool Kirk wanted, he had arranged for the peony plant to be dug up and moved to the front yard. I hoped the exquisite flowers would continue to thrive in their new location.

The workers outside wouldn't interfere with cleaning out that hutch today. I hoped to pack the dishes and deliver them to Aunt Lucy's home. I'd also stop to buy a box of those Italian cookies she loved. Sweeten her up before having that strenuous conversation, recommending she receive regular assistance or move into an assisted living facility like Summer Wind.

I enjoyed watching the pair of rugged-looking men take off their shirts, exposing their tan skin that glistened in the sun. The two laborers dug around the bush carefully, hoping not to disturb the roots. Perhaps in several weeks, the entire backyard would be transformed, highlighting an inground pool surrounded by a cement patio—a different view than watching the birds and butterflies flutter around the peonies.

"Okay, it's you and me today, hutch. Bring it on!" I decided to wash the dainty cups and saucers first. The sink was filled with hot, soapy water. The delicate pieces were gently washed one at a time to prevent chips or scratches in the gold gilding. I hand-dried and swathed each piece individually with bubble wrap for the trip to Aunt Lucy's. While packaging the last cup, a flash of red lights outside caught my attention. I carefully moved the box out of the way to peek through the front window. Two police cruisers had parked in front of the house, blocking the driveway. The handsome, shirtless men with the task of moving the peony plant were shouting, but I couldn't make out their panicked words.

I opened the front door and stepped across the rich green grass toward an officer who stood next to his car, across from the workers who ceased speaking in my presence. "What's going on, Officer? Did someone get hurt?"

The officer sized me up in my white Bermuda shorts and teal blouse. "Ma'am, are you the homeowner?"

"This was my mother's house. She recently passed, and I'm getting her affairs in order. What brings you here?" I glanced at the two landscapers, who seemed to do everything in their power to avoid making eye contact with me.

"Your backyard's a crime scene, ma'am."

"Crime scene?" I faced the tree relocators. "What happened?"

Their eyes swayed from each other to the officer, ignoring me.

"Can someone tell me what this is about?" I shouted.

The workers shrugged and twisted their backs from me.

A second officer hurried from the backyard. He approached his partner, breathlessly affirming, "CSI's on their way. Let's seal off the yard. Did you get their statements?"

I grew tired of being ignored. "This is my family home. I demand to know exactly why you're sealing off my property and why a crime scene investigation is suddenly occurring!"

"Your name, ma'am?" The first officer who had spoken to me asked.

"Victoria Ursini. My brother has been the legal property owner since my mother passed."

"Ms. Ursini, these two workers were digging up a shrub in the yard. They came across…well…a *skull* caught in its roots."

"A skull? A *human* skull was found beneath the peonies?"

Officer number two replied, "It *was* a human all right. We have to secure the perimeter. How long have you been staying here?"

I was too stunned to respond immediately. "I'm actually staying at a hotel. There was a break-in lately."

"Someone broke in? When was that?"

"A couple of nights ago. It was reported. I spoke with Officer Scott Kane."

The second officer jotted my words down in his notebook. "We'll be sure to contact him about that case."

"So w-w-what do I do? What happens next?" My nervous, animated hand gestures were extreme enough to burn hundreds of calories. I couldn't think of who to contact first: Kirk, Tony, Tommy, or Danny? Since we might need an attorney, I chose Danny first.

As I dialed, the first officer said, "Ma'am, you can't stay here. We can't allow you back inside."

"My pocketbook is in the kitchen. The lights are on."

"With your permission to enter, I'll get your things."

This sounded like a game my CIA character once played with a suspect; allowing officers access to the house would give them permission to look around. I held up my pointer finger, requesting he wait a moment.

Danny answered my call, and before he could say *hello*, my fast-spoken words about this wild situation blew him away.

"Don't let them enter without a warrant, Vicki. Make them do things by the book. At least that should stall them until I get there."

I texted my brothers and Tommy while I waited for Danny to arrive. My eyes remained glued to my cell, impatiently waiting for the bleep of a response.

A team arrived in multiple vehicles, wearing uniforms with CSI insignia. They carried equipment in toolboxes and duffel bags to the backyard. A woman stopped to speak to the officers first on the scene, pointing around the perimeter and shouting instructions to her crew. They all glanced in my direction simultaneously before trailing to the quarantined space.

Danny's Lincoln parked across the street just in time to prevent me from having a nervous breakdown. He waved from a distance. Then he stopped to speak to one of the officers standing in an authoritative, guard-like position.

More uniforms arrived in cruisers. By now, the whole neighborhood stood on the sidewalk or in the street, trying to catch a glimpse of the activity at the Ursini house. An older gent in a white muscle tee and camo bathing suit asked the officer some questions, who firmly suggested the man have a nice day and move along.

Danny treaded at a quick pace near me when another cop decisively raised his arm like he was directing traffic. Danny pointed in my direction, assertively waving his hands as his face turned the color of a tomato.

I approached to hear their conversation.

"You can come inside with us, Sergeant. My client was inside this house when the remains were found. She just wants to get her things and ensure the house is properly closed," Danny argued. "Let her get in there for a few minutes. You can observe every step she takes."

The sergeant reluctantly nodded. "Officer Turcio!" he yelled to the first officer I had met, divulging his name. "Please escort Ms. Ursini and her lawyer inside. Make sure she doesn't touch a thing except her pocketbook."

"Depending on what they find in the yard, Vicki, they might want to get inside at some point, but they'll need a warrant."

"What happens next? What should I expect?"

"Let them do their job. The CSI crew is no joke. They'll dig up the whole yard, searching for any other skeletal remains. They only have the skull now, but they need to see what else might be buried back there. Maybe they'll find more bones, torn clothing, or something to identify the remains. It's definitely a human skull, and from what the officer said, whoever they were, they've been buried back there for quite some time."

"Jesus!"

Officer Turcio followed me through the living room, dining room, and kitchen, where my purse hung from the top of a chair. I attempted to place the glass I drank from into the dishwasher, but Turcio stopped me. "Got everything you need now, ma'am?"

I absently nodded and returned the used glass to the table. I glanced at Danny, who softly said, "Vicki, you won't want to be here. This news has already erupted. Go back to the Montgomery to avoid the media. I'll be in touch as soon as I hear anything."

Could I ever avoid a scandal in this town?

CHAPTER 24

Sylvia's home—my childhood residence should feel warm and cozy. Instead, it transitioned to a crime scene. I considered a tagline for a soon-to-be documentary titled *Who Lies Beneath the Peony Bush*. The fresh image of a possible victim sprang to life—Uncle Gary. At the time when the man left my aunt, I had a busy college life with boys, friends, and launching a modeling career. When I asked why my aunt and uncle divorced, Sylvia said, "Don't ask, and whatever you do, don't mention it in front of Aunt Lu. She'll start crying again."

Sylvia was never one to be exceptionally tidy or work in the yard. Suddenly, a peony plant emerged. I searched my brain to recall when the flowers mysteriously appeared. When Tommy and I chatted by video, and I introduced him to Sylvia's house and yard, he thought that shrub looked out of place in that spot. I never gave much consideration to Sylvia's impulsive decisions. Now I had a million questions, and she wasn't here to answer them.

Urgently, I drove to Aunt Lucy's apartment to escape from the hungry reporters Danny warned me about. The Ursini family making headlines again is not something to discuss with my frail aunt over the phone. Not only because of the disturbing nature of today's scandal, but an in-person visit would allow me to carefully observe her reaction. Would she look horrified? Surprised? Or did my aunt know exactly whose bones were buried beneath the tranquil peonies?

Gary Connors, the husband she adored and continued to glorify decades after their divorce. The man Sylvia might have had an affair with, according to some forty-year-old argument Bridget and Claudia overheard. That wasn't information I'd share with the police, of course. Let them manage their investigation their way, and I'd talk to Danny and Tommy about hiring a private investigator to track down my uncle Gary to determine if he was either still alive or lay entangled with the roots of a peony bush.

A middle-aged couple skated out of the building complex, distracted by a trivial conversation, which allowed me to slip inside without announcing myself. I walked along the first floor, stopping before apartment 122, and impatiently exhaled before knocking.

Her eyes widened, showing her surprise to see me at the opposite side of the door. Her hair hadn't been combed. Plump, dark circles swelled beneath her eyes. She wore a red-printed housecoat and pink slippers. "Victoria, this is a surprise." Her left hand brushed through her white strands, acknowledging she hadn't fixed herself up for company. When she smiled, black spaces showed between a couple of teeth where her implants should be. Aunt Lucy moved her walker out of the way to let me in. "Don't just stand out in the hall. Come in."

"Sorry I didn't call first. It's been quite a day already, and it's barely noon."

"Would you like some tea?" she asked cordially, eying me up and down, detecting my jitters.

"Got anything stronger?" I snickered.

"Oh, my, what's got you all wound up today?" My aunt had the power to discern my moods and ailments.

"Before you hear about it on the news or in the papers…how about you sit down?"

She staggered across the tan Berber carpet. It took her a few moments to wiggle herself into a comfortable position on the brown recliner. She let out a breath and a cough. "Did something happen? Are your brothers all right? Good heavens, Victoria, what's wrong?"

"Kirk decided to have a pool dug in Mom's yard since he plans to move in."

She shrugged.

"The pool would take up quite a bit of space, and Mom's peonies…well, I wanted to salvage that bush, so Kirk hired someone to dig it up and replant it in the front." I rambled fast and nervously while Aunt Lucy listened intently without so much as a blink.

"They found a skull. A *human* skull, Aunt Lucy."

"What? How could that be?" Her fingers stroked her chin.

"The police were called, and my mother's house is now considered a *crime scene*. Seems like the skull's been there for quite some time."

"Really? Oh, dear, that's horrible!"

"They have a crime scene unit sifting through the dirt in search of any other bones or clues to identify the remains. Until they gather more evidence, they don't know how long this person was buried there. Mom moved into that house after I was born. I hope whoever was buried there died long before Mom bought the place. Do you know anything about the history of that house, Aunt Lucy?"

"Me? I was just a teenager when your mother moved in there. I still lived at home with your grandparents. Your grandpa helped Sylvia buy that house. She was a single woman with a newborn. Your grandma insisted that Sylvia lie to the neighbors about her *husband* dying, pretending to be a widower to avoid ugly rumors. Oh, how times have changed." She sighed. "If the previous owners of the house had something to do with that skull, I'm sure the police could look into old records to find a name…if they're still alive. A lot of years have passed, ya know."

"Why did my mother plant a peony bush in that odd spot? She didn't have a green thumb, but she loved those peonies. Why plant those delicate white flowers in the exact space above a dead body?"

"Victoria, are you asking me if your mother knew that her backyard was someone's final resting place?" Her cheeks grew a flustered shade of crimson. "Jeez, she must've planted those flowers at least forty years ago."

My dark eyes locked on hers. "A dead body buried beneath a bush she planted herself seems awfully suspicious. I have to ask you...do you have any idea who's buried there? You were my mother's greatest confidant. You were sisters."

Aunt Lucy shook her head feverishly. "Victoria, my sister was a lot of things, but if you're implying that she murdered somebody—well, that's absurd!"

Either my aunt had a fantastic poker face, or she had no idea about the mysterious body found. But I had my own theories.

"I have to ask you another question. I hope you'll be honest with me, even if it means betraying my mother's trust. Mom's gone now. There's no reason to keep her secrets anymore."

She swept her hand across her face, burrowing her fingers into the lines around her lips.

"Since I was a young girl, I have been so curious about my father. I used to fantasize about Dean Martin in the role of my dad. I watched all his movies, searched for a resemblance between us in pictures, and listened to all his songs. She allowed me to hold onto that ridiculous fantasy without setting me straight. Apparently, I asked too many questions about whatever kind of relationship they had. One day, out of pure frustration, she harshly told me to drop it and stop asking. I marched away from her, slammed my bedroom door, and cried myself to sleep that night."

"Oh, princess."

"I'm asking you, Aunt Lucy, did she ever tell you who my father actually is? Whoever he is or was won't change my life now. I don't *need* a father. I've gone more than sixty years without one. But I crave to know this part of me that's been missing. I have more family roots—an unfamiliar connection with others entwined by blood."

Her eyes swayed across the room, staring at an empty spot on the wall as if patiently gathering her thoughts before she spoke. "My big sister was a gorgeous woman back in her day. All the men adored her. When she danced on stage at the Flamingo, every eye in the room zoomed in on her perfect figure, long legs, and swiveling hips. She'd never admit this to you, dear, but she had *many* admirers."

I knew that, but I didn't disrupt my aunt from continuing.

"I know that today those paternity tests are as easy to get as a flu shot, but not in the '50s. The truth is, Victoria, she didn't know who your father was. There were several random men in her life before she got pregnant. She didn't tell me their names. A woman's indiscretions with men were kept hush. As for Dean Martin, if there was an *affair*, it happened long before you were conceived. I'm so sorry that the unknown hurts you. Your mother wasn't perfect. No mother is. Perhaps her secret was meant to be buried with her."

I didn't believe her. It was an easy, lazy way to escape honesty, but I accepted the hand she offered and squeezed her fingertips. "Sometimes, my mother made it difficult to believe anything she told me, Aunt Lucy. I loved her, but her exaggerations could be intolerable. If she told me the sky looked like rain, I'd rush to the window to see for myself."

She shrugged. "Your mother loved to entertain. That was just her way. Adding dramatic embellishments was a part of her charm."

"Well, what you call charming, I call excruciatingly insufferable. Did you two ever go at it? I mean, did my mother ever aggravate you with her whimsical tales or affairs?" I laughed when I asked the question to keep the mood light, though I hoped to uncover the heinous argument my friends described.

"Oh, sure, we had our sisterly spats."

"Spill! I'd love to hear your stories."

"Stories? About fighting with your mother? Oh, it's been too long. Maybe back when we shared a bedroom growing up. We fought over the lack of privacy, shoes, and blouses."

"How about boys?"

"Boys? Nah, she was a few years older than me. We were never interested in the same boys."

"When did you and Uncle Gary marry?"

"Nineteen fifty-nine. We had a beautiful June wedding. You were the flower girl, Victoria. You always looked like a beautiful princess, but on my wedding day, you were positively stunning!"

"I remember seeing pictures. I wore a lovely white silk dress. I know how much you loved Uncle Gary. I never asked you this before, but what happened? Why did you get divorced?"

She rolled her eyes and shook her head. "I don't like to talk about the sad moments in life. We should always be grateful and appreciate the happy times. I believe people enter our lives for a reason or a season. There's some kind of spiritual, purifying justification why some people don't stick around."

"I'm just curious. The last time I remember seeing Uncle Gary was maybe in the early '70s. Surprisingly, one day when I came home during a school break, Mom told me you two split up. Nobody told me any details."

"Back then, no one liked that vile word, *divorce*, a shameful, scandalous event. Gary and I weren't blessed with children. By the time we divorced, I was considered an old maid. At least, I felt like one."

"You? Never!" I giggled.

"I didn't have your mother's vivacious personality, Victoria. And admittedly, I felt sad for a long time after my marriage ended. It took me a while to get over losing your uncle. God, he was a hot ticket."

Her words forced a chuckle out of me. "He certainly was handsome. He was a few years older than you, right? Born when? Nineteen thirty-three or so?"

"That's right, May 14, 1933."

"Is he still alive? Did you ever hear from him, Aunt Lucy? Does he live nearby?"

"What's with all the questions?"

"I'm feeling a bit nostalgic, I guess. Some exes try to get back with their first love. We're both adults now. You can tell me if Uncle Gary ever had a change of heart. Did he ever crawl back, begging for forgiveness?" I laughed as I finished that dramatic sentence.

She snickered. "You're too much, my dear. Life isn't one of those drama shows you used to act in. No, I don't recall ever seeing Gary after we divorced." She let out a hearty breath. "When you get to be my age, you pay attention to the obituaries. Never saw his. Not sure where he's living these days. He was a ladies' man. That became the real problem in our marriage. Now you know why I divorced that ass. I used to wish syphilis on him. But at some point, I stopped caring about what had happened to him. I choose to think of happy memories, including my initial romance with Gary. Rehashing painful recollections does no one any good."

I nodded along with her story and released a snort, thinking about her wishing a horrible disease like syphilis on her ex.

I needed a distraction from what was happening at Sylvia's house, wondering if they found more bones or something to identify the remains. Who had been resting beneath those dainty white peonies? To lighten things up and ensure my aunt didn't watch the news or stay focused on her cheating husband and the pain that went along with that, I suggested we binge-watch season one of *Sex in the City*.

My cell buzzed with a breaking news event: *Skeletal remains found at the home where actress Victoria Ursini grew up.* Everyone started to text me: Kirk, Tony, Danny, and even Tommy. I casually stepped into the other room to return phone calls, telling my aunt I'd order us tuna sandwiches from Cinquini's Deli to be delivered.

Kirk and Tony were equally shocked when I confirmed the news story. Kirk planned to drive to the house to see exactly what was unfolding.

Tommy grew concerned about the evolving turmoil.

I couldn't properly grieve Sylvia with the increasing chaos suffocating me. With Aunt Lucy sitting not too far away, I couldn't get into the weeds of details with Tommy, but I promised him I was okay, taking my meds, and I'd call him later.

Danny and I texted back and forth between my aunt's questions about the four sexy women on TV. I asked Danny through a text about hiring a PI to look into the whereabouts of Gary Connors. He recommended his PI, Wayne Zullo. Now that I had my uncle's date of birth, Wayne had a decent starting point.

CHAPTER 25

A full twenty-four hours ticked away at a dreadfully slow pace. Metro wouldn't provide any information, nor would they let us inside Sylvia's house. Tommy and I spoke at great lengths last night after my foreboding day. He wasn't happy I canceled my flight home, but I couldn't leave Vegas yet, not until that skull found in the yard had a name associated with it. Although Tommy understood my rationale for staying in Vegas, he blew out a breath of agitation. I knew his lingering annoyance stemmed from missing me. We didn't fight often, and we always made up promptly. Life was much too short to deal with long bouts of bitterness.

I thought about Sylvia and the promise I had made about not selling her house. The recent events added more clarity to her final wish; perhaps she needed to keep the identity of whoever rested beneath those romantic peonies a secret. Should the house be sold, new owners could have uncovered Sylvia's skeletons—literally.

Sylvia had always been a good storyteller. Although I highly doubted she kept such a great confidence of this magnitude to herself, assuming she knew about the corpse in her yard. Her secrets might have died with her, but there were two allies in her life: my aunt Lucy, who offered no explanation or even a mere hint of having a clue, and Beverly Perrin. One of them must know the identity of the person buried in the backyard, and if not, maybe they can shed light on who my biological father was.

Beverly lived in a townhouse on Diamond Lane in Henderson. Her son Chad made a good living as a dentist. I remembered Sylvia telling me that Chad set his mother up nicely in a decent home near her children after her husband died.

Before showing up unannounced at Aunt Bev's home, I stopped by Callie's Sugar Factory and picked up a few of their unique cupcakes, a hot cup of tea for me, and decaf coffee for Beverly.

When I arrived, she looked both surprised and rather delighted that I dropped in on her without warning, carrying goodies. "I rarely get to eat sweets like cupcakes these days. I better gobble one up before my daughter comes over and reminds me about my elevated cholesterol."

I chuckled and introduced her to the cupcake selection I brought filled with yummy sweetness like coconut, hazelnut ganache, and maraschino cherry.

Aunt Bev chose the toasted almond flavor. "I saw that news briefing late last night. What's that all about?"

I felt my shoulders droop as I groaned.

"At my age, I take more cat naps during the day, which keeps me up late enough to watch *The Late Late Show with James Corden*. Did they really find a body in Syl's yard?"

Since she knew the situation, she could have had time to practice showcasing a clueless expression.

"Yes, it is horrible, and I'm concerned, Aunt Bev. Someone planted flowers over a *dead body*. I'm sure the cops believe my mother buried that person there and covered them with a peony plant."

"Sylvia was no murderer, Vicki! You don't know where those bones came from. Don't be so quick to judge. Syl's not here anymore to speak for herself. It looks like I'll have to do some defending!"

"I want to defend my mother, but we don't have all the facts."

"And it's not your job to gather them. Let Metro take the lead. If they have questions, they'll come sniffin' around. You obviously don't know anything, and Sylvia can't answer their questions."

"I'd love to clear my mother's name."

"You have no idea who's buried out there or how that person died. Don't jump to conclusions. Syl's yard was wide open for anyone to access it. You don't know if your mother knew anything. Maybe that body was buried there hundreds of years ago."

"I'm anxious for the medical examiner to find that out. But you're right. My mind is all over the place with theories and a burning desire to clear Mom's name."

Aunt Bev's objection to mulling over theories told me that if she had information about the person who once sported that skull, she wouldn't expose any details to me.

"My aunt claimed she had no knowledge. If my mother knew anything about this situation, she would've told one of you. Ya know, Aunt Lucy still talks about Uncle Gary. After all this time, she seems lost without him."

Beverly made a *hmpf* sound.

"What is it?"

She shook her head. "Your aunt was always a bit…nuts."

My brows lifted in surprise. "Nuts? Aunt Lucy is so sweet."

"Don't let her battle with MS fool you, honey. If she was so *lost* without Gary, she wouldn't have—"

"Wouldn't have…what?"

"That woman *drove* Gary away. Your mom and I talked about Lucy all the time. Gary—" She whistled. "What a *gorgeous* man! He messed around a little behind Lucy's back, making her nuttier than a starving squirrel. She followed him around, possessive and jealous. Tossed out accusations anytime he even looked at another woman. Well, everything blew up one night. That *sweet* aunt of yours attacked him."

"Attacked him?"

"Syl never told you any of this?"

I shook my head in total shock.

"Lucy whacked him in the head with a frying pan. The whole side of his face turned black and blue. Saw it with my own eyes. Gary showed up at the Flamingo that night. I still worked there, tending bar, so I know it was…oh, maybe around 1973 or so. I saw what a mess his face looked like and bought him a drink. He told me Lucy went on a rampage after he worked late that evening. She accused him of cheating on her, picked up a hot frying pan with oil still sizzling in it, and smacked him hard. He was done with her. Told me he wasn't going home again. I let him sleep in the office that night. I would've taken him home with me to sleep on the couch, but if your aunt ever caught him at my house, my face might have gotten welted up like Gary's. I didn't want that kind of trouble."

Aunt Lucy battled bipolar disorder like she battled multiple sclerosis. Before her diagnosis, she wasn't medicated to control her abrasive behaviors. The highs and lows of extreme levels probably triggered her outbursts, like whacking her cheating husband with a frying pan.

I pondered about the wild things I did anytime I went off my meds, thinking I was miraculously cured. I had driven down some pretty somber paths when noncompliant with treatment.

Beverly snickered. "Oh, I would've *loved* to take advantage of that delicious hunk of a man, but your mother would've been peeved at me, and Lucy's jealousy could be pretty damn scary. There's something else that doesn't sit right with me that you should know. Your mother checked in on Lucy every day."

"I know that."

"It started to become too much of a chore for her. She recommended Lucy consider moving into an assisted living complex so she'd always have help, but your aunt didn't like that idea. Syl told me that Lucy got so angry with her that she threw her out of her apartment. It was a day or two before her accident."

"What?"

"I bet sweet ole Aunt Lu never mentioned that argument with her sister."

I rubbed my chin, contemplating. I procrastinated bringing up the assisted living facility with her yesterday. It would've been too intense of a discussion while we impatiently awaited details about the skull and the police investigation.

"If your aunt was able to drive a car, she'd be a suspect in my book for killing Sylvia."

"You really think my aunt could've murdered her sister?" I shivered at the impossible thought.

Beverly sighed, then lifted her brows. "Well, she's got anger issues, and she's snapped before."

I needed a moment to compose myself while my brain digested this information. Details I feared about that skull belonging to Uncle Gary could be real. I sipped my tea in silence.

Beverly patiently observed my quiet demeanor without saying a word and bit into the delicious cupcake she selected, making smacking sounds and licking her fingers. "Vic, this is so good. Aren't you going to have one?"

"No, you can share them with your family." I couldn't ask her if she agreed with my theory about who lay beneath the peonies. She had already warned me to wait for the cops to investigate. My brown eyes met her blue ones. "You know so much history about my mother and my family, Aunt Bev. I'd appreciate your candor."

"About?"

I paused before finding the nerve to ask such an arduous question. "Did my mother tell you who my father is?"

Her head jolted fast enough to get whiplash. She placed her coffee cup on the table, released a lengthy groan, and used a napkin to wipe some frosting from her fingers.

"I don't want the mystery of my paternity to die with my mother or anyone else who may have the answers I'm looking for. Whoever it is, I can handle it…even if it's Uncle Gary."

A coughing fit took over Beverly. "Gary?" she spat out between coughs. "You think *Gary* is your father?"

"My mother kept it so quiet. I had to wonder if there was a scandal lurking around the truth. Friends of mine said they overheard Aunt Lucy accusing my mother of sleeping with Gary. Did she?"

"Oh, honey, I'm sorry that you ever thought such a thing. I told you, your aunt accused *everyone* of sleeping with Gary, even your mother and me. But Syl wouldn't have done that to her sister. Not in a million years!"

I felt relieved. "Can you tell me, Bev? The truth."

139

Beverly blew out a deep breath and sipped her coffee. "Victoria, you're not a child anymore. I'll tell you what I know." She looked up to the heavens. "Sorry if I'm interfering with your wishes, Syl." Her blue eyes seemed to deepen as they set upon me. "Did you ever stop and think that maybe there's a good reason why your mom never told you the truth?"

"I have to know. Please."

She cleared her throat before speaking, "I remember him well but *not* fondly. A mafioso type who hung around the Flamingo. The kind of guy who got whatever he demanded from people, especially women and their bodies."

"Demanded?" I hesitated when a look of pity washed across Beverly's face. "Are you saying my mother was raped?"

Beverly didn't confirm or deny such a painful notion. "When Syl's pregnancy started to show, she couldn't dance anymore. She could've waitressed. Instead, she took a leave of absence because she didn't want that gangster to know she was pregnant. She feared him, and she didn't want him in your life. I'm sorry, sweetie, but I'm telling you what she confided in me, and she didn't want you to know about that maniac. She literally hid throughout her entire pregnancy from everyone except her family to avoid that psychopath."

I let out an embarrassing snort. "So it wasn't Dean Martin?"

Bev huffed. "Whatever might have gone on between Syl and Dean ended before she was pregnant with you. I guess it was easier for her to give you a fantasy to consider than telling a young girl her daddy pilfered, assaulted, and killed for a living."

"Who was he? Tell me you remember his name."

"Oh, Victoria. Would you really want to know if that loser was the sperm donor? He wouldn't have been a good father. If he was in your life, who knows the kind of negative impact his involvement would've had? I agreed with your mom's silence, and I've kept it quiet all these years."

"I need to know, Aunt Bev. She protected me as a mother would. She did her job. Hell, I'm an old lady now and a curious one."

"Uh, okay. Okay." She emitted a soft moan before uttering, "Marco Fiore. The guy gave me the creeps." Her eyes squinted, either from thinking hard or acknowledging a headache. "Now don't quote me on this, but I think he disappeared. He stopped coming around the Flamingo all of a sudden. Back in the day, that's where many wise guys hung out since gangsters ran the place."

"I'm rather familiar with the history."

"People were looking for him. Cops. The mob. He might have high-tailed it out of Vegas, or his body will never be found."

"Or he's buried in my mother's backyard."

"Oh, no, Victoria! Syl avoided Marco like the plague, and he moved on to some other girl to harass. Lord knows your mother didn't want to spend any time with him or have you around that monster."

"Thanks for being honest with me, Aunt Bev."

"I hope I don't regret telling you this. Move on with your life, Victoria. Leave the past behind."

*****

Later that evening, I searched online for Marco Fiore, who could have been born in the '30s. Nothing. Nada. Zilch. The last name was pretty common, but the ages of the men I found were wrong. He disappeared long before the birth of the Internet. Even with his alleged criminal record, I couldn't find any information about him on my own.

Was I the product of rape? Poor Sylvia! Knowing this explained a lot. Thankfully, she loved me enough not to have mistreated me, considering my tainted conception. I understood why she had difficulty telling me about the *sperm donor*, as Aunt Bev put it.

A hundred ideas marinated in my brain. What if Marco wanted to know if he had a daughter and showed up on Sylvia's doorstep? Maybe Sylvia killed him to protect me, or his murder was in self-defense. I didn't know what to believe, and I couldn't stop myself from envisioning these wild notions while the police continued their investigation.

I drowned my sorrows by playing Elvis music off my iPhone, starting with "Love Me Tender." When the tears plummeted, I skipped to a more upbeat scale, "Burning Love."

Tommy returned my call. The words rolled off my tongue too fast for him to process immediately. I thought with his history, being associated with both the Russo and Toscano crime families, he might have crossed paths with Marco at some point. Marco Fiore's name didn't ring any bells, but he could've disappeared before Tommy's family moved to Vegas in the '60s.

Still, my mind drifted to Uncle Gary. If Aunt Bev was wrong about Sylvia's relationship with him, he could have fathered Kirk or me. Easier to make up fairy tales or remain silent about our paternal DNA than to tell a child that their father was their aunt's husband.

News like that could sever an artery between sisters.

CHAPTER 26

Conniving

The Clippers fan stirred with excitement. Time quickly approached. He arranged his plan well. Thought about every detail with the greatest precision.

His body had grown strong with his daily exercise regimen, but it took a long time to get to this point in life. His limp was barely noticeable after the last operation. The man never feared working hard to reach goals. But everyone gave up on him throughout his life—his parents, siblings, friends, and son. So much had been taken from him. This time he planned to take back a mere piece of what he was due.

Anticipation bubbled within his belly and flourished like oxygen raging through his blood. He picked up his white-lined pad and perused the final tasks to check off his list today in preparation for the party tomorrow night.

These wealthy socialites would finally know what it felt like to have their lives ripped apart—a depraved level of loss they deserved.

And they wouldn't see it coming.

CHAPTER 27

Days passed at a painfully slow rate before the police asked Kirk, Tony, and me to meet them at the station. I neglected to share my theory with anyone else, including my brothers, about Uncle Gary being the victim or that he could've fathered Kirk or me, causing a rift between the sisters and possibly the man's demise. I didn't want to plant seeds of misery in their minds. Tony would hear me out, but Kirk would vigorously defend Sylvia. If my brothers conceived their own theories, they weren't inclined to divulge them.

I arrived at the station on Martin Luther King Boulevard and met Kirk and Tony outside the main entrance.

"Do you think they identified the body? They've been so tight-lipped about any further evidence they found. Even the media is salivating for a juicy morsel of gossip," Kirk said with the dramatic flair he had been known for.

"Thank God we've not hit the news for the last couple of days," Tony added.

"Actually, it aired on *Inside Edition* last night," I sadly muttered. "Let's go in and hear what they have to say."

We checked in with the officer at the main desk and waited. After a few minutes, intently curious about the information we might gain today, three men in suits of various tones of gray approached us.

"I'm Detective Jessup. Which one of you is Tony Curtis Ianni?" the man wearing a faint shade of gray asked.

Tony raised two fingers.

"Come with me, sir," Jessup directed.

"What about us?" Kirk asked.

"I'm Detective Drago. You must be Kirk Douglas Ursini. Hmm, Kirk Douglas. Tony Curtis. Cute." The detective's dry, humorless tone made Kirk's eyes roll. He grew accustomed to being teased about his name. "Follow me, Mr. Ursini."

I glanced at the remaining man in a medium-gray suit and crooked plain black tie. "I guess I'm to follow you?"

"Victoria Grace Ursini, I presume."

I nodded.

He raised his arm, holding a folder with a few papers sticking out. He glanced at the floor, confirming nothing had slipped out of the folder, then he opened the door for me. "Right this way." He leaped in front of me, leading me through a hallway and into the working area, where several cops sat at desks. I spotted Kirk entering a room with Drago, but I didn't see Tony. I imagined he sat behind one of the closed doors we had just walked past.

"Can I offer you soda or water?" he asked.

"No, thank you."

The man still hadn't properly introduced himself.

When I filmed *Rising 51* several years ago, I worked with a law enforcement consultant who shed light on the inner workings of investigations, so I could learn to play the part of a CIA agent and some of the games they enacted.

The detectives divided us up to assess our individual reactions to whatever details they garnered from their analysis. Once they revealed the specifics they *chose* to share, they'd interrogate us for information and compare notes later. If they weren't planning on grilling us, they'd simply use the phone without the hoopla of an in-person meeting.

He opened the door to a brightly lit room with a standard rectangular table, a few chairs around it, and a large mirror. I couldn't help but wonder who stood on the opposite side, watching this performance. A tremor raced through me, feeling a bit uncomfortable and unprepared like the media ambush Jeffrey coordinated after Sylvia's funeral.

He waited for me to sit before he spoke. "So, Victoria Grace. Who was that?"

"Who was who?" I asked, already failing his Q&A.

"Your brothers are Tony Curtis and Kirk Douglas. I can't think of a Victoria Grace."

I laughed with the intent of emitting charm. "Actually, my mother considered naming me Grace Kelly, but she loved the name Victoria. She said there was a character named Victoria on *Secret Storm,* that old soap opera from eons ago." I displayed a wide, endearing smile. "Oh, and you are?"

He tilted his head slightly and parted his lips, realizing he had neglected to formally introduce himself. "Detective Ed Notaro." He smiled. "I watched your show, *Rising 51*. Cool series." His polite game of praise grew tiresome.

"Thank you, Detective. Did you find out about the skull? When can we access our mother's house?" I asked to move things along.

He opened his folder and glanced at it for several seconds, taunting me with the knowledge he had that I didn't. "The ME's report says the bones in question were of a man between the age of thirty and forty. Death occurred in the neighborhood of the mid-seventies."

My thoughts dashed all over the place. Aunt Bev told me she last saw Uncle Gary around 1973 when he told her he planned to divorce my aunt. I was in college. The timing fit.

"Did you identify the remains?"

Notaro smiled without answering my question.

"I'm not sure why you brought us all down here. I lived on campus at UNLV, oh, from 1973 to 1977. My brothers, jeez, were only in elementary school. If you have specific questions, please ask me so we can help figure this out."

"Your mother owned the house on Orchard Lane at the time of this man's death. CSI believes those flowers were planted on top of the body to hide the grave. Over time, the roots entangled around the corpse."

I was certain I made an expression of anguish as a sound of trepidation escaped my lips. "You don't believe my mother had anything to do with this, do you?" My heart pounded so hard; I worried my chest would explode.

"We're still investigating, Ms. Ursini. You say you were in college, but the University of Nevada is a short drive from your mother's home. You were old enough to see and hear things that went on in that house."

I sighed. "If you're asking me if I know anything about the body, I can assure you, I have no answers. If my mother had any knowledge, it's too late to ask her. Are you able to release a name and cause of death? Perhaps if I knew who he was, I could tell you if I ever met him."

Notaro slapped the folder on the table. "We managed to ID him as a man named Kettner."

I was certain confusion smeared across my face. Thankfully, it wasn't Uncle Gary, which completely blew my theory out of the water.

"Rodney Kettner," Notaro iterated.

"I'm not familiar with that name. Who is he?"

"Kettner *was* connected to your mother. His age falls in line with the ME's report. We found mostly all his bones and some torn pieces of cloth in your mother's yard. Kettner had a couple of broken bones from his youth that matched our findings. He's been missing since 1976."

"Do you have any information about why he'd be in my mother's yard? H-h-how did he die?"

"He was murdered."

"Murdered? How do you know that?" My voice cracked like an egg.

"Blunt force trauma to the back of his head. He didn't see it coming. We may never find the murder weapon so many decades later."

"I don't remember ever meeting someone named Rodney Kettner. You said he's connected to my mother."

"Your mother was his girlfriend. Kettner went to prison for counterfeiting and fraud crimes."

147

Counterfeiting! My head ached, connecting this man's death to the fake money and chips we found. Why did Sylvia hold onto that evidence? Was she his partner in crime?

"She was with Kettner when he got busted at a casino, the Thunderbird, in '74. He tried to pass fake chips and had a couple thousand in counterfeit cash on him. The detectives cleared your mother and let her go. She claimed to have no knowledge of Kettner's crimes, and they had no real evidence to charge her.

"Kettner got paroled in '76 after serving two years. He never met with his parole officer. Nobody ever heard from him after his release. A warrant was issued for his arrest, thinking he had skipped town. No one suspected his death or burial in your mother's backyard."

I shook my head in disbelief. "That's quite a story." Nervous and breathless, I added, "I'm speechless."

"Then I learned your brother, *Kirk Douglas*, got picked up for using fake money at a local restaurant. How about that? Your mother may be dead, but her name is all over this case as not only being in on the counterfeit operation with Kettner but also for his murder."

"It's so hard for me to imagine my own mother committing murder, Detective. What actual evidence do you have that she *killed* Kettner?"

"Uh, the fact that his remains were buried in her yard gives us plenty of reason to like her for this. We might be able to close this homicide case."

I hated hearing that they weren't looking too deeply into this crime. Sylvia was dead, but I didn't want her name tarnished as a murder suspect. "Surely, this Rodney Kettner character had other enemies. My mother was a thin, petite woman who couldn't have weighed more than 110 pounds. She would not have had the strength to kill a man, dig a hole, and bury the body."

"It's possible she had help. Maybe someone else was involved. As I stated from the beginning, we're still gathering facts. We wanted you and your brothers to know where things stood. You can access the house now. We've already gone through it. So glad you didn't throw out all her things yet." He snickered somewhat diabolically.

CHAPTER 28

Kirk, Tony, and I arrived at Sylvia's house, eager to step inside and compare stories. I didn't like the way Notaro laughed, indicating they had already gone through her things. If they found anything in the house related to Kettner's murder, he didn't say.

When we opened the front door and looked inside, you'd think a bomb went off or a tornado whipped through each room. The boxes we had spent hours neatly packing and piling were dumped out and ransacked. Clothing, shoes, gadgets, and knickknacks were spread across the floor or spilled out of boxes. A few dishes from the kitchen cupboard were shattered on the white tile. Most of the other rooms had already been emptied. They tore apart some of the furniture Kirk planned to keep when he moved in.

Tears began to fall. My mother's entire life had been rummaged through and blanketed across the living room carpet.

"What the hell! I can't believe they did this!" Kirk shouted my precise emotions.

My eyes wavered to the corner of the dining room. "The china! It's gone!" I raced to the empty hutch and opened the bottom cabinet to discover the dusty, delicate pieces stacked inside. At first glance, no chips or broken fragments were noticed. I exhaled slowly. At least they properly handled our great-grandmother's dinnerware. The rest of the place required serious tidying.

I dashed to the lanai to assess the yard, and Kirk followed me.

The peony plant was gone, evidence in the murder case. And the yard had been utterly shredded to mounds of dried dirt with flecks of dead grass.

Kirk stared at the desolate space and stated, "Don't worry about the yard. It would've been dug up for the pool I'm adding anyway."

I stormed away from the lanai, furious at the mess the police left.

Tony perused a document placed on the dining room table. "They had a warrant. Legal consent to tear through this place. They've got a murder to solve. The body was found on the premises, and we handed them over all that counterfeit money and fake chips. I can't believe our mother would've actually murdered a guy. This is so surreal!"

"She didn't. I know what you're both thinking, *here comes Kirk to her rescue again*. I'm always defending her to you two! I hope you can trust *my* instincts for a change. No way in hell do I believe she murdered anyone. At least not intentionally. Self-defense, maybe." His head swiveled back and forth, thinking.

"I'm going to hire a PI to look into Rodney Kettner. He might not find out anything more than what the police told us, but I want to try." I hoped Danny's PI friend, Wayne Zullo, could give us information the cops wouldn't. Wayne was still investigating Uncle Gary too.

"Thanks, Vic, for believing in our mother and my instincts," Kirk replied.

Somehow, I managed a smile for Kirk. "Let's start repacking this stuff up. We can take it to the Salvation Army or toss it. I can't stand to see this house looking like such a mess anymore."

An hour into cleaning and reorganizing, Leann arrived with three cups of coffee and tea for me. She actually thought of me and considered my preferences. It was a nice change of pace, getting along with her while she contributed some hard work as a member of this family.

With the four of us cleaning, it didn't take long to finish. Admittedly, I chose to throw out more of Sylvia's things than I had originally planned. Anything that broke during the police search got dumped. Trash pickup was scheduled every Monday morning, so we tossed many bags and boxes to the curb to clear out the house. The few remaining boxes to donate to charity were placed in the empty garage.

"How about we pick up Aunt Lucy and go out for a real dinner tonight…on me," I suggested. "It's been an excruciating day, and I'm beat. Plus, I need to eat something healthy. Maybe a nice piece of salmon from the Beachcomber."

Everyone agreed.

Leann wanted to change her clothes, so she and Tony said they'd pick up Aunt Lucy and meet us at the seafood restaurant at six.

"Why don't you invite Tara, Kirk?" I asked.

"No," he firmly answered.

"Have you tried to contact her since that night?"

"I can't call her after that. She probably thinks I'm a major loser with a criminal record."

"The news will broadcast everything we learned today at some point about Mom's involvement with Rodney Kettner's counterfeit scam. It was great news to hear that Detective Drago dropped the counterfeit charges against you. This investigation around Kettner's death proves we weren't involved with the counterfeit money we discovered."

"A woman like Tara won't give me the time of day. I'm not calling her, Vic. Let it go."

The angry, emotional tone in my brother's voice was enough to tell me to back off.

Danny's number displayed on my cell as Kirk walked out of the house. "Hey, Danny. How are you?"

"Good, Vicki. You?"

I had no desire to relive my day at that moment. "Fine. What's up?"

"Wayne got some info about your uncle, Gary Connors."

"Oh, great. What did he learn?"

"Gary Connors moved to Sparks in 1974. Your aunt and uncle's divorce didn't finalize until '75. He remarried and had two daughters. Died in 2016 from pneumonia. Wayne got you his credit score, kid's names, job information, and—"

I cut Danny off, reassured Uncle Gary lived a long, full life, and he wasn't buried in the backyard. "No, I don't need all those details, but please send Wayne my thanks along with my payment."

"Sure. I thought this news would bring you peace."

"I've got some more work for him if he can handle it."

"What's the job?"

"I need him to look into a man named Rodney Kettner." I spelled out Kettner for him before continuing. "Kettner was identified as the body buried in my mother's yard. He was connected in some way to my mother in the '70s. He served time from 1974 to 1976 for counterfeiting."

"I take it Kettner is the reason you found counterfeit money in your mom's house?"

"You got it! My mother was with Kettner when he got arrested, but they had no evidence tying her to Kettner's counterfeit operation, so they released her. Kettner got paroled in '76, and no one ever heard from him after that."

"Jesus, and all these years, he was buried in your mother's yard."

"I don't expect Wayne to solve the mystery of his death or salvage my mother's questionable reputation, but I want to know about this guy and his connection to my mother."

"Yeah, I'll get him on it. Oh, I received notification that those counterfeit charges against Kirk were dropped."

"Thanks to this new evidence."

"He must be relieved."

"Very much so."

"Well, do you need anything else, Vicki?"

"Can Wayne also look into a man named Marco Fiore? He was a mobster who hung out at the Flamingo in the '50s. I can't seem to find anything about him, and at some point, he left town."

"By *left town*, do you mean physically or spiritually?"

"That's unknown. Unfortunately, outside of him being a man with no scruples mixed up with people at the Flamingo, I have no other details to offer. Danny, you've been so amazing since I came to town."

"We're family, Vicki. Happy to help. Besides, Wayne's doing all the legwork. I'm just the middleman. May I ask why you want to know about Marco Fiore?"

"Uh...he's another man who had a connection to my mother before his disappearance."

"I see," he responded suspiciously but didn't press me for specifics.

CHAPTER 29

The Beachcomber was hectic on a steamy Nevada evening. Fortunately, Aunt Lucy insisted that Tony call and make reservations so we wouldn't have a terribly long wait.

Kirk selected linguini and clams, Tony ordered the lazy man's lobster, and Aunt Lucy and Leann heard the stuffed jumbo shrimp special and nearly drooled at the vivid imagery described by our waitress. I stuck with the healthy broiled salmon with mixed greens.

Tony entertained us with a story about Mandalay Bay's casino when security took down a man streaking through the gaming tables and slots. Things like that don't just happen in the movies.

Aunt Lucy laughed so hard, she choked on her green tea.

I quickly changed the dinner conversation to a grim subject and asked my aunt a pertinent question since no one else would. "Have you ever heard of a man named Rodney Kettner? Someone our mother might have dated in the mid-seventies."

Forks dropped, and everyone stopped chewing as the spotlight shined upon Aunt Lucy.

"Kettner?" She paused and scratched her head. "Is that spelled with a C or a K?"

"It's spelled K-E-T-T-N-E-R." I ran through what the police insinuated about Rodney and Sylvia's relationship. "I don't suppose that name rings a bell with you, does it?"

"You said that was back in the mid-seventies? Oh, princess, how in the world could I remember one of the many men in your mother's life from over forty years ago?"

"Rodney was a con man. If Mom brought him around the family, Grandpa wouldn't have approved. Gramps had a strong sixth sense about people."

"Do you have a photograph of him? Maybe if I saw his face, I'd remember."

"Well, I might be able to get a copy of an old mugshot from the detectives."

"I googled him. Didn't find anything about his life, and I don't remember him," Tony said.

"You were like six, Tony," Kirk teased. "Maybe Mom knew better than to have him over while we were home. We could've been hanging out with Grandpa at his market, or Tony and I could have been with Burt. Who knows? I just hope the media doesn't attack Mom. She's not around to defend herself. What will all her friends at church think?"

"This is not your responsibility," Aunt Lucy responded with a firm tone. "Your mother wasn't perfect, but she'd never murder someone. What can the police do now? She's deceased. They can't arrest her."

"They can slander her name."

"Thank God she's not here. I mean, what would an old woman do in prison besides rot or kill herself?" Aunt Lucy added with surprising melodrama.

"Can we change the subject, please?" Kirk demanded. He ventured on to the upcoming Tom Cruise *Mission: Impossible-Fallout* movie.

Leann glanced at her phone again; her eyes had been glued to it since we arrived. I wouldn't complain aloud, especially because we were finally getting along for a change.

155

"Holy crap! I got it!" Leann yelled loudly enough for several surrounding tables to hear.

"Got what, hon?" Tony asked.

"I snagged that Rios Roast coffee commercial! Yes! I can't believe it. It's a nationwide commercial!" Her face radiated a warm glow when Tony kissed her and congratulated her.

"That's great, Leann," I said.

She sent me a half-smile in return, but what more could I expect? Leann blamed *me* for not making a more prominent name for herself in an acting career.

Leann had little experience when she and Tony first started dating. When I filmed *Rising 51*, I promised to get her a role in at least one episode. The most I managed to do was get her in as a snarky waitress with one measly line she didn't say very well. Her acting wasn't up to par, but she pushed and pushed, expecting me to launch her career and get her better parts. The show's producers rejected her, but she condemned *me*.

From that moment on, she alleged that I didn't like the competition. Tony stood up for me, but he loved Leann and the life they created together. I certainly wasn't preventing her from getting other jobs; her lack of talent was the cause. But I felt very happy for her and this open door she managed to pass through.

Tony ordered a bottle of Riesling, Leann's favorite white wine. Aunt Lucy and I stuck to drinking tea. We all raised our glasses for a proper toast. Tony announced, "To Leann for pursuing her dreams. I'm sure this is just the start of making them come true. I'm so proud of you."

Leann blushed, but she loved the attention and couldn't wait to shine in the spotlight.

CHAPTER 30

Depriving

The happy birthday song began in honor of Francesca's fifth birth day. The back room of the Italian-American club was reserved for the occasion. A clown and a magician were hired to entertain the sixty attendees. Colorful balloons in bunches filled every table with a *Disney Frozen* theme. The cake decor of light blue with silver trim displayed the image of Elsa, cascading from the top layer to the bottom. The *Disney* heroine's blue gown with white speckles of snowflakes trailed along each layer.

Francesca's brown eyes burst open wide at the sight. She craved being the center of attention. The five-year-old jammed her finger into the bottom layer and helped herself to a taste. Her father laughed and took many pictures while her mother sat near her baby sister. Everyone cheered, standing around the birthday girl. No one paid any attention to the uninvited guest who carried a tray of frosted sugar cookies that matched the cake in blue and silver colors.

His Clippers cap stayed in the Ford parked up a block; it wouldn't have gone with the black pants and white dress shirt he wore to blend in with the staff's attire.

He dyed his hair a darker color and had worked hard over the last few months at growing a thick beard and mustache that he could later shave.

The moment finally arrived. Francesca's mom joined her hus-band to capture more photographs of Francesca's wondrous expres-sions. Everyone watched the silly, energetic birthday girl and the extravagant cake with sparkling candles. The lights had been lowered for an added effect during the birthday song.

The man captivated the little one's attention from the back of the room. First, with a cookie and then a small unicorn beanie he picked up and stuffed inside his pocket. The infectious smile he teased her with made her chuckle. He encouraged her with a hand gesture to play with the toy and enjoy a cookie that matched the *Frozen* theme. When she stepped within inches of the stranger, hold-ing the ends of her pink polka dot dress, she snatched the unicorn and giggled a precious smile beneath dark-brown eyes and a mass of gorgeous blond curls.

That was when he covered Francesca's baby sister's mouth, lifted her tiny figure off the floor, and scurried around the sharp corner to the exit as the last word of the birthday song left the breaths of her family members, giving all their attention to Francesca.

CHAPTER 31

Tommy and I established a date every night at nine thirty Pacific Standard Time. He'd be wide awake, preparing for his workday in Paris or enjoying coffee and a toasted baguette slice. I felt grateful for the technology to keep in touch with him. Unfortunately, FaceTime didn't have the luxury of using the sense of touch. I yearned to be near him, smelling his cologne and feeling his scratchy, stubbly chin when he kissed me. Perhaps in the future, a grand invention would allow such sensations. Not in my lifetime.

My family stories stunned Tommy. Tough to shock a man like Tommy Cavallo, who lived and breathed in a sketchy world of corruption and lust while building a billion-dollar empire. Somehow, my average family and the bewildering skeletons in the closets—or in Sylvia's case—the backyard, left him flabbergasted.

He offered to have one of his contacts investigate Rodney Kettner, but I explained Danny's PI already had the details. "That's my boy," Tommy said, proud of everything his son accomplished. He respected Danny as an honorable man, an intelligent attorney, and a loving husband and father.

"When are you coming home?" he asked the same question daily.

"Soon, I hope. I'd like to stay here a little while longer to ensure no new surprises come up. Maybe I'll learn something about this Rodney Kettner character. They might even dig up more dirt on Sylvia. They already like her for murdering him, and she's gone. She won't go to jail, but I don't want her name demolished by the tabloids since she's unable to defend herself."

He groaned. "I get it. Did you ask Danny to investigate Marco Fiore?"

"Yes, although I'm not sure I want to verify what a dirtbag he was."

"I still think you should take that DNA test. You could have relatives that would show as a match. Maybe you'll learn more about him from other people in his life. Besides, you don't know for sure this Fiore guy is your father. You're going solely on the word of an elderly lady."

"I doubt Aunt Bev would lie to me now. It makes sense why Sylvia never wanted me to know the truth. I'm not sure I can handle any more *truth*."

"I won't push. You sound exhausted."

"I think I could sleep tonight without the extra melatonin."

CHAPTER 32

On Saturday morning, I awoke in my suite at the Montgomery to the sound of voices on the television. I fell asleep watching a *Blue Bloods* rerun after my call with Tommy. CBS News reported some local stories and the weather. Another hot, sticky July day was expected.

I ordered from room service a tomato and cheese omelet, whole-wheat toast, and hot tea before I showered and dressed for the day.

The locket Sylvia left me remained in place around my neck. I opened it, reminiscing about the fond memory of the photo inside. I was too young to recall the specific event, but Sylvia shared the story with me enough times to form my own remembrance. Christmas Eve with the traditional Feast of the Seven Fishes, an Italian banquet at Grandma and Grandpa's house. They purchased a beautiful white angel to sit atop the Christmas tree that year. Sylvia lifted me up high so I could carefully place the delicate-looking angel myself. Then she hugged me and called me her sweet little angel. Grandpa snapped that black-and-white photo of us near the tree. I wore a look of pride to have hung the angel that year, and Sylvia's eyes gleamed with happiness.

My smile grew. I loved that she left me this locket with a warm recollection to hold onto, acknowledging that some of my childhood memories could be cherished without any jarring outcomes.

Breakfast arrived. I needed a hearty meal before tackling the fragile dishes today. I wanted to finally finish cleaning and packing them up to give to Aunt Lucy, per Sylvia's wishes, the final chore I hoped to accomplish before I flew home to Tommy.

While enjoying the tasty eggs, an amber alert was announced. A little girl went missing from a birthday party last night. The eighteen-month-old, Caterina Maroni, had a mass of curly blond hair, brown eyes and looked perfectly precious. "Maroni," I muttered. "I know that name." As soon as my mind connected the dots, the news anchor reported the girl to be the granddaughter of the former senator, Louis Maroni. Caterina Maroni's father was Michael Maroni—Angie Russo's cousin.

Tommy told me about his romance with Angie Russo in his younger years, as explained in his autobiography. He fell hard for Angie decades ago while married to Sadie. Their long-term affair ended abruptly. Despite their bitter breakup, Angie played an integral part in helping us live safely in Paris with our identity change. Our lovely apartment with the gorgeous Eiffel Tower view belonged to Angie. I had only met her a couple of times, but Tommy considered her a strong ally. He trusted Angie and still cared for her well-being. He'd want to know about this incident that involved a member of her family.

I glanced at the clock. Tommy was probably on the boat entertaining a group of tourists, but I texted him this information. He had quite a tumultuous history with the Russo and Maroni families, thoroughly illustrated in his memoirs.

Although they were criminals who supported Jeffrey's political campaign, I enjoyed Louis and his wife, Katie's, company. When Jeffrey and I were married, we sometimes engaged in lovely dinners with the Maronis. I didn't realize the criminal ties they held back then. My introduction to the Maronis first occurred when Jeffrey needed to secure Louis's support to run for governor—before I met Tommy.

Who would've taken an innocent toddler? Another crime family with a grudge? Katie and Louis must be frantic with worry.

*****

Caterina Maroni barely left my mind as I drove to Sylvia's house. Tommy hadn't replied to my text yet. He didn't have good cell service on the Seine.

It felt good to walk into a clean house with some furniture pieces Kirk chose to keep when he settled in. Tony brought the last few boxes in the garage to the Salvation Army. The curb was cluttered with remnants to discard. Anything else left to do would be up to Kirk to handle when he moved in permanently. Danny already advised we had clearance from the probate court to legally take control of Sylvia's estate.

I approached the hutch in the dining room. "Well, let's get this last part done." I started with the plates, washing and drying each piece one at a time, wrapping them in bubble wrap, and placing them within a cardboard box. I worked my way through the dessert plates and bowls, grateful I had already washed the teacups and saucers the day Kettner's body had been unearthed.

Once we moved the hutch to Aunt Lucy's house, I'd be unwrapping all these dishes and setting them up for her. The final two items, a platter and a large pasta bowl, sat at the bottom of the cabinet. A productive feeling ran through me, knowing I had nearly completed this daunting project. I also realized how fortunate it was that none of these fragile pieces were damaged during the police search.

I placed the bowl atop the platter. When I lifted the pair, something lightly tapped my leg and foot like a gentle breeze. I glanced down and witnessed an envelope, unsure where it came from or what it was.

With great care, I placed the platter and bowl on the dining room table and picked up two white letter envelopes stuck together. One said, *To Kirk from Mom.* The other said, *To Tony from Mom.* Instantly, it occurred to me. Sylvia mentioned in a note that she left us each a letter. With so much happening as of late, I had completely forgotten. The envelopes had been carelessly torn open. The police must have read them when they conducted their search. They had the warrant to explore all of Sylvia's possessions, no matter how personal, apparently.

But where was my envelope? My head peeked inside the cabinet. I lifted the china bowl and platter. She left a note for each of us. Had she intentionally left these letters in the hutch for us to find? Or did the cops find them somewhere else in the house when they conducted their search?

I texted Kirk and Tony, advising them of my findings.

Kirk replied that he had to work until noon. Tony's text said his shift at the casino started at two, and he was in the middle of a project at home. But he could be here soon.

I couldn't believe it! That psychic medium, Eve, had given me a message from Sylvia, specifying pink and gold colors, the same colors in the china pattern. Eve told me Sylvia had spoken to her, saying, "Think, Victoria, about my treasures." At the time, I assumed it had to do with the money and casino chips we found. But Sylvia used to hide cash in the empty sugar bowl. If she purchased tickets to a show, she'd tuck them behind a plate in this hutch—the place where she kept her treasures. These letters had been here the whole time. I had to find mine.

I stormed to the kitchen in search of a flashlight, then I dashed back to the cabinet and flicked the switch of the flashlight to illuminate the inside of the hutch. My aging eyes didn't see very well in such dim spaces.

No envelope.

The hutch was empty.

I paced around for a bit before plunging through the boxes we set by the curb, pending the arrival of the trash collectors. Perhaps the envelope meant for me got thrown out in error unless the police had confiscated it.

I rummaged through my purse for Detective Notaro's business card. If he or his team of investigators seized an envelope addressed to me, I wanted it. His brief voice mail message played, followed by an ominous beep. "Detective, this is Victoria Ursini. Please call me back. I'm looking for something at my mother's house, and I wanted to know if any of the officers who searched the house took something for your investigation."

Kirk's truck pulled into the driveway around twelve thirty. He found me frantically delving through the boxes piled by the curb like a madwoman. I wasn't sure how much time had passed since I began this scavenger hunt.

"What are you doing?"

"I can't find *my* envelope from Mom. Yours and Tony's are inside on the dining room table. I found them with the china! Looks like the police opened them and read them when they ransacked the place, but there isn't one for me."

"Relax, Vicki. Come inside. If we still can't find it, I'll help you go through these boxes. Mom said there was a letter for each of us, so yours must be here."

My hands trembled. I had no idea what Sylvia would have said to me in writing, but I'd like to think she'd revive a wonderful childhood memory like that Christmas when I hung the angel atop the tree.

Kirk staggered around the table as if my letter would magically appear in view. I pushed his envelope on the table toward him, but he didn't touch it.

"Hey! Where are you guys?" Tony's loud voice startled me.

"In here!" The house was small enough for Tony to easily follow my voice to the dining room. I picked up his envelope and handed it to him.

His lids were raised when he noticed the top had been ripped. "You read it?"

"Of course not. The police must have read them when they searched the place." Irritation released between my words.

"What's wrong?"

"She can't find her letter," Kirk said.

"It wasn't with ours?"

"Well, read, guys. Tell me what she had to say to you in your letters."

"Probably nothing different than what she'd tell us directly. I'm not opening it until we help you look. How did you stumble upon these?" Tony asked.

I explained how they fell from beneath the platter I carried.

Tony lifted the platter and the bowl as if I hadn't already done so. "Hand me the flashlight." He grabbed the light from my fingers and then scrunched to the floor. There was a tiny gap between the hutch and the floor beneath a floral design at the bottom of the antiquated piece. He flashed the light underneath within the tiny gap. "Sorry, Vic. If she wrote us a letter, there's one for you too. It's just not here."

My heart felt crushed. "I insist you take some time to read what she wrote to you."

They opened their mouths but instantly relented as if they'd ever win a fight with me.

"I can't wait to hear what she put in writing. It'll give me some consolation. Please."

While they became engulfed in their private moment with Sylvia, my eyes scanned the room, thinking. What did I miss? Was there another place where she could've left something for me?

Tony raised his head and smiled thoughtfully when he made eye contact with me. Kirk was still reading intently. His letter had several pages. It seemed Sylvia wrote Kirk a novel.

Tony stood and stepped near me to speak without disturbing Kirk. "Mom said some nice things and gave me advice. She said my dad was a great man and a wonderful father, but she just didn't *love* him. Hmm." He huffed and massaged his cheek.

"You're very lucky, Tony, to have Burt as your dad."

"Mom mentioned having a truly great love, but she didn't say who. God, I hope it wasn't that Kettner guy. No clue who stayed around long enough for me to notice that she found love in her life, but it wasn't my father."

I had to wonder myself. I hadn't witnessed an actual love interest for Sylvia.

"I know who it was," Kirk announced with surprise.

Tony and I swung our heads toward Kirk. His eyes widened, and his cheeks flushed when he rambled, "You're not gonna believe this. Mom's true love was *my* father."

Kirk stood then paced in a circle, biting the tips of his nails.

"Are you gonna tell us who your dad is or what?" Tony asked my precise, impatient thought.

"Shh! Give me a second while I process all of this. Holy shit! This is…huge! Things are starting to make sense. My whole life is coming together!"

I glanced at Tony, who was ready to jump out of his skin like me. "Bro, I gotta get to work soon. Tell us!"

"Mom's one true love was a married man she had an affair with and became pregnant with me."

I pondered quietly—*Uncle Gary.*

"Her whole life and world revolved around this man, so she could spend time with him…her one true love. This guy, he's been in my life all along since I was a kid. He coached my baseball team."

Uncle Gary didn't coach baseball, I realized.

"The church choir. My wedding to Lacy. He married us!"

"Wait, Pastor Gordon married you. Josh Steele's father was the man she loved?" My animated arms flung from my hips to my head.

Kirk shuddered. He picked up her letter as if he had to reread her words for verification. "Yes, she said they fell in love, but in his position back in the '60s, he couldn't get divorced. He wouldn't leave his wife, Georgina, and his sons. That's why Mom got so involved with the church. She wanted to be near him. She wanted him to be close to me, so he could participate in my life without anyone catching on as to why. Damn it! I knew my father my entire life, and she never told me!" Kirk, Sylvia's protector, fumed with anger toward her for the first time.

"Listen, I know how hard this is for you. Believe me, I get it. I may never learn who *my* father is. I'm not saying it was right, but if Mom had outed their affair back in 1968, Pastor Gordon would have lost his family and his career in town. The church might have relocated him away from everyone he loved to another parish in another state for having an affair with a woman from his flock. I'm sure he was conflicted. If he wasn't, why would he have coached your baseball team? I remember how much singing talent he said you had. He spent a lot of time having one-on-one sessions with you outside the choir. The fact that he married you and Lacy years ago is a big deal.

He obviously wanted to be at your wedding, and the only way he could've done that was to officiate."

"That's not even the half of it, guys," Kirk continued. "Mom started to distance herself from the church. Gordon was put in a nursing home recently. His family committed him there because he has Alzheimer's disease. Mom would drive to the facility to spend time with him, and she got caught. Someone overheard them talking. Somebody learned about their affair and my biology. She said in her letter that she felt threatened by the Steeles. She didn't name names, but there's only one person with something to lose. Look, she dated this last page a couple of days before the car accident." He took a breath to show us the dated addendum to the letter she had left him. "What if it wasn't an accident at all?"

"Kirk, slow down," I suggested, acknowledging Kirk's fanciful theatrics inherited from Sylvia.

My cell rang. Detective Notaro was returning my call. "Detective, hello. Thanks for getting back to me so quickly. Something is missing from my mother's house. Did your team make a list of anything they might have taken when they conducted that search?"

"What went missing, Ms. Ursini?"

"A letter in an envelope with my name on it can't be found, and there are two letters addressed to my brothers that were opened."

"Letters? I don't recall anyone opening personal mail, and there was nothing to seize. Your mother didn't have a computer. We didn't find anything related to Kettner. We didn't find any additional counterfeit money or poker chips. It's possible this letter could've been misplaced while you were packing up the place."

"I'd appreciate it if you'd check."

"Well, I've got several open cases that take precedence over a missing letter, Ms. Ursini, but I'll make a note of it."

"There's something else. It relates to my mother's car accident." I paused, thinking about the fear shining through Sylvia's written words in Kirk's letter. "We have reason to believe her car crash might not have been an accident."

CHAPTER 33

Sylvia had provided Kirk with specific details about Gordon Steele, the man she loved wholeheartedly. Pastor, a mere title and only a part of his identity. He was a huge Bengals fan, an exceptional bowler, and he could dance like Fred Astaire. She told Kirk about Gordon's Alzheimer's diagnosis. He started to say things that made little sense, and his short-term memory suffered the most. Sylvia believed Gordon erroneously informed someone in his family about Kirk being his son—the reason he wound up at Acorn Hill. They sent him away from all that was familiar to him to ensure his silence from an embarrassing circumstance his family couldn't face.

After a thorough review of Sylvia's letter, I encouraged Kirk to drive to the Acorn Hill facility where Gordon lived, and I willingly accompanied him.

We stopped at the accident scene that claimed Sylvia's life— where Route 147 met Lexington Road. The place where a dark-blue truck hit Sylvia's Chevy Impala with enough force to kill her. I cried, thinking of the pain she must have felt, alone on this gloomy stretch of road for an unknown length of time.

When we arrived at Acorn Hill, the woman at the information desk looked up Gordon's room number and directed us to it. The place resembled a hospital with staff in scrubs, pushing people in wheelchairs and dispensing medication. Then that hospital smell hit me: bleach, disinfectant, and urine filled my nostrils. The residents were dressed in normal, comfortable attire like T-shirts and sweatpants or khakis with elastic waists. As we shuffled down the sterile-looking hall, rooms appeared neat, with colorful bedspreads crisply placed atop each twin bed without a wrinkle. People roamed freely. Some walked the hallway alone. Others congregated in small groups, watching us apprehensively as we walked by.

When we reached the room with the Steele name posted on the wall, Kirk stood in the doorway for a moment. He quietly observed Gordon—his father—sitting back in an old brown recliner, wearing tan khakis and a red plaid shirt. His eyes were set on a rerun of *I Love Lucy*, the episode when she met Superman. Gordon laughed, watching the crazy redhead locked outside on the ledge of her New York apartment when George Reeves, as Superman, flew out to save her.

Gordon must have noticed through peripheral vision someone standing in the doorframe. His lips formed a generous smile, and his eyes lifted when they set upon Kirk.

I began to weep at the touching moment when Gordon waved Kirk over, patting the bed and encouraging Kirk to sit beside him. "Your mother was the most amazing, feistiest woman I ever met! If this disease had a heart, it would make me forget that she's gone." He sobbed. Surprisingly, despite Alzheimer's, Gordon knew exactly who Kirk and I were.

"I'll miss her. She'd visit me a few nights a week. Good God in heaven, I'll miss her adoring smile and that laugh of hers. What spunk!" He looked at Kirk and said, "She told me she was gonna tell you the truth. And if she couldn't say the words, she'd put it in writing."

"You're my father?" Kirk stated out loud, pleading for verbal confirmation.

Gordon nodded once firmly and shed a tear before patting Kirk's back. "So many times, I wanted to tell you, son. I'm sorry I wasn't a strong enough man or godly enough. You'd think I would've acted more honorably in my position."

"Why didn't you?" Kirk asked.

"Oh, son. My family. My other sons. I always considered you mine, even if you didn't pay attention to the clues. Your mother understood, for the most part. Boy, when other men paid her attention, that would surely fire me up. She did it on purpose. How she loved to get a rise out of me!" He laughed. "Sometimes we fought because we couldn't be together. Syl would get angry and date other men, telling me she had had enough and she was done with me. That's how your brother Tony was conceived. She ended our relationship and started to date Burt. Oh, I knew she could have another man in her life if she wanted one. She could've settled down with any guy, but she and I had something special, even if we couldn't share it with anyone.

"Your mother's involvement with the church kept her close to me. It kept *you* close to me, Kirk. We made it work to the best of our abilities. Your mother owned my heart, no matter what anybody thinks. I helped her financially to support you and ensure she could afford the house you lived in."

He placed his hand upon Kirk's and said with a raspy voice, "I'm so happy it's finally out in the open. You are my son, Kirk Douglas." Gordon chuckled. "Your mama always loved those old movie stars!" He opened his arms wide, waiting patiently for Kirk to embrace him.

It took Kirk a moment, but he slowly stepped into Gordon's welcoming arms for an endearing hug.

As Kirk pulled away, Gordon's eyes absorbed his dark features and athletic build. "You look so much like her, you know? Tell me, do you have her diamond ring? The one with the gold filigree."

"Er, yes."

"I gave her that ring. She never wore it on her left ring finger, but it was my way of showing my commitment and love for her. I'm glad she made sure you got it, Kirk."

I signaled Kirk, pointing to the door, advising I'd step out for a bit to give the father and son duo some privacy. I felt slightly envious that both my brothers knew who their fathers were now, yet my paternity still had a giant question mark next to it.

Kirk might have some time to spend with Gordon before Alzheimer's took his mind completely. In spite of the symptoms of the awful disease culminating in Gordon's retention, his love for Sylvia hadn't faltered.

I exited the building and strolled around the lovely grounds. Numerous flower sprays, blooming bushes, and a man-made lake drew my attention behind the property. I walked past a cement patio with tables and chairs for residents to sit outside and visit with their families beneath umbrellas to block the unbearable heat and sun's rays. A few swans waddled to the water for a refreshing swim. At least Gordon lived in a peaceful setting. I stepped closer to the water and sat on a wooden bench to watch the magnificent birds dive for nibbles of food.

A small feather floated through the air, smoothly drifting with the gentle breeze and landing beside me on the bench. Looking up at the tree branches swaying above me, I was astonished to see a light brown bird with a warm red tone to its wings, a female cardinal who soon flew to another branch where her mate sat. Male cardinals had vibrant red bodies with black faces around the bills. Puddles filled my sockets as I felt Sylvia's presence, happy and relieved that Kirk and Gordon had finally found each other. I wished her peace as I lifted the fluffy feather and placed it inside the pocket of my white capri pants, a memento of the day I learned so much more about her than I ever knew.

Thirty minutes had passed before I found my way back to Gordon's room to check on Kirk. The two sang a gospel song in a quiet tone—a song Kirk soloed in the choir when he was a child, "Bless the Beasts and the Children." He maintained a beautiful singing voice, clearly inherited from his father. Gordon remembered the words at first, but abruptly started to struggle, stammering through the second verse. With tremendous patience, Kirk placed his hand over Gordon's and finished the song, carrying Gordon through to the end.

An immediate shift in Gordon's expression was noticeable. Crossed brows in time with a fading smile. His eyes squinted as he moaned, "How'd you get in my cell? You don't belong in my cell!" He angrily hollered, "Guard! Guard!"

Kirk and I were astounded by the instantaneous change in the man's demeanor as fast as the flip of a switch.

A nurse popped her head in. "Are you all right, Gordon?" she asked calmly. She drew near, firmly securing his wrist in her hand to check his pulse.

He struggled in her grasp and tugged at her arm. "Don't let her put me back in chains! She's the devil!" he shrieked.

Kirk lowered his head in devastation but gently placed his hand upon Gordon's shoulder. "You're safe. I won't let anyone hurt you."

Gordon jumped at Kirk's touch but soon relaxed. He stopped fighting with the nurse and eased back into the chair, closing his eyes.

The nurse said, "His day started off better than usual."

"I'm his son. May I ask you questions about his condition?"

"Uh, well, I'd need to talk to a supervisor. I've never seen you here before. The supervisor has to check to see if your name is on the list of people we can give information to."

Kirk nodded. "Never mind. I won't be on that list. I'm merely concerned about his health. Is there anything you can tell me?"

"What you just witnessed happens pretty often. We're all trained to handle elderly patients with disorders of the mind. When Gordon has good moments, he's very charming." She glanced sympathetically at Gordon. "Then there are incidents when he blurts out words that don't make sense. He always calls this place his *prison*." The nurse ensured Gordon rested comfortably before she skipped out of the room.

"This is a prison. My prison. Where I belong," Gordan announced. His eyes remained closed as if talking in his sleep.

"Kirk, maybe we stayed too long. Our visit is overwhelming him," I said.

He nodded in agreement. "Gordon, we'll let you rest, but I promise I'll be back to visit."

"How are the peonies?"

Kirk cocked his head and moved closer, wondering if he heard Gordon's question correctly. "Mom's flowers?"

"I planted those for Sylvia. Her favorite flower. Beautiful and delicate like her. Something so lovely and dainty to disguise the ugliness beneath them."

I was certain I would get a crick in my neck from the sharp twist of my head.

Kirk cautiously squatted beside Gordon at eye level. "What ugliness lies beneath the peonies, Gordon?"

"True evil. Satan himself. He tried to hurt your mother. Taint her with his vicious whispers and monstrous plots. I rescued her from Lucifer. He would've killed her and taken her to hell with him!"

We listened intently to the confused words of a man with a horrible disease that damaged his mind and memory, but the unexpected details were adding up. His wild dialogue actually made sense.

"Gordon, how did you rescue Sylvia from…the devil?" Kirk looked uncomfortable, enabling the man's confusion, placating his distorted words, but he hoped to glean pivotal details.

"Those lovely white flowers brought peace after the apocalypse. I told Sylvia to dream of me when she looked at them. Don't be frightened. I'll always protect you, Sylvia," Gordon said, looking through Kirk as if he wasn't standing before him.

*****

Kirk and I left Acorn Hill with a million ideas running rampant through our heads. We gained far more information than we had anticipated.

"Do you think Gordon killed Rodney Kettner, protecting Mom in some way from him? Did he cover up his crime with those flowers?"

"We don't know what happened that night, Vic. We're not going to get the whole story. I'm not sure we can trust Gordon's memory."

"I know. I can't help but feel somewhat relieved that Mom probably didn't kill that man. Maybe Gordon walked in on them. Kettner had just been released from prison. Maybe he wanted Mom *physically*, and Gordon stopped him."

The drive back to Vegas was despondently quiet until Kirk said, "I don't want the cops to know. Gordon's living in hell as it is. I can't have the police questioning him, even if it might get Mom off the hook for Kettner's death. In his unstable mental state, the police won't take him seriously. Maybe it's enough that we have some peace of mind, believing she didn't outright murder a man, no matter how terrible Kettner was."

I agreed, accepting the fact that whatever happened on the night of Kettner's death would be buried with Gordon when his time came.

Kirk reached into his back pocket, held up a plastic bag with a red toothbrush in it, and dangled it before my eyes. "I swiped this from his bathroom."

I exposed an impish grin. "Ingenious."

CHAPTER 34

Calculating

Caterina cried herself to sleep again last night, missing her mommy. She was just a baby. She'd forget all about the abominable clan she had the displeasure of being born into. This blond curly Q was special.

The media focused on the amber alert again this morning, showing the Maroni family looking sad and hopeless, pleading into the camera for the safe return of their precious Caterina. The FBI became involved because of the corrupt organization her family led. With their criminal history, the cops would be investigating their enemies. He was sure they wouldn't look in his direction; his immense confidence bordered on cockiness.

He removed his Clippers cap and placed it on the bathroom vanity near his razors and shaving cream. He had to clip off the bulk of his beard and mustache before shaving his entire face and head to be as smooth as a baby's bottom. He laughed at the analogy. When he finished, his different look and bald head actually made him appear youthful.

His task list had a checkmark next to almost every item. He slid the kitchen drawer open and reached inside for the scissors, validating their sharpness by pricking the tip into his middle finger. He waved his hand, then sucked up the speck of blood that dripped.

He carried the scissors to the crib and watched Caterina sleeping soundly. His thumb and pointer finger wrapped through the holes of the tool. Slowly, he lowered the sharp blade into the crib as she squirmed in her sleep. The sharp edge neared Caterina's throat. He began slicing away at her pretty golden curls while she slept.

For the next leg of their adventure, Caterina needed to look like a boy.

CHAPTER 35

My brothers and I caught the end of Sunday worship at the First Congregational Church on Willow Street. We sat in the back pew and listened to Pastor Josh preach about loving thy neighbor and promoting acts of kindness.

Deception and corruption became embedded throughout my first marriage to Jeffrey. I was no stranger to duplicity. The whole world learned of my infidelity, unaware of the love and devotion I shared with Tommy.

I couldn't judge Sylvia or Pastor Gordon for falling in love and giving in to their desires. But setting out to murder her to avoid a scandalous affair, shrouded by the divinity of the church, had been the biggest con of all.

Before Josh blessed his parishioners with a day of peace, Kirk, Tony, and I slipped from the pew and walked around the corner to the office in the back, where Josh was expected to enter after he bid farewell to his adoring fans.

A smooth-sounding singer and organist played "How Great Thou Art" as people slowly moved to leave and get on with their day of peace per the pastor's wishes.

Voices from Josh's office were heard over the organ beats and the soprano's pretty hymn.

Without so much as a knock, I opened the door and stepped inside the room with my brothers taking their stance at my side. Josh's wife, Debbie, and his mother, Georgina, sat in the antiquated floral fabric chairs in the corner of the room. "Debbie, Mrs. Steele, so sorry if we disrupted your conversation."

Debbie's surprised reaction to our unexpected visit appeared obvious through her wide eyes and lifted brows. "Oh, hello, Ursini family." She chuckled awkwardly as if startled.

A small desk sat in the center of the room with three multicolored fabric chairs around it. Religious images hung upon the walls. A shiny white statue of the Madonna and child stood prominently in the corner. A large wooden cross dangled in the center of the main wall behind the cherry desk.

"Did you folks need something?" Georgina asked, then coughed harshly. She had aged over the years, looking like a ninety-five-year-old, but I didn't think she had reached that milestone yet. Her deep-set wrinkles and white hair added to her years. Her posture drooped, and her hands trembled, securing a walking cane slumped across her lap.

Kirk's voice disrupted my assessment of the ill, elderly woman. "We're waiting for Josh."

"Josh may be a while. He loves mingling with his faithful parishioners." Debbie smiled broadly, highlighting her perfectly straight teeth. "I'll tell him you were looking for him. Unless you had an appointment?"

"How about we simply wait back here and keep you company?" Tony decisively suggested, crossing his arms.

Debbie and Georgina's eyes met, exchanging awkward glances, unaccustomed to my youngest brother's assertive nature.

Josh entered. "Well, now, it looks like there's a party going on. Why wasn't I invited?" Josh smiled with enough sincerity to make me vomit.

Debbie chuckled as Josh removed his holy cloak to reveal his minister garb.

"You're the guest of honor," Kirk said.

"Am I? I'm intrigued." Josh placed his hands on his hips. "Would you like to sit?" He stepped behind his mother and gently kissed her cheek. "Are you comfortable, Mother?" he asked.

Georgina tapped Josh's hand that rested upon her shoulder. "I'm fine, son." She smiled at Josh like his followers, worshipping the ground he walked on.

I whispered to Kirk, "Maybe we should speak to Josh *alone*."

Josh's eyes narrowed, looking concerned. "If you folks need to speak with me privately, I'm sure Debbie can escort my mother home."

Kirk released his anger. "I think they should all hear this!"

I hoped Georgina Steele wouldn't keel over from Kirk's sudden aggression.

"You stand up on that altar, rattling off godly quotes with your holier than thou-ness, but to remain silent about my father...*our* father is malicious."

"What? Kirk, what did you say?" Josh asked with a confused expression as his hazel eyes swayed toward me. "Victoria, what's he talking about?" The shock on Josh's face could have been a fantastic pretense, but he appeared genuinely bewildered.

However, I couldn't help but notice the not-so-surprised look on Georgina's face. Her twitchy body language exuded a high level of discomfort.

"Take a breath," I whispered, resting my hand on Kirk's chest. I turned to face Josh. "Our mother wrote Kirk a letter before she died." I signaled Kirk to finish.

"In it, she revealed that *Gordon* is my biological father."

"What? Surely, you're not serious," he said, gently touching his mother's shoulders.

"Outrageous!" Georgina barked. "My husband couldn't possibly be your father!"

"A DNA test will tell us the truth."

"How dare you! You won't wreck my husband's reputation or Joshua's standing with the church with these lies!" Georgina slammed her hand onto the arm of the chair.

Josh's face shimmered a light shade of pink, but surprisingly, he remained calm. "Mother, if this story is true, we should confirm it. I can't imagine it to be true, but Kirk has a right to know. He obviously feels very strongly about his theory, and we've got nothing to hide."

"No! An outlandish claim like this could sully the family name. Your loyal parishioners will find out."

I shook my head, confused. I believed for certain Josh knew all along. It would be *his* name slung through the mud as the pastor of this congregation. This was his father's doing. It was of no reflection on Josh or his abilities as a pastor. I doubted he'd lose his career because the family name suffered some abrasions to its reputation, but he had the most to lose if Gordon's secret became exposed. "You really had no idea, Josh?"

"Vicki, don't let him fool you." Tony's hands lifted, showing resentment. "Someone threatened our mother, probably *killed* her."

"What? Sylvia was *murdered?*" Josh shook his head back and forth. "She never said a word about any of this to me. My father certainly didn't tell me they were *involved...intimately.*" He gazed in his mother's direction without making direct eye contact, then cleared his throat before speaking, "I was only about thirteen when Kirk was born. How would I have known? And you believe hearing this *uncomfortable* detail would make me want to harm or even *kill* your mother? I adored Sylvia's fiery personality and wisdom. I'm not sure what shocks me more, the fact that I might have another brother or that you think I'm capable of harming an elderly woman."

"You should all be *ashamed* of yourselves. Get out!" Georgina yelled, pointing her crooked, arthritic finger toward the door. "You will never get DNA from my dear Gordon."

"I already did," Kirk retorted, considering the toothbrush he swiped from Gordon's bathroom.

"You...what?" Georgina's blue eyes grayed when her brows rose in anger.

"Yesterday, I went to the Acorn Hill Assisted Living Center to visit Gordon." Kirk looked directly at Josh as he finished his sentence. "He was quite lucid during most of my visit when he confirmed that he was my father. I managed to get a DNA sample. The test results, when they come in, will confirm the truth. He professed his love for my mother but couldn't acknowledge me as his son back in 1968."

"Shut up! How dare you speak like that in front of me," Georgina shrieked with fury pouring out with a lone teardrop. She clutched at her heart and started panting.

"Mother? Are you all right?"

Georgina's gasps intensified. She couldn't catch her breath.

"I'm calling an ambulance! Josh, this is far too much for your mother to hear. Make them leave!" Debbie insisted.

"Perhaps we can continue this conversation later. My mother needs medical care."

I turned to Kirk and said, "Come on. We can sort this out with Josh *alone* after you get the test results." I nudged Kirk to leave.

Tony interjected in Kirk's defense. "My brother has a right to know his paternity even if none of you can accept it or will admit to it." He looked directly at Josh and said, "Can you accept the reality of this? Acknowledge Kirk as your half-brother?"

Josh pursed his lips, his mind abuzz with a million thoughts. He embraced his mother to help alleviate her stress. "This is a lot for me to process, but *if* we are brothers, I...I suppose I'd welcome him. Yes, Yes, I will accept whatever the test results reveal."

Georgina slapped Josh hard with the same hand that held her heart moments ago. Her breathing suddenly steadied. I wasn't sure if she was angry that Josh stopped tending to her pseudo-health crisis or that he intended to recognize Kirk as his brother.

"If that's how you really feel, then who else knew the truth? My mother's letter said someone warned her to stay quiet—a threat if you ask me. She wanted me to know my paternity but feared the backlash from all of you. Shortly after writing that letter, her car gets run off the road by a dark-blue truck that *kills* her."

"Dark-blue truck?" Josh queried as if seeking validation.

A tall, lean man in a business suit strolled into the room without knocking. He stood erect and authoritative as his eyes assessed the temperature of the people in the room. "I'm Detective Boyle, leading the investigation of Sylvia Ursini's hit-and-run. Mr. Ursini and I had a lengthy discussion last night. I'm here to talk to Pastor

Joshua Steele." His eyes moved directly toward Josh, his attire giving away his identity as the pastor.

Debbie spoke up, "The night of Sylvia's accident, Josh and I were up north at a retreat with dozens of people. You must be out of your mind if you think my husband had anything to do with that accident."

My personal experiences influenced my hypotheses, thinking about the various times I believed Jeffrey cheated on me. Also, when Tommy and I met and fell in love, Jeffrey's sixth sense kicked in, corroborating my infidelity. "You know, I was married once." *Twice, really*, I thought, but no one in this room knew about my clandestine marriage to Tommy. "Most people can tell when their spouse cheats. There's a change in their look and touch or lack thereof. This sick feeling just creeps up inside you like something is wrong, but you can't quite put your finger on it. A spouse always knows or, at the very least, *suspects*." Slowly, I moved closer to Georgina. "How long did you know about Gordon's affair with our mother?"

"You are way out of line, Victoria!" Georgina spat out with a ferocious grin, no longer exhibiting frailty.

"Am I? It's clear you didn't want anyone in your social setting to know your husband cheated on you."

"This is ridiculous!" the old woman squawked.

"Victoria, stop. Please don't speak to my mother that way."

I ignored Josh's compassionate plea. "Were you angry enough to kill her, Georgina? Run her car off the road to keep her mouth shut? She wasn't perfect. She didn't come from wealth. She made her own way and established independence. She created the best life she possibly could for her three children."

"Look at all of you *mongrels*. Three different fathers and a floozy dancer for a mother. The police say she *murdered* a man and buried him in her yard. What kind of woman does that? What was my husband thinking, carrying on with the likes of Sylvia Ursini? I should've had his head examined years ago!"

"So you did know years ago. You knew about their affair and about Kirk." I proved my theory in front of Detective Boyle.

She sneered and added, "Gordon knew to return to his life and marriage to *me*. If you're suggesting I killed that woman, it's a ludicrous concept. I don't drive anymore. Haven't driven a car in at least eight years. Look at me! I can barely walk without support." She lifted the curved handle of the cane on her lap.

"How about you all come down to the station, and I'll take your statements. We'll figure this out," Boyle persuasively recommended.

"We're waiting for an ambulance to take Georgina to the hospital," Debbie declared. Although the old bat looked strong to me.

In walked Terrance Fontaine, the organist with the beautiful voice who sang at Mom's funeral. "Sorry, Pastor Josh, am I disrupting something? You said you wanted to talk to me after service." He began biting his fingernails as he observed the large group in the room.

"It can wait, Terrance. Enjoy the rest of your day."

Terrance took a few steps away from the door when Josh's face lit up. His usual pink tone transformed to paleness.

"Terrance, wait a minute. Whatever happened to that truck you drove? I haven't seen it in a few weeks. A Ford, right? Dark blue."

Everyone's head turned in Terrance's direction.

"It was just giving me some trouble." Terrance shrugged. "It's in the shop getting serviced." He nodded definitively, smiling awkwardly, then turned to move.

As Boyle stepped near the doorway and opened his mouth to speak, Terrance darted toward the front of the church.

Everyone raced out of the room, watching Boyle chase him down, shouting to a few officers standing near the entrance, "Stop him!"

The officers rushed inside, but Terrance skated to the left to evade their attack.

An officer stood at each exit. Terrance's escape routes were blocked. He dashed up the lengthy spiral stairway that led to the choir loft with Boyle and the officers hot on his trail.

A rush flew through me, anxiety bubbling as I watched this scene play out like a *Chicago PD* rerun.

Voices screeched, echoing inside the church walls.

Terrance stood near the railing of the choir loft. "Stop!" he yelled. "Don't come any closer." He pushed his spry body on top of the railing, then sat, dangling his feet over the ledge and gnawing on his nails. The drop was long, though the fall probably wouldn't kill him, but it would hurt like hell.

"Terrance, what's got you so worked up? I only wanted to ask about your truck," Boyle calmly affirmed.

"No, no, no. I'm *not* going back to jail!" He thrust his head to look below his swaying feet, staring down at all who eagerly awaited the next move of a desperate man.

Josh called up to him, "God forgives, Terrance. We've been friends for a long time. I know what a good man you are, Terrance. Your mother wouldn't want you to get hurt, so why don't you come down from there and talk to me? You can talk to *me*, your friend."

"I'm sorry, Pastor Josh. I'm so sorry. You were in trouble." Terrance murmured through tears when he spoke. "I wanted to help you."

"Help me? I love that you wanted to help me, Terrance. What did you do to help?" Josh stared up at Terrance, speaking with a delicate, trusting tone.

"It's not my fault," he cried.

"Come off that railing, and we can talk about it. Just the two of us."

I knew that was a lie, but Josh's kind words and compassion shone through, making an emotional connection with Terrance.

"She made me! She made me help her." Tears gushed between his words.

"Who?"

I looked right at Georgina, who continued to shuffle slowly in our direction, using her cane with some help from her daughter-in-law.

The paramedics arrived with their supplies. Debbie raised her arm to flag them down. I'd bet money that Georgina's blood pressure was rising. The EMTs raced to the old woman and helped her to sit in a pew.

"Pastor Josh, you saved my life years ago when I was using. I nearly died, but you didn't give up on me. The church rescued me.

You helped me get my life back. I love singing here. I wanted to repay you for all you've done for me. I didn't mean to hurt her. I just had to stop her from telling anyone about your father." A thick stream of tears fell from Terrance's eyes. "She…she went to see your father. I overheard them talking about telling everyone the truth. She didn't care what it would do to you and your job here. She only cared about herself! She was so selfish! I wanted to stop her from telling Pastor Gordon's secret."

"Who did you work with, Terrance?" Kirk shouted up to him. "You said a woman made you do it." Kirk looked at Georgina, who feigned outrage at his allegation behind an oxygen mask a paramedic had placed over her mouth.

The police inched closer to Terrance from behind while he was distracted by the crowd below him.

"Don't come closer! Stay away from me," he ordered the officers who were spreading out around the distraught man.

"Tell us, Terrance," Boyle insisted. "Why should *you* take all the blame if someone made you do it? If you cooperate, everything will be okay."

Terrance wore a look of defeat. He removed his hand from the ledge that secured his body and pointed his finger down in Georgina's direction. All heads turned toward her. She looked like she'd faint until Terrance continued, saying, "Debbie told me I had to help her stop Sylvia. Debbie knew about Pastor Gordon and Sylvia. He told Debbie about his feelings for Sylvia during one of his episodes. She made me look for anything Sylvia might have written about her relations with him in her house. Sylvia told Pastor Gordon she put things in writing. She wrote Kirk a letter to tell him about their relationship, but I couldn't find it."

Terrance had broken inside my mother's house that night. I chased him away before he found the letters. Mousy, demure Debbie from school went to great lengths to protect her husband's family name and her life as a pastor's wife.

"You don't know what you're talking about, Terrance," Debbie argued, shaking her head with nervous animation. She left Georgina's side and dashed to Josh. "He's lying! Trying to cast blame on someone else to save himself!"

"I have text messages she sent me," Terrance added.

"That's preposterous. Shut up, Terrance. Just shut up or…or… jump already!"

An officer quickly moved in and grabbed Terrance from behind.

Terrance's balance became compromised when he moved to prevent capture. The weight of his body slipped off the railing and swung over the ledge, but the officer grabbed his arm to prevent him from falling to the floor below.

Terrance shrieked. The creaking sound of his arm snapping like a twig, dislocating from his shoulder, made me cringe. The officer held onto his wounded arm tightly. Terrance screamed in agony as his ligaments began to shred. His legs floundered in the air above us. One of his brown slip-on shoes dropped and bounced off the floor below.

Boyle raced closer to the officer, grabbed Terrance's healthy arm, and pulled him up and over to the other side. The pressure from the pull caused Terrance to squeal in pain from his injury.

Debbie pleaded to Josh, who looked as confused as the rest of us.

"Why, Deb?" Josh asked with great patience, fighting shock and anger while everyone else listened, moving closer to them.

Debbie shifted back and forth. "Terrance is lying. You've got to believe me!"

"Terrance says he has proof. The truth will come out." He stared into his wife's penitent eyes as if reading her mind, discerning her fear. "My god, what have you done?"

"I did nothing! I'm not saying a word to the police without an attorney," Debbie coldly specified.

By this time, Boyle had Terrance secured in handcuffs and staggering down the spiral stairs minus a shoe, whimpering. "Officer Holt, the suspect needs medical attention. Stay with him through the examination, then bring him to the station. Officer Whitney, cuff Mrs. Steele and read her her rights."

Officer Whitney took out his handcuffs as he approached Debbie, who squirmed and positioned her body before Josh, pleading for protection from the arrest and, most likely, the scandal about to fall upon the Steeles. A far more significant scandal than the affair between a pastor and one of his followers. Debbie drew intimately close to Josh, preying on his compassion. She brushed the tip of her head against his cheek, seeking comfort.

"Are those necessary?" Josh asked, holding onto Debbie as if he didn't want to let her go, unable to fathom her possible accountability in Sylvia's death.

"Yes, sir. I'm afraid they are," Whitney replied.

Boyle looked in Kirk's direction. "Relax, Mr. Ursini. I'll be in touch once we get to the bottom of this."

As much as we wanted to follow the police cars to the station, we had to wait, but we weren't very patient.

CHAPTER 36

Detective Boyle contacted Kirk Sunday evening. Terrance confessed; he wasn't leaving that jail cell. He had been charged with vehicular homicide and breaking and entering.

Debbie's arrest cited conspiracy to commit murder. She refused to speak. Her only words were to profess her innocence, demanding to be released on bond.

Terrance shared his cell phone with Boyle, giving him access to the emails and text messages that insinuated Debbie's involvement. Not only did the Steeles have to deal with the revelation of Kirk's paternity, but they also had a murder charge demolishing the family's reputation.

Boyle wouldn't offer specific details about the case, but he confirmed the evidence started to mount. Without a confession from Debbie, a jury would decide her fate.

Sylvia would have justice for losing her exuberant life prematurely.

We were all on edge that afternoon, but we needed to tell Aunt Lucy what we discovered about Sylvia's death and Gordon being Kirk's father before she heard it on the local news or through the grapevine in town. Her poker face made me question her ignorance about Kirk's paternity. If Sylvia and Gordon were in love, I found it hard to believe my aunt was kept in complete darkness. Perhaps that was a secret shared between sisters.

Tony and Leann ordered Chinese food for us to eat at Aunt Lucy's apartment.

I picked up the boxes of dinnerware I had cleaned yesterday and brought her the lovely set with mauve flowers and gold gilding. Tony and Kirk would have to tackle bringing the large hutch on their own. I needed to return to Paris this week; I had been away from home for twenty-one days—a long time to be apart from the man I loved.

If I learned anything from Sylvia's life, I learned to feel blessed and grateful to have such a wondrous love with Tommy. Like her, I didn't have the ability to share my love for Tommy with anyone. Sylvia and I both loved men behind closed doors, in the shadow of seclusion. Once the world believed Tommy had died in 2010, we were able to make our relationship work under the radar, away from Tommy's enemies, for our own safety. We couldn't openly flaunt our love in Vegas, but in Paris, we were free. Sadly, Sylvia never experienced such a luxury.

Aunt Lucy cried at the thought of someone taking her sister's life in such a horrible manner. However, she was appreciative that the criminals were caught and charged. She turned on the TV to a local news station in case the arrests of Terrance and Debbie made headlines while I picked at the vegetable lo mein on my plate. None of us truly enjoyed the meal after the day's events, learning Sylvia's death had been taken as punishment for wanting to expose Kirk as Gordon's son.

The ABC anchor, Lucas Malone, blurted Jeffrey's name after he reported on the missing Caterina Maroni—the second full day of her kidnapping.

"Shh, hold on," I interrupted Leann chatting about her upcoming commercial takes, and turned up the volume to hear about this little girl still apart from her family and why Jeffrey was making headlines.

Malone announced, "I'm being told that the former governor, Jeffrey Atkins, will be on the air at any moment with an announcement."

"Man, that guy doesn't stop talking. He must love listening to the sound of his own voice," Tony mocked.

"That's what I get for marrying a politician who loves publicity and being in the spotlight like a moth attracted to a flame."

"If he's not whining about losing the election years ago, he's got something negative to say about you," Aunt Lucy grumbled.

"Shh!" I watched as Jeffrey's face lit up the screen. He wore an expensive-looking black suit, a white-striped shirt, and his signature red tie.

Microphones surrounded him as he began to speak. "Thank you. I'll try to keep this brief, but I feel this news is important for the future of Nevada and my role in improving the economy, creating new jobs, and lowering taxes."

"What's he doing? Running for governor again? The next election is in a few months."

"Shh!"

"As you all know, I *wrongly* lost the election for governor back in 2012. Certain *bogus* reporters slandered my name and reputation. All of it had been based on the ramblings of a *con man's* memoirs. That scam artist, as you all know, is Tommy Cavallo. He lied about everything, folks. In fact, his written words are a complete farce, and I have proof."

"What the hell are you up to, Jeffrey?" I murmured.

"My ex-wife flew into Las Vegas for her mother's funeral earlier this month." Jeffrey stopped and glanced up at the heavens. "Rest in peace, Mom." He lowered his head to be back at eye level for the cameras. "What you don't know is that Victoria Ursini has been using a false identity."

Light whispers in the crowd were heard.

"That's right. She's been using the alias *Charisse LaSalle-McGee* in Paris, France. You know, those phony news stations would talk about Victoria living in Montana. She hasn't been in Montana. She's been living in Paris, and she wasn't alone. If you noticed, I mentioned she had a hyphenated name."

"Oh, shit! No, no, no, no, no!" I said more loudly than I expected. "How did he—?"

"I have evidence that Tommy Cavallo, former owner of the Montgomery Hotel and Casino, is very much *alive!*"

Gasps could be heard from his audience of journalists and his supporters. Reporters wanted to ask questions, but Jeffrey ignored them.

I grabbed my cell and called Tommy, immediately hearing his voice mail message. I urgently advised in a text that he call me back because our covers had been breached. I texted Danny next. My fingers moved nearly as fast as my brain, ignoring the questions my family spouted in the background.

"Vic, what the hell? Is this true?" Kirk probed.

I held up my hand, fingers outstretched, barely paying attention to their questions, staring back at the TV to hear what else my deplorable ex had to say.

"You probably think I'm exaggerating or outright lying, but friends, I'm not the liar here. I got railroaded from office because of the *lies* Cavallo generated years ago. He lied to the police, his family, and anyone who bought his autobiography, which is pure *fiction*. Cavallo deceived everybody, hiding out in another country, leaving a trail of broken promises, mocking inaccuracies about me, and skirting criminal charges. Charges like fraud, to start, and larceny, followed by racketeering. And you know who he trusted with this information—Victoria Ursini, who's been hiding with him."

"Governor Atkins, what evidence do you have?" a reporter inquired.

"Cavallo has been using the name Timothy McGee in Paris, France. He acts as a tour guide while Victoria Ursini, excuse me, *Charisse LaSalle-McGee*, works at the Musée d'Orsay, which coincidentally is the location where the Camille Pissarro painting, *the Boulevard Montmartre at Twilight, 1897*, had been shipped. Is it a coincidence that this painting suddenly reappeared shortly after Cavallo's alleged death?" Jeffrey laughed heinously.

"Where's the evidence, Governor?"

I shouted at the TV, "Yeah, where's your evidence, Jeffrey? Why the hell do they still call him *governor*? You lost, Jeffrey. Get over it!" My stomach twisted in knots as I released my frustration through angry words. Jeffrey uncovered our names and jobs, publicly offering Tommy up for his nemeses to find.

"How about photographs?" He immediately held up a collage of pictures of Tommy on his boat along the Seine River. "Wow, he's sure aged, hasn't he? But this is Tommy Cavallo, alive and well, living in Paris. I also have several testimonies from the staff at the Musée d'Orsay, who corroborated that Victoria Ursini is working there under the alias, Charisse LaSalle-McGee."

"Governor Atkins, how did you come across this information?" a journalist asked.

He smiled this Cheshire cat grin. "I can assure you that the information obtained was legally acquired."

"Of course, you won't share *how* you acquired this, Jeffrey. Jackass!" I yelled, forgetting my family sat around me, wearing stunned expressions.

"With Ms. Ursini back in town, it wasn't difficult to obtain her cell phone number. I needed to prove my innocence and win back the trust of the people of this great state. I hired a well-known, competent business to launch a full investigation at my own expense."

"Governor, are you saying you managed to triangulate her movements using her cell phone?"

"The methods used were aboveboard and legal."

I kept glancing at my phone, no reply from Tommy. "Aboveboard and legal, my ass!"

"Governor, will you run for office again?"

"That's a great question. Sadly, it's a little too late to throw my hat in the ring for this year's election, but I promise you, in four years, I will be back."

People in the background cheered.

"I have every intention of reclaiming the governor's office. Maybe even the White House!"

The cameras flicked back to the newsroom, where Lucas Malone summed up Jeffrey's bit.

Tommy had been outed. Where would we go to find security from his enemies now?

The sound of my brothers' voices resonated, but I couldn't focus on their words. Jeffrey's insatiable hunger for retribution could cost Tommy his life and crumble my whole world.

"Vic, is it true? Is Tommy alive?"

I didn't know what to say, and I couldn't face them.

"Lack of response says a whole lot, Vic. If what Jeffrey said was wrong, you'd call him a liar."

"Give her a moment," Aunt Lucy insisted. "Can't you see the anguish on her face?" My aunt always came to my rescue.

A text from Danny rang through, so I called him and stepped into Aunt Lucy's bedroom for privacy, explaining the urgency of this situation to Danny. I heard the constant bleeps of his cell phone on my end, exploding with texts and calls from the people in his life who heard Jeffrey's announcement.

"I've got to contact Pop before I say anything to anybody, especially the media," Danny said, breathless and concerned.

"He might be asleep. It's 4:00 a.m. in Paris. He didn't answer my call. I'm so worried!"

"Jesus, my wife, my kids, my *mother*. Uh, my mom called and texted several times in the last two minutes. She must have watched Atkins's theatrics in front of the camera."

"You've got a lot to deal with on your end, Danny." I stepped back into the other room, gazing at my family members, whispering their own theories. "So do I. Please have him call me if you hear from him first. I'll do the same."

"Damn, it is true! You've been with Tommy all these years?" Kirk sought affirmation.

I had been overpowered. Defeated. There was no point in keeping this secret any longer. I gave a simple, definitive nod.

"That's amazing!" Tony said with glee.

"Amazing? You're not pissed at me?"

"Your private life is your business. We assumed you wanted to avoid Jeffrey, and believe me, we all get it. Shit, if you managed to make your life with Tommy work all these years, that's pretty spectacular," Tony replied.

"Maybe I feel a little bad that you didn't trust us enough to tell us the truth," Kirk added.

I shook my head. "Trust had nothing to do with it. You read Tommy's book. There really are some dangerous people after him. He needed to escape and hide out for his own protection. You knew where I was and how to contact me. I…well…I just omitted the fact that Tommy was with me."

"Jesus. Now Jeffrey outed him."

"You see why I'm freaking out? I can't reach Tommy right now. He's not answering my messages. He has no idea everyone knows he's alive and where he is. What if a hit man shows up, and—" I grabbed my purse and sprinted toward the door.

"Where are you going?" Kirk questioned with worry in his tone.

"I've got to get to Paris."

"Wait!" Tony, the most rational of us, stopped me by tugging my arm. "You're not walking into a danger zone. Tommy would want you to be safe. What if he calls you when you're on a plane for fourteen hours?"

"I can't just sit here and wait."

"It's only been a few minutes since this aired. Give him time to call you, Vicki."

"Jeffrey caused all this trouble because he got a hold of my cell number. Unbelievable! Detective Notaro had my cell when he was investigating the Kettner case. Maybe Jeffrey has resources within Metro. Tommy's life is in jeopardy!"

Both Aunt Lucy and Leann appeared shocked and disoriented, quietly sitting back without saying a word about the debut of my nervous breakdown.

"I'm sorry, ladies. This must seem so crazy to you both."

"Nonsense. You're entitled to worry," Aunt Lucy said, shaking her head empathetically.

"Maybe you shouldn't have come home." Kirk lowered his head, saddened to have to say that.

"No. I won't be sorry for seeing our mother before she died. I have no regrets about coming back to Vegas. My only regret in this life is marrying Jeffrey. He wooed me with his charm, launching my acting career. I fell for his flattery and ambitious career goals."

Then a distant thought echoed in the back of my head, so soft and subtle, it barely made sense. My feet paced around the room in a couple of circles, leading me directly in front of Leann. "Hey, tell us again how you got that commercial."

"What?" she asked hesitantly.

"Yeah, the Rios Roast organization has a huge marketing plan with a healthy budget. It's incredible that your few acting credits awarded you a commercial with a company of that magnitude."

Tony interrupted my provoking implication. "Lay off, Vicki. Why are you bringing that up?"

"I'm curious. You need serious credentials and an agent to land such a gig."

"Well, I auditioned. They loved me," Leann responded, perfectly poised with raised, shaky brows.

"Okay, but what did you do to get them to even notice you? Again, you don't have an agent to get you in the door."

"Vicki." Agitation sparked through Tony's tone.

"Jeffrey got you that commercial, didn't he?"

"What are you talking about?" Tony screamed, raising his arms in anger.

"Admit it, Leann. I'll find out. Jeffrey knows the Rios family and people high up in the corporation. My god, Rios Roast was the first commercial he helped *me* get. What exactly did you have to do for that role?"

"What are you suggesting?" Leann snarled.

"Vicki, come on."

I disrupted Tony's uncomfortable defense. "Tony, do you keep my private cell number in your phone?"

He glared at me. "Yeah, so?"

"Are you aware Leann has a habit of looking through your phone? She knows your passcode. I caught her more than once."

"No way. Leann wouldn't give your number to Jeffrey, knowing how much I hate his guts." Tony's blue eyes glanced at Leann, who had the word *guilty* written all over her face. She wasn't a decent enough actress to disguise her betrayal. "Tell her, babe. You'd never do that. Not…for…a commercial." The light bulb shined brightly over Tony's head.

A popular commercial for a massive business like Rios Roast could make or break Leann in the business she had been so desperate to receive an invitation into.

He noticed the mortified expression she wore. "No. You didn't."

"Baby, I had no idea what he'd do. I figured he'd call her to talk or whatever. Bother her to make her crazy, or worst-case scenario, he'd sic the media on her personal number. All she'd have to do is get a new number. Big deal!" She looked at me. "I swear, I didn't know how he'd use that info. I didn't know you were hiding out with Tommy. How could I have known that?"

Tony stormed away from her, but she latched onto his arms frantically.

"Baby, I swear to God, I didn't think he'd do something like that, but for me…I could finally have a serious commercial under my belt. Get a bigger role. Make more money for us so we can get out of that dinky house."

"You are unbelievable. You should've talked to me about it first. You didn't come to me because you knew it would piss me off, and I wouldn't want you to hand over my sister's number to that asshole. I'd forbid it!" Tony shouted at the top of his lungs. "Go home. We'll talk about this later…if I come home."

"W-w-where will you go?"

"Just don't expect me home. Not tonight."

"Come home with me, Tony. We'll talk *privately*," Leann pleaded, her somber eyes evading the rest of us.

Tony turned his back on her and marched to the bathroom, slamming the door hard enough to shake the walls.

Leann studied the frowns we all wore and staggered out of Aunt Lucy's apartment alone.

CHAPTER 37

Time dragged, impatiently waiting, feeling mystified. I paced around Sylvia's living room, flipping TV channels all night, though I couldn't focus on any late-night program. The anger and hatred I shouldered for Jeffrey festered. This bitter taste regurgitated from deep within, harvesting the sickest fears I could conjure.

Kirk and Tony spent the night babysitting me and keeping my brain occupied between drifts of restless sleep. Tony didn't want to see Leann so soon after their argument, and Kirk was concerned about my enraged state.

Tommy missed our regularly scheduled evening call. I grew even more worried that he was in trouble. I refused to take my sleeping aid, fearing I'd miss Tommy's eventual call—that never came.

When the sun rose, my heart ached, acknowledging the fact that he never responded to my pleas, filling his voice mail box. A grim reality screamed that he hadn't listened to my messages at all. Was he being held captive and tortured by an enemy? He wouldn't intentionally worry me, ignoring my calls.

Good Morning America highlighted turbulent politics, the missing Caterina Maroni, and a deadly mass shooting in Philadelphia that ruptured during the night.

Danny summarized his investigation in spurts through texts. He contacted Tommy's attorney, Len Stein, and Tommy's good pal, Jim, hoping one of them had news.

They didn't.

Danny had a lot of people to answer to. He must be exhausted, creatively explaining to his family why he kept such a happy event a secret. I hoped they would understand the ramifications if too many people were allowed entry to such imperative, life-threatening secrets.

If Tommy didn't reach out to us soon, the miserable actuality I dreaded to conclude was that he could be dead—for real this time. Danny surely held the same fear, but neither of us found the courage to say those bitter words aloud.

Would this news hit the media in Paris? I had the number of a retired neighbor, a widower named Jacques, who lived two doors down and always recited the news highlights. He'd remind me to bring an umbrella if rain was due, share what he'd learn about a local terror attack, or describe an accident that might impact my drive to work. Tommy helped him with some heavy jobs around his apartment. The maintenance crew often took their sweet time fixing appliances. Jacques liked Tommy, and he spoke decent English. I searched for his number in my cell and dialed. By the third chime, he answered.

"Salut Jacques. C'est Charisse d'à côté."

"Ahh, bonjour, Charisse."

"Jacques, pardon, I've been away and trying to locate Tommy. Would you mind knocking on our door and checking on him?"

"Attendez."

I held on with bated breath when I heard Jacques place his phone down and step away.

Several minutes passed as I paced laps around the kitchen table before the movement of Jacques's phone could be heard.

"Pas de réponse, mais la porte a été déverrouillée."

"English, please, Jacques."

Jacques cleared his throat and spoke with a thick accent. "Your door iz unlocked. Your huzbun, he iz not home. I peered inside all ze rooms."

Shit! I thought. Tommy locked the door even when he collected our mail.

"Vous allez bien, Charisse?"

"Yes, everything is okay," I woefully lied.

"Shall I lock ze door for you?"

"Oui. Merci beaucoup, Monsieur." I hung up, feeling more worried than before I called Jacques—if that was possible. On a positive note, if Tommy or I hit Paris's prime news outlets like Reuters or the Le Monde daily paper, Jacques would have mentioned it.

My brothers tried to distract me. Tony ran to the store to fill the fridge as if I had an appetite. Kirk suggested we walk around the neighborhood and release my frustrations with exercise.

"Guys, go to work. You have jobs."

"And leave you alone to rush to the airport? Forget it."

I shook my head. "I agree with you. I couldn't be trapped for so many hours on a plane, unable to communicate with anyone without losing my mind. He'll contact me when he can. I have to believe that." Although I spoke with confidence, my stomach twisted in uncertain despair.

CHAPTER 38

Manipulating

In between bouts of tantrums, the little one played hide and seek with his Clippers cap. She liked it when he covered her precious pink cheeks with the tip of his cap. When he raised it, he'd make a silly face, stick his tongue out, or cross his eyes to make her giggle.

He knew she'd soon forget all about the family she once lived with. He scooped her up in his arms and carried her to the picture window he obscured with thick brown curtains. His eyes peeked between the creases of the drapes to view the wooded area lined with cedar, fir, and willow trees that stretched out for acres, far from the main road that saw little traffic—the place his parents owned and rarely used when they were alive.

Caterina scrambled about, so he placed her on his knee and bounced her up and down, generating loud, rambunctious, whinny sounds of a horse.

Yup, she'd learn to love him, he was sure. He skipped with her to the kitchen and grabbed a honey crisp apple. "You like apples, little one?" He wouldn't refer to her as Caterina. She needed a different name. He considered unisex names like Jessie, Mackenzie, or Casey until he finally settled on the perfect one.

She reached her tiny fingers out to hold a peeled apple slice without saying a word. She didn't speak much, with the exception of saying simple words like *mama*, *yes*, and *no*. She would point to items of interest like the unicorn stuffed animal he purchased for her, books he could read to her, and food she liked. He did his homework, researching the types of food and beverages an eighteen-month-old could eat.

He waited for his contact to be in touch with the paperwork and legal documents he required to flee the country with his *grandson, Riley*, to thwart the amber alert.

CHAPTER 39

Why hadn't Tommy called me yet? I couldn't bear to spend another full day stuck inside this house with my brothers nervously monitoring my every move. Last night, I chewed a melatonin gummy, but my bubbling blood raced through me with such intensity, I couldn't relax. My eyes closed from time to time through the night, but I didn't sleep for more than thirty-minute intervals. I felt wild, chaotic, and exhausted simultaneously. Even the lithium that controlled my moods couldn't alleviate this stressful disturbance.

Reporters called Sylvia's house phone. Some overzealous journalists were brazen enough to knock on the front door. Others were inappropriately curious about the backyard, photographing the grass remnants and dirt the CSI team left after exhuming Rodney Kettner's bones.

Kirk and Tony were zonked out, snoring loudly, overtired from watching my nervous animations. Before they woke, I fixed my hair and makeup, brushed my teeth, and drove to the Montgomery. I needed a change of scenery and some fresh clothes from my suite. To prevent my brothers from worrying, I texted them my plans and told them not to miss another day of work.

Needless to say, Kirk and Tony were not happy that I went AWOL, judging by the irritated tones in the texts they returned, but I assured them I'd check in later, and I wouldn't hop on a plane Paris-bound.

After watching a brief segment about Tommy's life and memoirs on *Good Morning America* in my suite, I ordered room service while the anchor switched to the recent massacre in Philadelphia. Perhaps eating would waste time and give me the motivation I needed to get through the anticipated miserable day of worrying. I couldn't think about much else besides Tommy.

Skimming through online news articles, some journalists declared Jeffrey a vengeful man, trying to win back the support of the people to regain power through unjust means. Others required more hard proof that Tommy still lived and breathed, wanting to speak with me, but I refused to give a statement to anyone. Then there were Jeffrey's supporters, who must suffer from stiff necks from constantly staring at their idol, standing high on the imperial pedestal where he placed himself.

Breakfast arrived moments before a text chimed in, distracting me from spreading a thin layer of light cream cheese on a toasted sesame bagel. My stomach tightened with anticipation as I lifted my cell, praying it would be Tommy.

It was Danny checking in on me, curious if I had heard any news. He indicated he'd be working from home again today. I texted him back, suggesting we commiserate together, inviting myself to his home in Summerlin.

He returned a thumbs-up emoticon and added, "I'll let security know to expect you."

*****

I thought about my last visit to Danny's house, meeting Eve, the medium with mystifying abilities. Danny believed she was a charlatan, but divine influences were nothing to joke about. Today, security guards surrounded the perimeter of his estate as if it were a walled fortress protecting a royal family from a rebellious society. My ID was checked and approved to enter through the iron gate to access the magnificent house.

A couple of vehicles were parked outside the garages. To avoid blocking anyone, I parked at the end of the pavement that led to the cobblestone path to the front door.

The sprinkler system flicked on, suddenly drenching the deep green grass and lovely flowers in the garden around the elongated front porch. As I stepped closer to the entrance, Danny stood at the door, leaning against the frame, displaying a slight smirk, reminding me so much of his father.

"You okay?" he asked, probably noticing the severe dark circles below my eyes.

"Antsy, nervous, and…well…a complete wreck. You?"

He released a trivial snicker. "Same."

The sound of children's laughter from somewhere inside brightened my mood. Other voices were heard down the hallway as I followed Danny to the kitchen. The closer to the kitchen we stepped, the heavier the aroma of cinnamon filled my nostrils, a pleasant scent that tickled my taste buds, even though I wasn't hungry.

"Coffee? Wait, you're a tea drinker," he questioned, seeking confirmation.

I nodded for tea, then my eyes met the others in the room. "Hello, Bianca, Sadie." I wondered why Sadie was here on a Tuesday morning. I suppose with all the commotion that upended our lives, she had a reason to be close to Danny and his children.

A man standing behind Sadie's chair sent me a smile. "Vicki, right? Hi, I'm Hank."

"It's nice to meet you, Hank." I stretched my arm out to shake his hand.

Hank and Sadie had been a couple since she and Tommy divorced in the mid-eighties. He was a handsome African American man who showed a sweet, gentle smile.

"Vicki, sit. Relax," Bianca suggested.

"How are you holding up?" Sadie asked me.

I shrugged, feeling an intense chill from her side of the table. Sadie, Hank, and Bianca stared directly into my eyes. I needed to ease the uncomfortable tension mounting in the room. "I'm sure you have questions."

"My son filled us in. We're all still shocked, thinking Tommy was dead all this time. How could he stay away from Danny and his grandchildren?" Sadie snapped.

"Mom, we talked about this." Danny mouthed the words, "I'm sorry," to me, standing behind his mother, out of her view.

"I'd like Vicki's perspective." Sadie's request sounded both urgent and frigid.

All eyes were upon me. I surveyed the hall to ensure none of the children stood nearby before I spoke. "I know you read Tommy's book. You're aware that people wanted to hurt him. Attempts were made on his life. He worried more about his family than himself. If someone planned to use him for target practice, he didn't want any of you to be caught in the cross fire. Your safety meant more to him. He was forced to stay away from you to assure your protection, so that's what he did. He found a way to disappear, and I had the option to stay behind and live my life without him or run away with him. I couldn't let him go. I love that man with my whole heart, and I wouldn't trade the last nine years we had together in Paris for anything. And now I'm falling apart, wondering where he is and if I'll ever see him again." I could feel the tears flow, soaking my cheeks.

Hank handed me a tissue as Sadie placed her hand atop mine. "I'm sorry you're going through this, Vicki. We all know Tommy's a survivor. Wherever he is or whatever he's doing, I'm sure you'll see him again." She released a slight chuckle. "That ex-husband of mine is way too stubborn to let anybody get something over on him."

I couldn't help but smile. Sadie was right. Tommy had a stubborn soul and tough disposition, but he wasn't invincible. Spending time with Danny and his family opened the door to hope.

The kids gathered around the kitchen table, waiting for a piece of Bianca's delicious cinnamon coffee cake.

Kristina, TJ, and Tyler welcomed me with warm hugs. They were silly yet polite when they joked with their grammy and grampy. Hank asked the kids if they were ready to go for a swim, keeping them distracted with fun activities to pass the time.

I stretched my neck from the kitchen, noticing Emma lazily stepping into the living room with her head sunk to her feet. "Excuse me," I said aloud for anyone around the table to hear. I picked up my tea and walked into the room where Emma sat quietly, entertained by a *Harry Potter* book. "Hi, Emma. Whatcha doin'?" I asked.

She glanced in my direction and woefully replied, "Reading."

"Do you think I'm too old to read *Harry Potter*?"

She shrugged, though her eyes remained focused on her book.

I inched closer. "Hey, you know, you're nearly thirteen now. Can I share something with you about your poppy?"

With a serious eye glare, she briefly glanced my way.

"Your poppy told me lots of stories about you."

Harry Potter suddenly became less interesting to Emma. She closed the book and raised her brows. "Like what?"

"Oh, he told me that when you were little, you loved the big pool at his house. You would turn the music up on the stereo really loud and bounce around to the songs. He also told me you were a beautiful ballet dancer. He has photos of you in your various tutus. Hmm, there's one outfit he loved the most, the blue one with the white trim and gold sequins."

Her eyes sparkled as a partial smile displayed. "That's my favorite!" Her frown returned as she lowered her head. "Why did Poppy stay away so long? Didn't he know how much I'd miss him?"

"Oh, sweetheart, believe me, it's been hard for him to stay away. But he kept tabs on you, and I can prove it!"

Her porcelain skin flushed nearly the color of her strawberry blond hair when a full smile lit up her face. "Really?"

"Uh-huh. He knows about your performance in *The Nutcracker*. You came in first place in the sixth-grade spelling bee. You wore a beautiful royal blue lace dress to the seventh-grade spring dance and danced with a cute blond boy named *Liam*." I whispered the boy's name so no one would hear, inciting a giggle from Emma. "He also knows about the perfect ten you earned on your bar routine. You've become quite a gymnast! Let's see…he said you flew more than two feet over those bars, performed a gorgeous handstand, and your… what's that word for when you finish your performance and land on your feet?" I jumped to my feet, straightened my body, and stretched my arms up high, imitating the act.

207

"My dismount!"

"Yes, Poppy said your dismount was pure perfection!"

"Poppy saw all that? Really? He had been watching!" Her blue eyes shimmered.

"He was always watching after you, Emma, and he always will."

She delighted me with a generous hug.

CHAPTER 40

Kirk and Tony returned to work after keeping me company again last night at the house. I couldn't handle them waiting around all day, watching me tread another deep trail of worries into the living room carpet.

Bianca welcomed me to stop by again if the four walls of Sylvia's house started to crush me. They were trapped inside their house too, avoiding publicity and worrying about Tommy as much as I was. Perhaps if we commiserated together, time would fly at a quicker pace, prompting a call, text, or email from Tommy. The unknown—a dastardly, sinful palace of uncertainty, where subtle waves of hope briefly entered, only to dissipate and melt away.

I heard the squealing sound of brakes. An unmarked police car pulled into the driveway. I recognized Detective Ed Notaro stepping out.

The case of the counterfeit loot had been closed, or so I thought. Detective Boyle kept Kirk in the loop with any updates regarding my mother's death. Debbie Steele continued to give the cops the silent treatment. Did Notaro have more information about Kettner's death?

I paused by the window, waiting for his knock, holding my breath. When his hand rapped against the door, I slowly exhaled before opening it. "Detective, what brings you by?"

He huffed, "I'm glad I found you here, Ms. Ursini. I've got some questions for you. I'll need you to come to the station."

I released a quick burst of a chuckle. "The station? What's this about?"

Notaro placed his hands on his hips and exposed a serious look. I couldn't tell if he was angry or irritated that he stood before me, making this request. "Some questions arose about a stolen painting that went missing from Mr. Jeffrey Atkins's possession several years ago."

He didn't refer to Jeffrey as the governor or former governor; perhaps he wasn't a fan.

Despite the sick feeling in the pit of my gut, I managed a smile. "I could answer your questions right here if that's okay, Detective."

"Sorry, Ms. Ursini. I need you to come with me."

*****

Before Jeffrey and I were married, I secretly searched for the Pissarro painting, the treasure stolen from my grandfather by his former business partner, Matthew Winters. Only Grandpa and his most trusted allies knew I funded the recovery mission.

Sylvia had grown excited about my life and engagement to Jeffrey. I developed a fruitful career, secured a wealthy, powerful man who adored me, and, in time, I returned Grandpa's precious masterpiece to him after removing it from Trey Winters's wall. Trey, the grandson of Matthew Winters, turned out to be an unscrupulous character, but I believed I could handle him and the situation all on my own. I thought I had everything I wanted in life, including happiness.

Then the threats began. Terrible intimidation tactics, complete with rodents and snakes. I confided in Jeffrey about stealing that painting for my grandfather. After all, Grandpa bought that painting legitimately from a European art dealer, or so he claimed.

During World War II, the Pissarro painting was stolen by German soldiers under Hitler's command. It hadn't been seen since the early 1940s. When the war ended, Hitler, being a sore loser, ordered his soldiers to destroy all the art and sculptures he stole throughout Europe just so no one else could enjoy them. Somehow, the Pissarro painting escaped a devastating fate and landed in my grandfather's hands. Its journey of surviving destruction remained a mystery.

Jeffrey's political career was on the line if the truth about his fiancé stealing the Pissarro painting from someone's home was unveiled. He needed me by his side as his wife. Marrying a successful actress helped Jeffrey win the mayoral race in Fernley, Nevada, where he lived and grew up. Because he helped my acting career take off, I had to reciprocate by assisting him in achieving his political goals.

He dealt with the Winters family, ensuring they wouldn't bother me again, neutralizing their catty threats. I loved Jeffrey at that moment, rescuing me from such a prickly predicament.

Had I maintained my daily regimen of lithium at that time, none of this would've occurred. That luscious rush! The thrill of the risks I took when searching for that painting caused a massive uptick in my moods, feeling invincible. Nothing could stop me. And Jeffrey's devotion and help triggered lust and a pulsating erotic reaction to his help. Sex between us turned wickedly hot and satisfying.

Our life was fantastic until my fuse started to dull, evoking hopelessness and severe gloom that tore me apart from the seams, bit by bit.

Aunt Lucy recognized the signs. She knew I went off my meds despite my habitual lies. I didn't believe I was ill. I convinced myself that I felt fine. It was my aunt who persuaded me to seek help.

After seeing a therapist and accepting my fate and a lifetime of medication, those wondrous highs and extreme lows mellowed somewhere in the middle of a state of normalcy. I realized the horrendous errors in judgment I had made. Any emotion I had for Jeffrey was triggered by the arousal of an intolerable condition I suffered from. I suddenly felt nothing for him, and I got scared. What if this medication dampened my ability to feel love and fulfillment from sex entirely? I searched my heart for love for Jeffrey, but the emotion vanished. I blamed the meds. I blamed my bipolar disorder. I blamed *myself*.

I stayed in the marriage for a long time, hoping to feel something exciting again. Ultimately, I needed a break from Jeffrey and our marriage. When I tried to discuss it with him, I realized what he had done. Jeffrey taped my confession about stealing the priceless Pissarro painting and nearly killing Trey Winters in the process. Trey OD'd the night I took the art. It was unclear if the Rohypnol I slipped in his whiskey added to his downfall, but the drug showed up in his tox report, proving he'd been roofied, but Trey couldn't prove it was *me* who gave him that drug—not until Jeffrey captured my confession on tape and blackmailed me to keep me tied to him.

When I met Tommy at the Montgomery in 2005, at first, our attraction led to what I thought would be a harmless one-night stand. Trusting men wasn't in my nature, but I actually felt something for Tommy, a fantastic energy and burst of desire—what I no longer felt for Jeffrey. I had hope. Hope that the medication didn't completely diminish an emotional, sensuous connection to a man's touch.

Little did I know that meeting Tommy and spending one night with him would make me crave more. God, he was sexy, funny, and kind. We couldn't stay apart from each other. Even when Tommy learned about my marital commitment, our hearts entangled, securing roots that deepened. I knew I loved him, and my bipolar disorder had been under control. My love for Tommy made me feel whole again. But I was legally bound to Jeffrey.

Divorcing Jeffrey became a grueling priority. We desperately searched for my taped confession. It took a great deal of effort and energy, but once we obtained the tape, we found a way to covertly send the Pissarro painting on a triumphant journey to France.

CHAPTER 41

I said absolutely nothing to Detective Notaro on the ride to the Metro station. My brain raced in overdrive, madly curious if Jeffrey attempted to press charges against me and what questions Notaro would ask. He hadn't read me my rights—yet.

Notaro sat me in a box with one of those large two-way mirrors. I refrained from waving to whoever stood on the opposite side. Perhaps Jeffrey weaseled his way in to observe the inquisition.

"Would you like some water or coffee?"

"No, thank you. I am curious what questions you have or how I can help you."

Notaro opened a brown briefcase and removed a folder. He kept this folder close to his frame, out of my sight. For all I knew, that folder might be empty like a ploy my character, Lexi Thorpe, used on an episode of *Rising 51* once to catch a bad guy who'd been lying through his teeth.

"In June of 2010, it's been alleged that someone unlawfully entered a secure area and stole a valuable painting." Notaro's eyes fixated on me, but I said nothing. "The priceless painting was replaced with a forgery. Shortly thereafter, said painting was opened by a curator at the d'Orsay Museum in Paris. I'm sure you know where I'm going with this, Ms. Ursini."

I offered no response, maintaining a stonelike expression.

He huffed in irritation. "Do you have any knowledge as to how the Camille Pissarro painting, *the Boulevard Montmartre at Twilight, 1897,* found its way to Paris, France, after it went missing nearly seventy years ago?"

"You've offered me a beverage, Detective, but you didn't offer me an attorney."

"These are some pretty basic questions that shouldn't warrant an attorney, Ms. Ursini."

I shrugged. "I'm afraid I can't answer your questions."

"Can't or won't? A lot of pieces are missing from this puzzle. I'm a damn good detective, and I will learn the truth with or without your help. I'd think you'd be inclined to cooperate and spare your family any additional public humiliation, considering how often you've been on the news recently."

"May I use my cell to make a call, please?" I asked politely with a widening smile.

Notaro looked at me as if I had asked for something completely unheard of.

"If I'm merely here to answer questions and not under arrest, I'm free to make a call. Frankly, I should be free to leave. I understand my rights, Detective. And I won't talk to you without an attorney."

Notaro grabbed his paperwork, plopped it in his briefcase, slammed the case shut, and marched outside the box.

I was certain that Notaro and others might be observing through the mirror or the small camera placed in the upper corner of the room. To prevent them from eavesdropping on a phone call, I sent two SOS text messages that included multiple exclamation marks.

Forty minutes passed, waiting in that box. I knew I wasn't alone. Detectives, possibly Jeffrey, watched my every move, praying I'd break. On the outside, I broadcasted a confident vibe, remembering Sylvia's advice to never let them see me sweat. On the inside, my confidence felt as sturdy as Jell-O. No one had proof of my involvement with the Pissarro painting except for the chapters in Tommy's memoirs.

Tommy. God, I wished I knew where he was! Three days without communication, while a lingering threat loomed, made me crazy, irritable, and frankly, pissed off. I'd like to think my intuition would be burning if he was caught and killed by enemies. He had to be alive. I chanted that positive belief constantly. If Tommy wasn't being held against his will, how could he make me wait so long without contact? He must know his absence was sending me over the edge, on the brink of self-destruction. All these inner thoughts raced through my mind, but I assured my presence looked calm to the observers on the other side of the mirror. I wouldn't allow them to see me sweat.

The door flung open. In stepped Notaro, holding that same folder with Danny on his heels.

"Detective Notaro and I had a conversation. I advised him that you are incapable of explaining any details written in my father's book. The words of a man who's been declared deceased would not be your responsibility, even if questions about his death were recently called into question. The painting is located in France. If someone wants that painting, perhaps they should discuss this with the French authorities and *prove* rightful ownership."

An ingenious tactic. Jeffrey would never win such a battle. He'd look like a thief himself, demanding a prominent museum relinquish that artwork.

"Counselor, lack of cooperation on the part of your client tells me she's got something to hide."

"What evidence do you have that suggests Ms. Ursini had a hand in the painting's disappearance from someone's storage room *besides* the book you referenced or the insinuations of her bitter ex-husband?"

Notaro paused and bit his lip in frustration. "She's free to leave." His scowl grew more intense before he brashly opened the door.

No sooner did I stand from my properly posed position in the metal chair when two men, wearing black suits and angry faces, charged inside.

My body felt stiff from sitting for so long, but their presence forced me to instantly stand erect.

"Who the hell are you?" Notaro asked.

"Agents Ortega and Frye." They flashed federal badges.

"What's the FBI want?" Flames seemed to spark from Notaro's reddened ears.

"We're taking over this case." Ortega reached for the folder Notaro held. "May I?"

Notaro pulled his file back. "Hold on. I still have some legwork to do."

"Not your job any longer, Detective. The FBI's in charge of this investigation now." Frye maintained a commanding stance and held out his hand to retrieve the file.

"Wait a minute. This relates to a theft that took place in *my* jurisdiction."

"The alleged theft of a priceless piece of art from the Second World War is a *federal* matter."

Danny's gray eyes found their way to me with a look of terror, but I kept my cool while all these men fought over who planned to arrest me or, at the very least, detain me.

Another man, older, bald, wearing a cheap brown suit and scuffed shoes, fought his way through the door. "Notaro, let it go. The feds are taking it on. My hands are tied."

"But…but, Captain."

"Come with us, Ms. Ursini," Agent Ortega directed with a firm tug of my arm.

"I'm Daniel Cavallo, Ms. Ursini's attorney."

Agent Frye held his arm out, "Right this way, Counselor."

When we exited the room, I noticed Jeffrey approach the captain. *Damn you, Jeffrey,* I thought. Didn't he have something better to do than to find ways to harass me? Shouldn't he be planning on reclaiming the governor title in four years? His devilish smile sparkled in my direction, believing he won the war, witnessing me in the custody of FBI agents, triggering blistering reviews by the tabloids of my questionable morality.

"Uh, excuse me, agents." Jeffrey took out his business cards, holding a couple between his fingers for them.

Frye and Ortega stopped upon Jeffrey's request. Frye took a card while Ortega ignored Jeffrey.

"I expect to be kept apprised of your investigation," Jeffrey instructed as Frye, Ortega, Danny, and I strode by him.

We neared a black Chevy Tahoe parked on the side of the Metro station. Agent Frye opened the back door for me to enter.

"Where are you taking my client?" Danny asked in an assertive tone.

Frye and Ortega scanned the area with eagle eyes, assuring no one else was within earshot. Frye's bitter brown eyes stared at me and asked, "Where are we taking you, Mrs. McGee?"

"Mrs. McGee?" Danny muttered, sounding perplexed that they used my alias.

"Drop me off at my mother's house at 67 Orchard Lane, please. Danny, you can meet me there. I promise I'll explain everything."

*****

Frye and Ortega ran through some legalities with me on the drive to Orchard Lane. They escorted me inside to assure my safety and bypassed Danny on their way out the front door, nodding a solid farewell to him without uttering a word.

Danny's fingers rummaged through his brown hair in bewilderment when he raced toward me. "What the hell just happened?"

"Danny, there are some things your father and I never shared with you. It wasn't necessary to divulge these details before. But now that your father's been outed, I've no idea what more will come. He took precautions when it came to everyone he loved. Faking his death and letting you and your family think he died had been an extreme yet essential part of the plan if we were to escape our pasts and stay alive."

"You both knew I hated being kept in the dark, but I got over it. What was that show downtown just now? The FBI swooped in as if you were headed to federal prison. Instead, they acted as your Uber ride."

"Tommy and I are protected by the FBI."

Danny dropped his briefcase by the kitchen table on the white linoleum, plopped into a chair, and blew out a hearty breath. "Go on."

"He did this for me, really. If Jeffrey or Trey Winters ever attempted to press charges against me for my part in taking back the Pissarro painting, your father didn't want me to get arrested. Charges were piling up against Tommy too. His involvement with the Toscano family and the crimes they committed at the Montgomery years ago hung over his head. Tommy worried he'd see the inside of a jail cell. He had no choice but to work with the Toscanos when he first inherited the hotel, you know that. The Toscanos would've killed him if he tried to end their partnership or blabbed to the cops about extortion and money laundering crimes."

"What kind of deal did he make with the feds? Obviously, they're not protecting you both out of the goodness of their hearts."

"In exchange for my full immunity related to the theft of the Pissarro art and the action I took to acquire it, we returned the Pissarro painting to the feds, who ensured it got back to France where it belonged. Tommy received complete amnesty for his association with the Toscanos by paying the government some lofty fines to make up for estimated unpaid taxes. He also gave them some excellent tips on open cases they couldn't solve without any inside information. Do you remember a few years ago when Gino Toscano got arrested for murdering the guy nicknamed *the Shrimp?*"

"Albert 'the Shrimp' Piccone. The *man in steel* case made national headlines. Are you saying Pop helped them nab Gino Toscano? Pop's name never came up in the trial."

"Your father sent the feds in the right direction. It took time until the FBI snagged many of Gino's soldiers. Tommy wasn't intricately involved in any of those crimes. He merely knew enough info to work with the feds and steer them down the right path to solve a few murders, local gambling scams, and some white-collar crimes. The Toscano family crumbled because of the numerous arrests made thanks to your pop. They didn't need Tommy to take the stand in court, not when the actual criminals who went down for the crimes named Gino as a high-ranking captain giving the orders. Apparently,

Gino believed someone inside his organization ratted him out because several soldiers started singing for better deals. Gino had no clue this started with Tommy. I mean, why would he? Tommy *died*."

"You're in the witness protection program," Danny logically concluded.

"Technically, yes. With your pop's hefty bank account, we agreed to fund the move ourselves with new identities. The assets he bequeathed to friends and family were his personal possessions. No one can charge us with fraud because we go by Tim McGee and Charisse LaSalle-McGee in Paris. Tommy's death certificate and our name changes were handled through WITSEC, and only certain law officials have access to our files."

"Thank God there's no threat of prison for either of you."

"Do you really think he would've told the whole world in his memoirs about my stealing the Pissarro painting and what happened to Trey Winters if I'd be harmed legally? He outright exposed secrets that could've sent me to jail if we didn't broker this deal. Jeffrey's allegations about fraud and theft are pointless. I don't really care about his personal attack on me and my character, but that bastard told the whole world that Tommy is alive. And if word got out that we're *protected*, his enemies would wonder who he gave up. I asked Frye and Ortega if they had heard anything yet."

"And?"

I shook my head. "They've been trying to contact their connection in France, but they're also MIA."

"That doesn't make me feel better."

"Me neither. When I returned to Vegas earlier this month for my mother's funeral, your father worried that Jeffrey would antagonize me or find a way to use the theft of that painting against me. Ortega had been our FBI contact from the start. Tommy advised him of my arrival in Vegas. I knew to contact Ortega if I ran into trouble—like when Tommy first went missing and today.

"Your pop isn't proud of this. He didn't want you to know of the compromises he felt he had to make. I blame myself. I was young and made it my mission to return that painting to my grandfather. I went about it the wrong way, with disastrous consequences. Tommy helped put away murderers and left a gaping hole in the Toscano organization for our exonerations. It took time to forgive ourselves for our past missteps. I guess there's no statute of limitations on regret."

Danny glanced at his watch.

"You've got someplace to be?"

"No, but I do have hotel business. I've been working from home since Atkins made his public announcement about Pop being alive."

"Go! I'm fine. Thank you for coming today and trying to get me out of a jam."

"Ortega and Frye really rescued you."

"Sorry, I guess I used you as a distraction until they arrived. I said I needed to contact an attorney. I didn't want Detective Notaro to know I texted Agent Ortega too."

Danny nodded. "Come home with me. Bianca and my mother would like the company."

I gave it some thought. "You know, after all the craziness this morning and getting very little sleep as of late, I think I'm going to lie down for a bit. But if you hear anything, call me."

"You do the same, Vicki."

My body required rest, and my brain needed to shut off. Overcome with emotion, rehashing our escape from our previous lives in Vegas, I slid beneath the silver covers of Sylvia's bed and drifted off to the wonderful place called dreamland.

CHAPTER 42

The sound of a vehicle parking disrupted a beautiful dream. Tommy and I were serenaded by a Venetian gondolier wearing a black-and-white striped shirt and a straw hat. I could feel the motion of the small vessel gently rocking me back and forth, curled in Tommy's muscular arms, bathed in the glow of the warm sun over calm waters. The taste of Tommy's lips piqued my desire as he offered me a generous kiss while the gondolier sang a romantic Italian tune.

Another type of noise pumped my lids open drearily. I had finally experienced a deep, restful sleep after several days. I lifted my cell beside me to read the time, four twenty-two. I'd been asleep for four hours. No new calls or texts from Tommy, so I laid back down to rest.

An obnoxiously loud thumping sound prompted my eyes to burst open.

My torso bounced up instantly. I slowly sat at the edge of the bed, taking a moment to stand. Feeling overtired these days triggered mild vertigo when making sudden movements. I stepped wearily to the front door to see who woke me from the heavenly sleep I craved. If this was a reporter, I'd lose my mind.

I pushed back the curtains from the window and noticed three people standing outside with their backs facing me. The black

Chevy SUV in the driveway told me agents Ortega and Frye must have returned; perhaps they had news about Tommy. That thought instantly energized me.

When I opened the door, one of the men in a navy-blue jacket and matching cap raced inside. The other two, wearing business suits, remained outside on the porch, and they weren't Ortega and Frye.

"What is this? Who are—"

His cap lifted, and my heart danced a quick-paced jive. "Tommy!" I fell into his large arms, breathed in the spicy fragrance of an unfamiliar shampoo he used, and squeezed him hard enough to tear my rotator cuff. I pulled away to devour his lips, melting into the sweet taste of his mouth and tongue. I hoped this wasn't a dream, a mere fantasy of our reunion. When reality set in, I did what any normal Italian American woman would do: I punched his chest hard. "Where have you been? I've been worried sick!"

"It's good to see you too, babe. You have no idea what I've been through this week."

"What *you've* been through? I wasn't sure if you were alive or dead!"

"Listen to me." He took my hands in his. "There's so much to tell you, but right now, I've got somewhere to be. I had to see you. I knew you'd be worried. Danny too. Listen, when I get back later, I'll fill you in. Then you can tell Danny I'm safe."

"You're leaving?"

"Babe, I don't have time to explain. Time is of the essence."

"I'm going with you."

"No, it's best you stay behind. I wanted you to see for yourself that I'm okay."

"After everything I've been through this week, I won't sit here and worry about you any longer. Is that the police outside? FBI?"

"FBI but—"

"No buts, Tommy Cavallo. If time is of the essence, you can fill me in along the way. You aren't leaving my sight!"

Tommy sighed in defeat, placed his cap back on his head, and opened the door. I thought he planned to leave without me while I slipped my sandals on, but he signaled the agents and said, "Make room for one more. My wife is joining us."

We entered the back of a black SUV with tinted windows, and I melted into the cozy leather seat.

"Honey, I couldn't communicate with anyone. Or I should say, these two wouldn't *let* me contact anyone. These are federal agents Beauchamp and Jourdain, stationed in Paris."

Beauchamp, a stoic-looking female agent, frowned at me as her male counterpart, Jourdain, started the car without so much as a wave.

"They got me out of France and into the US safely, but unfortunately, it took some time and a painful amount of paperwork once they learned my cover was blown. Not to mention the absurd amount of hours it takes to fly here. I had to leave my cell behind to prevent anyone from possibly tracking me. Atkins! He frickin' demolished our identities!"

"I tried to contact you. Warn you about Jeffrey's announcement."

"I'm sure you did. These FBI agents are good at their jobs. They discovered we'd been breached *before* Atkins announced it publicly. They realized someone was tracking me and looking into our lives in Paris. I'm so sorry I couldn't get word to you. If you did that to me, I'd be livid, but it was a necessity to the plan."

"Plan?"

"You don't think I flew all this way into the trenches without a plan, do you?"

I lifted my cell.

"What are you doing?"

"I'm telling Danny you're safe. He's been so worried. Like me."

Jourdain, our driver, suddenly decided to speak. "No, madam. No!" he yelled with a thick French accent.

I decided I did not like Jourdain.

"Hold off." Tommy lowered my cell into my lap with his palm. "Just a little while longer. Danny's waited this long. What's another hour or so?"

"A lifetime! That's what it felt like over these last few days!"

"I promise to make it up to you. All of you."

I whispered, preventing the agents from listening, "What is this plan, and where are we going?"

"The plan is to get our lives back, our former lives." Tommy moved toward the agents in the front seat. "Can you drive any faster?"

Jourdain raised his fingers from the steering wheel in frustration. "I'm going as fast as I can, monsieur."

Tommy clutched my hand and pulled me into his arms. How I missed that feeling of security. He placed his hand inside his front pants pocket and pulled out my wedding rings. "I didn't leave Paris without these."

I raised my left hand so he could slip the rings back on my finger where they belonged.

The car raced down Freeway 15 and exited off the ramp to Sahara Avenue—the road that led to Rancho Circle.

"Wait. Are we going to—"

Tommy smirked.

"What are you doing, Tommy? What is this plan?"

He gave me a brief summary.

I prayed to God we wouldn't regret this.

When we reached our destination, we stopped at a booth near a closed gate. Two men in business suits stepped out, armed with pistols in their holsters. Agent Jourdain spoke broken English when he flashed his credentials and advised of the important information he had for the residents.

One of the men stepped backward a few paces to his post and made a phone call, obviously seeking authorization for us to enter through the iron gate.

With permission, Jourdain drove up the lengthy path to the desolate mansion perched at the top.

I squeezed Tommy's hand hard with worry, but he patted the top of my fingers and kissed me. "It'll be okay." He nodded definitively, though I questioned his true confidence level.

Tommy's dreary description of the Russo estate in his memoirs met my expectations. Grimly rustic from the outside with a sinister aura that could attract evil spirits. The architecture looked impeccable. The rich green grass had been recently mowed. I lowered the window and smelled the fresh aroma of orange and apricot trees.

Several vehicles were parked out front when Jourdain pulled the SUV in line behind the others.

The agents stepped outside the car, and in a protective stance, they took in the surroundings. I noticed the weapons they packed when they slipped on light jackets exhibiting the FBI insignia.

"Should we wear bulletproof vests or something?"

"This isn't TV, honey. Trust me, please."

Beauchamp walked to the front entrance alone. I couldn't see who had opened the door, but she was allowed entry. Jourdain stayed behind, standing outside our vehicle.

"She's teeing everything up for us, sweetheart. Come here." He kissed me hard. "I missed you so much. When this is over, we'll celebrate with anything you want to do. Anywhere you want to go."

"I just want you *safe*," I said, placing my head into the crook of his neck.

Jourdain glanced at his buzzing cell. He tapped on the window then opened the back door and peeped inside, announcing, "It's time."

"Here we go." Tommy took hold of my hand and held it firmly as we trailed behind Jourdain into the home where Angie Russo once resided with her infamous uncle, the late Vince Russo, the former ruler of the Russo crime family. Today, Vince's daughter, Katie, lived here with her husband, Louis Maroni.

The moment we strode through the door, gasps were heard, followed by someone saying, "Holy shit!"

I doubted the people in the room even noticed Agent Jourdain or me.

"As I live and breathe. The stories are true. Tommy Cavallo is alive." A petite woman who looked about my age, with salt-and-pepper hair, said with surprise. "You've got more lives than a precocious feline," she added in a cool, shifty tone. "After all these years and your *presumed* death, I never expected to see you in my home again."

"Hello, Katie, Louis," Tommy said with a friendly smile. His gray eyes scanned the room to see familiar faces. "Wow, Michael,

Louie, David." He pointed to Katie and Louis's three adult sons. When Angie came into view, standing in the back, he smiled at the sight of her, his first love from his younger years. "Hi, Angie. I didn't expect to see you here."

"Angie's been a great support to us during this tragic time." Katie stood beside her cousin and draped an arm around Angie's shoulder.

"What are you doing here, Tommy?" Angie asked with surprise in her voice. She knew Tommy and I had been alive and hiding in Paris—a secret she kept from her powerful Mafia family, the people who had the rationale to want Tommy dead. Angie's uncle had threatened Tommy multiple times during Tommy and Angie's relationship, especially after their affair ended. Vince Russo had been a suspect in the car bombing in 2010, the wake-up call Tommy answered, convinced he should go into hiding.

Michael began shouting, "What the hell is going on? This agent here told us there was a lead on my daughter's whereabouts. Why are *you* here, Cavallo? You've got a lot of nerve showing up right now when my family is going through hell! Did you have something to do with Caterina's disappearance?" The blond-haired man lunged at Tommy, but Agent Jourdain stepped in front of us, adding a protective layer, raising his arms, and warning Michael to back off.

A tall woman stood beside Michael, crying furiously, most likely Caterina's mother. "Please. I beg you. Please, where is our baby girl?" she murmured through tears.

Michael placed a comforting arm around his wife.

Tommy spoke rapidly, "I found your daughter, Michael. These agents with me today contacted their local colleagues to bring your daughter home to you."

Michael's wife managed a hopeful smile, wiping her eyes with a tissue.

"Where is she, Cavallo? How do you know where my daughter is if you didn't take her!" Michael yelled angrily.

"Michael, let him speak!" Angie commanded. "I know how desperate you are to get Caterina back but give him a chance."

"My wife, Vicki, has been in Vegas, so she saw the news. She told me what happened to your little girl. I had a hunch and got the right people involved to investigate. You were looking in all the wrong places. Yeah, you probably have a long list of enemies who'd want to destroy you and damage your business, but this was personal. Too personal."

Beauchamp interrupted Tommy, "Agents are approaching the scene."

"Scene? What scene?" Michael desperately asked.

Beauchamp raised a hand for him to be patient.

CHAPTER 43

Reconciling

The white Ford Focus contained two suitcases, a diaper bag, and young Riley Frederickson, according to the fake passport and birth certificate he had created.

The air felt thick and balmy. Their new life over the border in Canada would be much cooler than the sticky Nevada heat. He was about to carefully buckle Riley into the car seat in the back but realized he had left behind the unicorn stuffed animal she loved. His plan worked perfectly so far, and he was prepared to leave for the airport ten minutes ahead of schedule. Going back inside the log cabin in the woods for her favorite toy was worth avoiding a temper tantrum later.

"Come on, Riley. Let's get your unicorn."

She fidgeted with insistence to get down and walk, squiggling from his grasp.

"All right, Riley." He placed her down gently but coerced her to hold his hand. "You've got to stay close to me, Riley." He spoke her new name constantly so she'd adapt to it.

He opened the door and entered. His eyes perused the den in search of the fluffy white unicorn with the rainbow horn.

Riley let go of his hand and trotted to the kitchen as he searched for the toy. Maybe it was in the bedroom, he wondered as his tall frame moved quickly. She might have to do without it on this trip if he couldn't find it in the next couple of minutes. He lifted the crib mattress and the blanket curled up on the floor. He checked the closet. No sign of the unicorn. Well, it looked too girly, anyway. Riley had to be a boy on this journey.

He trekked into the den, but the toddler escaped his sight. "Riley!" he called out loudly. "Where'd you go?" He left her alone for only a moment. His head swerved to the open front door. Alarmed, he raced outside to witness her twirling in circles near a purple azalea shrub, giggling through the dizzy sensation in the warm sun. "There you are. You can't wander off like that." His voice sounded angry, causing the little girl to rub her eyes and wiggle her chin. He picked her up and ambled back to the front door to secure the lock when the sound of a distant car was detected, traveling nearer.

His head whipped to the driveway. His eyes focused on a sedan pulling up. Then another sedan, and another.

The hunters found their prey.

He picked up the tot, dashed inside, and locked the door.

All he could do was pace in a circle, bouncing the toddler nervously, and wondering how they figured it out. How did they know who he was and where to find him?

*****

"I'll ask you again, Cavallo. Who...has...my...daughter?"

"Your father," Tommy calmly spoke, staring directly into Michael's black eyes.

Michael's head swerved toward Louis, the man he considered to be his father, confused.

"That's absurd! I didn't kidnap my granddaughter," Louis angrily retorted.

"Not *you*, Louis. Brett Corbyn, Michael's *biological* father," Tommy expressed with confidence.

"Brett? He hasn't been involved in Michael's life—ever," Katie bellowed.

Tommy shrugged a bit smugly. "Maybe that's the problem. It seems that Brett attempted to make contact, but you never let him see Michael when he was growing up."

"He never tried when Michael was a baby!"

"Yeah, well, he was recovering from a near-death experience in 1971, before Michael's birth."

Tommy didn't go into any further details, but he revealed in his memoirs that Vince Russo had to get even with the high school basketball player who got his daughter pregnant and didn't want to bear the responsibility of fatherhood back then. So Vince allegedly took his life's dream away, having him beaten so severely; it took him years to recover. Brett Corbyn never played basketball again and never had a chance to get to know the son he created.

Katie stared at the agents. "Is this true? You've confirmed Brett Corbyn has my granddaughter?"

Beauchamp gazed at her phone. "We believe this, Mrs. Maroni. If it weren't for Mr. Cavallo, Corbyn might have taken the girl out of the country."

"This is crazy!" Michael ran his hands through his blond hair. "Why would he do this?"

Tommy replied, "You'll have to ask him that question, but maybe he regretted not being in your life. We have no reason to believe Caterina has been harmed. In fact, it seemed like he was taking good care of her."

Jourdain added, "Yes, we've got Corbyn on camera at Target purchasing clothing, toys, baby food, and diapers."

Angie's brown eyes widened with surprise. "Tommy? You did all this? Why didn't you call?"

Tommy sent Angie a sincere smile. "I didn't want to give any of you false hope. Not until we could prove Brett actually had her. It was just a hunch I had when I first heard of her disappearance. Once the feds thoroughly looked at Brett's life, a witness reported seeing him with a blond toddler. The FBI discovered a cabin in the woods in the same vicinity the witness mentioned that the Corbyn family owns."

"Where is he? Where's Corbyn? Give me the address!" Michael angrily ordered.

*****

If only he fought the need to go back inside and get that damn stuffed toy, they'd be on their way to the airport, headed to Vancouver.

"Riley," he said calmly. "Listen, sweetheart. I know you're too young to understand this. Too young to ever remember me."

She smiled at him and pulled off his Clippers hat.

He placed the hat on her head and played their last game of hide and seek. He tried to make the funny faces she adored, but the tears he shed averted any ounce of silliness.

A loud knocking came from the door. "Mr. Corbyn! FBI! Open up!"

Gently, he held onto Riley. "I'm your grandpa." He smoothed her shaved head with the blond tone, regretting the need to cut off her pretty curls for the trip. "Your blond hair is just like mine when I was little like you. Your daddy has our blond hair too. They never allowed me to see my son. Those people turned your dad into a criminal! A *monster*! He doesn't even acknowledge me."

"Last chance, Corbyn!"

The little one cried in fear of the vehement banging at the door.

The agents heard her cries and broke the door down. One by one, they stormed inside the room, guns drawn. They didn't have far to go when they saw Caterina Maroni comfortably sitting atop Brett Corbyn's lap, wearing his favorite basketball team's hat, seeking protection from the man who kidnapped her.

Corbyn raised his arms high in the air, taking in a final scent of his granddaughter, lulling her fears with gentle humming.

"Don't move!" someone hollered at him.

A female agent inched closer, concealing her gun, knowing her team had her covered. "There, there, sweet Caterina. I'm gonna take you to see your mommy and daddy," she said softly as she carefully lifted her off Corbyn's lap.

Corbyn's eyes caught sight of the white unicorn toy hiding behind the television. He lifted his arms higher at an agent's firm demand.

Two muscular men surged atop him, flung his body to the floor, and flipped him onto his stomach as one agent quickly cuffed his hands behind his back, securing him to the floor with his knees.

"No, wait! The toy over there. It's her favorite. Please give it to her so she won't cry," he pleaded.

The agents looked at the toy but did nothing except read Brett Corbyn his rights.

*****

Beauchamp shouted, "We've got her! Caterina is with an FBI agent. She's safe. They're taking her to Centennial Hills Hospital to be examined. You can meet her in the ER."

"Where's Corbyn?" Michael asked. His intense, thug-like expression startled me.

"He'll be going to jail for a long time, Mr. Maroni," Jourdain affirmed.

Michael took his wife by the hand. "We're getting our baby girl back today! Let's go." He looked at Tommy. His angry sneer washed away as he extended his hand in gratitude.

Tommy eagerly accepted Michael's hand and shook it. "I'm happy I could help, Michael." He gazed in the direction of Michael's brothers, Louie and David. "I know you might not remember, but you and your family were once *very* important to me. I've known you since birth."

Michael merely nodded. He pulled his car keys from his pocket and anxiously rushed out the door with his wife and brothers trailing behind.

Katie and Louis scrambled to follow their sons out the door.

"Wait...hold on a sec, please." Tommy stood before them, preventing their exit.

Katie appeared agitated, practically stomping over her own feet to bypass Tommy. "Our granddaughter needs us."

232

"Caterina will be examined first, then she'll see her parents. Katie, I'm only asking for a moment of your time."

Katie huffed but turned to remain inside.

My eyes wavered to Angie, who approached me and placed her arm around my shoulder. She whispered in my ear, "Don't look so nervous, Vicki. Tommy found Caterina, something we've not been able to do. I'll help ease any tension from my end as necessary." Her face lit up, showcasing a lovely, trusting smile.

Tommy spoke like he took center stage as everyone gathered around him. "I'm hoping to let bygones be bygones. I was once part of your family through Angie." His eyes briefly shifted in Angie's direction. "When our relationship ended, the tables turned, and your family considered me an enemy. That was years ago. Today, I helped *save* your family."

"Are you bargaining with me, using my granddaughter as leverage?" Katie asked smugly.

"If this were a bargaining chip, I would've held my knowledge about Caterina's location hostage and traded it in exchange for my safety, as well as my family's. I'd never risk a child's life, no matter who her family is or what vendettas remain from decades ago. How much longer would you have taken to find her without my help? Corbyn had a passport made for her with a different name. He planned to take her out of the country. You never would've known where she was, if she was safe, or even alive."

"I, for one, am very grateful, Tommy," Angie announced. "Katie, Louis, this is wonderful news! We owe Tommy a great deal of thanks today."

Katie's eyes moved up and down Tommy's body suspiciously.

"Katie, it's time to let go of old grudges. Caterina has been found! Let Tommy and his family have peace in their lives." Angie grasped Katie's hands, facing her stern expression.

Katie spoke to Tommy while looking into Angie's beseeching eyes. "I'm not happy about how you portrayed my family in that book you wrote."

Angie squeezed Katie's hands. "Katie, please find forgiveness in your heart for Tommy and his family. Do it for *me*."

Katie's frown turned upright. Several uncomfortable seconds passed. Her body twisted toward Tommy. "Angie's right. She's been staying here since Caterina was taken from us, keeping me calm. If Angie was able to forgive you for past sins, I suppose…I could too."

Tommy approached Katie, took her by the hand, and pulled her in, offering a generous hug that almost made the frosty woman chuckle—almost.

We said quick goodbyes in the foyer when Angie, Katie, and Louis raced out the door and headed to Centennial Hills to greet little Caterina while Tommy and I followed Beauchamp and Jourdain to their car.

"Monsieur Cavallo, we have to follow up on Brett Corbyn's arrest and complete more administrative duties than you'd care to know about. What are we to do with you and your wife now?" Jourdain asked as he turned the ignition in the SUV.

"If you could drop us off in Summerlin, that would make my day."

I rummaged through my purse to find my cell. "I must call Danny and prepare him for this wonderful surprise."

"No," Tommy said.

"What?"

"*I'll* call my son and tell him myself." Tommy lifted his hand, requesting the use of my cell.

CHAPTER 44

Upon arrival at Danny's house, the whole family paraded outside across the lawn to greet Tommy. The kids jumped up and down, holding signs, saying, "We love you, Poppy!" "Welcome Home, Poppy!" "We missed you!"

Tommy was overcome with emotion, energized to see his descendants in person. I handed him a tissue from my purse to wipe his tears before he rushed out of the FBI vehicle, greeting his family one by one. I wanted him to savor this moment, relishing every precious glimpse of the faces he hadn't seen outside of photographs and videos for nine years.

He finally met TJ and Tyler in person for the first time. "Look at these grandsons of mine!" He punched the air before the boys. "Has your dad taught you any boxing moves?"

"We like karate!" TJ shouted and started to show off some kicks while Tyler chopped away at Tommy's arm, complete with sound effects.

Kristina raced into her poppy's arms, interrupting her brothers' karate-chopping exhibition, and held onto Tommy's neck. She pulled herself back slightly and looked carefully at his face, squeezing his cheeks with her palms. "You look *old*, Poppy," she said, causing hysterics among the crowd.

"Who looks old? Me?" Tommy laughed and announced loudly for everyone to hear, "Well, I am old!" He kissed Kristina's forehead and placed her down on the grass when he made eye contact with beautiful Emma, who would turn thirteen in a couple of months.

My eyes watched the lengthy hug between Tommy and Emma intently. Tommy dried the tears that plopped from her blue eyes. He had developed an amazing connection with his firstborn grandchild. "You and me—we've got a lot of catching up to do."

Emma shook her head and released a hearty giggle.

Danny nudged Tommy along to a family of four. I hadn't met them before, but I knew who they were because of their apparent Chinese features; it was Tommy's late brother John's family. DNA evidence concluded a few years ago that Haley Beck-Wu was John's daughter. She and Danny connected and planted roots together as family and business partners in the Montgomery.

"It's so nice to meet you, Uncle Tommy," Haley said with a smile.

"Uncle Tommy. I *love* that! Boy, do I have some fantastic stories about your pop, Haley. He'd be so proud of you. I wish John had the chance to know you." He leaned in and wrapped his arms around his niece. Thinking of John often conjured a swirl of emotions.

Haley introduced Tommy and me to her husband, Richard, and their children, Elizabeth and Greyson.

Tommy embraced John's grandchildren tightly, surely feeling close to him at that moment.

He soon came face-to-face with Sadie, his ex-wife, and her partner, Hank. Tommy nodded in her direction and shook Hank's hand. He met Sadie's impassive blue eyes a second time. "It's been a long time, huh, Sadie."

Sadie whispered, "I'm glad you're alive, Tommy. Danny really needs you." Through clenched teeth, she added, "But if our grandchildren weren't here right now, I'd tell you what I really think of you for this *dying* stunt and for the *personal* details you exposed to the world in your book about my family and me!" Turning to Hank, she calmly announced, "I'm ready to go." The couple made a hasty exit.

Rather than contributing to an argument with his ex-wife, Tommy shook off her disgruntled words. He remained quiet and focused his gray eyes across Danny's lawn, watching his grandchildren, grandniece, and grandnephew running around. The girls performed backbends and cartwheels. The boys looked like they were playing a game of tag, or maybe it was football. It was hard to tell for sure. They seemed to love chasing each other.

I slipped my arm around his waist.

Tommy clapped his hands loudly for everyone to gather around him, though he had already gained everyone's attention through his commanding presence. "It's good to be home again. Usually, I'm not at a loss for words, but, uh...right now—" A tear drizzled down his cheek.

Danny came to his rescue. "Pop, I ordered a banquet of your favorite dishes. The patio is set up in the backyard. Bianca's making coffee and tea. How about we head back there, and you can breathe for a moment."

"Oh! Before news of your return to town hits the media, I've got to tell *my* family." Tony was working at Mandalay Bay. Kirk didn't answer his phone. I left messages. Aunt Lucy sounded delighted that Tommy was home with me and couldn't wait to meet him. When my brothers called me back, they were thrilled that everything worked out and Tommy was safe.

Danny pulled up a lawn chair and sat across from Tommy and me. "Pop," he whispered. "Is it really safe for you to be here? What the hell happened?"

"I'll fill you in on the details when we're alone, but yes, we're safe."

"Wait," I said in a low tone. "What about Jeffrey? You eased the tension with the Russos, but Jeffrey is on a mission to destroy us. And what about the Toscano family?"

Tommy glanced around, confirming privacy. "Did you hear about that mass shooting in Philly the other day?"

Danny and I nodded. That story made national headlines.

"According to the FBI, the most powerful Toscano captains met at the restaurant where that shooting occurred. There were no survivors. Gino Toscano died in prison back in 2013. There's nobody left in the Toscano family who'd care about me and whether I lived or died. The Russos might have something to worry about. I got the distinct feeling the FBI thinks the Russos ordered that hit, believing the Toscanos kidnapped Caterina. The Russos and Toscanos have been at war since Gino's suspicious death. Whoever may be left in the Toscano family will be too busy seeking retaliation against the Russos to think about me. Too much time has passed. Anyone I dealt with decades ago is dead."

"And Jeffrey?" I asked.

"Jeffrey's an annoying little gnat. If he wanted me dead, he had my location and could've had someone take me out in Paris. Instead, he publicly revealed our identities to hurt *you*. He doesn't have the juice to kill me. He's a crooked politician, but he's no murderer. It was either the Toscanos or the Russos."

"You made peace with the Russos, Pop? Through Angie, I'm guessing."

"It's a hell of a story, son. Let's save it for later. Tonight, I want to get reacquainted with my family." He placed his hands lovingly around Danny's face and stared at him with pride, overcome with emotion.

In every conceivable manner, the family is a
link to our past, bridge to our future.

—Alex Haley

CHAPTER 45

Waking up in Tommy's arms in the Montgomery suite gave me that sense of comfort and security I felt in Paris. We were free! Free to be together anywhere we choose. I could show off our relationship with my family and friends. We could parade around town, dine out along the busy Vegas Strip, and gamble at the Montgomery with no threat of violence hanging over our heads. We would, however, have to deal with the intrusive media for a while, unfortunately.

"Babe, I was thinking," Tommy muttered as he kissed that ticklish spot on my neck the way I adored. "Now that we can live wherever we desire, maybe I'll buy us a place here in Vegas."

"You want to leave Paris?"

"Not entirely. I'll talk to Angie about buying back that apartment and making it officially ours. We can visit Paris anytime. But let's face it, Vegas is really home with our families. The Russos *sort of* like me again," he snickered. "Not that they'd want to spend holidays with me, but we established a truce. I'll stay out of their way, and we can reestablish ourselves here."

I smiled. "I love that plan. Before we head back to Paris, you need an official introduction to my family. I know you arranged to spend the day with Danny and the kids, but tonight, I'll plan dinner with the Ursinis. They can't wait to meet you! I wish you had the opportunity to meet Sylvia."

"Yeah, babe. Me too. I look forward to getting to know the rest of the Ursini crew. I told Danny we'd be over around nine this morning. He and Bianca are arranging a brunch."

"Actually, you go ahead and spend some quality time with them first. I have a breakfast date this morning. I'll see you at Danny's when I'm finished."

"A breakfast *date*? Hmm, should I be worried?" he asked playfully.

"Yes," I said teasingly, then gasped as Tommy slipped his arm beneath my bare body and moved me on top of him. "It's not that kind of date. It's family business. There are a couple of messes that need to be cleaned up."

"You're hot when you talk about *family business*," Tommy said with that look of lust trickling from his gray eyes that made me swoon for his affection. I kissed him hard, passion exploding. We had to make up for lost time.

After we showered and dressed for the day, someone knocked hard on the door.

For the time being, Danny hired two of his best security guards to follow us around for protection.

Tommy peered through the peephole at one of the guards, who signaled it was okay to open the door. When the door swung open, Tommy burst into laughter.

I stepped a little closer to see what caused his sudden amusement.

"Hey, hey, hey, Tommy C. in the flesh!" Rob Lubitski shouted as he and his brother made their way inside our suite.

"Rob! Jack! It's great to see you guys. Do you remember Vicki, my wife?"

I approached the Lubitski brothers, Tommy's former business partners, for a playfully informal greeting. They welcomed me with open arms.

"Someone else followed us up here to say hello," Rob said. He stepped aside, allowing Tommy's former assistant to be seen, wearing an enormous smile.

"Phyllis!" Tommy shouted before squeezing his arms around her petite frame, lifting her off her feet.

She barely had a chance to catch her breath at the sight of his presence. "I had to come up here and see you for myself. I couldn't believe it when I heard you were alive." Phyllis approached me and draped her arm around my neck, leaving a peck on my cheek.

"Danny contacted us. We thought you'd like a ride to Summerlin this morning."

"What's this? Chauffeuring during your retirement years? The Montgomery didn't leave you enough retirement funds," Tommy joked.

"Hey, at least we kept the place afloat after your disappearing act." Jack laughed.

"I can tell you're going to have an entertaining drive to Danny's house," I said.

"Aren't you coming, Vicki?" Rob showed off his genuine smile when he stopped me.

"I wouldn't dream of interfering with your reunion this morning, fellas. I've actually got somewhere to be." I pointed to the two security officers. "Which one of you is my shadow this morning?"

Tommy rushed toward me, offering a warm hug and sensual kiss. "I'll see you in a little while."

"I promise I won't be too far behind you."

"I've got some work to do, but I expect you to stop by and say hello to the new team in charge," Phyllis insisted as she pointed her finger at Rob and Jack. "*Their* offspring, Bobby and Rebecca, and of course, me. I'm still helping them run the place!"

"Come here, Phyllis. Give me another hug."

When Tommy finally released Phyllis from his arms, she joined my guard and me on the brief walk to the elevator. I couldn't help but smile wide, listening to the hysterics from the suite. Tommy reuniting with two of his best friends made me abundantly happy.

CHAPTER 46

I sat at an end booth in the café on the first floor of the Montgomery. I looked forward to meeting up with Tommy at Danny's home. Tommy promised he'd ease the children's heavy hearts by answering their questions as best as possible, keeping his responses at a PG level for the kids.

My bodyguard, Andre Manning, a tall African American man with a stocky build, stood in front of the booth, displaying broad shoulders and thick arms in a crossed position. He looked tough as nails but spoke with a friendly, smooth-sounding voice.

The aroma of pancakes and maple syrup filled the air. As delicious as it smelled, I only ordered a cup of tea that was boiling hot. I let it steep for a few moments when I noticed my breakfast companion inching her way near me. The pretty lady waved in my direction. Her blond hair was pulled back in a French braid with the end hanging over her shoulder. She looked confused when Andre stepped out in front of her.

"She's okay, Andre. Thank you."

Andre nodded and allowed her to walk toward me, then he moved back to his protective stance with his back facing me, surveilling our surroundings.

"Good morning," she said before she took the seat across from me.

"Thank you for meeting me here, Tara. I'm glad you were available."

"I dropped off Fiona, my daughter, at her friend's house for the day. I've got some time before my shift starts. I'm curious why you contacted me at work yesterday, so eager to talk."

"I didn't realize you had a daughter. How old is she?"

"Ten going on thirty." She laughed and rolled her eyes.

I smiled. "Sounds like a typical preteen. You know, I would've come to see you directly, but I'm sure you've watched the news." I pointed to Andre's back, alluding to the fact that security was of the essence. "I *hate* to pry when it comes to my brothers' *friendships*, but with so many unusual revelations we discovered after our mother's passing, I decided I needed to stick my nose in a place where it doesn't really belong. I know that night you and Kirk had dinner together ended in disaster. The charges against him were just a misunderstanding."

"I figured that was the case. I just don't get it," Tara said with her hand covering her lips.

I shook my head. "You see, we found that money in our mother's house. None of us had any idea it was fake. It looked so real, albeit *old* bills."

Her shoulders drooped. "I'm not talking about the money, Ms. Ursini."

"Please, call me Vicki."

Tara smiled and nodded. "I knew there had to be more to that story, but Kirk never returned my calls. I really liked him and hoped to get to know him better. I wondered if he had an issue because I'm a single mother. Fiona's father is active in her life. We're just no longer together. I'm not looking for a *daddy* for her."

Suddenly, I grew flustered. Did Kirk decide Tara wasn't the one for him, or was he embarrassed by being handcuffed in front of her at that posh restaurant? If Kirk didn't respond to Tara's messages, this impromptu meeting would soon turn incredibly awkward. "Tara, we were raised by a single mom. I highly doubt your daughter is an issue." No matter what Kirk's problem was, I didn't believe for a second that he wouldn't date a single mother.

From the corner of my eye, I observed Kirk heading in our direction. He gave a thorough once-over to Andre, who awaited my signal to let him through. When Kirk moved around the enormous man, he sent me a confused grin about my unexpected bodyguard. When he noticed Tara sitting across from me, his eyes bulged. "Tara?"

Tara rustled in her seat, wearing a sheepish grin, when she looked at him.

I jumped out of the booth, unsure what to do at this distressing moment. "Kirk, hi. Please, join us."

He barely said a word but gazed at Tara, whose porcelain skin turned beet red.

Tara's fingers trembled. She moved them beneath the table atop her lap and twisted her head away.

I moved a few steps from the table and Tara to speak somewhat privately to Kirk. "I asked Tara to meet me here. She didn't know you were coming. I'm sorry I interfered."

Kirk's eyes remained focused on Tara. He ignored my convoluted explanation and apology. "Tara, it's good to see you," he said politely in a cool but positive tone.

Her head flung toward him, and she smiled genuinely.

Kirk pointed to the beige cushioned seat where Tara sat. "May I?"

She scooted further in to give him enough room to sit beside her—a good sign.

A waitress approached our table to take our order. "Uh, I've got someplace to be. Kirk, Tara, stay and order whatever you'd like." It didn't seem that they heard me.

I caught the waitress's attention with a slight wave of my hand. "Charge their breakfast to my suite, please." I gave her the room number, then tapped Andre's shoulder. "My work here is done. Time to meet up with my husband." Even after an amazing night together, I hungered to be close to Tommy again. I stopped and glanced up at Andre. "Oh, I don't have a car today."

Andre smiled. "I'll drive you, ma'am."

I attempted to say goodbye to Kirk and Tara, but they were chatting so nicely that I decided not to disrupt them.

CHAPTER 47

Classic rock music blared from Danny's patio. The sound of Kiss's popular tune, "Rock and Roll All Nite," played, but there was something unfamiliar about it. When I scurried to the backyard with Andre a safe distance behind me, I realized they had set up a karaoke machine. Good Lord, Tommy was singing—terribly!

TJ and Tyler plugged their ears and narrowed their eyes at the rancid noise.

Emma laughed while Kristina shouted, "Poppy, stop!"

Tommy intentionally sang worse than usual just to make them laugh.

TJ chased Tommy around the patio, attempting to steal his mic.

I witnessed Bianca laughing and teasing Tommy about his lack of musicality.

Jack and Rob Lubitski didn't stick around. They respected that Tommy needed some quality time with his family, but they promised to plan a guy's night out so he could reconnect and reminisce with his pals.

TJ and Tyler talked about a little league baseball game they wanted their poppy to attend. Kristina started guitar lessons and played some notes of a ballad she'd been practicing. We praised her talent as she plucked at the chords. Emma coyly mentioned a gymnastic event she'd be competing in next month. She didn't come out and ask, but Tommy said he wouldn't miss it for the world, which made her smile.

Danny coordinated a tag football game. Bianca and I committed to a cheerleader role. Tommy jumped right in for a friendly game with his son and grandchildren until the heat became too insufferable. We all slipped on swimsuits and plunged into the refreshing pool.

The day seemed perfect. I felt bad when the time came to leave.

The boys had a little meltdown when Tommy started to hug them all goodbye. He gathered his family together. "I know I've been gone a long time. And yes, Vicki and I eventually have to head back to Paris…briefly. We're going to search for a house close by."

"You're moving back to Vegas permanently, Pop?"

"That's fantastic!" Bianca clapped her hands, kissed Tommy on the cheek, and hugged him tightly.

"We plan to keep the apartment in Paris, but yes, Vegas is and always will be our home. All of you are my home…my heart." He pointed to each of his grandchildren and flicked Kristina on the nose, causing her to giggle. "You can't get rid of me even if you tried! So no sad faces because we've got to go right now, okay? We'll see you soon. That's a promise."

CHAPTER 48

Since Tony had the day off, I asked him to pick up the trays of eggplant rollatini, stuffed sole, and a garden salad I ordered from Ricciardi's Ristorante for dinner this evening. He offered to pick up Aunt Lucy too.

Introductions to Tommy went smoothly, and the food tasted delectable. Italians always eased into conversation over good food and pleasant company. Tommy went out of his way to ensure Aunt Lucy was comfortable. He kept refilling her plate with food and her mug with tea.

"Oh, boy, you'll have to roll me out of here. I'm so stuffed!" Aunt Lucy giggled and snorted, causing laughter among the rest of us.

"You've got her laugh, babe," Tommy cited with witty appeal.

I smiled and released a slight snort, triggering an eruption of laughter and more teasing. Instinctively, I raised my hand to play-fully slap him as Aunt Lucy released a series of snorts.

Tony made martinis for Kirk and himself the way Sylvia liked them. As they sipped from the rims, Aunt Lucy said, "I used to love a good martini. *The dirtier, the better!* Shouldn't drink 'em anymore with all the medication I'm on."

"One won't hurt you, Auntie. You aren't driving," Tony said.

I signaled him a firm no, but my aunt perked up and said, "Make me one, Tony. It won't kill me."

Tony turned to fix her a drink, and I whispered, "Easy on the alcohol. She could get light-headed."

"She can indulge this one time."

Tommy and Tony went back and forth, sharing wild casino stories.

"Tony, if you ever get tired working at Mandalay Bay, I've got connections at the Montgomery."

Tony shook Tommy's hand. "I'll keep that in mind, Tommy. Thanks."

Kirk sipped the strong martini Tony made and said, "Hey, when I called you that day in Paris to tell you about Mom's car accident, you canceled a vacation. Where were you going?"

"Ahh, China—Beijing, Shanghai, Hong Kong," I conveyed with a sigh.

"I rescheduled our vacation for next year, March 2020," Tommy announced.

My lids raised in surprise. "You did?"

"March seems far away right now, I know, but at the time when I rescheduled it, I wasn't sure you'd be able to get more time off from work this year after this leave of absence you took. Now that we plan to move back to Vegas—"

"Actually, I quit my job at the museum this morning."

Tommy's head jolted toward me. "You quit?"

"I love our families and *you* more." I turned to address the others. "Like Tommy said, we will buy a house in Vegas. Paris will be a beautiful place we *visit*. Las Vegas is home. I'd have to quit my job anyway. Besides, Jeffrey contacted the people I worked with to confirm the alias I used, and with all the press about Rodney Kettner, I'm not sure the Musée d'Orsay would have allowed me to remain employed. I'm afraid that man's name will be deeply stitched into our lives for a long time. Maybe forever."

"That pig deserved more than a hammer to his head!" Aunt Lucy mumbled between sips of the dirty martini she swiftly consumed.

My head snapped in her direction. "You mean Kettner? What hammer?"

Silence occupied the room until Kirk's deep voice rang out, processing what our aunt had just said. "Aunt Lucy, the police didn't release any details about the murder weapon. The news never speculated it was a *hammer*."

"Jeez, you acted like you never heard of Rodney Kettner. Why did you lie?" I asked, quite outraged.

Aunt Lucy's fingers swept across her lips. Her cheeks flushed as her body stirred in her seat.

"Aunt Lucy, what do you know? You've got to tell us!" Tony's voice elevated, but he didn't want to yell at our frail aunt.

"Oh!" she puffed, then covered her mouth with her hand, realizing the alcohol made her slip. "Your mother was never involved with Rodney Kettner." She paused to catch her breath. "I was."

I gasped. Kirk and Tony's mouths dropped. Tommy raised his brows.

"My sister knew about my relationship with Rod. Uh, he turned out to be such a disappointment, but he paid me attention at a time when I needed it. Gary left me, and…well, let's just say I had trouble coping with the travesty of divorce. I lived alone in that house filled with memories of Gary, constant reminders of the devastation I suffered, failing at marriage.

"Rod got himself into some trouble, working for some mob types. I knew about the money he made and helped him stash some of it away. He'd make the money and sell it to some wise guy who funneled it through a few casinos. I found the danger rather exhilarating! Your mom knew something about living a fast life. I had finally started to experience that *rush*! But I never dreamed of the consequences to come.

"When Syl realized Rod was using me to hide his dirty money, she knew where to find him. She confronted him and warned him to stay away from me and to leave me out of his crimes." Aunt Lucy let out a quick snicker. "Sylvia was always the star in the family. Nobody *ever* noticed me. I was the quiet, shy one, but we looked so much alike. Syl was well-known in town as the Flamingo's exotic dancer, the single mom, and the hostess at the Flamingo's nightclub.

"The night they arrested Rodney is the same night Syl gave him hell and warned him to stay away from me. She didn't tell the cops anything about me or that I was really Rod's girl. She protected me like a big sister does. I was a bit *fragile* in those days, and I hadn't been diagnosed with MS or bipolar yet. Fortunately, the police let Sylvia go. They assumed she'd been dating Rod because she matched the description of his girlfriend. Me!

"Syl and I argued for days about it. She didn't want me living alone anymore. I guess she didn't trust me to make good decisions. So I moved in with your grandparents. When Rodney got out of jail, he searched for me, but I had sold the house Gary and I lived in. He tracked Syl down because he couldn't find me. He wanted me and his money, which I had hidden in a laundry bag and stashed in my closet at your grandparent's house. Syl didn't have the money the night Rodney showed up looking for me and his loot. I had it.

"He got really angry with your mother and attacked her for not telling him where to find me. He threatened he'd be back if she didn't tell him. Thankfully, you boys were little then and spent the weekend with your grandparents. Victoria, you were living on campus.

"Pastor Gordon arrived to see Sylvia the night Rodney showed up unannounced. Apparently, Gordon walked into the house and witnessed Rodney hurting your mother. Rod had her body pinned to the kitchen table, and he started strangling her until she told him where to find me. She almost *died* to protect me that night. Thank God Gordon got there when he did. He picked up the first thing he noticed sitting on the counter, a hammer, and whacked Rodney on the back of his head. Gordon didn't have a reason to be visiting Sylvia, a single mother and one of his parishioners, so late at night. He and Sylvia dug Rod's grave. They should've given more thought to where to dig, but they didn't want to bury the body where it bordered the neighbors' property lines, and they couldn't risk being discovered driving with a body in the trunk of a car.

"They both feared being part of a scandal. Gordon saved your mother's life. In a way, he saved mine too. Gordon counseled Sylvia, always telling her that they did what they had to do to protect their love and me. He killed the man to defend Sylvia. To help her see the blessing that she survived a near-death experience and that his love rescued her, he planted that peony plant. Peonies were her favorite flower. Those delicate buds grew into elegant blossoms—an endearing image for Sylvia to acknowledge the beauty of the love she had for Gordon…and me. That man put his own life, career, and freedom on the line to protect us.

"Those flowers symbolize love and loyalty. That's why your mother nurtured them. Rodney's death was another reason she couldn't tell you that Gordon was your father, Kirk. I'm sorry, but I had to protect your mother and Gordon."

My aunt's description of events was like finding that one missing wedge in a million-piece puzzle. Kirk made eye contact with me, surely sharing the same thoughts I had, following our recent visit to Gordon at the nursing home.

Aunt Lucy continued, "I hate that Rodney's bones were found, bringing up such a tortured memory from the past. I hate it even more that your mother is the number one suspect." Her dark eyes, moist and red, swayed to Kirk. "It's my fault Rodney Kettner entered our lives at all. And I don't want Gordon's name dragged through the mud now, Kirk. His mind isn't good. He saved your mother's life. Would it do anyone good to tell the truth now?"

Kirk said, "I hate that our mother's name has been portrayed negatively in the news. People will always think the worst. Mom kept this secret for decades! I doubt she'd want this to come out now, especially if it hurt Gordon. Their affair's already been outed, but murder—even in self-defense—is a completely different circumstance she wouldn't want us to validate. Let the cops suspect all they want. Nobody knows the truth…except for us."

"I agree with you, Kirk, but *only* because it's what Mom would want. She could've told Georgina about her affair with Gordon years ago to split up his family to have him for herself. She *never* did that. She protected Gordon because he was the love of her life. She was far from perfect, but she ensured Gordon and Kirk bonded through the church, even if no one else could know he was Kirk's father."

Tony added, "I don't like that the gossips in town will think cynically about Mom, but I agree—we need to honor her by keeping this quiet."

"I have a question," Tommy asked. "Aunt Lucy, how did the counterfeit money end up in Sylvia's house before she died?"

My aunt shook her head and shrugged. "Well, after Rodney's death, Sylvia took it from me. She said she'd destroy it. I handed her the laundry bag containing a hundred thousand dollars in counterfeit dough and about the same amount in casino chips."

Kirk shrieked. "We only found around ten grand and a couple thousand in chips."

"Are you positive of that amount, Aunt Lucy?" Tony asked.

"Look, kids. I've got MS, bipolar, and high blood pressure. I'm old, weak, achy, and numb, but my mind is still sharp. There was a hundred grand in that laundry bag in cash and another hundred grand in poker chips. Syl said she'd destroy it for me. As far as I knew, she had. I was nearly as surprised as you were to learn she still had some of it in this house."

"Where'd the rest of it go?" A question I asked that we might never get an answer to.

CHAPTER 49

Waking up the following day, I realized I had slept serenely through the night with Tommy by my side and without melatonin. My body twisted to feel the warmth of Tommy's flesh. As my arm stretched out, absently patting the empty side of the bed, I raised my lids. A faint sound of whispers was heard from the other room. I sat up, stretched, and yawned, then reached for my bathrobe before shuffling to the other room to observe Tommy speaking with Phyllis. "Good morning."

"Did we wake you?" Tommy asked as he approached me for a morning kiss.

"Sorry, Vicki." Phyllis played with her fingers. Her brown eyes darted around the room.

"You were sleeping so soundly. I closed the bedroom door. I didn't have the heart to disrupt you."

My eyes flowed back and forth between the two, suspecting something was up. "So what's going on? Phyllis wouldn't be here at… eight in the morning." It suddenly occurred to me that I hadn't slept this late in ages.

"I'll let you two talk privately." Phyllis glanced at Tommy. "You let me know what you want to do next."

Tommy returned a firm nod and scratched his head. "Thanks, Phyllis," he said as she left our suite.

"What aren't you telling me?"

"Phyllis called. You slept through the ringing," he said to distract me.

"And?"

He sighed. "The media is outside the hotel, blocking every entrance."

"Well, we knew they'd want a statement from the reincarnated man."

"Atkins is out there, firing up his supporters, wanting to prove my book is fiction, citing fraud charges, and blaming *me* for his election loss years ago." He rolled his eyes.

I darted to the window to peek at the rallying crowd below, saying, "There won't be any charges. We're covered under our deal with the FBI."

"That can't go public."

"We can't be holed up inside forever either. What's our next move?" I asked.

"I think I need to try something new and different—like honesty."

"Can you be honest without telling the masses that you gave up the Toscanos for our freedom?"

"Okay, honesty *with limits*. Why don't you shower and change for the upcoming insurgence while I jot down my thoughts and call Danny for legal advice."

Danny's instant response was to wait for him to arrive and brief us on what we should or shouldn't say. We were concerned Jeffrey might incite a riot, especially when we learned he held a bullhorn, riling the crowd.

*****

Our bodyguards walked beside Tommy and me as Danny escorted us through the corridors to the east side entrance of the Montgomery, where reporters were advised to wait for us. We hoped to give this one interview, one time, so we could move on with our lives. It would be inevitable that the paparazzi would follow us around for a while.

Tommy looked handsome in a dark-blue Versace suit we had delivered from the men's clothing store in the shopping mall attached to the Montgomery.

We trailed behind Danny to the podium at the top of the stairway that overlooked a perfectly manicured lawn with a colorful rose garden in shades of pink, red, and white. A layer of security guards stood in formation at the bottom of the steps, leaving hardly a hairline gap of space between them. Danny positioned himself on Tommy's left side while I stood on his right in a maroon and black dress, feeling anxious.

Cameras snapped.

My eyes squinted from the blinding sun. I envisioned Sylvia uttering, "Smile, Victoria, so the camera captures your charm and beauty."

"Good morning!" Tommy spoke into the microphone with a hearty, fresh tone. "It's so good to see you all again after my...*hiatus.*"

Many people chuckled at the vivacious energy Tommy projected to his audience.

Some booed.

He held up his novel, *Love Affair: Tommy's Memoirs,* with the stunning cover, showcasing brushstrokes of orange and yellow that coated the sky at sunset, overlooking the Vegas Strip, displaying the Eiffel replica at the Paris Hotel. "My book sure made a lot of noise in this town." He chuckled. "Allow me to clear up a few things. The details in my book are as accurate as they are entertaining. My point was to do just that—*entertain* people through authentic experiences."

A reporter shouted, "We're glad you're alive, Mr. Cavallo, but your book stresses your *death.*"

"No," Tommy stated matter-of-factly. "My book acknowledges my belief that someone *wanted* to kill me. Yes, I named some people who topped my list of suspects. You know about the car bomb and the death threats I received. That's all true, and no one has been held accountable for those incidents and the threats against my family. But my published memoirs never outright stated that I passed away. My story ends with the final statement: *This is the end of Tommy's memoirs and life as he knew it.* A true statement. My life as Tommy Cavallo ended, and a completely different lifestyle and identity emerged."

"You were declared dead! A medical doctor signed a death certificate." Jeffrey blurted out through a bright red bullhorn that matched his tie to ensure his voice radiated over the herd that monopolized the entire front lot of the Montgomery. "You were legally...pronounced...*dead*, Cavallo! You're a complete fraud, and you should be behind bars!"

"Mr. Atkins, glad you could make my *welcome home* party." Tommy smiled, knowing all the attention had shined on him. It seemed he missed the powerful glow the spotlight bestowed.

Danny warned Tommy not to let Jeffrey goad him. Remaining calm and never referring to him as the *former governor* would hurt Jeffrey more. Calling him Mr. Atkins was a polite dig.

"There were legal avenues I pursued to protect my family and me from harm. I *feared* for my life. I can't help that the media and my audience of readers took my memoirs and the announcement of my presumed death to heart and created a work of fantasy fiction. I had no control over what journalists published and implied after they read my memoirs. Because I thought my life and my family's lives were in jeopardy, I chose to go into hiding for protection from my enemies. Changing my name and leaving my former life behind was a choice I made, funded by my personal bank account and within my rights as someone who had been savagely threatened by an unknown assailant. A necessary, legal precaution that probably *saved* my life."

Another reporter asked, "Mr. Cavallo, have any threats been made against you since your identity was exposed? Was the perpetrator revealed?"

"I discussed my unique situation with law enforcement. Because Mr. Atkins publicly exposed me, I can only hope my family and I remain safe. My personal attorney—" he tapped Danny's shoulder— "is working on reclaiming my former life and name for me to legally use again. I was honest with the FBI. They're not charging me with fraud or any other crime. People read too much into the details of my book and created a false narrative. Now I appreciate and respect the press and the power it yields. Media personalities manage to shape the perspectives of viewers. Documentaries were written, citing theories on who killed me and why. I couldn't believe the reaction my story garnered."

"Based on your book and your death certificate, Cavallo!" Jeffrey hollered through that infuriating bullhorn. "Again, you committed fraud. I will personally see to it that you are held accountable for your crimes."

"It's so interesting that you use the phrase *based on* my book, Mr. Atkins. Yes, my memoirs focused on my life story and my personal thoughts about the death threats I received. I had no *proof* of who was behind the threats or if those situations were mere accidents. But everyone else wanted to solve my *death* and point fingers at the alleged suspects. In fact, you were a suspect, Mr. Atkins, *based on* the words written in my book."

"Did your memoirs lie about your criminal connections? Or when you indicated that you formulated a plan to seek revenge on me and steal from me while having an affair with my wife?"

Tommy's jaw twitched the moment Jeffrey referenced me. "My memoirs are based on *facts* like the way you blackmailed Victoria, forcing her to stay married to you, and the illegal funds that went into your campaign for governor years ago." Tommy's eyes drifted away from Jeffrey to face the crowd. "When Mr. Atkins was governor, he threatened to ruin my business when he learned Vicki and I fell in love. My memoirs are based on indisputable facts. If law enforcement had hard evidence about my business affiliations, my former business partners and I would've gone to prison decades ago. As far as Vicki and me, our affair happened. It wasn't an ideal circumstance, but it also wasn't illegal. Nor was any plan we discussed to free her from her marriage to Mr. Atkins."

"You think I'm here because of Victoria Ursini, seeking revenge? For what? Vicki brought me nothing but problems between her theft of that Pissarro painting and her mental health problems. The woman suffers from bipolar disorder."

I gulped. I had never publicly addressed the condition I lived with. Jeffrey couldn't sink any lower, exposing a personal battle I had worked hard to manage. This genetic disposition I inherited and the struggles I went through were horrific until medication put me back on track.

Tommy's happy look quickly transformed into a frown. In his memoirs, he revealed a lot of personal information but nothing about the vile, mood-altering condition I dealt with.

I stepped in front of Tommy calmly and reached for the microphone. Through a bright smile, I could hear Sylvia's voice telling me, "Reach for the stars, despite their distance, and never give up." I cleared my throat. "Jeffrey, you have every right to bring your concerns to the police. I encourage you to do whatever you feel is necessary. Since you're using Tommy's memoirs as evidence, how about I quote a few important lines from his story that highlight his true fears."

I opened Tommy's book and turned to chapter 7 first, stating, "If the mob didn't get what they wanted, they'd destroy the Montgomery, and we'd be *lucky to remain breathing*." I skipped to chapter 13 next, announcing, "If I could find a way to be rid of my partners, I would—*unless they had me killed*." Next, I flipped to chapter 26 to recite, "I didn't have a choice *unless I preferred death*."

A few people gasped.

I kept going. "They embezzled money, skimming the casino *against my will*. Tommy also states, '*If I wanted to survive, I couldn't stop the Toscanos.*'" I stared directly into the flashing red dot of a TV camera, bathing in the warmth the luscious spotlight emitted. "I can continue quoting this book, filled with the terrifying ordeal Tommy lived through. As for me, I'm far from perfect. I've made mistakes. Yes, I was diagnosed with bipolar disorder, which I faithfully take medication to control now. Having a mental health condition is nothing to be ashamed of if you seek help and maintain a healthy regimen, as I do today. Tommy mentioned our cooperation with the FBI. They are not filing any charges. Their investigation concluded, and we are free to get back to our lives. If you have concerns about how the FBI handled this case, you can certainly talk to them."

Jeffrey's face matched the shade of his red tie, mortified and angry.

"Ms. Ursini!" A reporter shouted.

I pointed in her direction, encouraging her to ask a question.

"What's next for you and Mr. Cavallo? Will you return to acting? Go back to Paris?"

"As long as Tommy and I are together, we'll make any place we land home. I'm excited to see where our life will take us." I grabbed Tommy's hand. "I've got the love of my life by my side, and we'll continue to create a splendid future *together*."

Jeffrey forcefully disrupted the friendly Q&A, blowing smoke through that menacing bullhorn. "Did the police solve who killed Rodney Kettner? The man buried in your mother's yard? Your mother is their number one suspect."

Calmly, I replied, "I'm sure Metro will make a statement if they solve the mystery surrounding that man's death. Sylvia Ursini is innocent unless *proven* guilty."

Danny approached the microphone. "That's all the time we have for today, folks. Thank you for coming."

I took over the microphone to make one final statement. "Jeffrey, I hope you find peace and happiness in your life." My smile oozed sincerity. I meant what I said, even if I laid it on a bit thick. Perhaps if Jeffrey found passion in something other than vengeance, he'd move on with his life and forget all about me.

The reporters began spouting questions, but they weren't for Tommy or me.

"Mr. Atkins, how do you feel about revealing Tommy's whereabouts and his classified identity that could cost him his life? You could've put him and Ms. Ursini in grave danger."

"Mr. Cavallo stated that everything in his book is accurate. Mr. Atkins, can you explain your involvement in the threats made against him and extorting Ms. Ursini?"

"Former Governor Atkins, please describe your affiliation with members of the Russo crime family, who allegedly supported your campaign years ago financially."

"Do you still plan to run for governor in four years?"

We left Jeffrey in defense mode. He became the bull's-eye for target practice as our security detail escorted Danny, Tommy, and me back inside the Montgomery.

"He did not expect you to turn the tables on him. Excellent job, sweetheart!" Tommy smiled at me with pride.

"I can only hope this will force him to leave us alone now. Let him focus on his next political campaign or anything else."

Danny was rapidly texting someone. "My PI, Wayne, wants to stop by later this afternoon and meet you in person, Vicki. He has info on those two men you inquired about."

CHAPTER 50

I was slightly startled when a herculean man strolled inside our suite, dragging his cowboy boots behind Danny, towering well over six feet. His delightful smile tapered his rough look, putting me at ease.

"Wayne Zullo, this is my father, Tommy Cavallo."

"It's a pleasure to meet you, sir." Wayne nodded, stuffing his hands in his pockets. Danny advised us that Wayne was a germophobe who never shook hands.

"His wife, Vicki Ursini."

"Hello, Wayne. It's nice to meet you. I appreciate all the work you've put into helping locate Gary Connors. And now I hear you've got information on Marco Fiore and Rodney Kettner. I'm anxious to find out what you learned."

Wayne followed us to the living room area of our suite. Tommy and I sat together on the loveseat. Danny sunk into an armchair.

"Please take a seat," I insisted because Wayne remained standing. "Can I get you something to eat or drink?"

"No, thank you," Wayne said as he sat on the tan sofa opposite Tommy and me. He pulled out his folder and perused the documents. "Marco Fiore. This was tough. Had to go about it old-school-like."

"I like this guy." Tommy chuckled.

Wayne grinned and continued, "Fiore seemed to fall off the face of the earth. He made a lot of enemies, especially after swindling his boss. His wife *hated* him. I'm talking pure, venomous hate. He wasn't the faithful type. Never home. Gambled with their savings. One day, she said, he never came home, and she was pretty happy about that. I found the police report his wife filed in 1962. He's listed as a missing person, but no record of him ever being found."

"His remains are probably restrained at the bottom of Lake Mead," Tommy surmised.

"Or he changed his name to hide from his enemies. Frankly, his wife's a strong suspect if he was murdered. She detested the man," Wayne added. "She filed papers to declare Fiore deceased in 1965 so she could remarry."

"Could he still be alive?" I questioned.

"There's no proof of his actual death, just legal paperwork. Sorry, I couldn't give you anything more tangible."

"That's okay, Wayne. It's something," I said aloud as my brain digested these details. I took a moment to compose myself, worried I might not uncover the truth about my paternity.

Wayne opened another folder and reviewed the contents. "Then there's Rodney Kettner, arrested for a few petty crimes. He never did time until he got caught making counterfeit money. I found a connection with some local gangsters in the '60s and '70s. He'd make money for them to wash through local businesses and casinos.

"According to the police report, your mother was with him when he got busted. She was brought in for questioning but later released. She copped to being involved with Kettner but swore she had no idea about the counterfeit racket he ran. The police couldn't tie her to anything except having bad taste in men."

I couldn't help but snicker, thinking how the police reports never mentioned my aunt. Sylvia went out of her way to protect her younger, fragile sister.

"He had a business partner, a financier who looks clean from arrests. He did well for himself until his death several years ago. A guy named Perrin."

"Perrin? You mean Lance Perrin?" I screeched with surprise.

"You know him?" Tommy and Danny asked in stereo.

"Lance Perrin was my aunt Bev's husband."

"Perrin and Kettner had some kind of racket going on in the '70s. I couldn't get pertinent details, but Perrin was somehow involved with the counterfeit scam back then."

"I think I need to pay Aunt Bev a visit."

"Call her. See if she's home," Tommy suggested.

"I know exactly where she is." I paused to verify the time on my Apple watch. "It's Friday afternoon."

CHAPTER 51

Every Friday, Sylvia and Aunt Bev ate at Margaritaville within the historic Flamingo resort to keep the reflections from long ago fresh in their minds. Sylvia once told me that if either of them won big, they'd enjoy a more luxurious meal at Bugsy and Meyer's Steakhouse. Once their bellies were full, they would wander around the casino, talk to the other regulars, and play slots or roulette. It became a fun routine that made them feel youthful.

We entered the Flamingo and headed in the direction of Margaritaville, assuming Beverly continued her traditional Friday afternoon outing without Sylvia.

Tommy stopped in front of Bugsy's bar and sucked in a deep breath. "Ah, Bugsy. What a vision he had. He built the first luxurious resort in this desert, and his place still stands." He cleared his throat and said, "I was…oh, still in diapers back then. Long before your time, sweetheart."

As I smiled, I couldn't help but notice a petite woman sitting at Bugsy's bar through the dim red lights. Her short platinum hair and firm posture for a senior citizen looked familiar. I tapped Tommy's shoulder and pointed to our ten o'clock. "There she is. That's Aunt Bev."

We glided along the pink and gray carpet toward the barstools where Beverly sat, laughing loudly with a couple of gentlemen in her age range, obscuring the sounds from the ballgame airing on the TV set above.

She spotted us approaching. "Victoria!" She stood with open arms, seeking a warm embrace. Her eyes swayed in Tommy's direction. "Well, this handsome man must be the lucky fella who married you." She showed off her flirtatious grin and hugged Tommy. "Hey, boys, this is Syl's daughter, Victoria, and her husband, Tommy." She pointed to a tall, slim man dressed in a snazzy suit and tie. "This is Oscar." Next, she flicked her finger at a stubby, stockier man in a cream-colored polo shirt and khaki pants who smelled like Old Spice. "And this is Carter. Boys, this is that Tommy Cavallo character, owner of the Montgomery. The one everyone thought was dead."

The men made the connection, shook Tommy's hand, and joked about teaching them how to come back to life someday.

Tommy entertained Oscar and Carter while I whispered to Beverly, "We need to speak with you privately. I hate to break up your party, but it's important."

She nodded with suspicion and waved her hand at her friends, saying, "Buy me another drink, fellas. I've gotta talk to the kids here for a minute."

We made our way to an empty table with a few chairs positioned around it in the lounge for privacy.

Tommy snickered and whispered into my ear, "No one's called me a *kid* in decades."

Aunt Bev took a moment to hold onto the chair as she carefully sat. Her exuberant charm often shrouded her senior status, much like Sylvia. She'd never reveal to anyone the aches and pains she suffered from, judging by the slight smell of Bengay blended with her perfume. "I get the feeling bumping into you here wasn't happenstance. You could've called me."

"It's good to know you're keeping with tradition. I remembered your Friday plans with my mother. I didn't want to take you away from your fun, but I couldn't wait another day."

"Okay. What do you need?" Her eyes squinted with curiosity.

"I did some research on Rodney Kettner. You know, the man found in my mother's backyard. The man people thought was involved with her."

The color in Beverly's face began to drain.

"I know it was actually Aunt Lucy who got tangled up with him, and my mother protected her from the fallout."

Beverly leaned back against the chair in sheer silence. Her shoulders drooped.

"I learned that Kettner had a partner—your husband."

She rolled her eyes and clicked her tongue in frustration. "Victoria, you aren't a mother, so maybe you just don't get it." Beverly looked at Tommy. "You're a father, right?"

"Yes, ma'am."

"You wrote that book. How does it feel having your son know all your intimate secrets and faults?"

Tommy twisted his head and shrugged, understanding the direction Beverly traveled.

"There are some things children don't need to know about their parents' lives. Rodney Kettner was one of those things. Stop digging up dirt about your mother. Sylvia loved you more than you could ever know. Why drag the memory of her in the gutter for some matters dating back to her younger days, in need of money to raise three kids on her own? People in town judged her for never marrying after having three children. She didn't make much money working in this joint. She made more as a dancer, but as she aged, she couldn't do that job anymore. How else could she support her family? I mean, your grandparents were very generous when it came to helping both their daughters and you kids, but they weren't wealthy."

"Aunt Bev, I'm not here to tarnish my mother's name or judge her. I just want to understand what happened. I learned that Lance was Kettner's partner, and the money my brothers and I found was only a small portion of it. Where did the rest of it go?"

She huffed, peeked over her shoulder, and whispered, "Lance managed the casino here at the Flamingo back in the day. That's how we met. Mr. Carlino was the big boss then. The kind of guy you didn't ask questions to when he gave you an order. He wanted

Lance to act as the middleman, a protective layer between him and Kettner. Kettner brought Lance the dough for Carlino, who used his boys to wash it through other casinos in town. When Rod got pinched and sent to jail, Carlino became enraged and took it out on Lance. Jeez, what awful luck Syl had, being with Kettner when apprehended, rousing a huge problem for her. You see, Carlino had a few cops on his payroll who reported back to him. Lance's life was on the line. So was your mother's since Carlino assumed she knew about the money and where he stashed it. Because the cops released your mother, Carlino thought either she was innocent, or she gave Kettner up to take the wrap alone. And let me tell you something, Carlino *never* believed anyone was innocent.

"Carlino might've killed her if she didn't prove her worth to him. Lance convinced Sylvia to get the rest of the money from Lucy and sell it to Carlino. He'd pay for it, but Carlino had to be more cautious with the amount he purchased since the cops were still investigating Kettner's counterfeit ring. Instead of taking the entire amount, he took a few grand here and there. He bought most of the fake chips and sold them on the streets. He paid Lance 30 percent of face value, which he split with Sylvia. That was a fortune in the '70s! Every month or so, Carlino's guys came around for more chips and cash. It went on for a while until they got caught running a car theft ring in town. They all went to jail. Some were charged with more serious crimes like murder and died in prison."

"So the money left in her house was whatever Carlino didn't buy back. Why'd she keep it?" I asked.

"Carlino's soldiers went to jail, but he didn't. He went into hiding—location unknown to me. Lance worried someone might come looking for it someday. He told Sylvia to hold onto it, just in case. I knew she hid it somewhere. Obviously, that's how you found it after she died. Syl never talked about it again, and I had no interest in bringing that subject up. She *never* told me about Rodney's death." Beverly's eyes focused on her friends at the bar, chatting with a petite silver-haired woman. "That's all I know, kids. I didn't want to dishonor your mother by telling you this stuff." She turned to face Tommy. "You, of all people, know what would've happened if Lance and Sylvia rejected Carlino's demands. And if he ever sent someone to see Lance for the rest of that money, they needed to have it readily available."

Tommy nodded, looked my way, and shrugged in agreement. "I think we understand, Beverly."

"Help a lady out of this chair, will ya? That woman over there is stealing my dates!" Aunt Bev started to shuffle away but stopped in her tracks and added, "Let this go, Victoria. You've got this handsome man in your life to devote your attention to. Leave your mother's past alone."

CHAPTER 52

"Are you satisfied with what Bev told you?" Tommy asked as I pulled the Mercedes out of the Flamingo's parking lot.

"I guess it makes sense. I could see why Sylvia would want to pick up some extra money, although it was *illegal*. She could've gone to prison if she got caught. She's lucky she didn't get killed!"

"Listen, I knew of Carlino. He was a heavy hitter at the same time I worked with the Toscano family. I wasn't involved, but I know the Toscanos bought counterfeit dough in small amounts. Couldn't get caught with too much at once. If the cops caught you with too many fake bills, it'd be obvious that some illegal racket was going on. They'd make small, irrelevant purchases to prove how good of an artist the counterfeiter was. Then they'd gradually work up to more expensive merchandise or throw it down on a blackjack table at another casino.

"Your mother got swept up in the commotion to protect your aunt. Sylvia was a brave woman and maybe more loyal to her family than you give her credit for. Look, babe, I understand why you have issues with her. You didn't have a father growing up, and she kept a lot of secrets. But you had your grandfather. He was your father figure. He introduced you to art. You turned out good. You know, you've got some of Sylvia's spunk too. I love that spunk! Think about the risks you took to return the Pissarro painting to your grandfather years ago."

"Well, I wasn't taking my meds at that time."

"Okay, but what about the risks you took just to be with me? I think you're more like Sylvia than you realize."

I raced into the right lane to access the freeway.

"Whoa! Where are you going?" Tommy roared with surprise.

"We're taking a slight detour."

*****

We arrived at the Pine Rock Cemetery, pulled through the tall black iron gate, and drove through the arteries within the massive space. Tommy didn't have to ask why we were there.

I recognized the sweet acacia tree with yellow blossoms in the area where we buried Sylvia a few weeks ago. We exited the car after I parked it off to the side of the narrow road. Tommy took my hand and allowed me to lead him over the grass and markers of other deceased individuals. My heart thumped when I noticed the shiny headstone my brothers and I selected was in place, highlighting her full name and the dates of her existence. The onyx plaque looked beautiful with the simple yet eloquent caption: *Beloved Mother, Sister, Friend*.

"Mom, there's someone I'd like you to meet—my husband, Tommy."

He cleared his throat as if about to speak, then he turned his head and caught my eye. "Do you think I can have a private moment with her?" He showed his delightful smirk.

I smiled and stepped a few paces back as Tommy squatted, placed his hand on the tombstone, and bowed his head for a few moments. As he stood to his feet, I heard him whisper, "Thank you."

"Did you just thank her?"

He wrapped his arms around me. "I thanked her for raising you to become the woman you are. If it weren't for you, I wouldn't be this happy. I'm greatly indebted to Sylvia."

We strutted back to the Mercedes arm in arm until Tommy abruptly stopped. "I've been thinking."

"About?"

"I can't believe I'm saying this, but maybe it's time I retire."

"What? You swore you'd *never* say that word."

"If we're moving back to Vegas, I can't run the tour business in Paris. Remi Archambault took over since I unexpectedly left France. He's having a great time. He might buy the business or at least run it for me until I sell it. Don't worry. I'll find something to do in this town to keep me busy and out of your hair. I know you love me, but I'd probably get on your nerves at some point, turning into a complete bore."

I laughed. "One thing you're *not*, Tommy Cavallo, is boring."

CHAPTER 53

Kirk and Tony finally planned to move the hutch to Aunt Lucy's apartment. I thought I'd help set the dishes in place once the piece was settled in its new home. Finally, I'd have that chat with Aunt Lucy about getting her extra assistance or convincing her to move into an assisted living facility. Her name slowly drifted to the top of the waiting list at Summer Wind.

Tommy made plans this afternoon with his old buddies, Jack, Rob, Len, Jim, and his retired PI friend, Larry. I was thrilled he got to spend time with his friends before we returned to Paris. He promised his grandchildren we'd stick around to see Emma's upcoming gymnastic event, Kristina's music performance, and one of TJ and Tyler's baseball games. We had a lot to clean up in our Paris apartment before securing our roots back in Vegas.

Kirk completely moved into our childhood home on Orchard Lane, and it seemed that Tara would be spending a great deal of time here with her daughter, Fiona. Tara planted a lovely pair of white peony plants in the front yard on either side of the porch—a sincere act since Kirk explained Sylvia's love for the peonies that the police destroyed in the backyard. I wasn't certain how much information Kirk shared with Tara about the symbolic connection of the peonies to the loyalty and love Sylvia had for her sister and Gordon.

"Once we get this hutch out of here, I'll start painting. We picked out some new colors to make this place feel like home for all of us," Kirk explained.

"Hmm, *we* and *us?*" My widening smile caused Tara to blush. "I'm happy for you."

Tony stumbled in, carrying pizza boxes.

"We can always count on you for food, Tony." I laughed.

"Fiona, we got anchovies just for you," Kirk teased the young girl.

Fiona scrunched her nose. "Eww, I won't eat those disgusting things, Kirk."

Tony smiled at Fiona, saying, "I got you covered, Fi. Mozzarella for you." He fist-bumped her hand, spun around me, and walked briskly to the kitchen.

I followed him to catch a moment alone with my youngest brother. "How are you?"

He made no eye contact with me as he fumbled through the drawers for silverware and paper plates. "Good. Why?"

"Tony, you and Leann were together a long time."

"I'm fine. Maybe what she did to you was a wake-up call for me. One that I should've answered a long time ago."

"You stayed with Leann because you obviously loved her. Look, don't let what she did to me be the reason you don't work things out with her."

"She's selfish. She didn't give a damn what your ex would've done to you or how he'd hurt you. All she cared about was getting that frickin' commercial. I don't want her back."

"Have you talked to her?"

"Only to ask when she's moving out. She'll be out of my house next weekend. Kirk's going to have some company here until she's gone. I can't even look at her. I'm done."

"I can get you a room at the Montgomery. You'll be closer to work, and you'll have some privacy. I can easily make the arrangements. In fact, I insist."

Laughter came from the other room. Kirk and Tara were saying something cutesy and silly.

Tony smiled. "Hmm, yeah, they don't need a mopey extra wheel hanging around this place, even if it's only for a week." He dashed past me with a slice of mozzarella in hand.

I knew this breakup with Leann hurt more than he'd divulge. Tony, the brave, stoic marine, didn't show emotion like Kirk and me.

It took two strong men fifteen minutes to get the heavy hutch out the door and down the front steps. Another seven minutes to carefully place it in the back of Kirk's pickup truck that Tara and I lined with thick old blankets. Thankfully, Aunt Lucy lived on the first floor of her apartment building. They could wheel it through the main entrance on their moving cart.

Kirk stumbled onto the lawn and lay down to allow the prickly grass to cool his warm body. He playfully pulled Tara down beside him. "In another week, the ground will be dug for our new pool! Soon we'll be diving into the water anytime we want to cool off."

"I can't wait to swim," Fiona shrieked and clapped.

A dark-gray Nissan Rogue pulled into the driveway. We recognized the passengers before they stepped from the vehicle to greet us.

Kirk pushed his body up from the lawn, then helped Tara to stand beside him.

To lighten the mood, I approached Josh Steele with a smile. "Hello, Josh."

"Hi, Victoria." Josh reached out to embrace me. His hold felt awkward.

His younger brother, Drew, hugged me, saying, "It's nice to see you again, Victoria. Been a long time."

My eyes wavered toward Kirk, who didn't move from his spot on the lawn to greet his half brothers. Tony made no effort to welcome them either.

The Steele brothers must have sensed the thorny mood emitting from Kirk and Tony, receiving nothing but lengthy stares and partial grins.

Josh opened the conversation. "Kirk, we hoped to talk with you. I've called."

"I've been busy," Kirk replied with bitterness lurking in his tone.

"I see. Drew and I spoke with our father the other day."

"How is he?" Kirk asked.

Drew chimed in, "He had a few good mental health moments when we spoke. He confirmed everything you said. His love for your mother...and...you. I suspect the paternity test you took will confirm this."

"I don't have the test results yet if that's why you're here."

"No. I mean, that's not why we're here." Josh paused and stared attentively at Kirk's face. "I'm sorry. I never noticed it before."

"What's that?" Kirk asked.

Josh tapped Drew's arm and pointed at Kirk. "Your stance. Your height. The stern chin. Characteristics we Steeles have, Kirk."

Although Kirk inherited Sylvia's dark, Italian features like me, Josh's perception was accurate. Kirk stood much taller than Tony, the same six feet, two-inch height as Josh and Drew. We all instantly noticed the subtle Steele similarities.

Tara nudged Kirk, realizing they were putting in some effort, extending an olive branch.

"I guess I never noticed," Kirk muttered. He turned to Tara to introduce her. "This is Tara, my girlfriend, and her daughter, Fiona."

Josh and Drew took a moment to shake their hands.

"Kirk, if you're open to it, we plan to drive to Acorn Hill to visit Dad tomorrow afternoon. Would you like to join us?" Drew suggested, wearing a sincere smile.

"Oh. Um. Tara and I had—"

Tara shook her head and whispered, "Our plans can wait, Kirk."

Kirk contemplated, then stuttered, "I...I guess that would be okay."

"This isn't weird at all, is it?" Josh released an awkward laugh. "I remember you as a baby, having no clue about our deep connection." Josh turned his body to face Tony and me. "I'm deeply sorry for any trouble my family caused all of you, especially your mother's death. To think my own wife had something to do with—" He stopped suddenly, unable to continue. His left hand raised and covered his mouth, seeping shame and mounds of remorse.

Drew draped an arm around Josh's shoulder.

"I heard Debbie still pleads her innocence, despite the evidence the cops have against her," Kirk stated. "I'm staying apprised of the case. But I realize now that you had nothing to do with it. And I suppose I should apologize for thinking you were involved, Josh."

"I understand why you questioned me. Had I known the truth, I would've welcomed you to our family sooner. Maybe Sylvia would still be alive. I certainly wouldn't blame you for running far in the opposite direction."

"Well, you're in the business of forgiveness. I'm sure it wasn't easy for either of you to come here and invite me to visit Gordon with you." Kirk paused, thinking. "I appreciate the gesture." He held out his hand.

Josh accepted Kirk's hand and smiled. Drew stepped before Kirk next and shook his hand firmly.

"I know this is none of my business, Josh, but what's next for you and Debbie?" I questioned.

Josh huffed. "I have no idea. To reiterate Kirk's words, I'm in the business of forgiveness. But excusing my wife for conspiracy to commit harm to another human being—a friend and parishioner who *died* because of her actions is difficult to digest."

"I didn't mean to pry."

"Oh, you're not the first person to ask me that question, Victoria. I think about what advice I'd give to someone else."

"Which would be?" Kirk's brows raised, yearning for Josh's reply.

"Don't make any sudden decisions when emotionally charged."

Drew sadly gazed at Josh with similar hazel eyes, saying, "You don't have to make any hasty decisions right now."

We all nodded, unsure what a proper response would be besides silence.

"We're driving up to Acorn Hill after worship tomorrow. Can you meet us around two?"

"Maybe I'll attend tomorrow's service and drive up with you."

Kirk's response compelled Josh and Drew to smile brightly.

CHAPTER 54

The time had arrived for Tommy and me to return to Paris after becoming completely immersed in our families. Although we loved our life in Paris, we lived in seclusion. Since Tommy reclaimed his freedom, we were eager to make Las Vegas our primary residence. It would be a couple of months until we could move into our new home in Summerlin, minutes from Danny's home. Until then, we needed to prepare our Paris apartment for a lengthy reprieve, uncertain when we'd return.

I needed to go through my belongings to determine what I'd bring back to the States and what could stay behind. As I entered the kitchen in search of a marker to label boxes, Tommy slipped a French vanilla coffee pod into the machine.

"Would you like some tea?" he asked me.

"Uh, not right now," I said, realizing Tommy's eyes followed each step I took to the kitchen drawer. "What is it?"

"As much as I love this apartment, it's hard being in Paris again. I'm happy we got our lives back. We'll see our families regularly without keeping crucial secrets from them. I'm really looking forward to getting to know my niece, Haley, better." He smirked. "I smile anytime I see her. Those green eyes allow me to feel John's presence. I wish you knew him, hon."

"In a way, I do. I can visualize him through the stories you've shared and the pictures you've shown me. A medium once said, '*Cardinals appear when angels are near.*'"

Tommy laughed. "Cardinals, huh?"

I couldn't help but giggle. "I know it sounds strange. Maybe you need to meet Eve and have an engaging reading for yourself."

"I don't need a psychic or a red bird to talk to the dead. As long as I've got you with me, let's live spontaneously. Did your aunt check out that assisted living facility?"

"Not yet, but she realizes she's getting older and needs help. This facility is high-end, and she can keep Ginger and Giselle. She loved the pictures of the place. Tony and Kirk said they'd take her there for a visit. If she likes what she sees, she agrees to move, although my brothers aren't thrilled about transferring that heavy hutch again."

"We'll hire a moving company to take care of everything. Kirk and Tony have their own lives, and we have the means to help."

"Have I told you how wonderful you are?"

"Not today." His lips puckered up against mine. "Angie called me back. She said she'd prepare the paperwork to transfer ownership of this place to us. Perhaps we could bring the family here and show them all the attractions. Maybe Kirk would want to bring Tara here someday for a romantic getaway."

"Ooh la la. That's a great idea. I'm not ready to part with this place," I said, looking through the balcony door at the magnificent view of the Eiffel Tower.

"Me either." He glanced at his watch and sipped his coffee before placing the cover over the steaming thermal mug. "Gotta run to that meeting with Remi and the attorney."

"It's great that Remi wants to take over the business from you. Are you sure you want to give it up?"

He nodded. "I've got a million ideas buzzing through my brain of how to spend my time in Vegas."

I giggled, knowing he wouldn't retire completely.

He kissed my cheek goodbye, grabbed his keys, and dashed off to his business meeting.

As I began rummaging through my dresser drawers, I stumbled upon the DNA kit Tommy had bought me for my birthday last year. *Explore Your Roots!* I wouldn't want to know Marco Fiore if he still lived, using an alias after what I learned about him. Beverly implied that he raped Sylvia. She had her reasons to keep him out of my life. Aunt Lucy told me Sylvia dated a few men at that time. If there were other possibilities, maybe this DNA test could answer my questions.

This burning, nagging curiosity clawed its way into my head. I tore open the box, reviewed the simple instructions, and decided once and for all to spit into the small tube and mail my DNA to the lab. In four to six weeks, perhaps I'd gain some perspective about my paternity. The odds seemed slim, but I had to try.

CHAPTER 55

By the middle of September, Tommy and I settled into our 2,200-square-foot home. The ranch house we purchased was built in 2014. The inside looked immaculate. Besides a change of paint color in a couple of rooms, we were able to move right in. A building with four walls to dwell. A place to lounge, cook a meal, plan a future, and visit with the people we loved. I could create hearty vegetable and flower gardens in the spacious backyard. The sweet emotions Tommy and I developed through the years would transform this structure into a home.

Kirk had been spending time with Josh and Drew. Gordon's DNA test results revealed with 99.8 percent accuracy that he was Kirk's biological father. Although there was still some awkwardness to the situation, Josh and Drew made Kirk feel like family, even if their mother, Georgina, discouraged it. Kirk visited Gordon on occasion. He had good and bad days, but Kirk said Gordon always recognized him and called him son.

Another bonding moment between Kirk and Josh related to the church choir. Kirk helped with the music selections and singing hymns at Sunday worship until Josh found someone to permanently take over the position held by Terrance Fontaine, who had been sentenced to ten years for vehicular homicide. Ten years of his life for killing Sylvia didn't seem adequate.

Debbie Steele's trial was set to begin in the spring since she rejected a plea bargain from the DA. Josh didn't bail her out. He hadn't filed for divorce either. She could spend the rest of her life behind bars.

With a craving for pancakes and veggie sausage-like patties for breakfast on a Tuesday morning, Tommy helped me in the kitchen. He teased me, referring to the vegetable side dish as *fake* sausage, but he always ate a second helping.

School began for the grandkids. We agreed to watch them tonight, so Danny and Bianca could have a break, and we could spoil them. While flipping pancakes over the griddle, Tommy anxiously chattered about some activities we could do with the kids. Maybe we'd take them to the Hard Rock Café for dinner, following a superhero movie.

My cell buzzed, causing my eyes to skim through incoming email messages. My heart beat fast as my fingers tapped to access my inbox. "My DNA results are in! Can you watch the fake sausage while I check this out?" I needed my large-screen computer. Unfortunately, even with glasses, my eyes couldn't focus on my cell phone, and I wanted to absorb all the details.

"I'll turn the stove off. I want to see your results too!"

The moment had arrived, but admittedly my expectations were set pretty low. Most likely, Marco Fiore died decades ago. Unless he had siblings or another child who submitted their DNA to this same site, I couldn't verify any information I sought. My trembling fingers clicked on the twenty-two-inch computer monitor. I opened my email and clicked on the link to view my results. "Whoa! Okay, it looks like I'm 50 percent Italian, 46 percent French, 3 percent British and Irish, and a *speculative* 1 percent Russian. That's interesting. Hmm. Something doesn't add up," I said.

"What do you mean? It adds up to 100 percent."

"No, what doesn't add up is Marco Fiore. How does he factor in? I mean, he was part of the Italian Mafia, right? If Marco was my father, I'd have a higher Italian rate."

"Maybe you can't go by the story Beverly told you. These results support what Aunt Lucy knew about several men being in your mother's life."

Suddenly, I felt excited. Maybe that awful gangster wasn't my father after all.

"Can I navigate?" Tommy sat and took control of the mouse. He clicked on a tab that led me to DNA Relatives. "Let's see what this brings up." We waited several seconds until the screen refreshed. "You registered as your initials, VU?"

"I didn't want to put my whole name out there."

"That's smart. People will know who you are. Every crazy distant relative you have would contact you." Tommy pushed the mouse near my hand. "You drive. You may recognize some names."

The list noted the suspected relationship of each individual, the name they used on the website, and the matched percentage, with the strongest relationships starting at the top. My list of relatives began with someone named Marlene without a last name and the surprising relationship we shared. "Tommy, she shows as a half sister! Oh my god! This might actually work. I could discover my father through this Marlene woman!"

"Click on her and see what it says?"

First, I glanced down the list to see if there were any other close relationships. There were a couple of second cousins whose names were not familiar. I recognized a couple of last names of other distant cousins noted. I hadn't talked to them in many years but knew they shared Ursini blood. Could some of these unknown distant relatives be from my cloudy paternal side? I clicked on Marlene's name and read more about her DNA results and how close in comparison our numbers were—28.4 percent, which perceived us to be half sisters. Marlene's results showed percentage rates of French, British, Irish, and Russian in common with me, assuming this is her father's heritage. Her French numbers were far higher than mine. Lower numbers showed Finnish and Swiss backgrounds. Her mother also differed from mine.

I knew the Ursinis were Italian. Grandma had Sicilian roots, and Grandpa's ancestors hailed from Tuscany. The results mapped my Italian roots that were talked about my entire life. The map also indicated the regions Marlene and I shared, mostly in southern France, while Britain and Ireland areas connected us too.

"There's a link to send her a message." Tommy noticed.

"Uh, what do I say? God, this is so unbelievably uncomfortable. I think I need some time to think about it."

"Let me check on breakfast. I'll grab a tray, and we can eat in here."

I nodded, merely agreeing without processing his words. Marlene was my main lead. Whoever Marlene's father was would tell me everything I'd yearned to know my whole life. I clicked on the "Send a Message" icon and attempted to write a simple note. *Hi Marlene, it looks like we have a common parent. I don't know who my father is.* No, that sounded awfully desperate. I needed to give this some more thought.

Tommy stumbled into the room with two plates that held a couple of fluffy pancakes and two fake-sausage patties each. "I forgot your tea," he said before quietly stepping out again.

I stared at the computer, willing myself to think of the perfect message to send—something witty, maybe.

Tommy and I barely said a word over bites of our breakfast I barely tasted. He knew my brain worked in overdrive about this highly complex situation. If Marlene reviewed her DNA relatives often, she'd eventually notice she suddenly gained a half sister. But what if she didn't randomly check this site? Maybe my sending her a private message would gain her attention faster. I typed up a fairly direct introduction.

Dear Marlene,

My name is Vicki. I'm new to this site, but your name came up as close as a half sister. I'd love to try to figure this out. I hope to hear back from you.

It was a simple message that got straight to the point. I wouldn't give her my full name or date of birth yet. I wanted a reaction first. Then I sat and waited.

And waited.

And waited.

CHAPTER 56

Two days had passed since I emailed Marlene. I knew nothing about her except for her first name. Tommy wished she listed family last names, so he could hire Wayne Zullo to research her.

Tommy was stirring the pasta e fagioli I created for dinner, a thick version instead of a soupy one. We both preferred more ditalini in our recipe with added spices and a secret ingredient I'd never divulge.

I chopped a cucumber for the salad when my cell buzzed with a new email. I peeped at my phone to see a message from the DNA site—from Marlene. I dropped the knife and rushed to my computer, shouting, "She wrote me back!" to Tommy, who lowered the flame on the stovetop and raced me to the computer. I fiddled with the keyboard to access the site to read Marlene's message.

Hello Vicki,

I signed up on this site several years ago, so I don't check it often. The fascination with DNA relatives wore off, but your message both intrigued and confused me. My parents were married for over fifty years. I'm not sure what to think. Were you adopted? Did my mother have a child before marrying my father? Or could my father have gotten someone pregnant and not have known? He's still alive and swears he has no knowledge of another child. Unfortunately, my mother died two years ago, so I can't ask her. I hope to hear from you with additional details.

Sincerely,
Marlene

Maybe Marlene would be relieved to know that her parents married *after* my birth. So many ideas pummeled through me.

Tommy helped phrase my reply to Marlene without exposing too much personal information. My fingers quivered while strong shivers flew up my spine as I typed, edited, and reviewed my response ten times before pressing the send button, which read:

Thank you for replying to me, Marlene. I was born in Las Vegas, Nevada, to a single mother in 1955. I wasn't adopted. My mother is deceased now, and I never knew my father. If we share the same father, it's likely he did not realize my mother was pregnant. Did your father live in Vegas or visit in the early part of 1955?

Regards,
Vicki

I sat by the computer all night, biting my fingernails and pacing the hardwood floors.

Marlene didn't reply.

CHAPTER 57

Another two days flew by since I messaged Marlene. What if she didn't get my note? I couldn't focus on anything else. Tommy attempted to distract me with the artwork we had shipped from Paris that had recently arrived. He asked which pieces to add to which walls or if I wanted to buy some new contemporary work I admired. He hung my favorite copy of Giulio Romano's *Love Scene* on the wall above our bed. The Monet copy Sylvia bequeathed to me hung in the living room.

He rambled on about us spending time with each of his grand-children individually to become more acquainted with them one-on-one. The kids started to call me *Mimi Vicki*. Tommy chattered away about any random thought to take my mind off Marlene and her lack of response.

Then it happened. At 6:10 p.m., an email from the DNA site popped up.

My heart raced as if I just ran a five-mile marathon. Would Marlene accept this revelation, exposing having a half sister? Or would she tell me I was a crazy woman and completely repudiate the DNA results?

Tommy placed his hands on my shoulders. "Relax, babe. No matter how this goes, you and I have an amazing life. Whoever this woman and her father are won't change who you are."

I nodded and clicked on Marlene's message that read:

Hi Vicki,

I apologize for taking so long to write back. This is a lot to absorb, and I wanted to discuss the information you provided with my father, brother, and sister. My dad is pretty spry for eighty-seven years young, as he would say. He did visit Las Vegas in the '50s, although the exact year escapes his memory. He was in the Air Force in 1955. He admitted he met a woman at a casino on the Vegas Strip, the Flamingo. If you are open to this, it may be better to discuss this information by telephone. We hope to hear from you. My number is 239-555-0174.

Sincerely,
Marlene and family

"Wow! She mentioned the Flamingo, where your mother worked. What are you waiting for?" Tommy handed me my cell. "Call her, but block your phone number. I mean, we don't know anything about these people. Maybe they're pulling some scam."

"Honey, you can't really con someone with DNA results. I never put my true identity on the site. They don't know my last name yet."

"I've got a suspicious nature—with good reason. You're an actress and my wife. Odds are good they've heard of you unless they live on another planet."

To pacify Tommy's fears, I tapped into the settings of my cell phone and blocked my number from registering to protect my identity. With trembling fingers, I dialed Marlene's number, hit the green button to dial, and set the phone on speaker.

Marlene answered on the second ring. "Hello."

"H-h-hi. Is this Marlene?"

"This is she." Her voice cracked.

"Hi Marlene, this is Vicki. I just read your message. Is this a good time?"

"Vicki! Hello. Yes. Yes. I'm glad to hear from you. I'm putting you on speaker right now."

"Hi, Vicki!" was heard from several distant voices in the background.

"Wow, who's there?"

"I'm here with my brother Bruce, sister Chloe, and our father, Ray. Ray Laurant."

A sudden rush of relief washed through me the moment Marlene said his name was Ray Laurant instead of Marco Fiore. I needed a moment to compose myself. I looked at Tommy and muted the phone so the Laurants wouldn't hear me. "What if Marco changed his name?"

Tommy shrugged. "Maybe your aunt Bev was wrong, or Sylvia worried Marco *could be* your father."

"Vicki, are you still there?" Marlene asked.

I fought the tears but lost the battle. I hoped with everything in me that they couldn't tell I was crying or heard my teeth chattering from the extreme tension. I unmuted my phone. "Yes, I'm here. Sorry, I...I guess I'm a little...overwhelmed."

"Yeah, we are too, on this end," Marlene said, emoting a sense of polite anxiety.

"Uh, so let me ask you, Ray, how did you know my mother?"

"I was a lieutenant in the Air Force at that time. My captain had business in Nevada, and I was charged to fly him." Ray's voice became hoarse as he continued, "I'd never been to Vegas before, so I looked forward to checking the place out until I had to fly Captain Young back to the base. And boy, did I meet a gorgeous girl! Man, I couldn't take my eyes off her. Legs up to here."

I couldn't see his visual of my mother's legs, but the others in the room with him laughed. So did Tommy.

"Dad, stop it," Marlene scolded Ray.

"I'm telling the truth. She had long, raven hair and the darkest eyes I'd ever seen. An Italian beauty with an unusual last name. Something like Orchini or Erquini."

"It's Ursini, actually," I corrected.

"Yes, Ursini. That's it."

"Vicki, this is Bruce Laurant, your…uh…half brother. I have to ask, are you Victoria Ursini, the *actress*?"

Tommy raised his brows, showing his *I told you so* face.

"Hi, Bruce. Yes, I'm *that* Victoria Ursini."

"Whoa. Dad, Vicki's been in movies and TV shows. I loved *Nick of Time*, and my wife and I watched *Rising 51* faithfully when it was on," Bruce added.

"Is that right?" Ray answered, seemingly surprised, while the sound of women's whispers could be heard in the background, probably gossiping. "Tell me, how is your mother, Vicki?"

"Dad, remember I told you Vicki's mother passed away," Marlene said, empathy pouring in.

"Oh, yeah, yeah. I'm sorry to hear that. I didn't mean to bring that up."

"That's okay, Ray." At his age, he was entitled to forget things, especially after just discovering he had another daughter more than sixty years ago. "My mother was a very strong woman. Beautiful as you described."

"Oh, a pretty little thing. Younger than me. It was definitely the Flamingo where we met. At the time, I had no idea the place was run by hoodlums. My wife, Martha, and I watched a documentary on Vegas going back to the '40s when the Strip first livened up. I'd laugh, telling her I spent time at the Flamingo. Of course, I didn't tell her I met your mother." Ray laughed. "That wouldn't have gone over well."

Tommy whispered, "This guy is no mobster, babe. He was in the military. This isn't Marco Fiore incognito."

Reassured, I smiled with contentment and nodded in agreement with his theory.

"So, Ray, where did you go after you left Vegas?"

"Oh, I finished my time in the Air Force and later worked as a pilot for KLM airlines in Europe before I switched to Delta in the early '60s, met Martha, and had Marlene, Bruce, and Chloe. If your mom ever wanted to contact me to tell me about you, Vicki, it wouldn't have been easy for her to find me between the military and settling in Europe for several years." He cleared his throat and coughed a couple of times. "I honestly had no idea about you, dear. You need to know that. Had I known I had a daughter out there who might have needed me, I would've been there."

The sincerity seeping from Ray's words made my dark-brown eyes flood.

"Thank you for saying that, Ray. It's a pleasure to finally know who my father is and to have this conversation."

"Hi, Vicki. This is Bruce again. Are you still living in Las Vegas?"

"I've moved around a lot, but I'm back in Vegas again. Where are you all from?"

"Florida, West Coast. Hi, Vicki. I'm Chloe, the *baby* of the family. I wanted to say hi."

"She's forty-seven and still refers to herself as the *baby*," Marlene said with a loud cackle.

I laughed through my words. "Hi, Chloe. Tell me about yourselves."

"I have one son in high school. Bruce has a son and daughter in college. Marlene has two sons. One of them just had a baby girl last month. Daddy's first great-grandchild!" Chloe happily announced. "What about you, Vicki?"

"I don't have children."

Tommy made a coughing sound.

"Oh, I'm on speaker also. My husband, Tommy, is standing next to me."

They all greeted Tommy with warm hellos.

"Hi, Laurant family! Hey, is that spelled L-A-U-R-A-N-T?"

I slapped his hand, knowing he only confirmed the spelling so he could have them investigated.

"Yes, that's how we spell the name," Ray replied.

"It's Chloe again, Vicki. I don't know how feasible it is for you, but we discussed this before Marlene emailed you back. We'd love to meet you in person if you're open to it."

I smiled and paused to fight the tears. "I...I'd like that, Chloe. I'll have to get back to you. Tommy and I just moved into a new house, but perhaps we can talk again and discuss it."

"I couldn't be happier to meet you in person, dear. At eighty-seven, I don't know how many more days I've got left. Your mother was so much younger than me. I'm sorry to hear of Lucy's passing."

My head turned and darted to gauge Tommy's reaction, who appeared as confused as me, raising his brows, when Ray brought up *Lucy's* name.

"Ray, h-h-how exactly did you and my mother meet? I know it was a long time ago, but do you remember?"

"Well, it was in the casino at the bar. I sat beside her and noticed how pretty she was. I offered to buy her a drink." He hesitated and chuckled. "A dirty martini. *The dirtier, the better*, she said with a vibrant laugh."

My pulse raced, and my neck stiffened when I turned to Tommy, shocked to hear Ray talking about meeting my *aunt*, not Sylvia.

"Ray, did my mother work at the Flamingo when you met her?"

"Work there?" He paused, thinking. "Well, she got me into the nightclub to see a show. She might have worked there and pulled some strings to get me in without a ticket. But...wait a minute. Her sister starred in the show! She was one of the dancers on the stage. They looked a lot alike, but honestly, my eyes stayed focused on Lucy. If I didn't have to head back to the base per the captain's orders, I would've wanted to stay or at least go back and see her again. Hmm, funny how life takes you down different paths. Gosh, I feel like I'm doin' all the talkin' here. How about you tell us all about you, honey?"

Tommy's eyes widened, realizing the depth of this knowledge I had gained. My paternity had always been in question. I had no idea my mother's true identity was even more mystifying.

"Hmm, where...do I...start?" I stuttered, holding back more tears. I cleared my throat before giving them some of the very basics.

They could easily learn all about me through a Google search, with scandalous entanglements, especially if they read Tommy's memoirs.

My entire world just turned upside down. Could Ray have the Ursini sisters confused? Or did he just reveal the biggest secret two sisters could conceal? Aunt Lucy was a mere eighteen-year-old at the time of my birth. Sylvia was twenty-two and single herself. My life suddenly sounded like an exciting Friday cliffhanger on *The Young and the Restless*.

Although my thoughts were all over the place, I didn't correct Ray or tell him the only mother I knew my entire life was Lucy's older sister, Sylvia.

CHAPTER 58

We ended the call on a positive note, exchanging personal phone numbers and promises to keep in touch. I'd love to meet Ray in person someday, but right now, my body felt so numb I could barely sense the tears that oozed from my sockets.

Tommy took a step back, waiting patiently for my jumbled thoughts to decipher this madness.

"*What the hell?* Could Aunt Lucy be my mother, but Sylvia raised me?"

"Give yourself some time to let this news sink in. You can clear this up with Lucy once you calm down."

My mind spun with fury, deliberating about the similarities I shared specifically with Aunt Lucy as I paced the room. We had the same large foot size and the same laugh. Sylvia and Lucy always resembled each other as sisters often did. I used to think I resembled Sylvia, but maybe I looked more like Lucy. The biggest parallel: bipolar disorder, often a genetic, mental health condition. Sylvia didn't have it. Neither did Kirk or Tony. Grandma Ursini passed that horrible trait to Lucy and ultimately to me.

Tommy touched my shoulders, preventing my irate pacing from scuffing the hardwood floor. "*If* it's true, Lucy must've been too young. It's pretty amazing of Sylvia to raise her sister's child as her own. She kept you as part of the family. You weren't given up for adoption or placed in an orphanage. Whatever happened back in 1955, you were lucky and very much loved, honey."

I raced to the coat rack and slipped my windbreaker over my turquoise short-sleeved blouse. "Are you coming with me?"

Tommy muttered, "You ladies might need a moderator."

*****

Aunt Lucy's voice clicked through the speaker of the lobby in her apartment complex, "Who's there?"

"It's Victoria and Tommy."

"Oh, this is a surprise," she said before buzzing us access to enter.

"Babe, please take a breath. If you want her to be candid with you, you have to be *calm*. If she realizes how upset you are, she might withhold facts."

Though I understood what Tommy advised, I had lost all sense of common courtesies. I couldn't suppress my emotions at the moment. The 50 percent of hot Italian blood raged through my veins like wildfire.

Lucy stood in the doorway, holding onto her walker, smiling. She had changed for bed already, wearing a gold cat-patterned bathrobe over black pajamas. "What brings you by?" she asked me with open arms, waiting for the hug I normally greeted her with. Instead, I stomped around her and her walker, avoiding our usual embrace.

Tommy eased his way inside. "Hi there, beautiful." He kissed her on the cheek.

"Oh, you are too much, Tommy." She snorted through a quick laugh.

"I found my father. My actual birth father," I blurted before the door had a chance to close behind us.

"What? How?" she asked with knit brows.

"Have you ever seen the commercials about DNA kits to learn your genetic history?"

"Victoria, those are just nonsense."

"No, they aren't. Those tests are based on science and facts. DNA can't be tainted. DNA that I provided matched someone else in the system."

Lucy's body stiffened. Her left arm started circling in waves out into the air as if trying to regain a compromised balance.

Tommy quickly steadied her by grasping her arm and securing her petite body beside him. "How about you sit?" He guided her to the recliner. It took her a moment to settle, but I kept talking and pacing.

"I just got off the phone with a man named *Ray Laurant*. He used to be a pilot in the Air Force and happened to be in Vegas at the Flamingo the year I was born."

Lucy's eyes were glazed with tears. "You talked to Ray? How did you—"

"Ray eventually married and had three children. My DNA matched one of his children as a half-sibling. We started communicating, and I just hung up the phone with him. My *father*. He talked about meeting this young Italian beauty at the Flamingo. How stunned I was to hear him ask about my mother, *Lucy*."

Lucy turned her head away. Her hand covered her mouth. Then her lids closed.

"My god. It's true. You're my *birth* mother? Why did your sister raise me?"

Tommy sent me an uneasy gaze, detesting the conflict.

I'd known this woman my entire life as my aunt. I had a right to this anger exploding from within. I needed to understand what decisions were made decades ago that impacted my life—my whole existence.

"Lucy, I'm sure your situation back in 1955 must have been difficult. You were just a kid. You've got to understand Vicki's reaction to all the secrets. It's no surprise that she always wanted to know about her father. Just take a breath and a moment to collect yourself." Tommy's words were far gentler than I believed she deserved.

My perpetual nervous pacing resumed, hoping to hear more than a flood of excuses.

"She warned me this would happen someday," Lucy groaned. "Sylvia was always smarter than me. Older, wiser, more glamorous. You know, I idolized Syl. I'd hang out at the Flamingo and watch her up on that stage. Boy, I never had her courage. To put myself out there for everyone to see. Always the center of attention while I hid in the back corner, a wallflower, watching from afar with envy."

Reeling with impatience, I allowed her to continue, hoping she'd get straight to the point.

"Men fawned over her. No man ever looked at me the way they gawked at my sister. I'd observe Syl and Beverly flirt with men and wish I was brave enough to try. I had turned eighteen and was able to drink liquor in 1955. I remember sitting at the bar at the Flamingo, and this handsome man sat beside me. Our eyes met, and I saw *fireworks!* I tried not to act so shy. I thought, *What would Syl do?* And I acted on impulse. I'm sure I had a couple of drinks in me, which made me feel a little brave.

"I brought him to see Sylvia's show. She saw me sitting with a man in the audience and flew into protective mode. She didn't like me spending time with a military man, thinking he was only interested in sex. When she went back on stage for her second act, I encouraged Ray to spend time alone with me. That's what my big sister would've done. Well, that night, a foolish girl lost her virginity. Ray was a gentleman—sweet and handsome. He met up with me the next night too. But he had to leave town. I felt so alive and energized about the time I had with him, though I never saw him again."

"Obviously, you got pregnant."

Slowly, Lucy nodded. "Ray left town, and I didn't know how to find him. I never asked what base he'd be at. God, I was mortified and terrified at the same time! I told Sylvia. She helped me figure things out. She knew of a doctor who'd terminate the pregnancy if I chose. Despite it being illegal, I couldn't commit such a sin."

I sighed, realizing I could have been aborted.

"I had to tell my parents. Oh, they were so angry! Your grandpa wanted to get his hands on Ray. They had planned to keep you and raise you as their own. I was so scared. To be a pregnant teenage girl without a husband in 1955. That simply wasn't proper.

"My pregnancy sent my mother over the edge emotionally. She battled bipolar like you and I do, but she never really understood it or treated it. Grandpa was sick with worry, having to take care of her. My belly had already started to protrude. You know, I always had MS. I just never had a severe episode until my fifties to know any better. It doesn't mean I didn't have symptoms. Pain, numbness, jitters. Sometimes, life frustrated me, and I'd lash out. The mania made my emotions intolerable. So many highs and lows. Sometimes I'd have a bundle of energy, and other times I couldn't get out of bed. Add pregnancy hormones to that horrendous pot of stew, and well, I…tried to…kill myself. Sylvia stopped me from swallowing a bottle of pills."

I covered my mouth, suddenly understanding the devastation she dealt with. The medication she took today controlled her range of emotions. She wasn't diagnosed years ago to fathom the natural reaction to scattered feelings spread across a broad, emotional spectrum.

"Sylvia saved my life that night. She swore to protect my baby and me. Said she'd take you and raise you as her own. Her generous, loving gesture gave me hope to keep living, at least through the rest of the pregnancy. She didn't want me to hurt myself or the precious cargo I carried. Our parents helped out as best as they could, of course. And I had the pleasure of watching you grow up—my princess."

"I never saw adoption papers."

"No, we didn't go about it the legal, proper way. Hey, back in 1955, there weren't computers to track details like today. Your mother and I stayed inside throughout my pregnancy. We never left the house. We wanted everyone to believe that she was your mother, Victoria. No one could see she wasn't really pregnant. And no one could see my body grow the way it did. There was this guy at the Flamingo who really bothered Syl. He was a terrible man. Syl asked for a leave of absence. Told her boss she wanted to get away from him. Then you were born, and eventually, Syl went back to work and informed people she had a baby. People assumed her mysterious leave was maternal."

"This guy at the Flamingo who bothered her. Was his name Marco Fiore?" Tommy asked.

Lucy stopped to think. "I can't recall. What does that matter?"

"Aunt Bev thought Marco was my father."

Lucy's eyelids raised in irritation, her usual reaction to Beverly's name entering a conversation. "I don't know what your mother told Beverly. I used Sylvia's name at the doctor's office for my regular checkups and at the hospital where you were born. They all knew *me* as Sylvia Ursini. So all your records would show her as your mother. No one questioned my identity. They didn't ask for ID or social security numbers during that era. Even if they did, we looked too much alike for people who never met her to ask questions." Tears fell from Lucy's eyes.

I grabbed her hand. Somehow, my anger settled beneath the mountain of lies I had been fed my entire life.

"I thought dealing with an unplanned pregnancy would be the hardest thing I'd ever have to do." She shook her head and wiped her eyes. "No, the pregnancy and delivery were nothing! Handing you over to my sister to love and nurture your entire life was the most excruciating pain I could ever experience. Oh, how many times we'd fight about how she punished you or wanted you to be exactly like her, getting you into modeling and acting when you were just a baby. When you called her *mommy* for the first time, my heart shattered! But the one thing we agreed on was keeping this secret. We didn't want to upset your life. I got to be in your life as your aunt. Syl did the hard stuff. She really was your mother. And that's who she should always be to you."

Tommy draped an arm around Lucy and squeezed.

In the midst of agonizing silence, she pleaded, "Say something, Victoria."

I inhaled the dry air deeply and sat beside her. "This is too much for me. I...I don't know what to do or think about all this. I need time. I'm not sure how I feel."

"Syl and I lived with the truth our whole lives. You bonded us to be even closer, you know. There's nothing stronger than sisters who would die for each other. To be honest, after you grew up and asked so many questions about your father, she wanted to tell you the truth. Sylvia had second thoughts about staying quiet, but I forbid her. I made her promise to keep this secret. I worried this would really hurt you. I know you stay on your medication these days, but bipolar disorder can be unpredictable. I'd hate it if you got sucked back into that ugly black hole."

I bit my fingernails hazily, deep in thought.

"I knew she wrote you a letter, Victoria. She always kept things hidden in that china cabinet. I found it the last time she brought me to her house, and I…took it. Sure enough, in that letter, she shared our secret with you. I wasn't prepared for you to read it."

"You took the letter my mother wrote me! The one I searched for after her death." My heart suddenly sunk to my feet.

"I read your brother's letters to make sure Syl didn't write anything about this to them."

"Wait, that's why their letters were ripped open? I thought the police read them when they searched the house. My god, how could you do that? Those letters revealed her deepest, innermost emotions, and you stole that from me."

"I didn't *destroy* the letter. I kept it."

"Where is it?"

She attempted to stand but couldn't gather strength in her arms to lift her body from the chair.

Tommy said, "Tell me where you put it, Lucy. I'll get it."

She released a huff. "There's an old cigar box at the top of my closet in the bedroom. The letter is in there."

My eyes shot daggers her way.

"I couldn't bear it if you hated me, Victoria. I wanted to spare you pain."

"Maybe you didn't want your secrets exposed. Maybe this has nothing to do with me at all. It's all about you!"

"No!"

"Do you know how terrible I felt, wondering if that letter got thrown out by mistake when we cleaned out the house? Kirk learned who his father was. I desperately wanted to know what she'd say to me, and you denied me that right. You deprived me of all my rights!"

Her tears fell like rain. She reached for a tissue on the table beside her chair and blew her nose hard.

Tommy returned from the bedroom with an envelope in his hand. An envelope that had been torn open. He handed it to me.

I removed the paper from the envelope to ensure it was the letter I hoped to read. Seeing Sylvia's handwriting and her signature, signing it as *Mom*. "I feel I need to read this privately." I turned to Tommy, saying, "Let's go."

"Wait a minute. Lucy, are you okay? Can I get you anything before we leave?" Tommy asked, empathy souring.

She waved her hand, sobbing. In a bitty voice, she whispered to Tommy, "Take care of my princess."

*****

My head leaned against the passenger window, mindlessly watching the buildings float by.

Tommy attempted to speak to me, but I couldn't translate his words. He pulled into the garage and parked the black Cadillac he had purchased when we officially moved back home.

We sat quietly in the plush, cream-colored leather seats for a few moments.

"Are you all right? You got a complete, complicated education about your family history over the last couple of hours."

"I'm…processing."

"I thought for sure you'd read the letter Sylvia wrote by now."

"I just need a minute." I paused and closed my eyes before exiting the vehicle in a fog and making my way inside our home.

"How about a cup of green tea?"

I nodded. "What do I tell my brothers? Kirk and Tony, technically, are my first cousins."

"Don't go there. You were raised as siblings. They are your brothers, no matter how much DNA you share. Emotional connections are far more powerful than genetics."

I opened the letter, more prepared than ever to read the message Sylvia wished to convey. Tommy stood before me, watching my reaction to the ink spread about this paper. She always had neat penmanship.

Dearest Victoria,

You must know how proud I am of all you've achieved in life. Not only did you navigate your way through a fabulous career as a model and actress, but you did so much good for the community when you were the wife of a mayor and governor. I sang your praises whenever I had an audience. My friends would brag about their children's accomplishments, but they never held a candle to your success. Even with the negative publicity you endured, you always came out sparkling like diamonds, in my opinion. I know, I'm biased. Who cares if what people say is good or bad, right or wrong? When they *stop* talking about you altogether, that's when you have to worry.

I know I wasn't a typical mother. I didn't teach you how to darn a sock or make special recipes— except for my grilled cheese. Layer the bread with mayonnaise instead of butter, and add tomato and tuna for a heartier sandwich.

You were always as bright and independent as you were beautiful. I told you I named you after a woman from that soap opera I used to watch. Actually, you were named after Victoria Woodhull, a suffragist who helped pave the way for women in this country. I wrote a paper about her during my senior year in high school. I think I got a lousy B minus. Victoria Woodhull ran for the US presidency in the late 1800s. And you thought Hillary Clinton was the first female to run for president. No one took Woodhull's presidential run seriously. If I remember correctly, the officials didn't even bother to count her votes, thinking a woman could never hold such a powerful position. Victoria Woodhull was a smart, strong, independent woman who fought for what she believed in—the type of woman I wanted you to emulate.

For thirteen years, it was just you and me before your brothers were born. We bonded over face masks, manicures, and makeovers. I loved you with my whole heart. Although you are my flesh and blood, I have to tell you, sunshine, I didn't bring you into this world in the traditional way. If you're not sitting down, you probably should before you read further. Your aunt Lu found herself in some "trouble" years ago. She was much too young and incapable of being a single parent. You must be shocked right now as you read this. Times were different in 1955 than today. We allowed people to think that I gave birth to you as a way to protect you and my sister's reputation. Before you think Aunt Lu didn't want you, stop that thought! It's nonsense! Her mental health was never good, as you know. I always wanted to tell you this from the time you turned eighteen, but I couldn't go against Lucy's wishes. She felt torn and shattered giving you up. She didn't want you to resent her. She wanted you to always love her as the aunt who referred to you as "princess."

I'm telling you this now because somehow you think you'll feel more complete knowing the truth about your parentage. All you really need to know is that you had two women going to bat for you your whole life. Your aunt and I had some really nasty fights about how I raised you.

That's because we both loved you. I don't want you to resent either of us. Lucy carried you for nine months, but I'll be your mom forever.

You've yearned to know about your father since you were a young girl and observed your friends' dads playing with them or picking them up from school. I wish I could have given you the moon as fathers go. I couldn't be honest with you about the man because it would reveal our secret.

His name was Ray, and he was a pilot in the Air Force. You'd have to get the rest of the details from Lucy if she's still alive when you read this. Because he was in the military, she never saw him again. But she told me he was a kind man. She thought if he knew you existed, he would've been in your life. We don't know if he's alive or dead or where he lives. I don't think your aunt loved him. I think she loved the idea of being with a good man.

She was so concerned when she recognized the signs of bipolar you expressed as you grew up. I let her take the lead, having discussions with you since she lived with the same condition. We were so grateful you didn't have MS! When Lucy got diagnosed, we prayed daily that you didn't inherit that defective gene.

I know you found the love of your life and had the opportunity to experience what a rush love is. It was so unfortunate that Tommy Cavallo passed suddenly. I wish I had met him. But whenever you visited me during that time with Tommy, that glow on your face declared your true happiness.

Love secreted from your beautiful brown eyes. I also had that kind of love once, and I thank God for such a blessing to really know what true love is, even if I never married the man who owned my heart.

If you're reading this note, I must have moved on to the next level of God's plan for my spirit. Always remember you are braver than you think, stronger than you believe, and smarter than you give yourself credit for.

I recently read this poem on the church's bulletin board that someone found on the Internet; the author is unknown. "A messenger to tell you we're never far apart. My spirit will live on, forever in your heart. When you see a cardinal, you'll know these words are true. I'm never far away. I'll always be with you." I hope you think of me after I'm gone, at least whenever you see a cardinal soaring by. I'll always be with you, Victoria. You and your brothers are the most precious gifts in my life.

Love,
Mom

My body trembled as tears welled up. She mentioned cardinals, just like Eve had told me through her psychic sense.

In some strange way, I felt closer to Sylvia, I mean, *my mother*, than I had in years. She saved her sister and me, a selfless act that risked her reputation and future. The disconnect between us, inflated by my mind, had finally shattered. This revelation created a bridge that would forever link our hearts. I had never attained so much respect for anyone. My mother earned my loyalty and admiration.

Would my anger cease about Lucy stealing this letter to prevent me from learning the truth? The truth my mother wanted me to know, even if I had to wait until her death to discover it. It was too soon to tell.

Tommy handed me a steaming mug of green tea and held me tenderly in silence.

CHAPTER 59

On a Saturday in mid-November, Tommy and I flew into the Southwest Florida International Airport, rented a BMW, and drove along the flat Interstate 75, zipping by palm trees, golf courses, and shopping malls to the enchanting town of Naples.

Ray, my father, lived with my brother Bruce and his wife, Annie. I suggested we meet at a restaurant of their choice, but they preferred a more personal setting. To avoid overwhelming me at our first meeting, I'd only be meeting Ray, Marlene, Bruce, and Chloe today—no spouses, children, or Marlene's granddaughter. Bruce teased, saying if they didn't scare me away, I could meet the rest of the family on Sunday. I told Bruce I didn't scare easily.

The jitters swept through me the entire flight and while driving along the picturesque journey to Naples. I spoke with my new family members several times by phone since the test results introduced me to a new part of my existence. Lucy was accurate about Ray seeming kind and caring. He told me he couldn't wait to meet his oldest daughter for the first time.

Tommy parked on the street behind a Honda CRV. Three other cars sat in the brick driveway. The sun sparkled against the pretty ranch home where my father waited behind the cranberry-colored front door my eyes stared at, pondering if he felt as nervous as me.

"Take a breath, babe," Tommy encouraged. "When you're ready, we'll go in. This is something you've always wondered about. These people are welcoming you into their lives. There's nothing for you to fear. And I'll be right by your side."

"Well, thanks to Wayne Zullo investigating them, you're relieved no one has a record," I teased, causing Tommy to surge with laughter. I squeezed his hand and kissed him as my stomach swirled, performing somersaults. I squinted to observe a decorative, white plaque hanging on the door with the image of colorful flowers and a majestic red cardinal in the center. With a light-hearted gaze up into the blue sky through a few cottony clouds in search of heaven, I sent a wink to my mother. "I'm ready now, Tommy." I exhaled, then exited the vehicle.

Tommy picked up a large shopping bag from the back seat and carried it to the door. I didn't want to show up empty-handed. Because Ray's heritage was primarily from France, I shopped for gifts online. How cool it was to discover I had so much French blood running through my veins after living in Paris for nine years. I bought them each a charming Christmas ornament of the Eiffel Tower. Once I confirmed they enjoyed an occasional alcoholic beverage, I purchased a pair of Botticelli crystal champagne flutes from the St. Louis collection from Versailles and a bottle of Dom Perignon for each sibling. For Ray, I put together something much more personal that I hoped he'd appreciate.

A lump tore through my throat when Bruce opened the door, jiggling the placard with the brilliant red bird.

The family shuffled toward Tommy and me with warm greetings. We exchanged some current photographs, which helped me to identify everyone. But I spotted the elderly man standing in the back, leaning on a wooden cane. He had thin white patches of hair, dressed in a suit fit for Florida—beige in color, a white dress shirt, a blue plaid bowtie, and supportive dress shoes. Although my half-siblings were chatting away, my eyes swayed in Ray's direction. He held a large bouquet wrapped in lavender tissue paper.

The eighty-seven-year-old staggered toward me slowly, holding out a dozen red roses mixed with greens and baby's breath. "My, you are a beauty like Lucy, Victoria."

"The flowers are lovely, Ray. Thank you." I breathed in the fragrant buds.

Ray opened his arms.

I handed Tommy the bouquet before allowing myself to tumble into Ray's warm embrace. The scent of his musky cologne tickled my senses. A feeling of security overwhelmed me as he squeezed my petite frame and expelled a sentimental gasp. I held onto him tighter, not wanting to let go, igniting more tears. My mother left this world, but I now had a father. A father! All my life, I wished upon stars and birthday candles for this outcome. A new family to connect to and build relationships with. People who I might find similarities with that could bond us, entwining our hearts. Family stories to hear and new ones to devise. This wasn't a dream in which I had to pinch myself awake. I allowed myself to plunge into this powerful rush of energy charging through my blood. I found my father, thanks to Tommy and the DNA test he bought. The future would be up to Ray and me.

When Ray's grip relaxed, I noticed Marlene and Chloe releasing a waterfall of emotions through dark, expressive eyes. But when they smiled, I discovered our resemblance. We shared the same smile and dimples, a Laurant trait.

To break from the gushy introduction, I reached for tissues in my purse to wipe the sappiness from our faces.

Once composed, I handed out the gifts I had brought. They tore at the packages and loved my selections, especially the lavish champagne.

Chloe had a copy of Tommy's memoirs in hand. "Will you sign this for me, Tommy?"

He seemed surprised. Tommy's book had been released after his presumed death while we were in hiding. He never had a book signing. No one had ever asked him for his autograph before. He sent Chloe his remarkable smirk and happily signed the book with pride.

"Oh my gosh, I couldn't put it down. I can't believe what a thrilling life you led. You two went through a lot to be together. I'm happy for you."

"I've not read the book yet, but I heard the headlines. Chloe and Marlene talk about it constantly!" Bruce rolled his eyes.

"I'll bring my copy for your signature tomorrow, Tommy," Maureen imparted.

"Tomorrow. November seventeenth," Ray spoke up. "It's your birthday."

I showed off my Laurant dimples. "You knew?"

"After hearing about Tommy's book, the kids looked you up. I'm probably not supposed to say anything—"

"Daddy, you promised you'd be quiet!" Marlene shouted.

Ray jokingly waved his hands at Marlene to stifle her concerns. "We're going to celebrate your birthday with the rest of the family tomorrow."

"That's so sweet. Sounds like fun." The gift I brought Ray sat on the coffee table untouched. "Hey, how about you open this?"

"Oh, yes, of course." He chuckled as he slowly sunk his body into the chocolate brown sofa. He tapped the cushion, inviting me to sit beside him as he carefully removed the navy-blue bow and the green and blue-striped wrapping paper.

Everyone crowded around to see what I packed inside the box, which obviously differed from the gifts I gave my half-siblings.

Ray removed the top of the box and picked up a white digital photo album. I organized a chronological arrangement of my baby pictures that my mother had packed away. I found them in a box when cleaning out her closet. I scanned the photos to create this beautiful memory book online. I couldn't think of a more special gift than to share some of my best childhood memories with him. I included photos of my mother and Lucy.

"Wow, look at this! What a gorgeous baby you were!" Ray's unfocused eyes moved back and forth between the album and me, overwhelmed with surprise. He unfolded a hanky from his shirt pocket and blew his nose. His eyes focused on one photo in particular. He pointed to Aunt Lucy. As much as my mother and she resembled each other, Ray confidently recognized the young lady who captured his eyes years ago. "That's Lucy."

I nodded, but my smile faded. Before we planned this trip, I had explained to Ray and the others how Lucy's sister raised me as her own.

Tommy glanced at me with those gray eyes, signaling to look more upbeat.

"What a beautiful gift, Vicki," Marlene said as tears plopped from her eyes.

"Yes, thank you!" Ray beamed with delight, then he hugged me. "I'm sorry if I let the cat outa the bag about my time with Lucy. I feel like I flip-flopped your whole world."

I shook my head. "You cleared things up. I'm not saying it was easy to hear, but I'm grateful the truth has been freed."

His eyes shifted back to the photo album. "This is fantastic! Maybe you can walk me through each picture and tell me something about where you were and how old you were. Dang, I've got a lot of catching up to do."

"Me too, Ray. Me too."

CHAPTER 60

In spite of the jarring family secrets exposed, Tommy and I had so much to be grateful for this Thanksgiving. He suggested we celebrate the holiday in extravagance. He booked the Ring of Kerry banquet room at the Montgomery in the Ireland wing and arranged an elaborate Thanksgiving feast with the traditional turkey, stuffing, and mashed potatoes, plus some Italian specialties blended in to satisfy the Ursini family traditions.

Danny, Bianca, and our grandchildren were the first to arrive. Haley and her family trickled in behind them. The kids got to run around and release their energy before other guests came. Danny and Haley's children loved spending holidays together as a family, especially since Tommy was home with them where he belonged.

We opened up the invitation list to include Tommy's oldest and dearest friends and their families, including Len Stein and his wife, Dr. Wanda Sherman, who were instrumental in assisting with our undercover relocation to Paris in 2010. What a wonderful sight to watch Tommy and his tightest allies laugh, reminisce about the past, and make plans for the future.

Kirk, Tara, and Fiona entered with Aunt Lucy, whose reddened face told me she'd been crying. I hadn't been able to look at her the same since the truth came out. Tommy encouraged me to speak to a therapist and release my animosity. With battling bipolar, seeking therapy to address a traumatic event was essential to my mental health. I understood the choices two young sisters made in 1955, vowing silence and loyalty to each other. Therapy helped me to compartmentalize my frustration and anguish, and to think logically without focusing on the negative aspects. My anger with Lucy subsided, but I hadn't been able to completely reconcile with her.

As predicted, Kirk and Tony were stunned to learn my true genetic background, but they said they'd never think of me as anything but their older sister, no matter the percentage of DNA we shared. The pain of being lied to my entire life scorched my insides. But one thing Tommy stated was true: my life didn't change. Kirk and Tony were still my brothers. My mother was the late and great Sylvia Ursini, a famous showgirl from the Flamingo in the 1950s. She lived a hell of an exciting life, and she was brave enough to raise me as her own at a time when single mothers were chastised.

My feelings for Aunt Lucy were somewhat ambiguous. I still referred to her as my aunt, but I couldn't help but look at her differently, knowing she was my birth mother. We always shared characteristics as Ursini women, but now that I have learned the truth, I see much more of myself in her face and mannerisms.

We hired a moving company, though my brothers supervised Aunt Lucy's move into the assisted living facility, Summer Wind. Apparently, she loved it. The staff acted amiable and were quite helpful. The amenities were useful to accommodate her every need, and the beautiful place allowed her cats to remain with her. Ginger and Giselle were fortunate felines.

Tony showed up for Thanksgiving dinner alone, although I encouraged him to bring a date. He indicated he had to work the night shift later. He'd been working long hours and saving money. Perhaps staying busy with work prevented him from missing the relationship he had for years with Leann.

Tony's eyes perused the room as I chatted about my next visit to Florida before Christmas to see my new family again. Suddenly, Tony pointed to the open bar. "Hey, who's the woman with the red glasses standing alone?"

I smiled, clutched his hand, and escorted him to the bar where the pretty lady stood, wearing a blush-pink floral dress. "Hey, Phyllis. What are you drinking?" I asked.

"Rum and diet coke." Her eyes latched onto Tony as she sipped the last of her drink.

"Have I ever introduced you to my brother?"

Phyllis gulped. "This is your brother?"

"Yes, my youngest brother, Tony Ianni. Tony, this is Phyllis Santore. Phyllis helps keep the bosses here at the Montgomery in line. She's also a huge sci-fi fan, like you, Tony."

She giggled, causing Tony to smile in a way I hadn't seen him do in quite some time.

"Looks like you need another drink, Phyllis. May I?" Tony offered.

My grin widened. I stepped away to let them get acquainted. From a distance, I noticed Tommy waving at me. I marched up to the small stage to stand beside him with a microphone in hand. He tapped the mic to ensure it worked. The obnoxious sound grabbed everyone's attention.

Tommy stood before the happy faces in the crowd, then he reached for my hand to hold. "This is the greatest Thanksgiving in the history of all my Thanksgiving holidays. Man, do I have a lot to be thankful for, starting with this one." He kissed my forehead. "Danny and Bianca, my beautiful grandchildren, my in-laws—Kirk, Tony, and Lucy, my niece, Haley, and her family. And everyone else here—well, you're family too. Family equals love. It's *not* about DNA. Family is who you welcome into your life and your heart."

Surely Tommy added that last line of his speech for my benefit.

"I had to go without you all for nine years. That was tough! Thankfully, this woman here loved me enough to keep me in check. I would've gone crazy if she wasn't by my side. I will never take any of you for granted." Tommy raised his glass of fizzy seltzer with lime slices. "Alla mia famiglia! My family here today. It's good to be alive and well and home again. Salute!"

I caught a glimpse of my family, my aunt in particular. As difficult as it was, I approached their table and sat at the empty seat beside Aunt Lucy, whose pink, swollen eyes released a few tears at the sight of me. I rested my hand atop hers and squeezed. "Happy Thanksgiving, Aunt Lucy."

"Oh, Victoria. I'm so sorry."

"I know. I'm working through my issues." I blew out a heavy breath. "Like my husband said, we both have a lot to be thankful for. So tell me all about your new apartment. Maybe Tommy and I will stop by this weekend and check it out."

As Aunt Lucy started to speak, my eyes met Tommy's from across the room. He sent me a wink simultaneously with his beautiful smirk, happy to see me make peace with my aunt.

2020

Family is the anchor that holds us through life's storms.

—Unknown

CHAPTER 61

Relinquishing

A day in the life of Brett Corbyn had resulted in daily strip searches, use of communal toilets and showers, eating tasteless ramen noodle snacks and a scoop of mush they deemed edible after standing in a lengthy line for that slop they dared to call food. Inmates didn't sit around all day and do nothing. They were given responsibilities to learn skills and develop a good work ethic if released. Brett had been assigned to work in the chow hall, allowing him to sneak samples of the better-tasting options—if any.

When Brett arrived at this hell hole six months ago, he quickly learned to be vigilant in large, crowded areas like the chow hall and the yard for fresh air and exercise. Anyone could be abruptly butchered and left to die before the guards caught wind of a battered, bloodied corpse.

He earned a twenty-year sentence for kidnapping his granddaughter, Caterina. He wanted to be a part of his son's and grandchildren's lives, but Katie and Louis Maroni never allowed him the opportunity.

Brett's biggest regret was telling Katie he wasn't the father of her unborn child in 1971 when he knew damn well he was; too immature to offer a benevolent reaction to her surprising announcement. Fatherhood would've ruined Brett's future as a pro-basketball player and a lot of anticipated good times, living off the exuberant salary he expected to yield. He was much too young to settle down after high school graduation and raise a baby with a girl he had had a one-night stand with. But he followed his son, Michael Maroni, throughout his life. His son had been raised to become a ruthless thug like his adopted father and his notorious criminal grandfather, Vince Russo.

Brett had no proof, but he believed Vince Russo organized the brutal assault on him after the last basketball game he ever played. That attack was payback for walking away from Katie and her unborn child. Katie married Louis Maroni, a junior wise guy who entered the political realm. They squashed any legal parental rights Brett had. Michael probably had no idea of the hoops Brett jumped through to try to see him when he was little. The man had to focus on his physical recovery from the savage incident he endured.

The Corbyn family strongly encouraged Brett to back off. He nearly died the night of the attack. Brett felt angry that his family didn't stand by his side, willing to fight for his rights as Michael's biological father, but they feared the Russo family. All he wanted was for Michael to think of him and to know he cared.

Any shred of hope Brett dwelled on had faded away.

The chow hall became busy around noon with two long lines of criminals categorized as moderate risks for this prison. He felt lucky he wasn't sent to a maximum-security facility where the real criminals go: murderers, pedophiles, and rapists. There were murderers at this prison, but not the serial type—crimes like manslaughter, accidental deaths, or second degrees.

"Shit!" Brett said when he spotted a container of mayonnaise spilled across the floor. A few large guys laughed, knowing Brett was the sucker who had to clean up the mess they probably made intentionally. He wouldn't tangle with them. Legally, he'd been labeled as handicapped, still struggling with a minor limp—an easy target for cruel intentions in a joint like this. Brett hobbled away from the nasty snorts to retrieve a mop and bucket to clean up the thick sludge. As he accessed the maintenance closet and reached for the light switch, a hand fiercely grabbed him and yanked him inside.

In a nanosecond, a voice in the dim room growled, "Your *son* sends his regards."

Brett instantly felt the point of a shiv pierce through his gut once—twice—three times. The unbearable pain paralyzed his lower half. His fingers darted to the wound, feeling the warm syrupy blood expelling.

"My son thought of me? I bet he'll think of me every single day of his life now. Tell him I w-w-wish he k-k-killed me years a-g-g-o."

The assailant dashed from the room, ditching the blade in a nearby garbage pail.

Brett gasped for air, realizing he no longer had to fulfill the next 7,092 remaining days of his confinement. He lived in hell long enough. His body slid to the floor, leaving a thick slather of blood against the wall. His final breath was taken before another inmate discovered a puddle of crimson expanding beneath the maintenance closet door.

CHAPTER 62

I had been approached with an offer to act as a spokesperson for bipolar medications in a public service announcement to ease the stigma of living with a severe depressive disorder. Jeffrey's bitter words about my battle with this condition hit the tabloids, which portrayed him as a vengeful ex-husband. His skit went viral, so my name came up in conversations as a potential celebrity voice.

After I taped my first commercial, my agent contacted me with an opportunity to join the cast of *General Hospital* as a new villainess character. It would be a recurring role, not taking up too much of my time to tape in California, and the part sounded positively delicious!

Tommy revisited a longtime dream of having a Montgomery hotel in France. He consulted with Danny and the other Montgomery owners about a Paris hotel prime for the taking—a tremendous moneymaking opportunity. The team was all-in as long as Tommy acted as a consultant and worked through the process alongside them. I knew Tommy couldn't actually retire. He got back in the game, working by his son's side in a familiar business, in which he excelled.

We each kept our options open for short-term projects while enjoying time with family, friends, and each other.

Kirk, Tara, and Fiona happily lived in our childhood home on Orchard Lane, building a future as a family. Tony and Phyllis were spending a lot of time together. Tony told me he felt at home with Phyllis and her large Italian family.

I kept in contact with Ray and my new siblings regularly. Tommy and I planned to have them visit Vegas, comping their rooms at the Montgomery and showing them around our town.

In late February 2020, I had just hung up the phone with Ray, discussing their trip to Vegas. I hinted about seeing Lucy and making a stop at the Flamingo.

Tommy called out to me, sounding frantic. I raced into the living room, where he watched the evening news at an extremely high volume. He focused on each syllable the reporter uttered.

"What is it?" I asked.

"I think we need to postpone our China trip next month."

"Because of that strange virus? Is it getting worse?"

"Italy's goin' on lockdown. There's concern it'll hit the US soon. People are *dying*. It's pretty serious."

"Maybe the media is inflating the details," I suggested, hoping we didn't need to put off our vacation again.

"Well, we don't have to decide today, but I'll be paying attention to this coronavirus."

"I can't believe they named this thing after a beer." I snickered, while Tommy wore a sour expression. "Okay, we'll stay on top of it. Hopefully, nothing like what China and Italy are experiencing comes to the US. That would be like living through a bad sci-fi movie."

"We need to stay safe. I finally got my life back, spending time with Danny and my grandchildren. I don't want any of you to get sick. Hell, I don't want it either."

"An outbreak like this virus never happens in this country. I guess we just have to wait and see what comes of it."

"And pray." Tommy's tone instilled great concern.

CHAPTER 63

The whole world quickly changed. The virus ignited in China had rapidly spread to other countries, including the US, taking its sweet time infecting its victims. The Centers for Disease Control, the World Health Organization, and other prominent infectious disease organizations advised of the symptoms demonstrated in most people, like fever, coughing, and shortness of breath. COVID-19 didn't care about race, religion, sexual orientation, age, gender, or income. It didn't matter how much life someone had left in them to live. The vicious germs spread, hungering to settle in the lungs of unsuspecting hosts. The lucky ones were asymptomatic or developed minor flu-like symptoms. Others were hospitalized and placed on ventilators because their lungs were too impaired to take in oxygen without help. Many died.

Healthcare professionals were overworked with limited supplies to protect themselves from contracting the dreaded disease. Bodies were piled outdoors in trailers until they could safely be claimed by surviving family members. Funeral homes were booked solid. Because of strict social distancing requirements, people couldn't attend their loved ones' funerals.

When tests became available, people waited in line for hours, sitting in vehicles, possibly circulating the ravenous evil to anyone within six feet. Labs were overutilized, causing weeks of delays in distributing test results. Without knowing their results, those with no to mild symptoms could have spread the contagion further.

Police officers, firefighters, and paramedics needed to take extra precautions when called to service. They had a different kind of wicked killer to protect themselves from outside of gun-toting criminals and the massive flames of a fire. The coronavirus would sneak up on its prey without warning or sympathy for the destruction it caused.

Countries went into lockdown, prohibiting domestic and international travel. Many businesses closed, attributing to an outrageous rise in unemployment. Education transitioned to learning at home via web-based resources. School dances, athletics, and graduation ceremonies were negated.

Everyday life as we knew it changed. Masks became a necessary accessory. Grocery stores limited items to buy, like meat, cleaning supplies, and paper goods. Toilet paper couldn't be found anywhere. Some flew into a state of hoarding, making household items even more inaccessible.

Simple things we took for granted, like lingering inside brick-and-mortar stores or meeting friends for dinner indoors, were prohibited. Concerts and plays were canceled. Movie theaters and shopping malls closed. Brides and grooms had to postpone their wedding plans because states restricted gatherings of large numbers. Venues closed.

The Strip quieted like nothing we had ever witnessed, with a significant drop in reservations at the Montgomery and every other hotel in town. Entertainment had to be canceled. The food court and stores within the hotel had limited traffic. The casino required revamping to circulate air properly and to limit the number of people who entered. Gaming tables and slots were modified to allow six feet of space between seats.

The year 2020 might be considered one of the most disastrous times in American history, ranking high along with the birth of influenza and the Great Depression.

Tommy and I remained isolated within our Vegas home. We kept in contact with our families through electronic devices. We only left the house to grocery shop. Danny and his family would come by and speak to us through our front door every week. At least we got to see them, but we couldn't touch, hug, or kiss people outside our homes.

Bianca went back to teaching. With new at-home learning, teachers were needed to help or substitute if educators caught the virus. Bianca taught her children at home while using Zoom to access her classroom.

We couldn't travel to our Paris apartment. Tommy's purchase of the Paris hotel went through, but the COVID-19 crisis prevented profits. The tourism industry suffered.

The world drastically changed. Everyone learned to adapt to the continual culture shock.

We had no choice.

CHAPTER 64

Aunt Lucy loved living at Summer Wind. She didn't have to worry about cooking or cleaning, and the facility offered rideshares to take residents to doctor appointments and the grocery store. Unfortunately, complexes for the elderly became an easy hotspot for the coronavirus to target. Several seniors living at Summer Wind tested positive, as did the staff. They closed their doors, prohibiting visitors and family members of the residents from entering. This meant we could only check in on Aunt Lucy by telephone.

One day, she didn't answer my call. Given the troubled state of the world, I grew worried. I spoke with one of the staff members who advised that my aunt had developed COVID symptoms and her breathing labored. An ambulance was summoned to take Aunt Lucy to the hospital, and unfortunately, not even family could be with her.

The media alleged that when some found themselves hospital bound with COVID symptoms, they often never left the four walls of their sterile rooms. They died alone unless a compassionate nurse or doctor held their hands until they puffed their final breath.

Because Tara worked at Sunrise Hospital, she checked in on Aunt Lucy, who drifted into a state of unconsciousness, requiring a ventilator.

I wanted to see her. Although I had spoken to her regularly since Thanksgiving, we didn't discuss the explosive secret my mother and she had kept for decades again. What else could be said? The lies and the hurt still poked at my heart, but I reached the point of forgiveness, understanding Lucy's youthful decisions while unknowingly battling bipolar disorder.

After a few days in the hospital, her health continued to decline. I begged Tara to sneak me in to see her.

I wore long sleeves, long pants, and a face mask, and I wrapped my hair back in a scarf. Tara met me at the hospital entrance during her break. She looked exhausted, worn out from extensive double shifts. I felt grateful she could check in on Aunt Lucy and let her know we were all praying for her recovery.

Recently, Kirk told me he planned to propose to Tara. He had the diamond ring our mother left him from Gordon cleaned and polished for her. Fiona approved. He hadn't felt this happy or secure in a relationship before. Tara had no idea of the impending surprise.

Tara handed me additional protective gear, including gloves and a plastic face shield, before entering the area where the COVID patients rested. "She's not conscious, Vicki, but we believe she can hear you, so speak loudly to her," she said as we ambled down a narrow hall active with medical professionals, racing in and out of rooms.

Some sick patients sat in wheelchairs or lay on gurneys in the busy hallways.

"Thank you for doing this for me, Tara."

"I'm afraid you can't stay long. This could be the last time you see her. I'm sorry. I don't mean to sound so drastic and harsh, but unfortunately, she's not responding to treatment. With her age and medical conditions—"

I sighed. "I understand." When I reached the right room and peered inside, my god, what a horrendous sight to witness! Four people crammed together in a small space, lying completely immobile. Aunt Lucy lay in the first bed with the tubes from the ventilator breathing for her, noisily supplying her with oxygen. She looked so thin and frail, more than ever. The MS always made her appear weak, although Ursini women had strong spirits and a lot of fight in us.

An IV attached to her arm provided her with the nutrients her body craved. With the tube from the breathing machine jammed down her throat, she couldn't eat or drink.

I barely recognized her as I sat beside her on a metal stool with a gray cushion and slid the seat as close as possible to her motionless figure. "Aunt Lucy, it's Victoria," I spoke brashly as Tara advised. I looked around at the other patients, who didn't stir in their sleep or react to my loud voice. "Tara says she visits with you every day. I snuck in, Aunt Lucy. You'd be proud of my ingenuity. Kirk, Tony, and Tommy send their love. We're all rooting for you to fight this virus and come home."

The brazen moans from another patient made me jump off the stool. When the woman stopped groaning, my body sunk back onto the uncomfortable seat. "Ginger and Giselle are fine. They're adapting to living with Tommy and me, but they miss you. I'm not here to talk about your kitties. I snuck in because I had to see you. I need to say the words aloud to you. I understand the choices you made when you were a kid. Your options were limited. And I'm grateful that the woman who created me, who brought me into this world, had a ringside seat for all the main attractions in my life. We Ursini women can be brassy and bold, but we're also loving and fiercely loyal to our family. I got that from my mother. From *both* my mothers. I love you, and I forgive you." I squeezed her fingers, hoping she'd squeeze back, but her lifeless hand lay limp and cold. I prayed that she heard me.

I sat with her for a few more moments until Tara returned, signaling the need for my immediate departure. Through painful sobs, I whispered, "Goodbye, Aunt Lucy. Mom will be waiting for you. I trust she'll take care of you in heaven the way she did here." I brushed my glove-layered hand atop her ashen hair and shed an abundance of tears.

Too much protective gear covered my head to clean my face. Tara helped me remove the layers so I could scrub my hands with soap and water before grabbing a tissue to wipe away the massive flood that drained from my eyes and nose.

I had to get out of this awful place. I needed Tommy. I rushed home to snuggle in his welcoming arms, relieving the hurt I felt about losing another idyllic woman in my life. Aunt Lucy's death seemed inevitable.

In preparation for that imminent call, I secured the grave next to my mother's plot for her. She should rest beside her sister, beneath the acacia tree, for eternity.

CHAPTER 65

As she lay on her deathbed, oblivious to the machine that kept her breaths regular, Lucy Ursini reflected on various flashes of her life. Victoria, her princess, forgave her for the staggering secret she had maintained for years. Lucy had always been concerned that such exposure would have ended her relationship with the woman she gave birth to and adored.

Bipolar disorder, the root of all evil, was to blame, she thought. The disease toyed with her mind and emotions. Her outrageous suspicions caused her marital problems. She always pointed fingers at any good-looking woman who glanced in Gary's direction, even her sister. If only she had known to seek treatment for her wild outbursts and demented rationalizations, maybe her marriage would have survived her manic state.

Vivid images of Rodney Kettner holding her sister down, strangling Sylvia with his bare hands sparked an old, turbulent memory tucked far away along the outskirts of her mind. Lucy clasped the hammer lying on the counter tightly in her fist.

Sylvia whimpered, struggling to push the belligerent man off her as Lucy crept up from behind and struck Rodney's head with all her might. For once, Lucy had to protect Sylvia.

The scorching imagery of her smacking that bastard continuously caused her body to twitch through the nightmare. Every bit of anger and frustration she carried had relinquished with each thrust to Rodney's skull. A traumatic event suppressed in the depths of consciousness for decades. Somehow, through the shock, she convinced herself that Gordon had killed the man.

The blood. She wasn't prepared to see so much blood layering her pale skin, drenching her clothing.

When Gordon arrived for his rendezvous with Sylvia, he walked in on Lucy covered with spatters of Kettner's blood, and his cold body stretched across the kitchen tile. The hum of Sylvia's pleas instantly emerged, begging Gordon to help them and keep their confidence.

Pastor Gordon was a docile man. He'd never be able to kill a man like Rodney Kettner. If Lucy hadn't shown up when she did, Sylvia wouldn't have survived that violent ordeal.

Sylvia knew how to manipulate men, especially Gordon because he loved her so much. Even if the good preacher talked about this now, no one would believe a word that left his lips, thanks to his faltering mental state.

Lucy recited the same words continually in her mind, "The bond of sisters lasts forever," until her final breath was expelled.

*****

Her eyes leisurely opened to an astounding view. Lucy stared at the remains of her figure beside her. The machine next to the bed beeped a foreboding, lengthy tone. Her head bounced between the machine, her still body, and the team of health professionals who raced inside the room.

Kirk's girlfriend, Tara, sadly confirmed her time of death.

A warm breeze wrapped around her frame. Lucy realized she felt no pain. She had no breath, no coughing spell, no arthritis, and the unbearable numbness had departed. Her thoughts were clear and sound. Every happy memory from her birth flashed before her eyes. She had never felt so healthy and strong before. A unique, somehow familiar sensation overwhelmed her. She smiled and turned to face the wondrous phenomenon.

"Hey, Lu," Sylvia stated with a wide smirk. She appeared as a youthful dancer who showed off her long, graceful legs and hourglass shape.

"Hi ya, Syl. Gosh, you look gorgeous!" She admired Sylvia's shimmering silver corset feather dress that hugged her slim waist and puffed out around her thighs. The complementing feather headdress sparkled with strings of rhinestones and pearls, arching over her head nearly two feet high.

"We've been waiting for you."

"We?"

"Mommy, Daddy, Nana, and Poppy. Our whole ancestral line is eager to greet you."

Lucy gazed around the empty gray space, attempting to see beyond Sylvia's image. "Where are they?" she asked, as her focus raced back to the people standing around her lifeless body, lying still on the hospital bed.

"The *heaven* everyone fantasizes about in *that* world—we call it *home* on this side. You'll reunite with everyone soon. Just take my hand, sister." Sylvia gracefully stretched out her arm.

Lucy reached for Sylvia's hand but pulled back suddenly. "I... uh."

"There's no need to be scared, Lu. Where we're going has no fear, no pain, no sickness. All your glorious memories will stay intact. Your spirit will be chock-full of peace, love, and forgiveness."

"But Victoria. Kirk. Tony. With both of us gone—"

"They'll be all right. We'll always be with them. You'll see."

Lucy continued to look back upon her body, the flesh that once contained her soul. She observed Tara using her cell to inform Kirk of her passing. She could feel the strong love between them and the sadness they exchanged about her death. She closed her eyes, listening to their voices as clearly as if she had sat beside them.

Kirk notified Victoria immediately by phone.

Her heightened auditory sense heard the sadness in Victoria's cracked tone, and Lucy's keen telepathic perception visualized the shedding of tears. "It's so strange. I can hear them, see them, and feel their energy like a warm cozy blanket swathed around me."

Sylvia's eyes beamed brightly as her lips raised at the corners. "Trust me, Lu. That awareness will be enhanced once you come home with me. I've so much to show you. The bond of sisters lasts forever," she recited Lucy's final living thought, then she held out her hand again.

Lucy smiled with elation as she grasped Sylvia's delicate fingertips. With a quick blink, she instantly became enlightened about the next journey for her soul.

*****

Millions became infected with the coronavirus worldwide. By the end of 2020, in the US alone, more than 350,000 people succumbed to COVID-19 or complications from the disease. The virus, a global threat, destroyed lives, injured the economy, and caused emotional, financial, and physical unrest throughout the world.

Although many people perished, leaving loved ones behind to grieve, the country slowly strengthened. A vaccine was created and distributed in 2021 to subdue the effects of the pandemic. Only the ticking of time could soothe the anguish felt and the peril experienced worldwide. Through strength and resilience, the people of the United States of America withstood the battle, conquered multiple variants of the virus, and eventually healed.

Epilogue—2024

Those we love can never be more than a thought away, for as long as there's a memory, they live in our hearts to stay.

—Unknown

CHAPTER 66

Ray survived the worst of the pandemic without so much as a sniffle or a cough. Once traveling became safe, Ray spent two weeks with Tommy and me in Vegas. I extended the invitation to my siblings and their spouses as well, and we comped rooms for them at the Montgomery, but Ray, my father, stayed in our guest bedroom. It was nice to get to know them better and show my new family around the Vegas Strip. Ray and I were equally sorry he couldn't reunite with Lucy.

We flew to California for a few days so he could watch me perform on the set of *General Hospital*. The cast and crew were extremely accommodating. Ray's exuberant smile lit up the room as he watched me in action in front of the cameras, which included me slapping another character viciously across the face. Tommy looked amused, holding back laughter.

I prayed we would have more times like these together.

It was Sunday afternoon, May 5, 2024. I slipped into an elegant royal-blue dress trimmed with silver beads, preparing for a special dinner this evening. A familiar jingle from the TV caught my attention. Goose bumps sprang up on my arms as I glowered at the screen to witness Leann in a ruby-red bathrobe stretching out her arms and yawning before lethargically stepping into a kitchen, where the aromatic scent of Rios Roast coffee awakened her to start her day. "Oh, brother," I muttered, rolled my eyes, and clicked the remote to change the channel, grateful to be a tea drinker. I must give the mediocre actress credit for securing a few commercials.

My computer chimed, alerting me to an incoming video call from my Laurant siblings. We tried to talk virtually every couple of weeks, but today I didn't have much time to spend catching up.

After a few minutes of blasé chitchat, Tommy's footsteps were heard approaching from behind me, entering the camera's range.

"Hi, Tommy!" Marlene shouted and waved on camera.

"Hi, Laurant family!" he happily answered, leaning across the desk to view the screen.

"Hey, did you decide about that book option for a film deal?" Bruce asked.

"Your book was such a huge success. I'm confident the movie would be spectacular!" Chloe's animated hands flew across the screen, thrilled about the potential of Tommy's memoirs transitioning to film.

Tommy shrugged in return and rubbed his smoothly shaved chin. "Not yet," he replied.

We were uncertain about bringing further attention our way, and Tommy didn't want to distress the Russos and Toscanos. There was no reason to rejuvenate their anger and risk retaliation. He planned to decline the film offer.

"You look nice in that suit," Marlene flattered him, changing the subject.

I peeped at my watch and realized Tommy was already sharply dressed in his dark-gray suit and blue tie that harmonized with my dress. "Oh! I've got to finish getting ready! Sorry, gotta run! Talk soon."

Giselle jumped up to greet the family on the computer, her black tail waving in my face, seeking attention. Ginger grew jealous and darted near me, requiring snuggles.

"Have fun tonight! Bye!" Chloe exclaimed before clicking to leave the conversation.

Marlene and Bruce said their farewells.

"Okay, kitties, we've got a wedding to get to!"

CHAPTER 67

Later that evening, before friends and family, Tony and Phyllis exchanged vows, pledging to devote their lives to each other in sickness and in health, in good times and in bad—forever.

The Buckingham Palace room at the Montgomery was delightfully decorated with maroon and cream-colored linens. Tony requested centerpieces of white and pink peonies that complemented the color scheme—a gesture in remembrance of our mother. The hotel crew catered to Phyllis's precise specifications. It seemed she had envisioned this day for years, but she hadn't met the right man until she laid eyes on Tony that Thanksgiving Day in 2019. Dating throughout the pandemic didn't dissuade the beginning of their relationship. She soon moved into Tony's house in Paradise.

Phyllis looked stunning in a white satin, strapless mermaid gown with a strand of pearls around the waist and a hint of beads hugging along the edge of the sweetheart neckline. Her flaxen hair was pulled up into a dramatic bun, highlighted by a shimmering headband.

Tony wore a simple black suit with a formal necktie, looking incredibly handsome.

Kirk stood beside Tony as his best man during the ceremony. Tommy and I sat with Burt, Tara, and Fiona as the vows were exchanged.

I flashed back to Kirk and Tara's unique wedding in September 2020, with Tony by Kirk's side. The intimate ceremony was officiated by Pastor Josh in the backyard of their home on Orchard Lane. Gordon sat up front with his son, Drew, displaying smiling eyes throughout the event. He still suffered from moments of confusion, but he got through the wedding without incident. Everyone wore masks and adhered to social distancing rules.

Debbie Steele was released from prison after a jury miraculously found her not guilty of her part in my mother's death, leaving my brothers and me speechless. Josh never filed for divorce, but they no longer exuded a happy couple vibe, living day-to-day under false pretenses. She didn't dare show her face at Kirk's wedding. In fact, she rarely made an appearance at church. She may not reside behind bars, but the constant whispers, and loss of friendships and respect in town, imprisoned her. Her only ally in life seemed to be her poodle.

Tommy and I approached the smiling bride and groom as the waitstaff hurried to clear appetizer plates from tables in preparation for the main course.

I joked with Tony, saying, "Phyllis must be your soulmate because you *never* had an interest in marriage. I'm so happy for you both."

"If you and Tommy hadn't come home a few years ago, we wouldn't have met."

"Are you giving us *all* the credit for your happiness?"

His crystal blue eyes danced as he pulled his bride by his side. "*She* gets the credit for my happiness."

"You got that right, Tony. And this woman deserves to be happy." Tommy stepped closer and left a delicate kiss on Phyllis's cheek, causing her to blush.

Although today's event brought joy to everyone in attendance, Tony and Phyllis took a moment to reflect on those who were no longer with us: our mother, Aunt Lucy, and Phyllis's Nonna and Nonno, who became casualties of COVID before they could be vaccinated.

A light breath of air hit my ear, sending an intense quiver rushing through me. My mother's distinct voice was in my head, saying, "You've got more chapters to live through, Victoria. Keep turning the pages of life for your next adventure." I shook my head, feeling a tad dizzy.

"Whatcha thinking about?" Tommy wrapped his arms comfortably around my waist.

"How truly blessed we are." I scanned the decorated hall, surrounded by family and friends. "I sense my mother's energy. Her love and joy. All three of her kids are content and happy. Mom and Aunt Lucy are here, celebrating with us. I can't explain it, but I feel their presence as if they were standing right beside me."

"Hear that? They're playing our song!" Tommy took me by the hand when the DJ played Elvis's "The Wonder of You." He led me to the dance floor, twirled me beneath his arm, and hummed a few bars of the pretty melody, staring deeply into my brown eyes as we swayed to the music.

"You requested our song." My fingers caressed the back of his head through the bright gray strands. "I'm so happy we get to grow old together."

He displayed his infamous smirk. "Sweetheart, I'm already old. I need hearing aids, my restless legs keep me up at night, and I'm as blind as a bat without my glasses."

"Well, we *both* have some natural dents in our armor from aging. But look around, my love. You created so much in your life to be proud of, Tommy Cavallo. This hotel is still in business, even after the disastrous pandemic. And your family is together."

From our spot on the dance floor, I followed Tommy's eyes, gazing through the room. He observed Danny and Bianca laughing with Haley and her husband Richard, unable to stop talking. Whether their conversation focused on work, politics, or the upcoming family picnic they were organizing didn't matter. Danny and Haley grew close as cousins should. Tommy always searched for pieces of his departed brother when in Haley's presence. Our grandchildren shared a table with Haley's kids, our great-niece and great-nephew, acting silly, teasing each other.

He smiled, observing two of his closest friends, Jack and Rob Lubitski, who attended the wedding with their wives. We had dinner plans with them next week at Gilberti's.

Tommy's focus returned to me. "I know how lucky I am." His lips pressed against mine, then his face lit up as if he had a brainstorm, saying, "You know, maybe it's time we reschedule China, our next adventure together."

Your next adventure, the whispered words I swore my mother imparted moments ago.

"I want to make all your dreams come true, sweetheart."

I smiled, exposing my dimples. "You already have."

ABOUT THE AUTHOR

 Gina Marie Martini is an award-winning author of the drama series, *Entanglements.* She was born and raised in Connecticut, where she lives with her family. She earned a bachelor's degree in psychology and a master's degree in health administration. Gina maintains a full-time career in the health insurance industry with a background in behavioral health and clinical programs.

Follow her at www.ginamariemartini.com, Facebook, Instagram, and Twitter.